GAO XINGJIAN is the first Chinese recipient of the Nobel Prize in Literature. He was born in 1940 in Jiangxi province in eastern China, and has lived in France since 1987. Gao Xingjian is considered an artistic innovator in his native China, both in the visual arts and in literature. He is that rare multi-talented artist who exels as a novelist, playwright, essayist, director, and painter. Two novels, the internationally best-selling *Soul Mountain* and *One Man's Bible*, are available in English from Flamingo, as well as a volume of his art entitled *Return to Painting*.

MABEL LEE, PhD, is Honorary Associate Professor of Chinese at the University of Sydney and an authority on twentieth-century Chinese literature and history.

Praise for *Soul Mountain*:

'A rich soup of a book... Part novel, part philosophical tract, the genius of *Soul Mountain* lies in its not attempting to offer any answers. It instead belongs to that curious genre of intellectual quest dominated by the great German writer WG Sebald... A wonderfully broad portrait of a country caught between the ancient and the modern in a most fundamental way.'
Irish Times

'There is a sense throughout that Gao is running after things that are already vanishing. On the nature reserves, people are shooting bears and even pandas; stones inscribed with historical inscriptions have been dynamited to yield materials for bridges that were never built... *Soul Mountain* is Gao's attempt to bring back what is lost. In the end, his gift is to look beyond politics at the human condition.'
Sunday Times

'A picaresque novel on an epic scale... complex, rich and strange.'
Independent on Sunday

'A quirky, thick, playful monster of a book... both engaging and elegant.'
New York Times

'When he writes of his experiences in the real world, Gao transcends cultural barriers. A good story will out in any language, and when Gao is good he is staggeringly so. His writing about the Cultural Revolution is remarkable.'
Daily Telegraph

Also by Gao Xingjian

SOUL MOUNTAIN

ONE MAN'S BIBLE

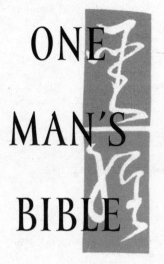

一個人的

Gao Xingjian

Translated from the Chinese by Mabel Lee

Flamingo
An Imprint of HarperCollinsPublishers

Flamingo
An imprint of HarperCollins *Publishers*
77–85 Fulham Palace Road,
Hammersmith, London W6 8JB

Flamingo is a registered trade mark of
HarperCollins Publishers Limited

www.**fire**and**water**.com

Published by Flamingo 2003
9 8 7 6 5 4 3 2 1

First published in Great Britain by Flamingo 2002

First published as *Yi ge ren de sheng jing* in Taipei, Taiwan,
by Lianjing Publishing House, 1999

ISBN 0 00 714242 0

Set in Galliard

Printed and bound in Great Britain by Clays Ltd, St Ives plc.

ONE

MAN'S

BIBLE

一個人的

1

It was not that he didn't remember he once had another sort of life. But, like the old yellowing photograph at home, which he did not burn, it was sad to think about, and far away, like another world that had disappeared forever. In his Beijing home, confiscated by the police, he had a family photo left by his dead father: it was a happy gathering, and everyone in the big family was present. His grandfather who was still alive at the time, his hair completely white, was reclined in a rocking chair, paralyzed and unable to speak. He, the eldest son and eldest grandson of the family, the only child in the photo, was squashed between his grandparents. He was wearing slit trousers that showed his little dick, and he had on his head an American-style boat-shaped cap. At the time, the eight-year War of Resistance against the Japanese had just ended, and the Civil War had not properly started. The photograph had been taken on a bright summer day in front of the round gateway in the garden, which was full of golden chrysanthemums and purple-red cockscombs. That was what he recalled of the garden, but the photo was water-stained and had turned a grayish yellow. Behind the round gateway was a two-story, English-style building with a winding walkway below and a balustrade upstairs. It was the big house he had lived in. He recalled that there were thirteen people in the photograph—an unlucky number—his parents, his paternal uncles and aunts, and also the wife of one of the uncles. Now, apart from an aunt in America and himself, all of them and the big house had vanished from this world.

While still in China, he had revisited the old city, looking for the old courtyard compound at the back of the bank where his father had once worked. He found only a few cheaply built cement residential buildings that would have been constructed a good number of years earlier. He asked people coming in and out if such a courtyard used to be there, but no one could say for sure. He remembered that at the rear gate of the courtyard, below the stone steps, there was a lake. At Duanwu Festival, his father and his bank colleagues would crowd on the stone steps to watch the dragon-boat race. There was the pounding of big gongs and drums, as dragon boats decorated with colorful streamers came to snatch the red packets hanging from bamboo poles put out by the houses around the lake. The red packets, of course, contained money. His third uncle, youngest uncle, and youngest aunt, once took him out on a boat to fish for the two-horned water chestnuts that grew in the lake. He had never been to the opposite side of the lake, but even if he went there and looked back, from that short distance, he would not have recognized this dreamlike memory.

This family had been decimated; it was too gentle and fragile for the times. It was destined to have no progeny. After his grandfather died, his father lost his job as bank manager and the family fell into rapid decline. His second uncle, who was keen on singing Peking Opera, was the only one to work with the new government authorities, and this was on account of his Democratic Personage title. Nevertheless, seven or eight years later he was labeled a rightist. Afterward, he grew sullen, barely spoke, and would doze off as soon as he sat down. Transformed into a listless, wizened old man, he held on for a few years, then quietly died. The members of this big family died of illness, drowned, committed suicide, went insane, or followed their husbands to prison farms and simply passed away, so that the only person left was a bastard like him. There was also his eldest aunt whose black shadow had once engulfed the whole family. She was said to have been alive and well a few years ago, but he had not seen her since that photo was taken. The husband of this aunt was a member of the Nationalist airforce. As ground personnel, he never dropped a bomb but he fled to Taiwan, where he died of some illness a few years later. He did not know how this aunt had managed to get to America, and had not bothered to find out.

However, on his tenth birthday—it was customary in those times to use the lunar calendar, so he was actually only nine—the family was a large one, and it was a big event. When he got out of bed that morning, he put on new clothes as well as a new pair of leather shoes; to have a child wear leather shoes in those days was indulgent. He also received lots of presents: a kite, a chess set, a geometrical puzzle, imported coloring pencils, a pop gun with a rubber stopper, and the *Complete Collection of Grimms' Fairy Tales* in two volumes with copperplate illustrations. His grandmother gave him three silver dollars wrapped in red paper: one Qing Dynasty "dragon ocean," one Yuan Shikai "big bald head," and one new silver dollar with Chiang Kai-shek in full military regalia. Each of the coins made a different sound. The Chiang Kai-shek one made a tinkle, compared with the clank of the thick and heavy Yuan Shikai "big bald head." He put these in his little leather suitcase, together with his stamp album and his colored marbles. Afterward, the whole family went out to eat steamed crab-roe dumplings in a garden restaurant with artificial mountains and a pond full of goldfish. A big round tabletop had to be used to seat everyone. For the first time, he was the center of attention in the family and he sat next to his grandmother in the seat where his grandfather, who had recently died, would have sat. It was as if they were waiting for him to become the bastion of the family. He bit into a dumpling, and hot liquid from the filling splashed his new clothes with grease. Nobody scolded him, they simply smiled, but he was greatly embarrassed. He remembered this, probably because he had just lost his childish ignorance and was aware of becoming a grown-up, and because he felt really stupid.

He also remembered that when his grandfather died, the mourning hall was hung with layers of coffin curtains, like the backstage of an opera theater, and it was much more fun than that birthday. A troupe of monks struck clappers and gongs as they chanted sutras. He lifted the coffin curtains, ran in and out of them, and had a good time. His mother got him to put on hemp shoes and he did, under duress, but adamantly refused to tie white cloth around his forehead, because it looked ugly. It was probably his grandmother's idea. However, his father had to tie white cloth around his head even though he was dressed in a white linen Western suit. The men who came to mourn were also mostly in suits and ties, and the women were all wearing *qipao* and high-heeled shoes. Among the guests was a woman who played the piano; she was a coloratura soprano and the tremble in her singing made it sound like the bleating of a lamb—of course this wasn't in the mourning hall but at the wake at home. It was the first time he'd heard singing like this and he couldn't stop laughing. His mother quietly scolded him right in his ear, but he couldn't help laughing out loud.

In his memory, the time of his grandfather's death was like a special festival, and there was an absence of grief. He thought the old man should have died much earlier. He had been paralyzed for a long time, and during the day was always reclining in the rocking chair; that he should return to heaven, sooner or later, was quite natural. Death in his grandfather's case was not frightening, but his mother's death terrified him. She had drowned in a river on a farm. Her bloated corpse was found floating in the water by peasants when they took the ducks down to the river in the morning. His mother had responded to the call of the Party to go to the farms to be reeducated. She died in the prime of life, at the age of thirty-eight, so her image in his heart was always beautiful.

A present he got as a child was a gold Parker fountain pen, given to him by Uncle Fang, one of his father's colleagues at the bank. He was playing with Uncle Fang's pen at the time and wouldn't put it down. The grown-ups all thought it was a good sign, and said the child was sure to become a writer. Uncle Fang was very generous and gave him the pen, it was not on that birthday but when he was younger, because he had written a piece about it in his diary when he was almost eight. He should have been going to school but, because he was frail and sick all the time, it was his mother who taught him to read and also to write with a brush, a stroke at a time, over the red character prototypes printed in the squares of the exercise books. He did not find it hard, and at times filled a book in a day, so his mother said it was enough of that, and got him to write a diary with a brush to save paper. Some composition booklets with small squares were bought for him and even if it took him half a day to fill a page, it counted as his assignment. His first diary piece read roughly: "Snow falling on the ground turns it pure white, people treading on it leave dirty footprints." His mother talked about it, and everyone in the family, as well as family acquaintances, knew about it. From that time he could not stop himself writing about his dreams and self-love, sowing the seeds of future disaster.

His father disapproved of his staying indoors all day reading and writing. A boy should be fun-loving, explore the world, know lots of people, distinguish himself; he did not think much of his son being a writer. His father thought of himself as a good drinker. Actually, he liked to show off more than he liked drinking. At the time, a game known as Charging Through the Pass involved downing a cup of liquor with each person at a banquet, and anyone who could make a round of three or five tables was a hero. Once his father was carried home unconscious and left downstairs in what used to be Grandfather's chair. None of the men were at home, and his grandmother, mother, and the maid couldn't get his father upstairs to bed. He recalled that a rope was lowered from the window upstairs and somehow both the chair and his father were slowly hauled up. His father hung high, swaying in midair, drunk and with a smile on his face. This was his father's great achievement, but he couldn't tell whether it was fantasy or not. With a child, memory and imagination are hard to separate.

For him, life before he was ten was like a dream. His childhood always seemed to be a dream world, even when his family was on the run as refugees. The truck was careering along a muddy mountain road in the rain and, all day long, he held a basket of oranges, which he ate under the tarpaulin covering. He once asked his mother if this had happened, and she said at the time oranges were cheap, and if you gave the villagers some money, they loaded them onto the truck next to the people. His father was working for a state-run bank, so armed guards, escorting the transport of banknotes, accompanied the family as it retreated with the bank.

The old home, now frequently appearing in dreams, was not the foreign-style house with the round doorway and the flower garden in which his grandfather had lived, but the old house with a well, left by his maternal grandmother. This little old woman, also dead, was forever rummaging in a big suitcase. In the dream, he is looking down at the house, which doesn't have a roof, at rooms divided by wooden walls. No one is there except for his grandmother who is frantically rummaging in the suitcase. He remembered that in the house there was an old-style leather suitcase that had been given a coat of paint and that in it, hidden under the clothes, was a parcel containing his grandmother's deeds to houses and land. The properties had been used to pay off debts or sold a long time before the new government authorities would have confiscated them. When his grandmother and mother burned that parcel of yellow, disintegrating papers, they were in a panic, but he hadn't reported them because no one came to investigate. However, had he in fact been questioned, he probably would have reported them, because his mother and grandmother were colluding to destroy criminal evidence, even if they did dearly love him.

That dream was several decades later, after he had been in the West for some time, in a small inn in the city of Tours in Central France. He had just woken up but was still in a daze. Behind the gauze curtain, old louvered shutters with peeling paint half-blocked the gloomy gray sky between the leaves of a plane tree. In the dream he'd just had, he was in that old two-story house, standing on the upstairs balcony that hadn't collapsed, leaning on a rickety wooden railing and looking down. Beyond the gate was a pumpkin patch where he used to catch crickets in the heaps of tiles and rubble among the vines. He clearly remembered that behind the wooden partition in the dream there were many rooms where guests used to stay. The guests had all disappeared just like his grandmother, just like his past life. In that life, memory and dream intermingle and the images transcend time and space.

Since he was the eldest son and eldest grandson, everyone in the family—including his maternal grandmother—had great expectations of him. However, his frequent bouts of illness from early childhood were a worry, and they had his fortune told many times; the first time, he recalled, was in a temple, when his parents took him with them to Lushan to escape the heat. The Immortal Grotto was a famous attraction. Next to it was a big temple with a vegetarian hall as well as tea stalls catering to tourists. It was cool inside the temple and there were not many visitors. In those times, people were carried up the mountain in sedan chairs, and he sat on his mother's lap tightly clutching the handrail in front of him, but couldn't help looking down the deep crevasse at the side. Before leaving China, he revisited the place, which, of course, already could be reached by bus, but couldn't find the temple. Even the ruins had vanished without a trace. However, he clearly remembered that on the wall of the visitors' hall in the temple there was a long scroll painting of Zhu Yuanzhang with a pockmarked face. The temple, it was said, was founded in the Ming Dynasty and, before becoming emperor, Zhu Yuanzhang was said to have sought refuge there. Something as concrete and complex as this could not have emerged from a child's imagination. Moreover, a few years ago, among the treasures of the Palace Museum in Taipei, he saw the scroll painting of Zhu Yuanzhang with a pockmarked face. So this temple had actually existed, and the memory had not been imagined, and the old monk's prediction had, in fact, come true. The old monk had warned in a loud voice: "This little one will suffer many disasters and hardships. It will be hard for him to survive!" The old monk even slapped him hard on the forehead. It gave him a fright but he didn't cry. He remembered this because he had always been spoiled and had never been slapped.

Many years later, he developed an interest in Chan Buddhism, and on rereading those Chan conundrums, he realized that the old monk had probably given him his first lesson in life.

He did have another sort of life, only afterward he simply forgot about it.

2

The curtain is partly open. Against the black shadow of the mountain, blocks of lit apartments loom. The sky above the mountain is gray, and the brilliant mass of lights from the night market shines onto the ledge of the window. The insides of the transparent postmodernist building opposite can be seen distinctly, and as the elevator slowly rises in its tubular frame to the level of your room you can even make out the figures of the people in it. With a long-range lens, from over there, it would certainly be possible to photograph the inside of your room, even how you make love with her could be photographed.

However, you do not have to hide, and there is nothing you must avoid doing. You are not a movie star or a television star, or an important politician, or a local Hong Kong magnate who's afraid of being exposed in the newspapers. You hold French travel documents as a political refugee and have been invited for this visit, your room has been booked and paid for by someone else. You presented your documents on checking into this big hotel, bought by the Mainland government, so your name has been entered into the computer at the reception desk in the lobby. On hearing your Beijing accent, the supervisor and the girl at the desk looked embarrassed but, in a few months, after Hong Kong is returned to China, they will also have to speak with a Beijing accent, and are probably taking lessons right now. It is their duty to keep tabs on what guests are doing, now that the proprietor is the government, so this episode of lovemaking in the nude that you have just indulged in will certainly have been videotaped. Also, for security reasons, in a big hotel, installing a few more video cameras would not be money wasted. Sitting on the bed, you have stopped sweating, feel cold, and want to turn off the buzzing air-conditioner.

"What are you thinking?" she asks.

"Nothing."

"Then what are you looking at?"

"The elevator going up and down in the building opposite. You can see the people inside the elevator, there's a couple kissing."

"I can't see them," she sits up in the bed.

You're talking about using a long-range lens.

"Close the curtains."

She is lying on her back, her white body completely bare except for the luxuriant clump of downy hair between her legs.

"They wanted to make a video but the hairs were too stark," you tease.

"Who are you talking about? Here? Who's making videos?"

You say it's a machine, that it's automatic.

"Impossible, this isn't China."

You say that the Mainland authorities have bought the hotel.

She sighs softly, sits up, and says: "You've got a phobia." She puts out her arm and runs her fingers through your hair. "Switch on the table lamp, I'll go and switch off the main light."

"No need. Just now we were in too much of a hurry for me to have a good look."

You utter sweet words, bend down to kiss her lustrous white belly in the bright light, and ask, "Do you feel cold?"

"A little," she laughs. "Want some more cognac?"

You say you'd like some coffee. She gets out of the bed, switches off the air-conditioner, plugs in the electric kettle and puts instant coffee into a cup. Her full breasts sway weightily.

"Don't you think I'm fat?" she says with a laugh. "Chinese women have better figures."

You say, not necessarily. You adore her breasts, their solidity, their sensuousness.

"Haven't you ever had . . . ?"

Facing you, she sits in the round chair by the window and leans back, tilting her head and letting you look as much as you want. She is blocking the illuminated building with the elevator, and the mountain behind looks darker. On this wonderful night, you say that her body is incredibly white, as if it's not real.

"And you want coffee so that you will be more awake?" There is scorn in her eyes.

"So that I can hold onto this instant better!"

You say that life, at times, is like a miracle and you are lucky to be alive. All this is pure coincidence and yet it is real and not a dream.

"I'd like always to be dreaming but it's just not possible. I prefer not to think of anything."

She sips the cognac and closes her eyes. She is a white German woman with very dark hair and long eyelashes. You get her to part her legs so you can see clearly and have her deeply imprinted in your memory. She says she doesn't want memories, only to feel this instant. You ask if she can feel you looking at her. She says she can feel you roaming over her body. Where have I roamed? you ask. She says from her toes to her waist, oh—she's gushing again, she says she wants you. You say you want her, too, but you also want to see how this body, so full of life, twists and turns.

"For a better photograph?" she asks, her eyes closed.

"Yes." Your eyes are fixed on her and scour her entire body.

"Can you photograph everything?"

"Nothing is left out."

"Aren't you afraid?"

"Of what?"

You say you have no inhibitions. She says she has even less. You say this is Hong Kong, and China is now far away from you. You get up and press against her. She asks you to switch off the main light, and you again enter her moist body.

"Are you deeply attracted to me?" She is slightly breathless.

"Yes, I'm buried." You say you are buried in her flesh.

"Flesh only?"

"Yes, and there are no memories, only this instant."

She says she also needs to be fused like this in darkness, in nebulous chaos.

"Just to feel the warmth of a woman. . . ."

"Men also have warmth. It's been a long time since. . . ."

"You've had a man?"

"Since I've had this sort of sensation, this trembling. . . ."

"Why?"

"I don't know, I don't know why. . . ."

"Try to say why!"

"I wouldn't be able to make myself clear. . . ."

"Is it because it happened so suddenly and was totally unexpected?"

"Don't ask."

But you want her to tell you! She says no. But you keep at her, keep taking it further, go on asking her. Is it because you've met by chance? Is it because you don't understand one another? Is it more exciting because you're strangers? Or does she simply seek after such thrills? She shakes her head each time to say no. She says she's known you a long time; even though many years have passed and she'd only seen you twice, your image stayed with her and grew more and more distinct. She also says that just now, a few hours ago, when she saw you she became excited. She says she doesn't casually go to bed with men, she isn't a slut, but she doesn't lack men either. Don't hurt her like this. . . . You're moved by her, need to be intimate with her and not just sexually. Hong Kong is a foreign place for you and for her. That small association with her is a memory from ten years ago on the other side of the sea, when you were still in China.

"It was in your home, one night in winter. . . ."

"That home was confiscated a long time ago."

"Your home was warm, special, it had a warm feeling."

"It was warm air piped in by a generator. The pipes were always very hot. Even in winter, only a single layer of clothing was needed inside. The two of you arrived in big padded overcoats with upturned collars."

"We were worried about being seen and getting you in trouble—"

"Yes, the regular plainclothes police were on duty at the front of the building. They finished at ten o'clock at night. It was pretty awful for the next shift in the howling winter wind."

"It was Peter who suddenly thought to drop in on you, without phoning. You were old friends, he said, and as he was taking me to your home it was best going at night to avoid being stopped and questioned."

"I didn't have a line installed because I didn't want friends talking carelessly on the phone, and also to avoid having anything to do with foreigners. Peter was an exception, he'd come to China to study Chinese. At the time he was passionate about Mao's Cultural Revolution and we used to argue often, but he'd been a friend for some time. How is he?"

"We separated long ago. He was a representative in the China office of a German company, found a Chinese girl, married her, and took her back to Germany. I heard that he's now the boss of a company he had started up. Back then, I'd only just arrived in Beijing to study. I didn't speak much Chinese and it was hard to make Chinese friends."

"I remember you, of course I remember you. As soon as you came through the door you took off your big padded coat and your scarf, and there stood a very beautiful young foreign woman!"

"With big breasts, right?"

"Of course, very big breasts. Blushing white skin and bright red lips even with no lipstick. Really sexy."

"You couldn't have known at the time!"

"You were so bright red, it was impossible not to notice."

"It was because it was too hot in the room and we'd been cycling for more than an hour."

"That night you sat quietly opposite me but didn't say much."

"I was struggling to understand what was being said. You and Peter were talking all the time, although I don't recall what about. I didn't know much Chinese at the time but I remember that night, I had a strange feeling."

You, of course, also remember that winter night, you had candles burning, which added to the warmth, and you couldn't tell if there was anyone downstairs watching your window. You had finally obtained a little apartment, a decent refuge, a home, and you had a fortress to protect yourself from the political storms outside. She sat on the carpet with her back against the bookcase. It was a clipped woollen carpet made for export, that had gone on the domestic market. Sold at a reduced price as a second-grade product, it was still expensive, exactly the amount of advance royalty you had received for your book. However, that book, which did not so much as touch on politics, stirred up a great deal of trouble for you. Her shirt collar was open and her skin was very white, and those long legs in sleek black stockings were enticing.

"Don't forget, you had a girl in your apartment. She was wearing very little and, unless I've remembered wrongly, she was barefoot."

"She was usually naked, and she was when the two of you came in the door."

"That's right, we had been sitting and drinking for some time before the girl quietly came out of the bedroom."

"You two were obviously not going to leave right away. I asked her to join us, so she put on a dress."

"She shook hands with us but didn't say a thing all night."

"Like you."

"That night was very special, I had never seen a Chinese home with that sort of atmosphere. . . ."

"It was special because a white German girl with bright red lips had suddenly arrived. . . ."

"And there was also a barefoot little Beijing girl who was lovely and slender. . . ."

"Flickering candlelight. . . ."

"We sat drinking in your warm, cozy apartment as we listened to the howling wind outside."

"It was unreal, just like it is now, and probably there are also people watching. . . ."

You again think that the room is probably being videotaped.

"Is it still unreal?"

She clamps you with her legs and you close your eyes to experience her, hugging the fullness of her body and mumbling, "There was no need to go before morning. . . ."

"Of course, there wasn't. . . ." she says. "At the time, I didn't want to leave. It was a bitterly cold winter night and we had to cycle for an hour. Peter wanted to go, and you didn't try to get us to stay."

"Yes, that's right." You say that it was the same with you. You had to cycle back with her to the barracks.

"What barracks?"

You say that she was a nurse in the army hospital and she couldn't stay out overnight.

She lets go of you and asks, "Who are you talking about?"

You're talking about her army hospital being in the barracks in the outer suburbs of Beijing. She used to come every Sunday morning, and on the Monday morning before three o'clock you had to set off and cycle for more than two hours to get her back to the barracks before dawn.

Shrinking back, she pushes you away, sits up and asks, "Are you talking about that Chinese girl?"

You open your eyes and see her glaring at you. You apologize and explain that it was she who started talking about the little lover you had at the time.

"Do you long for her a lot?"

After pondering, you say, "That's in the remote past. We lost contact long ago."

"And you've had no news about her?" She sits on her haunches.

"No." You also move away from her and sit on the edge of the bed.

"Don't you want to look for her?"

You say that China is already very distant from you. She says she understands. You say you have no homeland. She says her father is German but her mother is a Jew, so she has no homeland either. But she can't get away from her memories. You ask her why not? She says she isn't like you, she's a woman. You say oh, and stop talking.

3

He needed a nest, a refuge, he needed a home where he could be away from people, where he could have privacy as an individual and not be observed. He needed a soundproof room where he could shut the door and talk loudly without being heard so that he could say whatever he wanted to say, a domain where he as an individual could voice his thoughts. He could no longer be wrapped in a cocoon like a silent larva. He had to live and to experience, be able to groan or howl as he made wild love with a woman. He had to get a space to exist, he could no longer endure those years of repression, and he needed somewhere to discharge his reawakened lust.

At the time his small partitioned room could only hold a single bed, a desk and a bookshelf, and in winter, when he put in a coal stove with a metal pipe for warmth, it was hard to move around with another person in the room. The worker and his wife having intercourse, or their baby having a pee, on the other side of the very basic partition, could be heard clearly. Two other families lived in the building and they all shared the tap and drain in the courtyard, so whenever the girl visited his small room, she was observed by the neighbors. He had to leave the door partly open as they chatted and drank tea. His wife—a woman he'd married ten years earlier and from whom he'd been separated for almost as long—had gone to the Party committee of the Writers' Association, which had in turn arranged for the street committee to report on him. The Party interfered in everything, from his thinking and his writing to his private life.

When the girl first came looking for him, she was dressed in an oversized, padded army uniform with a red collar-badge. Her face flushed, she said she'd read his fiction and had been deeply moved by it. He was on guard with this girl in an army uniform. Looking at her childlike face, he asked how old she was. She said she was studying at the army medical college and was an intern at the army barracks. She said she was seventeen that year. An age, he thought, when girls easily fall in love.

He closed the door to his room. When he kissed the girl, he had not yet received legal approval for a divorce from his wife and, fondling the girl, he held his breath. He could hear the neighbors walking in the courtyard, turning on the tap, washing clothes, washing vegetables, and emptying dirty water into the drain.

He was increasingly aware of his need to have a home, but not just so that he could possess a woman. What he wanted first of all was a roof that kept out the wind and rain, and four soundproof walls. But he did not want to marry again. Those ten years of futile, legally binding marriage were enough. He needed to be free for a while. Also, he was suspicious of women, especially young, pretty, seemingly promising girls with whom he could easily become besotted. He had been betrayed and reported more than once. At the university, he had fallen in love with a girl in the same class whose looks and voice were so sweet. But this lovely girl was ambitious, so she wrote a voluntary confession of her own thinking for the Party branch secretary, including in it his negative comments on the revolutionary novel *Song of Youth*, which the Communist Youth League was promoting as compulsory reading for young people. The girl had not deliberately set out to harm him, and in fact had feelings for him. The more passionate a woman, the more she had to confess her emotions to the Party: it was like the religiously devout needing to confess the secrets of their inner hearts to a priest. The Communist Youth League considered his thinking too gloomy, but the charge was not too serious, and, while he could not be admitted to the League, he was allowed to graduate. In the case of his wife, the matter was serious. If what she had reported had been substantiated with a fragment of what he had written in secret, he would have been labeled a counterrevolutionary. Ah, in those revolutionary years even women were revolutionized into lunatics and monsters.

He could not trust this girl in an army uniform. She had come to ask him about literature. He said he was not permitted to be a teacher, and suggested that she go to night classes at a university. There were literature courses she could enroll in for a fee, and she would be issued with a certificate after a couple of years. The girl asked what books she should read. He told her it was best not to read textbooks; most libraries had reopened and all the books that had formerly been banned were worth reading. The girl said she wanted to study creative writing, but he urged her not to, because if she messed up it would set back her future prospects. He himself was having endless troubles, whereas a simple girl like her, in an army uniform and studying medicine, had a very secure future. The girl said that she was not so simple and that she was not what he thought. She wanted to know more, she wanted to understand life, and this didn't conflict with her wearing an army uniform and studying medicine.

It wasn't that the girl failed to attract him, but he preferred casual sex with uninhibited women who had already wallowed in the mire at the bottom of society. There was no need for him to waste his energy teaching this girl about life. Moreover, what was life? Only Heaven knew.

It was impossible to explain what life was and, even more so, what literature was to this girl who had come to learn. It was as impossible as explaining to the Party secretary who managed the Writers' Association that what he considered literature didn't require the direction or approval of anyone. That was why he was running into trouble all the time.

Confronted by this refreshing and lovely girl dressed in an army uniform, he was unmoved and certainly did not have any wild thoughts. It had not occurred to him to touch her, and certainly not to go to bed with her. The girl was returning some books she had borrowed from his shelves to read. Her face was flushed and, having just come in the door, she was still slightly out of breath. As usual, he made her a cup of tea, then got her to sit on the chair against the bookshelf behind the door while he sat sideways in the chair next to the desk, as he did when editors came to discuss his manuscripts. There was a cheap sofa in the little room, but it was winter and a stove heater had already been installed, so if the girl sat on the sofa, the metal chimney of the stove would have blocked her face, and it would have been hard to talk. Both were sitting at the desk when the girl began stroking the novels, formerly banned as reactionary and pornographic, which she had returned. It seemed that the girl had tasted the forbidden fruit, or that she knew what forbidden fruit was, and was therefore uneasy.

He became aware of the girl's flesh because her delicate hands, right next to him, were stroking the books. The girl saw him looking at her hands and hid them under the desk. She became even more flushed. He questioned the girl on what she thought of the protagonists, mainly the female protagonists. The behavior of the women in these books conformed neither to present social morality nor the teachings of the Party. But, he said, that probably was what was known as life, because life actually was without fixed measurements. If the girl wanted to report him later on, or if the Party at her workplace ordered her to confess her dealings with him, there were no serious errors in what he had said. His past experiences constantly reminded him to be sure of this. Ah, and that was also called life!

The girl later said Chairman Mao had lots of women. It was only then that he dared to kiss her. The girl closed her eyes and let him fondle her body, so electrically sensitive to his touch inside the big padded army uniform. The girl asked if she could borrow more of such books to read. She said she wanted to know about everything, that it was not terrifying. At this, he said if books become forbidden fruit, society becomes really terrifying. That was why so many people lost their lives in the so-called Cultural Revolution that had now officially ended. The girl said she knew all this and that she had even seen someone who had been beaten to death: there were flies crawling on the black blood from his nose. He was said to have been a counterrevolutionary, and no one would collect the corpse. She was only a child then. But don't think she's a child, she is an adult now.

He asked what did being an adult imply? She said don't forget that she is studying medicine, pouted, and gave a laugh. He then held her hand and kissed her lips that gradually yielded to him. Thereafter, she came often, returning books and borrowing books, always on Sunday, staying longer each time, sometimes from noon till dark. However, she had to catch the eight o'clock bus back to the military barracks in the outer suburbs. It was always in the evening, when the sound of vegetables being washed gradually died in the courtyard and the neighbors had shut their doors, that he shut his door and had some moments of intimacy with her. She would not take off her army uniform and always kept an eye on the clock on the desk, and, when it was almost time for the last bus, she would quickly button up.

More and more he needed a room to protect his privacy. With great difficulty, he had obtained a legal divorce, but the state ruled that for him to live with a woman, they had to be married. Furthermore, for a woman to register an application to marry him, he first had to have proper housing. Including the years he had worked on a farm during the Cultural Revolution, he had already worked for twenty years and, according to the regulations, he should have been allocated housing long ago. However, it took two more years of suffering, and many quarrels and angry outbursts with housing cadres, before he was finally allocated a small apartment. It was just before a leader of the Party, more senior than the head of the Writers' Association, targeted him for criticism. He got together all of his savings as well as an advance on part of the royalties for a book that it might or might not be possible to publish, and somehow secured a peaceful refuge.

The girl arrived at his newly allocated apartment, and the moment the spring lock on the door clicked, the two of them went wild with excitement. At the time, the painting wasn't finished, bits of plaster were everywhere, and there was no bed. Right there, on a sheet of plastic with bits of plaster sticking to it, he stripped her down to her slim young girl's body that had been hidden all this time under the loose army uniform. However, the girl begged him under no circumstances to penetrate her. The army medical college carried out a full physical examination once a year, and unmarried female nurses were tested to see if their hymens were intact. Before being enlisted, they had to undergo rigorous political and physical examinations, and, apart from routine medical duties, they could be sent at any time on missions to look after the health of senior officers. Her spouse had to be approved by her military seniors, and she could not marry before she was twenty-six, before which time she could not resign, because, it was said, state secrets would be involved.

He did everything but penetrate her, or, rather, he kept his promise. Although he didn't penetrate her, he did everything else he could possibly do. Soon the girl was dispatched on a mission to accompany a senior officer on an inspection of the Chinese-Vietnamese border. After that he didn't hear from her for a while.

Almost a year later, also in winter, the girl suddenly reappeared.

He had just come home late at night after drinking at a friend's home when he heard a quiet knocking on his door. The girl was wretched, crying, and said she had been waiting for a whole six hours outside and was frozen stiff. She couldn't wait in the hallway because she was afraid people would see her and ask who she was looking for. She had hidden in the workers' hut outside and it was awful waiting until she saw the light come on in the apartment. He quickly shut the door and had just drawn the curtains when the girl, still wrapped in her outrageously huge military overcoat and still not warm, said, "Elder Brother, take me!"

He took her on the carpet, rolling backward and forward, no, crossing rivers and seas. They were like two sleek fish, or, rather, two animals tearing at one another in battle. She began to sob, and he said cry as loudly as you want, you can't be heard outside. She wept and wailed, and then shouted. He said he was a wolf. She said no, you are my Elder Brother. He said he wanted to be a wolf, a savage, lustful, bloodsucking, wild animal. She said she understood her Elder Brother, she belonged to her Elder Brother, she wasn't afraid of anything. From now on she belonged only to her Elder Brother, what she regretted was that she had not given herself to him earlier. . . . He said, don't talk about it. . . .

Afterward, she said she wanted her parents to somehow think of a way of getting her out of the army. At the time, he had an invitation to travel overseas but wasn't able to leave. She said she would wait for him, she was her Elder Brother's little woman. He finally got a passport and visa, and it was she who urged him to leave quickly in case they changed their minds. He did not realize it would be a permanent separation. Maybe he was unwilling or refused to think about it so that the pain would not strike him right to the core of his heart.

He would not let her come to the airport to see him off, and she said she would not be able to get leave. Even if she got the first bus from the barracks into the city, then changed several buses to get to the airport, it was unlikely that she would get there before his plane took off.

Before that, it had not occurred to him that he might leave this country. On the runway, taking off at Beijing airport, there was an intense whirring as the plane shuddered and was then instantly airborne. He suddenly felt that maybe—at the time he felt only maybe—he would never return to the land below the window. This expanse of gray-brown earth that people called homeland was where he was born and had grown up, it was where he had been educated, had matured and had suffered, and where he never thought he would leave. But did he have a homeland? Could the gray-brown land and ice-clad rivers in motion under the wings of the plane count as his homeland? It was later that this question arose and the answer gradually became quite clear.

At the time he simply wanted to free himself, to leave the black shadow enveloping him, to be able to breathe happily for a while. To get his passport, he had waited almost a year and had made the rounds of all the relevant departments. He was a citizen of this country, not a criminal, and there was no reason to deprive him of the right to leave the country. Of course, this reason was different for different people, and it was always possible to find a reason.

As he went through the customs barrier, they asked what he had in his suitcase. He said he had no prohibited goods, just his everyday clothes. They asked him to open his suitcase. He unlocked it.

"What's in there?"

"An ink stone for grinding ink, I bought it not so long ago." What he meant was that it was not antique, that it was not a prohibited item. However, they could still use any excuse to detain him, so he couldn't help being tense. A thought flashed through his mind: this was not his country.

In the same instant, he seemed to hear, "Elder Brother—" He quickly held his breath to calm himself.

Finally he was allowed through. He fixed his suitcase and put it on the conveyor belt, zipped up his hand luggage, and headed toward the boarding gate. He heard shouting again, someone seemed to be shouting his name. He pretended not to hear and kept going, but still he looked back. The official who had just searched his luggage had been checking a few foreigners in the sectioned-off corridor and was in the process of letting them through.

At that moment, he heard a drawn-out shout, a woman was calling his name, it was coming from far away and floated above the din of the people in the departure hall. His gaze went above the partition at the entrance to customs, searching for where the sound was coming from. He saw someone in a big army overcoat and an army hat, hunched over the marble railing of the second floor, but he couldn't see the face clearly.

The night he said good-bye to her, as she gave herself to him, she said over and over into his ear, "Elder Brother, don't come back, don't come back. . . ." Was this a premonition? Or was she thinking of him? Could she see things more clearly? Or could she guess what was in his heart? At the time he said nothing, he still hadn't the courage to make this decision. But she had awakened him, awakened him to this thought. He didn't dare to confront it, was still unable to cut the bonds of love and hope, unable to abandon her.

He hoped the person in the green army uniform hunched over the railing wasn't her, turned and continued toward the boarding gate. The red light on the flight indicator was flashing. He heard behind him a forlorn scream, a drawn-out "Elder Brother—" It must be her. However, without looking back again, he went through the boarding gate.

4

Warm and moist, writhing flesh. Memories start returning but you know it's not her, that sensitive delicate body that had let you do anything you wanted. The big, robust body pressing hard on you with unrestrained lust and abandonment totally exhausts you. "Keep talking! That Chinese girl, how did you enjoy yourself with her and how did you abandon her just like that?" You say she was a perfect woman, the girl wanted only to be a little woman, and wasn't wanton and lustful like her. "Are you saying you don't like it?" she asks. You say of course you like it, it's what you dream about, this sheer, total abandonment. "You also wanted to make her, that girl of yours, become like this?"—"Yes!"—"Also turn into a spring?"—"Just like this," you convulse, breathless. "Are all women the same for you?"—"No."—"How are they different?"—"With her there was another sort of tension."—"How was it different?"—"There was a sort of love."—"So you didn't enjoy yourself with her?"—"I enjoyed her but it was different."—"Here it is just carnal lust."—"Yes."—"Who is sucking you?"—"A German girl."—"A one-night prostitute?"—"No," you call out her name, "Margarethe!"

At this she smiles, takes your head in her hands and kisses you.

She is straddling you, kneeling, but her legs relax as she turns to brush aside a loose tangle of hair hanging over her eyes.

"Didn't you call out the wrong name?" There is an odd ring in her voice.

"Aren't you Margarethe?" you ask back, not comprehending.

"It was I who said it first."

"Don't you remember? When you asked, your name had already come to my lips."

"But it was I who said it first."

"Didn't you want me to guess? You could have waited a second more."

"I was anxious at the time, I was afraid you wouldn't remember," she admits. "When the play finished, people from the audience were at the theater door waiting to talk with you; I was embarrassed."

"It was all right, they were friends."

"They left after a few words. Why didn't you go for drinks with them?"

"It was probably because I had a foreign girl with me that they didn't hassle me."

"Did you want to sleep with me then?"

"No, but I could tell that you were excited."

"I lived in China for years and, of course, understood the play. But do you think Hong Kong people would?"

"I don't know."

"A price has to be paid." She looks moody again.

"A very moody German girl," you say with a smile, trying to change the atmosphere.

"I've already told you that I'm not German."

"Right, you're a Jewish girl."

"Anyway, I'm a woman," she says wearily.

"That's even better," you say.

"Why is it better?" That odd ring in her voice returns.

You then say you had not had a Jewish woman before.

"Have you had lots of women?" Her eyes light up in the dark.

"I guess quite a lot since leaving China," you admit. There's no need to hide this from her.

"When you stay in hotels like this, do you always have women to keep you company?" she goes on to ask.

You're not as lucky as that. And when you stay in a big hotel like this, the theater group that invited you would be paying for it, you explain.

Her eyes become gentle and she lies down next to you. She says she likes your frankness, but that is not you as a person. You say you like her as a person and not just her body.

"That's good."

She says this with sincerity and she presses against you. You can feel that her body and her heart have softened. You say, of course, you remember her from that winter night. After that she came especially to see you, she said she happened to be passing. She was on the new bypass of the city ring road, saw your apartment block, and for no apparent reason dropped in. Maybe it was to look at the paintings in your apartment, they were unusual, just like a dream world. It was windy outside, the wind in Germany didn't howl, everything in Germany was sedate, stifling. That night, in the light of the candles, the paintings seemed to have something mystical about them and she wanted to see them clearly during the daytime.

"Were those all your paintings?" she asks.

You say you didn't hang other people's paintings in the apartment.

"Why?"

"The apartment was too small."

"Were you an artist as well?" she goes on to ask.

"Not officially," you say. "And, at the time, that was indeed the case."

"I don't understand."

You say, of course not, it's impossible for her to understand. It was China. A German art foundation had invited you to go there to paint, but the Chinese authorities would not agree to it.

"Why?"

You say even for you, it was impossible to know, but at the time you went everywhere trying to find out. Finally, through a friend, you got to the relevant department and found out that the official reason was that you were a writer and not an artist.

"Was that a reason? Why couldn't a writer also be an artist?"

You say it's impossible for her to understand, even if she does know the language. Things in China can't be explained by language alone.

"Then don't try."

She says she remembers that afternoon, the apartment was flooded with sunlight. She was sitting on the sofa examining the paintings and really wanted to buy one of them, but at the time she was a student and couldn't afford it. You said you would give it to her as a gift, but she refused, because it was something you had created. You said you often gave paintings as gifts to friends. Chinese people don't buy paintings, that is, among friends. She said she had only just met you, and couldn't really count as a friend, so it would be embarrassing to accept it. If you had a book of your paintings, you could give her a copy, or she could pay for it. You said paintings like yours couldn't get published in China, but, as she liked your work so much, it was all right to give her one of them. She says the painting is still hanging in her home in Frankfurt. For her, it is a special memory, a dream world, and one doesn't know where one is. It is an image in the mind.

"At the time, why did you insist on giving it to me? Do you remember the painting?" she asks.

You say you don't remember the painting but you remember wanting to paint her, wanting her to be your model. At the time, you had never painted a foreign girl.

"That would have been very dangerous," she says.

"Why?"

"It was nothing for me. I'm saying it would have been dangerous for you. You probably didn't say anything at the time because right then there was knocking at your door. You opened it, and it was someone who had come to check the electricity meter. You gave him a chair and he stood on it to read the meter behind the door, then, after making a note, left. Did you think he had really come to read the meter?"

You don't answer, you can't remember any of this. You say life in China sometimes appears in nightmares and you deliberately try to forget them, but from time to time they charge out of the subconscious.

"Didn't they warn people in advance that they would be coming?"

You say that in China anything is possible.

"I didn't go again because I was afraid of getting you into trouble," she says softly.

"I didn't think. . . ." you say.

You suddenly want to be affectionate, and put your hands on her abundant breasts.

She strokes the back of your hands and says, "You're very caring."

"You too, dear Margarethe." You smile and ask, "Are you leaving tomorrow?"

"Let me think. . . . I could stay longer but I'll have to change my plane ticket to Frankfurt. When do you return to Paris?"

"Next Tuesday. It's a cheap ticket and hard to change, but if I pay extra I can still change it."

"No, at the latest, I'll have to leave by the weekend," she says. "A Chinese delegation will be in Germany for a conference on Monday and I'll be interpreting. I'm not as free as you, I work for a boss."

"Then there are still four days." You count up the days.

"Tomorrow, no, one night has already passed, there are only three days," she says. "I'll phone the boss and ask for leave, change my ticket, then go to my hotel and bring my luggage across."

"What about this boss of yours?"

"He can get lost," she says. "My job here has been completed."

It is already light outside the window, and clouds swirl above the big building with the white pillars opposite. The peak is shrouded in mist and the lush vegetation on the mountain is the color of black jade. It looks like rain.

5

He did not know how he had returned to his home in Beijing. He couldn't find the key in his pocket, couldn't open the door, and was anxious people in the building would recognize him. He heard foot-steps coming down the stairs and quickly turned, pretending to be going down. The person coming from the floor above brushed past him: it was Old Liu, the department chief, his boss back when he was working as an editor years ago. Old Liu was unshaven and looked like he did when he was hauled out and denounced during the Cultural Revolution. He had protected this old cadre at the time and Old Liu wouldn't have forgotten this, so he told him that he couldn't find the key to his apartment. Old Liu hesitated, then said, "Your apartment's been reallocated." At this he remembered that his apartment had been confiscated. "Would you be able to find somewhere for me to stay?" he asked. A worried frown appeared on Old Liu's face, but, giving the matter some thought, he said: "It will have to go through the building management committee, it won't be easy. Why did you have to come back?" He said he had purchased a return plane ticket, he hadn't thought. . . . However, he should have. After being overseas for many years, how easily he had forgotten the difficulties he had experienced in China. Someone else was coming down the stairs. Old Liu pretended not to know him and hurried downstairs and out the front door. He quickly followed to avoid anyone else recognizing him, but when he got outside Old Liu had vanished. The sky was filled with flying dust, it seemed to be one of Beijing's early-spring dust storms, but he couldn't be sure if it was spring or autumn. He was wearing a single layer of clothing and felt cold. Suddenly he remembered that Old Liu had jumped out of the office building and had been dead for years. He must quickly escape. He went to stop a taxi on the street to take him to the airport but realized that the customs officials would immediately see from his documents that he was a public enemy. He was troubled about having become a public enemy and even more troubled that he had no place to stay in this town where he had spent more than half of his life. He arrived at a commune in the suburbs to see if he could rent a room in the village. A peasant with a hoe took him to a shed covered with thin plastic, and pointed his hoe at a row of cement *kang* inside. The place must have been a cellar for storing cabbages in winter, which they had converted with a layer of cement. Probably there has been some progress, he thought. He had slept on the ground at the reform-through-labor farm in a big communal bed: the ground was spread with straw and people slept one next to the other, each with a forty-centimeter bed space, not as wide as these *kang*. Here, it was one person to a *kang,* much larger than the single cement lot in the cemetery where he had buried the ashes of his parents together, so there was nothing for him to complain about. Inside, he found more *kang* downstairs. If he rented, he would choose a downstairs *kang* where it was more soundproof. He said his wife liked singing. Good heaven! There was a woman with him. . . . He woke up. It had been a nightmare.

He had not had that sort of nightmare for a long time, and if he had dreams they didn't have much to do with China. Abroad, he met people from China and they would all tell him to go back and have a look: Beijing has changed a lot, you wouldn't know it, and there are more five-star hotels than in Paris! When people said it was possible to make a fortune in China today, he would ask if they had made a fortune. And if they went on and said that surely he thought about China, he would say both of his parents were dead. What about being homesick? He had already committed such feelings to the grave. He had left the country ten years ago and refused to think about the past. He believed he had broken with it a long time ago.

He was now a free-flying bird. This inner freedom had no attachments, was like the clouds, the wind. God had not conferred this freedom upon him, he had paid dearly for it, and only he knew just how precious it was. He no longer tied himself to a woman. A wife and children were burdens too heavy for him.

When he closed his eyes his mind began to roam, and only with his eyes closed did he not feel others watching and observing him. With his eyes closed, there was freedom and he could wander within the female cavern, a wonderful place. He once visited a perfectly preserved limestone cave in the Massif Central of France. The tourists entered one after the other, holding onto the iron rail of their individual cable cars. The huge cavern, illuminated by orange light, had layers of walls with twisting folds and numerous wet, dripping stalactites and stalagmites. This deep fathomless cavity created by nature was like a huge womb. In this dark natural cavern he was minute, like a single sperm, moreover an infertile sperm, roaming about happy and contented; this was a freedom that exists after release from lust.

Before he had sexually awakened, as a child, he would travel on the back of the goose in the children's books his mother had bought for him. Or, like Andersen's homeless waif with a bronze pig, he would mount the bronze pig to roam the noble mansions of Florence at night. But he could still remember that his first experience of female warmth didn't come from his mother but from a servant called Mama Li who used to bathe him. He would splash around naked in the tub, then Mama Li would grab him and carry him against her warm breasts to his bed, scratch him where he itched, and coax him to sleep. This young peasant woman didn't worry about taking a bath and combing her hair in front of him when he was a child. He could still remember her big white breasts hanging like pears, and her oiled, shiny, waist-length black hair. She used a bone comb to smooth out her hair and folded it into a big bun that was tied into a net and then fixed onto her head. At the time, his mother had a hairdresser's perm, and combing it wasn't as much trouble. As a child, the cruelest thing he saw was Mama Li being beaten up. Her husband came to look for her and wanted to drag her off, but she clung desperately to a leg of the table and wouldn't let go. The man grabbed her hair by the bun and banged her head on the floor until blood from her forehead dripped onto the tiles. Even his mother could not stop the man. Only then did he find out that Mama Li had fled from the village because she couldn't endure her husband's bullying. But she wasn't able to buy her freedom even by giving the man her indigo print bag with the silver coins and a silver bracelet in it, all of her wages for several years of work.

Freedom is not a human right conferred by Heaven. Nor does the freedom to dream come at birth: it is a capacity and an awareness that needs to be defended. Moreover, even dreams can be assailed by nightmares.

"I warn comrades to note that they want to restore capitalism. I am talking about the Ox Demons and Snake Spirits, high up, and down below, from the Party Center down to provincial cadres! Where they exist in the Party Center, we must relentlessly drag them out, we must safeguard the purity of the Party and not let the glory of the Party be sullied! Are there any here among you? I would not dare to vouch that there are not. Aha, you thousands gathered at this meeting, are all of you so pure and clean? Are there none groping for fish in muddy waters, colluding with higher ups and jumping down below? They want to confuse the battle lines of our class struggle; I urge all comrades to be on the alert and to sharpen their eyes. All who oppose Chairman Mao, all who oppose the Party Center and all who oppose socialism must be dragged out!"

As the voice of the official on the platform died down, everyone starting shouting slogans:

"Exterminate all Ox Demons and Snake Spirits!"

"I swear to protect Chairman Mao with my life!"

"I swear to protect the Party Center with my life!"

"If the enemy refuses to capitulate, it must be destroyed!"

All around him people took the lead in shouting, and he, too, had to shout out loudly so that he could be heard; he couldn't just make a show by raising his fist. He knew at this meeting that anyone who behaved differently from others would be noticed, and he could sense that he was being observed, arrows were pointing at his back, and he was sweating. He felt for the first time that maybe he was the enemy, and that very likely he, too, would be destroyed.

Maybe he belonged to the class that had to be destroyed. Then what class did his deceased parents belong to? His paternal great-grandfather wanted to be an official, donated a whole street of properties, but still couldn't manage to buy himself the black silk hat worn by officials. He went berserk, got up one night and torched everything, including the house he had kept to live in. That was during the Qing Dynasty, before his father was born. His maternal grandmother had mortgaged all the property left by his maternal grandfather, and was financially ruined by the time his mother was born. Neither of his parents had been involved in politics. However, his father's younger brother had performed a meritorious deed for the new government by stopping a sum of money at the bank from going to Taiwan, and that was how he had earned the title of Democratic Personage. They were all salaried workers, did not want for food and clothing, and lived comfortably, but they also lived in fear of losing their jobs. They had all welcomed the New China, and believed that the new nation would be better than the old one.

After "liberation," when the great armies of the "Communist bandits"—later called the "Communist Army," later still called the "Liberation Army," and then later officially named the "People's Liberation Army"—entered the city, both his parents felt liberated. Incessant war, bombing, fleeing as refugees and fear of robbery all seemed to have gone forever. His father did not like the old Nationalist government. His father had been a branch manager in a state-run bank, but in his father's own words, his failure to understand the nepotism and infighting cost him his job. Following that, for a while, he worked as a journalist with a small newspaper, but when it closed down, he could only sell off property in order to survive. He remembered the silver "big heads" in the shoebox under the five-drawer chest getting fewer by the day, and the gold bracelets disappearing from his mother's wrist. This very shoebox under the five-drawer chest had been used to hide a copy of *On the New Democracy,* printed on the coarse paper used in Mao Zedong's border region. The book had been smuggled into the city by his father's mysterious friend Big Brother Hu. This was the earliest publication he had seen of Mao Zedong's writings, and it was hidden with the silver dollars.

Big Brother Hu was a teacher in a middle school, and whenever he visited, any children were chased off. However, he quietly looked forward to this talk of "liberation" and deliberately went in and out of his parents' room. He heard bits that he understood. The fat postmaster, a landlord, said that the Communist bandits advocated sharing property and sharing wives, eating from one pot of food, and rejecting blood ties. He also said they engaged in rampant killings. His parents did not believe the postmaster. His father, laughing, said to his mother, "That maternal cousin of yours," that is, her father's maternal cousin, "is a Communist bandit with a pockmarked face, if he's still alive. . . ."

This maternal uncle had joined the underground Party in Shanghai long ago, while at university. Afterward, he left home and went off to Jiangxi province to take part in the revolution. Twenty years later this uncle was still alive and he eventually met him. His pock-marked face was not frightening, and, flushed with alcohol, he looked even more heroic. He had a resounding laugh but was asthmatic and said that during those years when he was a guerrilla fighter he couldn't get tobacco and often dried wild herbs to smoke. This maternal uncle came into the city with the big army, put notices in the newspapers to look for his family, then, through relatives, found out what had happened to this maternal cousin of his. Their meeting had something theatrical to it. His maternal uncle was worried about their not recognizing him, so he wrote in his letter that he could be identified on the railway platform by a white towel tied to the top of a bamboo pole. His soldier aide, a peasant lad from the countryside, was there waving a long bamboo pole over the heads of the thronging crowds. Sweat was pouring off the rim of the lad's army cap, but, regardless of the heat, he kept it strapped on to hide his scabby head.

Like his father, his maternal uncle was fond of drinking. Whenever he came he always brought a bottle of millet liquor and a big lotus-leaf parcel of chicken wings, goose liver, duck gizzards, duck feet, and pork tongue. These savory delicacies filled the whole table. The soldier aide would be sent away and the two men would chat, often until late into the night; his maternal uncle would then be escorted back to the army compound by his aide. This maternal uncle had so many stories to tell—from his early years in an old-style big family on the decline, to his experiences in the rolling battles during the guerrilla war. He would listen even when he couldn't keep his eyes open, and refused to go to bed even after his mother had told him several times.

Those stories came from a world totally alien to the children's stories he had read, and from children's stories he turned to worshipping revolutionary myths. This maternal uncle wanted to encourage him to write, and had him stay in his home for a few months. There were no children's books in the house but there was a set of *The Collected Works of Lu Xun*. This uncle's method of teaching was to have him read one of Lu Xun's stories during the day and then, after returning home from official duties, he would ask him to talk about it with him. He couldn't understand those old stories; moreover, at the time, he was more interested in catching cicadas in the weeds and rubble by the wall. His maternal uncle returned him to his mother and, with a loud laugh, conceded that he had failed.

His mother at the time was still young, not even thirty. She didn't want to rear a child or be a housewife anymore, and instead wholeheartedly threw herself into the new life; she started working and didn't have time to look after him. He had no problems with schoolwork and immediately became a good student in the class. He wore a red scarf and didn't join the boy students in their dirty talk about girls, or in their pranks. On Children's Festival Day on June 1, he was selected by the school to take part in the city celebrations at which he presented flowers to the exemplary workers of the city. One after the other, his parents had been honored as exemplary workers of their work units and awarded the prizes of enamel tea mugs and notebooks printed with their names. For him, those years were also lucky years. The Youth Palace often had singing and dancing programs, and he hoped that one day he would be able to go on stage to perform.

He attended a fiction recital, at which a teacher read a work by the Russian writer Vladimir Korolenko. The story took place on a snowswept night, and the first-person narrator was driving a jeep on a mountain road when the brakes failed. He saw a light on the cliff and struggled up to the house where there was an old woman. In the middle of the night, the howling wind made it impossible for the narrator to fall asleep and, listening to the wind, he seemed to hear someone sighing from time to time. Thinking he might as well get up, he found the old woman sitting by the solitary lamp in the room, facing the banging door. The narrator asked the woman why she hadn't gone to bed. Was she waiting for someone? She said she was waiting for her son. The narrator indicated that he could wait instead. It was then that she said her son was dead and that it was she who had pushed him down the mountain. The narrator naturally couldn't help questioning her about it. The old woman gave a long sigh and said her son deserted during the war and came back to the village, but she did not allow her deserter son into the house.

The story somehow moved him deeply and it made him feel that the world of adults was incomprehensible. Now it was he who had deserted. The thoughts that had circulated in his mind from childhood had determined that he would later be declared the enemy. However, he would never again return to the embrace of the homeland that had nurtured him.

He also recalled that the first time he thought hard about something was probably when he was eight, because of where it had taken place; it was soon after he had written his first diary entry. He was leaning out the window of his little room upstairs when he dropped the rubber ball he was holding. It bounced a few times, then rolled into the grass under an oleander bush. He begged his young uncle who was reading below in the courtyard to throw the ball back to him.

His young uncle said, "Lazy bones, you threw it down, so come down and pick it up yourself."

He said his mother told him he was not to come downstairs to play until he had finished writing his first diary entry.

His young uncle said, "But what if I pick it up and you toss it down again?"

He said he hadn't tossed it down, that the ball had dropped by itself. His young uncle reluctantly threw the ball into his window upstairs. Still leaning out the window, he went on to ask his young uncle, "The ball dropped down, but why didn't it bounce back? If it bounced back the distance it dropped, I wouldn't have had to trouble you to get it."

The young uncle said, "It's all very well for you to say so, but this has to do with physics."

He then asked, "What's physics?"

"It has to do with a basic theory and you wouldn't be able to understand."

His young uncle at the time was a middle-school student and greatly inspired his respect, especially with his talk of physics and some basic theory. He remembered these words and terms and thought that while the world looked ordinary, everything in fact was profound and unfathomable.

Afterward, his mother bought him a set of children's books, *Ten Thousand Whys*. He read through every volume but nothing impressed him, except for the question about the beginning of the world, which has always remained in his mind.

Remote childhood is hazy, but some bright spots float up in memories. When you pick up one end of a thread, memories that have been submerged by time gradually appear and, like a net emerging from the water, they are interconnected and infinite. The more you pull, the more threads seem to appear and disappear. Now that you have picked up one end and again pulled up a whole mass of happenings from different times, you can't start anywhere, can't find a thread to follow. It's impossible to sort them to put them into some sort of order. Human life is a net, you want to undo it a knot at a time, but only succeed in creating a tangled mess. Life is a muddled account that you can't work out.

6

A man you don't know has invited you for lunch at noon. The secretary said on the phone, "Our chairman of the board, Mr. Zhou, will pick you up punctually in the hotel lobby."

You arrive in the lobby, and, immediately, a fashionably dressed man walks up to you; he has broad shoulders and a solid build, a broad face and a square jaw. He presents his business card to you in both hands.

"I've been wanting to meet you for a long time." The man says he's seen your play and has boldly ventured to take up a bit of your time by inviting you to share a meal with him.

You get in his big Mercedes limousine, an obvious sign of wealth. The chairman of the board drives the car himself and asks what you would like to eat.

"Anything's fine. Hong Kong is a paradise for food," you say.

"It's different in Paris, the women there are all so wonderful." Mr. Zhou is smiling as he drives along.

"Not all are, some in the subways are tramps," you say. You start believing that the man really is a boss.

The car drives past the bay and enters the long underwater tunnel to Kowloon.

Mr. Zhou says, "We'll go to the racecourse, it'll be quiet at lunchtime and good for talking. It's not the racing season. Normally, if you go there for a meal, you have to be a member of the Jockey Club."

So, a wealthy man in Hong Kong likes your play. You start feeling curious.

The two of you are seated, and Mr. Zhou orders some plain food, stops joking about women, and becomes serious. Only a few of the tables are occupied in this spacious, comfortable dining room, and the waiters stand some way off quietly in the courtyard. It's not like most Hong Kong restaurants that are bustling and packed with customers all the time.

"I'm not bluffing. I swam here illegally from the Mainland. During the Cultural Revolution, I was doing hard labor on a military farm in Guangdong province. I had finished middle school, I wasn't stupid, and I wasn't going to sacrifice myself like that for the whole of my life."

"But crossing illegally was dangerous."

"Of course. At the time, both my parents were in prison, the house had been ransacked, and whichever way you looked at it, I was a mongrel offspring of the Five Black Categories."

"What if you came across sharks—"

"That wouldn't have been so bad, at least I'd have had a chance to fight it out to see if I was lucky. It was people I was frightened of, the searchlights of the patrol boats were sweeping the water all the time. When they found anyone trying to cross illegally, they'd just open fire."

"Then how did you get across?"

"I equipped myself with two basketball bladders, basketballs used to have a rubber bladder with a tube that one blew into."

"I know them, children used them for floats when they were learning to swim, plastic products weren't widely available in those days," you say, nodding.

"If boats came along, I'd let out the air and swim underwater. I practiced for a whole summer. I also took some drinking straws with me." Mr. Zhou has a smile on his face but it doesn't seem genuine. You sense that he is sad, and he no longer looks like a rich man.

"The good thing about Hong Kong is that you can somehow get by. I suddenly got rich and now no one knows my past. I changed my name a long time ago and people only know me as Zhou such-and-such, the chairman of the board of the company." A hint of arrogance plays at the corners of his mouth and eyes and once again he has the look of a rich man.

You know this is not directed at you. You're a total stranger and he hasn't hesitated to tell you all about his background. This arrogance has developed because of his present status.

"I liked your play but I don't think it can really be understood by Hong Kong people," he says.

"When they do understand, it will be too late." After a pause, you say, "One needs to have had a particular sort of experience."

"It's like that," he confirmed.

"Do you like plays?" you ask.

"I don't usually see plays," he says. "I go to the ballet and concerts, and I book tickets for famous singers, operas, and symphony groups from the West. I'm starting to enjoy some artistic things now, but I've never seen a play like yours before."

"I understand." You give a laugh, then ask, "Then why did you think to come and see this play?"

"A friend phoned and recommended it," he says.

"Does that mean that there are some Hong Kong people who do understand the play?"

"It was someone from the Mainland."

You say that you wrote the play when you were in China but that it can only be performed outside China. The things you're writing nowadays don't have much to do with China.

He says it's much the same for him. His wife and son were both born in Hong Kong and are genuine Hong Kong people, and he's been here for thirty years and also counts as a Hong Kong resident. His only dealings with the Mainland have been in business, and that was getting more and more difficult. However, for better or worse, he has managed to extract a big amount of capital from the place.

"Where are you thinking of investing?" you can't help asking.

"Australia," he says. "Seeing your play made me even more certain."

You say that your play doesn't really have a China background, it's about ordinary relationships between people.

He says he knows that. Anyway, he needs somewhere to go, just in case.

"But won't Australia have an aversion for Chinese if masses of Hong Kong people flood there?" you say.

"That's what I want to talk to you about."

"I don't know how it is in Australia, I live in Paris," you say.

"Then how is it in France?" he asks, looking right at you.

"There's racism everywhere, and naturally it occurs also in France," you say.

"It's hard for Chinese in the West. . . ." He picks up his half glass of orange juice, then puts it down again.

You feel some sympathy for him. He says he has a small family, born and bred in Hong Kong, and his business would be able to keep operating. Of course, there's no harm preparing for a way out.

He says he is honored that you agreed to have this very ordinary meal with him, and that, like you as a person, your writing is very frank.

You say, it is he who is frank. All Chinese live behind masks and it's quite hard to take off the masks.

"It's probably when there's no profit or loss for either party that people can become friends."

He says this incisively; he has clearly been through many ups and downs in his dealings with people.

A journalist is to interview you at three o'clock, and you have arranged to meet at a coffee shop in Wanchai. He says he can take you, but you say he is a busy man and there is no need for him to do this. He says should you come back to Hong Kong to feel free to look him up. You thank him for his kindness, say this is probably the last time you will put on a play in Hong Kong, but that in future you are sure to meet again, though, hopefully, not until he is in Australia. He quickly says no, no, if he goes to Paris he will certainly look you up. You leave him your address and telephone number, and he immediately writes his mobile phone number on his business card and gives it to you. He says to give a call if you need any help and that he hopes there will be an opportunity to meet again.

The journalist is a young woman wearing glasses. She gets up from a seat by the window overlooking the water as soon as you enter and waves to you. She takes off her glasses and says, "I normally don't wear glasses, but I've only seen your photographs in the papers and was afraid I wouldn't recognize you."

She puts her glasses into her handbag, takes out a tape recorder and asks, "Is it all right to use a tape recorder?"

You say that it doesn't bother you.

"When I interview, I insist on the accuracy of what I quote," she says. "Many journalists in Hong Kong will write anything. Sometimes Mainland writers get so angry that they demand corrections. Of course, I understand their situation. Anyway, I know that you're different, even if you do come from the Mainland."

"I don't have any superiors," you say with a smile.

She says her editor in chief is very good and generally doesn't touch what she writes, and whatever she writes is published. She can't stand restrictions; after 1997—there's that 1997 again—if she can't take it, she'll just leave.

"Where will you go, if you don't mind my asking?"

She says she holds a British passport for Hong Kong residents, so she can't get residence in England. She doesn't like England anyway. She's thinking of going to America but would prefer to go to Spain.

"Why Spain and not America?"

She bites her lip, smiles, and says she had a Spanish boyfriend. She met him when she went to Spain but they have broken off. Her present boyfriend is from Hong Kong. He's an architect and he doesn't want to leave.

"It's hard getting work elsewhere," she says. "Of course, I like Hong Kong best." She says she has been to many countries and that it's fun traveling, but it would be hard living in those places. Not so in Hong Kong, she and her parents were born in Hong Kong, she is a one-hundred-percent Hong Kong person. She has also done special research on Hong Kong history, literature, and changes in cultural practices. She's thinking of writing a book.

"What would you do if you went to America?" you ask.

"Further studies. I've already corresponded with a university."

"To study for a Ph.D.?"

"To study and maybe also to look for some work."

"What about your boyfriend?"

"I might get married before leaving, or . . . Actually, I don't know what to do." She doesn't seem to be nearsighted but her eyes have a faraway look. "Am I interviewing you or are you interviewing me?"

She pulls herself together and puts on the tape recorder. "All right, now please say something about your views on cultural policies after Hong Kong reverts to the Mainland, will plays in Hong Kong be affected? Such issues preoccupy the Hong Kong cultural world. You are from the Mainland, could you give your views about this?"

After the interview, you again take the ferry back to Kowloon to give instructions to the performers at the Cultural Centre Playhouse. When the play begins, you can return to the hotel to have a leisurely meal with Margarethe.

The sun is shining at an angle through the clouds onto the sea, and glistening waves lace the blue water, the cool breeze is better than the air-conditioning indoors. On Hong Kong Island on the other side of the water, the lush green mountains are densely crowded with tall buildings. As the sounds of the bustling city recede, a rhythmic clanging on the water becomes distinct. You turn and notice that the sound is coming from the construction site of the auditorium being built for the handover ceremony between Britain and China in 1997. The banging of pneumatic hammers reminds you that, at this very moment, Hong Kong is by the minute and second unstoppably becoming China. The glare of the sun on the waves makes you squint and you feel drowsy, the China that you thought you had left continues to perplex you, you must make a clean break with it. You want to go with Margarethe to that very European little street in Lan Kwai Fong, to find a bar with some jazz where you can get drunk.

7

Boom! Boom! Pneumatic hammers again and again, unhurried, spaced at three- or four-second intervals. The great, glorious, correct Party! More correct, more glorious, greater than God! Forever correct! Forever glorious! Forever great!

"Comrades, I'm here representing Chairman Mao and the Party Center!"

The senior cadre had a medium build and a broad ruddy face. He spoke with a Sichuan accent, looked to be in good health, and his speech and movements indicated that he'd led troops and fought battles. The Cultural Revolution had just begun and the senior cadres still in power—from Mao's wife Jiang Qing to Premier Zhou Enlai and Mao Zedong himself—all wore military uniforms. The senior cadre, accompanied by the workplace Party secretary, sat erect on the dais that was covered with red tablecloths in the auditorium. He noted the soldiers and political cadres guarding the side doors and the back door to the meeting.

It was almost midnight. The whole workplace with its more than a thousand staff, group after group, assembled in the auditorium. No empty seats were left, and gradually even the aisles had filled with people sitting in them. A soldier-turned-political-cadre, also wearing an old army uniform, conducted the singing. "Sailing the Seas Depends on the Helmsman" was sung daily by the troops in the ranks, but these literary people and administrative cadres couldn't sing the straining high notes of this paean. "The East Is Red" was set to a folk song everyone knew, but even that was a shambles when it was sung.

"I support my comrades in opening fire on the black gang opposing the Party, Socialism, and Mao Zedong Thought!"

The meeting instantly erupted into the shouting of slogans. He couldn't tell who started the shouting and was caught off guard, but he also involuntarily raised his arm. The slogan-shouting wasn't uniform, and the voice of the senior cadre boomed through the amplifier even more loudly and immediately drowned out any stragglers.

"I support my comrades in opening fire on all Ox Demons and Snake Spirits! Now, please note that I say *all* Ox Demons and Snake Spirits, all of those reactionary scoundrels skulking in dark corners waiting to jump out and act brazenly as soon as the climate is right. Chairman Mao put it well: 'Those reactionaries simply aren't going to be overthrown unless you strike them down!'"

At this, all around, people stood up and, with raised fists, began shouting loudly.

"Down with all Ox Demons and Snake Spirits!"

"Long live Chairman Mao!"

"Long live!"

"Long, long live!"

This time, the slogans rose and subsided in waves, which became more uniform and forceful. After this had been repeated a few times, the whole gathering was shouting uniformly, like an all-engulfing wave, like an unstoppable tide that instilled terror in people's hearts. He no longer dared to look around and, for the first time, perceived that these familiar slogans possessed a menacing power. Chairman Mao was not far away in Heaven, was not an idol that could be stored away, Chairman Mao had supreme power. He had to keep up with the shouting and he had to shout clearly and, moreover, absolutely without any hesitation.

"I just don't believe it! So many intellectuals have been crammed into this workplace of yours; can everyone assembled here really be so revolutionary? I'm not saying it's not good to have knowledge, I didn't say that. I'm talking about those two-faced counterrevolutionaries. In their writings, they use our revolutionary slogans, they put up the red flag to oppose the red flag, they say one thing but mean something else! I reckon, they would not have the guts to openly jump out to present themselves as counterrevolutionaries. Are there any such people at this gathering? Would any of you dare to stand up and say you oppose the Communist Party, oppose Mao Zedong Thought, and oppose Socialism? If there is, I invite you to come onto the dais to speak!"

The gathering fell silent, breathing virtually stopped, and the air congealed. If someone had dropped a needle, it would have been heard.

"But it is after all the world of the dictatorship of the proletariat! So they are forced to assume a disguise, take up our revolutionary slogans, and, with a shake, transform themselves. Wasn't I just now talking about groping for fish in muddy waters? While we are engaged in the Great Proletarian Cultural Revolution, they are out there fanning up evil winds and lighting malicious fires, colluding with people in high positions and jumping down to work on the people below. They are intent on wrecking every level of our Party in the workplace and are making out that we are a sinister gang. They are wicked and crafty! Comrades, you must be vigilant! Look around yourselves carefully and haul out all those enemies, scheming careerists, and despicable worms inside and outside the Party who have infiltrated our ranks!"

After the senior cadre departed, everyone quietly filed out, nobody daring to look at anyone else for fear of showing the terror in one's heart. But, back at the offices where all the lights were on, people came face to face with one another and everyone went through hurdles of confession and remorse. People all requested individual sessions, at which everyone, sobbing and weeping, reported their misdeeds to the Party. People were easily manipulated. They were softer than dough when they wanted to make themselves pure, although they were vicious when it came to exposing others. Around midnight, people were most vulnerable, wanting the comfort of their partner in bed, and it was at this particular time that the interrogations and confessions took place.

Some hours earlier, at the after-work political study session, everyone had a copy of Mao's *Selected Works* on the desk as they browsed through the newspapers or pretended to be doing something to fill in the two hours before they would go home, laughing and joking. Revolution was seething in the upper echelons of the Party but hadn't yet fallen onto the heads of the masses. When the person from the political department came into the office to tell people to stay for the all-staff meeting, it was already eight o'clock at night. Another two hours were wasted, and still there was no sign of people being assembled. Old Liu, the department chief, kept tamping more tobacco into the bowl of his pipe, and someone asked him how many more pipes he'd need to smoke. Old Liu smiled without replying, but it could be seen that he was deeply worried. Old Liu was normally not officious, and the fact that he had put up a poster about the Party committee had endeared him to everyone. However, when someone said you couldn't go wrong if you followed Old Liu, he immediately raised his pipe and corrected him, "We must follow Chairman Mao!" Everyone laughed. Right until then, it seemed that no one wanted this class struggle to erupt among colleagues in the same office. Furthermore, Old Liu was an old Party member from the time of the War of Resistance against Japan, and this was reflected in his salary and rank. And as for that curved leather chair with armrests in his department chief's office, not just anyone was entitled to it. His room that smelled of his pipe tobacco with its chocolate aroma still had a relaxed feeling.

After midnight the political cadres and the staid, expressionless Party secretaries separately ensconced themselves in their own offices. One after another, people went through the cycle of confession, remorse, crying if they wanted to, and then entered the phase of informing on one another. Big Sister Huang, in charge of receiving and dispatching documents, had her turn to speak ahead of him. Her husband, who had worked for the Nationalist Government, had abandoned her to run off with his mistress to Taiwan. The old woman said that the Party had given her a new life and, whimpering uncontrollably, took out her handkerchief to dry her eyes and nose. She was so frightened she was crying. He did not cry, but only he knew that sweat was running down his back.

The year he started university, when he was just seventeen and virtually still a child, he attended a struggle session against rightist senior students. It was in a lecture room with stairs, and new students had to sit on the floor at the front for their initiation in political education. As a name was called, the rightist student stood up, walked to the bottom of the stairs, and, head bowed, faced everyone. Sweat on the forehead and nose, tears and mucus splashing on the floor, the student would be absolutely wretched, just like a dog floundering in water. Those who came forward were fellow students, and, one by one, they went through the emotional routine of listing their anti-Party crimes. Some time later, these rightist students who never said anything and always sat at a separate table, leaving as soon as they had eaten, disappeared from the big dining hall. No one ever mentioned them again. It was as if they had never existed.

It was not until after he graduated that he heard the expression "reform through labor," there seemed to have been a taboo on any mention of it. He didn't know that his father had been investigated and sent to a reform-through-labor farm, he had only heard a few vague remarks about it from his mother. He had already left home and was in Beijing studying at university, and his mother had written about it in a letter, but as "labor training." When he returned home during summer vacation a year later, his father had returned from the farm and had been reinstated in his job but he had been smeared as a rightist. His parents kept all this from him and it was not until the Cultural Revolution, when he asked his father, that he found out that he had been implicated because of his old revolutionary maternal uncle. His father's workplace had a much higher percentage of rightists than the quota, so his father was not branded a rightist, instead he only had a salary cut and a record made in his file. His father's problem was that he had written a hundred-character piece on the news blackboard where he "spoke freely" in response to the Party's call for people to freely voice their views to help the Party improve people's work habits. At the time his father did not know that this was called "luring snakes out of their lairs."

What had happened to his father nine years earlier also happened to him. He fell into the same trap. Indeed, all he had done was put his signature on a poster. It had on it Chairman Mao's call—ALL OF YOU MUST CONCERN YOURSELVES WITH THE IMPORTANT AFFAIRS OF THE NATION—in bold-type print from the *People's Daily*. When he was on his way to work, someone was putting up the poster in the big hall downstairs and was soliciting signatures, so he took up a pen and signed his name. He was unaware of the motives of this anti-Party poster nor of the political motives of the person who had written it. He couldn't work it out, but he had to acknowledge that it was aimed at the Party Center. By signing his name, he lost his bearings as well as a class standpoint. Actually, he had no idea what class he belonged to—after all, he couldn't count as a member of the proletariat—and so he didn't have a clear class standpoint. If he didn't sign this poster then he would have signed a similar poster. He confessed to this. He had, without doubt, committed a political error and from that time on, it was on his file. His personal history was no longer clean.

Prior to that he had truly never thought to oppose the Party. He had no need to oppose anyone and simply hoped that people wouldn't disrupt him from dreaming. That night rudely awakened him and he could see his precarious situation: a political storm was raging everywhere and if he were to preserve himself he had to lose himself among the common people. He had to say what everyone else said and be able to show that he was the same as everyone else. He had to keep in step to lose himself among the masses, say what was stipulated by the Party, extinguish all doubts, and keep to the slogans. He had to join with colleagues in writing another poster to indicate his support for the Party Center leadership, denounce the previous poster, and admit his error, in order to avoid being labeled anti-Party.

The obedient will survive and the rebellious will perish. In the early morning, the corridors of the building were covered in new posters, there had been a change in the political climate: today was right and yesterday was wrong, people had turned into chameleons. A poster just put up by a political cadre gave him a shock.

"Renegade Liu so-and-so, you are called a renegade because you have gone against the basic principles of the Party! Renegade Liu so-and-so, you are called a renegade because you have betrayed Party secrets! Renegade Liu so-and-so, you are called a renegade because you are an opportunist and have profiteered all this time by concealing your landlord background to worm your way into the revolutionary camp! Renegade Liu so-and-so, you are called a renegade also because up to now you have sheltered your reactionary father by hiding him in your house to resist the dictatorship of the proletariat! You are a renegade, Liu so-and-so, because your class instincts are taking advantage of this movement. By confusing black with white to deceive the masses, you have jumped out to target the Party Center. You harbor evil motives!"

This inflammatory call for revolutionary action was intimidating. His immediate boss, Old Liu, thus relegated to a different class from everyone, was instantly isolated; he left the crowd around the poster, returned to his department-chief office, and shut the door. When he reemerged, he was no longer smoking his pipe, and no one dared to greet this former department chief.

After a full night of warfare, it had started to get light. He went to the lavatory and washed his face. The cold water revived him and he looked through the window into the distance at the stretch of gray-black roof tiles. People were probably still asleep and dreaming. Only the round top of the White Pagoda had been tinted by dawn and was becoming more and more distinct. For the first time it occurred to him that he probably was a concealed enemy, and if he wanted to go on living he would have to wear a mask.

"Please be careful of the carriage door, the next station is Admiralty." This had been spoken first in Cantonese and then in English. You had dozed off and gone past your station. The underground in Hong Kong is cleaner than it is in Paris, and Hong Kong and Hong Kong people are orderly, compared to Mainlanders. You will have to get off at the next stop to go back the other way so that you can return to the hotel for a nap. Tonight you don't know where you will wake up, but it will be in a bed with a foreign woman. You are irredeemable. Now you are not just the enemy, you are careering toward hell. However, memories for him *were* hell.

8

"Why don't you tell me about that Chinese girl of yours? How is she?" Margarethe puts down her glass of wine and raises her long black eyelashes, thick with mascara, to look at you across the small round table.

"I don't know, I suppose she's still in China," you mumble, trying to avoid the question.

"Why don't you get her out? Don't you ever think about her?" Her eyes are fixed on you.

"That was ten years ago, what's the point of bringing it up? If it's not brought up, then it's forgotten." You try to say this nonchalantly. What you want right now is to be romantic with her.

"Then how is it that you remembered me? That night, the first night we met in your home?"

"It's hard to say, sometimes the smallest incident remains clear, yet some other times I can't remember the names of people I know well, and sometimes I can't remember what I had been doing for many years—"

"Have you also forgotten her name?"

"Margarethe!" You squeeze her hand and say, "Memories are depressing, let's talk about something else."

"Not necessarily, there are also happy memories, especially of people one has loved."

"Of course, but it's best to forget what is in the past." You, in fact, can't think of the girl's name and can, instead, only recall pain. Her voice and face have also become blurred.

"Will you forget me, too?"

"When you're so vibrant, so full of life, how could I forget you?" You look at her eyes under her thick eyelashes, trying to change the subject.

"But her, you're not saying that she wasn't?" She doesn't avoid your eyes and looks directly at you as she says, "She was so young, delicate, lovely, and so sexy. She was sitting right in front of me, clutching her skirt around her legs, the front of her dress hung low and she clearly had nothing on underneath. It was in China, at that time, so it left a very deep impression."

"When you were knocking on the door, we were probably making love." Your lips part in a smile, it is best not to be too serious.

"You'll forget me just the same, and before many years." She pulls her hand back.

"But this is different, it's different!" you retort, unable to think of what to say, and not saying anything intelligent.

"For men, it doesn't matter which woman's body it is. It's all the same thing."

"No!"

But what can you say? Every woman wants to prove she's different and in that hopeless battle in bed, tries to find love in lust, always thinking that after the physical lust passes something will remain.

In this very fashionable Bar 97 on this little street in Lan Kwai Fong you sit facing her. You are close but there is a small round table between you, and you are trying to catch her eye. Loud rock music is playing, and the howling is in English. White clothing glows in the dark-blue fluorescent lights. The men with ties, mixing drinks behind the counter, and the hostesses are all tall Westerners. Margarethe, dressed all in black, is barely visible except for her bright red lipstick that shines and looks purple in the fluorescent lights. She seems unreal and is utterly stunning.

"Is it simply because I'm a Western woman?" She is staring at you with a slight frown and her voice seems to be coming from far away.

"No, it's not simply because you're a Western woman. How can I put it, you're in every sense a woman whereas she was still a girl." You seem to be lighthearted and joking.

"How else are we different?" She seems determined to find out everything.

In her unflinching gaze you detect something devious, and say, "She didn't know how to draw in, she could only give but didn't know how to enjoy. . . ."

"Of course, the woman would come to know, sooner or later. . . ." She stops looking at you, and her eyelashes, heavy with mascara, lower.

You think of her pulsating body, stiff but yielding, her moistness, her warmth, and her breathlessness, that all arouse your lust, and you fiercely say you're thinking of her again.

"No!" She cuts you short. "It's not me you are thinking about but her. You are only seeking compensation from my body."

"How can you say this, you are truly beautiful!"

"I don't believe you." She looks down and turns the glass with the tips of her fingers. This little movement is very seductive. She looks up and smiles, revealing the gully between her breasts that had been blocked by the shadow of her head, and says, "I'm too fat."

You start to say no but she stops you, "I'm quite aware of it."

"Aware of what?"

"I hate this body of mine." She suddenly turns frosty again, has a sip of wine, and says, "All right, you don't understand me, you don't know anything of my past and my life."

"Then tell me about it!" you coax her. "Of course I want to understand, I want to know everything, everything about you."

"No, all you want is to have sex with me."

All right, you can only try to wheedle your way out. "There's nothing bad about that, people have to go on living, the important thing is to be living in this instant. What has happened is in the past, there has to be a clean break."

"But there can't be a clean break. No, there can't be!" she insists.

"What if I have?" You wince. She is a serious woman, she was probably good at mathematics in middle school.

"No, you can't cut off memories, they remain submerged in your heart and from time to time they gush out. Of course, it's painful, but it can also give you strength."

You say that memories may give her strength but for you they are the same as nightmares.

"Dreams aren't real but memories are events that have actually happened and can't be erased." This is how she argues.

"Of course, and moreover, they haven't necessarily gone into the past." You give a sigh, and go along with her argument.

"They can resurface any time if you don't guard against them. Fascism is like that. If no one talks about it, doesn't expose it, doesn't condemn it, it can come back to life again!" She becomes agitated as she speaks and it is as if the suffering of each and every Jew weighs upon her.

"Then do you need to suffer?" you ask.

"It's not a question of need. The pain actually exists."

"So, do you want to take all of humankind's sufferings upon yourself? Or at least the sufferings of the Jewish race?" you respond.

"No, that race ceased to exist a long time ago, it has scattered all over the world. I am simply a Jew."

"Isn't that better? It's more like a person."

She needs to affirm her background, and what can you say to that? What you want is precisely to remove the China label from yourself.

You don't play the role of Christ, and don't take the weight of the cross of the race upon yourself, and you're lucky enough not to have been crushed to death. She's too immature to discuss politics and too intelligent to be a woman. Of course, you don't say the last two things out loud.

A few trendy Hong Kong teenagers arrive. Some of them have their hair tied in ponytails, but they are all men. The tall blond waitress seats them at the table next to yours. One of them says something to the woman, but the music is too loud, and she has to bend down. After listening, she smiles, showing her white teeth that glow in the fluorescent lights, and then moves another small, round table: apparently others are coming. A male couple, gently stroking each other's hands, is ordering drinks.

"After 1997, will they still let homosexuals meet publicly like this?" she moves close and asks in your ear.

"In China, it's not just a matter of not being able to meet publicly. If homosexuals are discovered, they are rounded up as vagrants and sent off to labor camps, or even executed." You had seen some Cultural Revolution cases in internal publications from the Public Security Office.

She moves away and leans back but doesn't say anything. The music is very loud.

"Shall we go out for a walk in the street?" you suggest.

She pushes away the almost empty glass and stands up. Both of you go out the door. The little street, a blaze of neon lights, is thronging with people. There are bars one after another, as well as some elegant cake shops and small restaurants.

"Will this bar still exist?" She is obviously asking about after 1997.

"Who knows? It's all business, as long as they can make a profit. The people here are like that, they don't have the guilt complex of the Germans," you say.

"Do you think all Germans have a guilt complex? After the Tiananmen events of 1989, the Germans kept doing business with China."

"Do you mind if we don't discuss politics?" you ask.

"But you can't escape politics," she says.

"Could we escape for a little while?" you ask her very politely and with the hint of a smile.

She looks at you, laughs, and says, "All right, let's have something to eat. I'm a little hungry."

"Chinese food or Western food?"

"Chinese food, of course. I like Hong Kong, it's always so full of life, and the food is good and cheap."

You take her into a small, brightly lit restaurant, crowded and noisy with customers. She addresses the fat waiter in Chinese, and you order some local dishes and a bottle of Shaoxing rice liquor. The waiter brings a bottle of Huadiao in a pot of hot water, puts down the pot as well as two cups, each containing a pickled plum. He says with a chuckle, "This young woman's Chinese is really—" He puts a thumb up and says, "Wonderful! Wonderful!"

She's pleased and says to you, "Germany is too lonely. I like it in China. In Germany, there is so much snow in winter, and, going home, there is hardly anyone on the streets, they're all shut up in their houses. Of course, the houses are large and not like they are in China, and there aren't the problems you've mentioned. I live on the top floor in Frankfurt, and it's the whole floor. If you come, you can stay at my place, there'll be a room for you."

"Won't I be in your room?"

"We're just friends," she says.

When you come out of the restaurant, there's a puddle on the road, so you walk to the right and she to the left, and the two of you walk with a distance between you. Your relationships with women have never been smooth, you always hit a snag and are left stranded. Probably nothing can help you. Getting someone into bed is easy, but understanding the person is difficult, and there are only ever chance encounters that provide temporary relief from the loneliness.

"I don't want to go back to the hotel right away, let's take a walk," she says.

Behind big front windows, the bar by the footpath is dimly lit and people are sitting around small tables with candles.

"Shall we go in?" you ask. "Or would you like to go somewhere by the sea where it will be more romantic?"

"I was born in Venice, so I grew up by the sea," she replies.

"Then you should count as Italian. That's a beautiful city, always bright and sunny."

You want to ease the tension and say that you have been to Piazza San Marco. At midnight, the bars and restaurants on both sides of the square were crowded, and musicians were playing in the open air on the side near the sea. You remember they were playing Ravel's *Bolero* and it drifted through the night scene. The girls in the square bought fluorescent bands from peddlers and wore them on their wrists, around their necks, in their hair, so green lights were moving everywhere. Beneath the stone bridges going out to sea, couples sat or lay in gondolas, some with little lanterns on their tall prows, and, rowed slowly by the boatmen, they glided toward the black, smooth surface of the sea. Hong Kong lacks this elegance but it is a paradise for food, drink, and commodities.

"All that's for the tourists," she says. "Did you go as a tourist?"

"I couldn't afford to be a tourist. I had been invited by an Italian writers' organization. I thought at the time it would be good to settle in Venice and find myself an Italian woman."

"It's a dead city with no vitality, which relies on tourists to keep going, it has no life," she cuts in.

"Still, people there lead happy lives."

You say that when you got back to the hotel, it was well after midnight, and no one was on the streets. In front of the hotel, two Italian girls were amusing themselves by dancing around a tape recorder on the ground. You watched them for quite some time; they were really happy and even tried to get you to talk and laugh with them. They were talking in Italian, and, even though you couldn't understand them, you could tell they were not tourists.

"Just as well you couldn't understand them, they were just baiting you," she says coldly, "they were a couple of prostitutes."

"Probably," you say, thinking back, "but they seemed passionate and very lovely."

"Italians are all passionate, but it's hard to say if those women were lovely."

"Aren't you being overly critical?" you say.

"You didn't hire them?" she asks instead.

"I wouldn't have had the money," you say.

"I'm not a prostitute," she says.

You say it was she who started talking about Italy.

"I've never been back."

"Then let's stop talking about Italy."

You look at her and feel dejected.

You return to the hotel and go to your room.

"How about if we don't make love?" she says.

"All right, but the double bed can't be separated."

You don't make a move.

"We can each sleep on our sides of the bed and we can sit up to talk."

"Talk until morning?"

"Haven't you ever slept with a woman without touching her?"

"Of course, with my former wife."

"That doesn't count, that was because you no longer loved her."

"It wasn't only a case of not loving her, I was also afraid she'd expose—"

"Your relationships with other women?"

"At the time it was impossible to have other women. I was afraid she'd expose my reactionary thinking."

"It was also because she didn't love you."

"It was also because she was terrified; terrified I would bring disaster upon her."

"What kind of disaster?"

"It's impossible to explain in a few words."

"Then it's best not to try. Haven't you ever slept with a woman you loved or liked and not made love?"

You think about it and say, "Yes."

"That was the right thing to do."

"How was it the right thing to do?"

"You must have respected her, respected her feelings!"

"Not necessarily. If you like a woman and don't touch her—that is, when you are sleeping in the same bed—it's very difficult." For you, anyway.

"You're quite honest," she says.

You thank her.

"No need, there's no proof yet, let's see."

"It's the truth, it actually happened. Afterward I regretted not having touched her but I was no longer able to find her."

"In other words, you respected her."

"No, it was also because of fear," you say.

"Fear of what? Fear that she would report you?"

You say it was not that former wife of yours, it was another woman. She would not have reported you. She was the one who had taken the initiative and, of course, you wanted to, but you were too afraid.

"Why?"

"I was afraid of being discovered by the neighbors. Those were terrifying times in China, I don't want to talk about those old happenings."

"Talk about them, you will feel better after you talk about them."

She seems to understand something of the human mind.

"But just don't talk about women." You think she's acting like a nun.

"Why not talk about women? Whether it's a man or a woman, they're human in the first instance and it's not only a sexual relationship. You and I should be the same."

You don't know what you should talk about with her. In any case, you can't immediately get into bed, so you try studying the well-ordered strokes in the set of color woodcut prints in gilded frames on the wall.

She removes the clasp in her hair, and her hair tumbles down. While taking off her clothes, she says her father went back to Germany afterward. Italy was poor, and it was easier to make money in Germany.

You don't ask about her mother, you remain carefully silent and try not to look at her. You think it's impossible to relive the beautiful dream of yesterday.

She takes a robe into the bathroom, leaving the door open, and, running the water, goes on to say, "After my mother died, I went to Germany to study Chinese; the Chinese programs in Germany are quite good."

"Why did you study Chinese?" you ask.

She says she wanted to distance herself from Germany. When a new fascism reared its head, they would again report her. She was referring to the neighbors in her street, the cultivated ladies and gentlemen she had to acknowledge with an insipid hello when they met outside. If she came upon them on weekends, while they were polishing their cars—their cars were as shiny as leather shoes—she'd have to stop to say a few words to them. But some day, as happened in Serbia not long ago, they or their children would betray, expel, gang-rape, and murder Jews.

"Fascism wasn't only in Germany, you never really lived in China. Fascism was no worse than the Cultural Revolution," you say coldly.

"But it wasn't the same. Fascism was genocide, it was simply because one had Jewish blood in one's body. It was different from ideologies and political beliefs, it didn't need theories." She raises her voice to argue.

"Your theories are dog shit! You don't understand China at all and you haven't experienced the Red Terror. It was an infectious disease that made people go mad!" You suddenly lose your temper.

She says nothing, and, wearing a loose gown and holding the bra she has taken off, she emerges from the bathroom, shrugs her shoulders at you, and sits on the bed, head bowed. With eye makeup and lipstick removed, her face is pale but it has a more feminine softness.

"Sorry, sexual repression," you explain with a bitter smile. "You go to sleep." You light a cigarette.

She stands up, walks over to you, presses you against her soft breasts, fondles your head, and says quietly, "You can sleep next to me but I don't have any lust, I just want to talk with you."

She needs to search for historical memories, and you need to forget them.

She needs to burden herself with the sufferings of the Jews and the racial humiliation of the Turks, but you need to receive from her body a confirmation that you are living at this instant.

She says, right now she has no feelings.

9

Late at night, after the criticism meeting at the workplace had ended, he went back to his room. Old Tan, who shared the room with him, had been locked up for interrogation in the meeting room of the workplace building, and would not be returning. He locked the room, lifted a corner of the curtain to see that all the lights were out in the neighboring homes of the courtyard, closed the curtain and carefully checked that there were no gaps. He then opened the coal stove, put a bucket next to it, and began to burn his manuscripts: a pile of diaries, and notes in several dozens of books of all sizes that he had kept since his university days. The belly of the stove was very small, and he had to pull apart a few pages at a time, then wait for the scorched paper to burn thoroughly and become white ash, before shoveling it into the bucket. The ash was ground to a paste: not the smallest fragment of unburned paper must remain.

An old photograph taken with his parents fell out of a diary. His father was wearing a suit and tie, and his mother was wearing a *qipao*. When his mother was alive and took out the clothes from the chest to air them, he had seen this silk *qipao* with orange-yellow flowers on an ink-blue background. In this faded photograph his parents were leaning against one another and smiling, and in between them was a skinny child with thin arms whose eyes were round with bewilderment as if he thought a bird would fly out of the box camera. Without hesitating, he stuffed the photograph into the fire. With a dull crackle, the edges began to burn. His parents had started curling up by the time he thought to retrieve it, but it was already too late, and he watched the photograph curl and then flatten out. His parents' image had turned into black-and-white ash, and the skinny child in the middle had started to go yellow. . . .

The way his parents were dressed, they would have counted as capitalists or managerial employees of a foreign firm. He had obliterated whatever he possibly could, done everything he could to cut off his past, wipe out his memories. Even recalling those times was a heavy burden.

Before he burned the manuscripts and diaries, he had witnessed a crowd of Red Guards beat an old woman to death in broad daylight. He was riding his bicycle near the soccer grounds of bustling Xidan around midday during the lunch break, so there were lots of people out on the main street. Ten or so teenagers, fifteen- or sixteen-year-old middle-school students—a few girls among them—wearing old army uniforms and red armbands with black writing on them, were using leather army belts to beat up an old woman who was sprawled on the ground. The old woman had a wooden placard with the words REACTIONARY LANDOWNER'S WIFE tied with wire around her neck. She could no longer move but was still wailing. People passing by all kept a certain distance and watched in silence. Not one person stepped forward to stop them. A civilian policeman wearing a blue hat and swinging his white gloves walked past and seemed to look with unseeing eyes. A girl in the group, who had her short hair tied into two little bunches and looked quite elegant in glasses with a light-colored frame, also started wielding her belt. The brass buckle struck a mass of disheveled gray hair with a thud, and the old woman's hands went up to clutch her head as she collapsed onto the ground. Blood oozed between her fingers, but she could no longer make a sound.

"Long live the Red Terror!" The Red Guard patrol riding in formation on their new Eternal brand bicycles shouted this slogan all the way along Chang'an Avenue.

They had also interrogated him. It was about ten o'clock at night, and he had just cycled past the front of the Diaoyutai State Guesthouse with its armed sentries. Up ahead, under the bright streetlight, were a few motorbikes with sidecars. The road was blocked by a line of youths in military uniforms, wearing red silk armbands with the black inscription: BEIJING RED GUARD UNITED ACTION COMMITTEE.

"Get off!"

He braked suddenly and almost fell off his bicycle.

"What background?"

"Professional."

"What work?"

He named his workplace.

"Have you got your work permit?"

Luckily, he had it on him, and he took it out to show them.

Another person on a bicycle was stopped, a youth with a flat-top haircut, at the time a self-deprecating sign for "offspring of dogs."

"You should be at home so late at night!"

They let him pass. He had just got on his bicycle when he heard the youth with the flat-top haircut behind mumble a few words and then being beaten until he was howling. He didn't dare to look back.

For several days on end, from late at night until early morning, he was in front of the stove and his eyes were red from the heat. During the day, he had to force himself to be wide awake to deal with the dangers that could crop up at any time. When the last pile of notebooks was burned, he stirred the ashes into a paste to make sure no traces remained, then poured a plate of leftover vegetables and half a bowl of noodles on top. Totally exhausted and unable to keep his eyelids open, he lay on the bed fully clothed but could not fall asleep. He recalled that at home there was still an old photograph that could stir up trouble. It was a group photograph of the War of Resistance National Salvation Theater Troupe of the YMCA, which his mother had joined when she was young. They were all wearing military uniforms that must have been presented to members of the troupe when they went to express their appreciation to officers and soldiers in the War of Resistance: the military caps had badges with the Nationalist insignia. If this photograph were seized it would definitely create problems, even if his mother had died some time ago. He didn't know whether his father had dealt with the photograph, but it was unsafe to write to alert him.

Among the manuscripts destroyed was a novel he had given a prominent elderly writer to read, hoping for a recommendation or, at least, approval of it. He did not expect that the old man would be stony-faced and without a word of encouragement to the younger generation. Finally, with a grave expression, the old writer sternly warned him: "Think carefully before committing anything to writing! Don't submit manuscripts casually. You don't understand the dangers of the written word."

He did not immediately understand. At dusk one day, in early summer, June, when the Cultural Revolution had just started, he went to the old man's home to ask for news about what was happening. As soon as he came in, the old man quickly closed the door and, staring at him, asked in a hushed voice, "Did anyone see you come in?"

"There's no one in the courtyard," he said.

The old man was not like the old cadres; nevertheless, when he instructed young people, he was forever saying our Party this and our Nation that. He was, after all, a famous person with revolutionary credentials. He spoke with a vigorous voice, and what he said was always measured and lucid. But now his voice had suddenly turned reedy, and trembled deep down in his throat as he said, "I'm a black-gang element, don't come here again. You're young, don't get involved. You've never been through the experience of struggles within the Party—"

The old man wouldn't let him finish his greetings, and, nervously opening the door a crack, peeped out and said, "Keep it for later, wait until all this passes, keep it for later, you don't know about the Yan'an Rectification Movement."

"What was the Yan'an Rectification Movement like?" he went on to stupidly ask.

"I'll tell you later, leave quickly, leave quickly!"

All this took place in less than a minute. One minute earlier he thought the struggles within the Party were somewhere far away, it had not crossed his mind that they were right in front of him.

Ten years later, he heard that the old man had been released from prison. By then, he too had returned from the countryside and was back in Beijing, so he went to see him. The old man was reduced to skin and bones, and one of his legs had been broken; he was propped up in a reclining chair and had a black Persian cat on his lap. A walking stick stood by the armrest.

"A cat's life is actually better than a human's."

The old man's lips parted in what seemed to be a smile, revealing the few front teeth he had left. As he stroked the old cat, his beady eyes in their sunken sockets glinted strangely, just like a cat's. The old man did not talk to him about his experiences in prison. It was not until he visited him in hospital, shortly before his death, that he said his greatest regret in life was that he had joined the Party.

Back then, when he left the old man's house, he thought about those manuscripts of his. They had nothing to do with the Party, but they could get him into trouble. Still, he hadn't decided to burn them, so he carried them on his back in a big bag to the home of Big Lu, a friend he'd made while in hospital with dysentery. Big Lu, born and bred in Beijing, had a big build and taught geography in a middle school. Trying to impress a pretty young woman, Big Lu got him to draft a series of love letters. Then, by the time Big Lu's newly wedded wife found out he'd been an accessory in the letter writing, she was already irreversibly married to Big Lu, so there was a special friendship between the three of them. Big Lu lived with his parents, and they had an apartment with a courtyard all to themselves, so it wasn't hard to hide a bag of things.

At the height of summer, August, the Red Guard movement started. Big Lu's wife suddenly phoned him at the office and arranged to meet him at noon in a shop that sold milk drinks and Western-style cakes. He thought the couple must have had an argument, so he hurried on his bicycle to the cake shop. The old shop sign had been taken down and replaced with a new one, with the slogan: SERVING THE WORKERS, PEASANTS, AND SOLDIERS. Inside the shop, above the seats, was a long slogan scrawled in black characters across the wall: OUT WITH ALL STINKING CAPITALIST OFFSPRING!

At first, the "destruction of the four olds" by the Red Guards, which had started in the middle schools, seemed to be children having a ruckus. However, the Great Leader's public letter addressed to them, affirming that "it is right to rebel," incited the young teenagers to violent action. Anyway, not being a stinking capitalist offspring, he went in. They were selling milk drinks, as usual, but before he had found somewhere to sit, Big Lu's wife came in, took his arm as if she were his girlfriend, and said, "I'm not hungry yet, let's go for a walk, there's something I have to buy."

When they had left the cake shop and were on the street, she quietly told him that Big Lu had been so intimidated by the Red Guards at the school that he had shaved his own head in advance. This was because his family owned their apartment. They did not count as capitalists, but even as petty entrepreneurs, they could be searched at any time by the Red Guards. She asked him to quickly take away that bag of his from the coal shed in the courtyard.

It was Lin who saved him. Early in the morning, soon after getting into work, Lin walked by several times in the corridor. His desk faced the corridor and he saw that Lin was signaling him. He came out of the office and followed Lin down to the end of the corridor, where there was a bend before the stairwell. As no one was coming, they stopped there. Lin quickly told him to hurry home to fix up his things, because the Red Guards from the workplace were about to set out to search the belongings of his roommate, Old Tan. He rushed down the stairs, cycled hard, and got back to his room in a lather of sweat. He piled all his own things onto his own bed and beside it. He also went through the drawers of Old Tan's desk. He found an old, pre-Liberation photograph of Old Tan, taken at university with a group of students. Everyone was in student uniform, wearing caps with the twelve-point white-sun insignia of the Nationalist Party. He rolled it into a little ball, went out of the courtyard, and tossed it into the deep pit of the public lavatory on the street. When he got back to the courtyard, the car from the workplace had already arrived.

Four Red Guards from the workplace entered the room, and Lin was among them. Lin knew he was a writer but had never seen any of his manuscripts. She was in love with him, and didn't care about his writings. She, of course, had not come because of his manuscripts, but because he had taken lots of photographs of her, not naked but in provocative poses. They had been taken before and after the two of them had illicit sex in the woods at Badaling, in the western suburbs of Beijing. If any of those were found, it would be seen at a glance that their relationship had gone past being colleagues or revolutionary comrades. Lin was a deputy-minister's daughter, and she was married. Her husband, from an old revolutionary family, was in the army, and worked in a research unit carrying out research on nothing less than rockets or some new weapons. He had not the slightest interest in defense secrets, but was infatuated with this beautiful woman. Lin had taken the initiative, and she was the more passionate.

Lin was deliberately casual and made a loud fuss, "This room of yours is really small! There's nowhere to sit."

She had been here before, of course, when Old Tan wasn't home, and she'd be wearing a low-cut dress—he'd pull down the zipper on the back, take out her breasts and kiss them—nothing like the army outfit she wore now. Her long hair that used to be in a plait had been cut and tied with rubber bands into two short bunches, the standard hairstyle for women soldiers in the forces, as well as for the Red Guards of the present.

"How about making some tea, I'm dying of thirst!"

Lin deliberately opened the door wide and, standing in the doorway, she fanned herself with her handkerchief. Because of her doing this, the neighbors in the courtyard, peering into the back window, would not get the wrong impression that he was being searched. She made it all seem cheerful, as if they had dropped in for a visit.

He quickly made tea for everyone. The others declined, but the seriousness of the search had evaporated; besides, they all knew one another. Before the wearing of red armbands, family backgrounds were indistinguishable and everyone appeared to be equal. The leader of the Red Guards, Danian, was a hefty youth who played table tennis with him at lunchtime, and the two got on well. Danian's father was political commissar of an army division. He was wearing his father's old, much-washed, faded khaki army cap, and also an old leather army belt that was no longer regulation gear. These gave him the air of being a blood-lineage successor to the revolution.

When the Red Guards first formed at the workplace, he and other youths without a Five Red Categories background accepted the invitation to attend a meeting. It was there that Danian first revealed what he was capable of. Seated at one end of the bench of the main table, he said to those who didn't qualify to be Red Guards, "You people attending our Red Guard meeting today count in our revolutionary ranks as fellow travelers!" Danian confronted him by calling out his name—"Of course, that includes you!"—to let him know that it referred to him as well. However, having read *The History of the USSR*, he knew precisely what "fellow traveler" signified. If Lin had not warned him, and those manuscripts of his were found, he would certainly have been destroyed by this fellow in this surprise attack.

Danian retained his air of formality and said, "We're here to search for reactionary criminal evidence on Tan Xinren, and this has nothing to do with you. Which are your belongings? Separate them from his."

He put on a smile and said, "I've already separated my things, is there something else I can do to help?"

They all said, "This is none of your business, this is none of your business. Which is his desk?"

"That's his, the drawers aren't locked."

He pointed it out, then stood to one side. This was all he could say in defense of his roommate, Tan. But at the same time, he had drawn a line of demarcation between Tan and himself. Only later did he find out that, just as he was going downstairs to get his bicycle to hurry home, a Red Guard notice had been posted in the front hall of the workplace building: "Seize Tan Xinren with his history as a counterrevolutionary!" Old Tan, immediately isolated in the workplace building, had lost his freedom.

They pulled out Old Tan's notebooks, translation manuscripts, letters, photographs, and English-language books. Tan translated some novels from English in his spare time, mostly prorevolutionary works by writers from Asia and Africa. However, there was an English novel with a half-naked foreign woman on the cover, and this was put to one side. From under the old-newspaper lining of a drawer, they pulled out a white envelope. It was found to contain several condoms.

"The old bastard is still at this sort of thing!"

Danian took one and waved it about. Everyone laughed.

It wasn't that the people involved were amused, but that everyone was putting on an act of being pure and chaste. He and Lin also laughed but avoided one another's eyes.

Later, at the mass meeting called to criticize him, they questioned Old Tan about the woman he had an "improper sexual relationship" with. It was intimated that Old Tan was involved in a spy network, and he was forced to name the woman, a widow. Immediately, the Red Guards at the woman's work unit were notified, and her home, too, was searched. Some heartrending classical poems in Tan's drawer, probably written for this woman, constituted irrefutable evidence of "anti-Party, anti-Socialist longings for the paradise of the past."

The Red Guards found two loose bricks in the house and pried them up.

"Should I go and borrow a spade from a neighbor?"

He had deliberately asked Danian this to avoid the pain of being subjected to a search. At the same time, he wanted to play a joke: they might as well dig three feet down and make an archaeological discovery. Terror only came afterward. He borrowed a pickax from the old retired worker next door, and they began digging, filled the room with dirt and bits of brick so that there was nowhere to step, then threw down the pickax and left.

It was afterward that he found out the surveillance unit at his workplace had been informed by the street committee that the sound of a wireless transmitter was coming from their room. The person who had reported it must have been the old retired worker next door. When Old Tan and he had gone off to work, the old man, who was at home, heard the crackle of the radio they had forgotten to turn off behind the locked door. He took it to be a secret transmitter and must have thought that if he could catch the enemy it would prove his total loyalty to the Leader and the Party. When he ran into the old codger in the courtyard after the search, the man's wrinkled old face was beaming with smiles. Disaster had thus brushed by him.

10

The lights are off, and you're lying in the dark on a bed with a woman, your bodies close to one another, and you are telling her about the Cultural Revolution. Nothing could be more futile, and only a Jewish woman with a German mind, who has learned Chinese, could possibly be interested.

"Shall I keep going?" you ask.

"I'm listening," she says.

You say there was a middle-aged woman who worked as an editor in your office. A political cadre summoned her and said there was a telephone call for her in the security office. She returned some minutes later to the office, tidied the proofs on her desk, and, looking at the expressionless faces in the office, announced that her husband had gassed himself and that she was going home to attend to things. The head of the office was in solitary confinement, and Old Liu, the department chief, had been labeled an alien-class element who had wormed his way into the Party, so she could only request leave from those left in the office. Early the following day, she wrote a poster, clearly drawing a line of demarcation between herself and her husband who had "cut himself off from both the people and the Party."

"Don't go on, it's heartbreaking," she whispers into your ear.

You say you have no desire to go on.

"Why was this happening?" she asks.

"Enemies had to be found; without enemies, how could the political authorities sustain their dictatorship?"

"But that's how it was with the Nazis!" She is excited. "You should write about all this!"

You say you are not a historian, you're lucky enough to have escaped, and there's no need for you to make another sacrifice to history.

"Then write about your own experiences, your personal experiences. You should write all this up, this is valuable!"

"Historically valuable? When the many thousands of tons of archives become public, it will just be a wad of scrap paper."

"But Solzhenytsin—"

You cut her short and say you're not a fighter and you're not a flag-bearer.

"But don't you think that some day things will change?" She needs to have faith.

You say you are not a fortune-teller, and you don't live in empty hope, and you will not be lining up in the streets to welcome it. You will not be returning to China during your lifetime, and there is no need for you to waste the little life you have left.

She softly apologizes for stirring up these memories, and says that to understand your suffering is to understand you, can't you see?

You say you got out of hell and don't want to go back.

"But you need to talk about it, and, while you are, maybe you will become less uptight about it." Her voice is gentle, she wants to comfort you.

You ask if she has ever played with sparrows, or watched children at it. A string is tied to one of the sparrow's legs while the child holds the other end of the string. The sparrow flaps its wings desperately but can't fly, and is tormented until it just closes its eyes and stops moving, strangled by the string. You say that, as a child, you used to catch praying mantises. That jade-green body with its long, thin legs and two pincers raised like meat cleavers looks ferocious, but when children tie a fine thread to one of its legs, it tosses and turns a few times, and then falls to pieces. You ask if she's had such experiences.

"People aren't sparrows!" she protests.

"And, of course, they're not praying mantises either," you say. "Nor are they heroes, and if they can't stand up to might and power, they can only flee."

The room floods with darkness so thick that it seems to be in motion.

"Press close to me." Her voice is suffused with gentleness. She's brought you pain and she's trying to comfort you.

Separated by her negligee, you embrace her soft body but can't generate lust. She caresses you, and her soft hands wander over your body, bestowing her feminine kindness upon you. You say you're mentally worked up and tense, and you close your eyes to loosen up and to feel her tenderness.

"Then talk about women," she softly teases by your ear like a solicitous lover. "Talk about her."

"Who?"

"That woman of yours, was her name Lin?"

You say she wasn't your woman, she was someone else's wife.

"Anyway, she was your lover. Did you have lots of women?"

"You should realize that in China, at that time, it was not possible to have lots of women."

You also add that Lin was your first woman. You say this, knowing that probably she will not believe you.

"Did you love her?" she asks.

You say that it was she who seduced you and that you didn't want to become involved in this sort of futile love.

"Do you still think about her?" she asks.

"Margarethe, why are you asking this?"

"I want to find out the status of women in your heart."

You say she was, of course, quite lovely. She was a recent university graduate, she was very pretty, and could even be called sexy. At that time, in China, not many dressed like her, in body-hugging dresses and mini high heels; for those times, she was quite flashy. As the daughter of a high-ranking cadre, she was in a superior position, she was arrogant and willful but totally unromantic. However, you were only able to live in your books and your fantasies, your routine work was dead-boring. There were always zealots who wanted to get into the Party in order to become bureaucrats. They organized extra Mao's *Selected Works* study groups for after work and hassled people to attend. Anyone who didn't attend was considered ideologically unsound. It was only after nine or ten o'clock in the evening, when you got back to your room and sat at your own desk by the light of your desk lamp, that you were able to lose yourself in reverie and write your own things: that was you. In the daytime, in that world alien to yourself, you were always in a daze and always dozed off at meetings, because you would have stayed up all night. You were nicknamed "Dream," and you even answered to "Sleepy Bug."

"Dream is a beautiful name." She's chuckling, and the sound reverberates in her robust chest.

You say it was, to some extent, a camouflage, otherwise you would have been hauled out for criticism long ago.

"Did she also call you that? Did she fall in love with you just like that?" she asks.

"Maybe."

You say of course you were fond of her, and it wasn't just pure lust. You were very wary of women who had been to university, because they all gravitated toward the light and always tried to achieve a sort of angelic purity. You knew that your own thoughts were dark, but you had been taught a lesson by your little experience of love at university. If what you raved on about in private came to be confessed by the woman in one of the thought-report sessions set up by the Party or the work unit, you, too, would have been put on the altar for sacrifice.

"But surely there were other women?"

"If you haven't lived in that environment, you wouldn't understand."

You ask whether she would want to make love with a Nazi who might expose her Jewish background.

"Don't mention the Nazis!"

"Sorry, but there is a similarity. They made use of the same psychology," you explain. "Lin, of course, wasn't like that, but she enjoyed many privileges because of her family. She didn't try to get into the Party; her parents, her family, were the Party. She didn't need to put on an act or go to report on her thinking to the Party secretary."

You say the first time she invited you to a meal was in an elegant dining room that was not open to the public. To get through the door, a pass was needed. Naturally, she paid, you didn't have a pass and didn't have the money to pay, and felt bad about it.

"I understand," she says softly.

You say Lin wanted you to take her husband's military pass so the two of you could take a room in the holiday guesthouse for high-ranking cadres and their families in the Summer Palace. She said you could pose as her husband. You said what if you were found out? She said you wouldn't be, and, if you wanted to, you could wear her husband's uniform.

"She was brave," she murmurs.

You say that you, however, were not, and this recklessness made you very anxious. Anyway, you made love with her. The first time was in her home. Her home was a huge courtyard complex occupied by her parents and the old doorkeeper who swept the yard and lit the stove. At night, they all went to bed early, and it was very quiet in the courtyard. It was she who initiated you into manhood, and, no matter what, you're grateful to her.

"That means you still love her." She props herself up on her elbows and looks at you in the dark.

"She taught me."

You reflect about it; rather than love, it was desire for her lovely body.

"What did she teach you?"

Her hair brushes against your face, and you see the faint gleam of the whites of her large eyes looking down at you.

"She took the initiative. She had just become a married woman," you say. "Anyway, at the time, I was over twenty and still a virgin. Don't you think it's hilarious?"

"Don't say that, at that time, in China, everyone was puritanical, I understand. . . ."

Her fingers play little games on your body. You say that you were not puritanical and that you also wanted her.

"Was it because you were repressed that you wanted to indulge yourself?"

"I wanted to indulge myself with a woman's body!" you say.

"And you also wanted a woman to indulge herself, right?" Her velvety voice is right by your ear. "Then fuck me, like you did those women of yours in China."

"Who?"

"Lin, or that girl whose name you've forgotten."

You turn and embrace her, lift her negligee, and slip into her. . . . "If you want to ejaculate, go ahead. . . ."—"Ejaculate in whose body?"—"A woman you want. . . ."—"A wanton woman?"—"Isn't that what you want?"—"You're a prostitute?"—"Yes."—"Have you ever sold yourself?"—"Yes, and not just once. . . ."—"Where?"—"In Italy. . . ."—"Who did you sell yourself to?"—"Anyone who wanted. . . ."—"You're cheap!"—"Not at all, you can't afford me, what I want is for you to suffer. . . ."—"That's all in the past."—"No, it's right by you. . . ."—"That deep place?"—"Yes."—"It's very deep, right inside to the end . . . maybe too deep. . . . Is that why you're squeezing hard, sucking?"—"You've ejaculated! Don't worry. . . ."—"Aren't you afraid?"—"Afraid of what?"—"What if you became pregnant?"—"I'd have an abortion."—"Are you crazy?"—"You're the one who's afraid, you want to indulge but you don't dare. Don't worry, I've taken something."—"When?"—"In the bathroom."—"Before coming to bed?"—"Yes, I knew you would fuck me."—"Then why did you torment me for so long?"— "Don't ask, if you want to, just use it . . . this body. . . ."—"The body of a prostitute?"—"I'm not a prostitute."—"I don't understand."—"Don't understand what?"—"What you said just now."— "What did I say?"—"You said you had sold yourself."—"It would be impossible for you to comprehend, impossible for you to understand, impossible for you to know!"—"I want to know everything about you!"—"If you want to use me, go ahead, but don't hurt me."—"But aren't you a prostitute?"—"No, I'm just a woman, one who became a woman too early."—"When?"—"When I was thirteen. . . ."—"Nonsense! Are you making it up?"

She shakes her head. You want her to tell you about it! She mutters that she doesn't know anything and doesn't want to know. . . . She needs to suffer and to experience ecstasy through suffering. You need women, need to ejaculate your lust and loneliness into the bodies of women. She says she pays because she, too, is lonely and longs for understanding. Pays for love and enjoyment? Yes, she just wants and so she gives and also pays. And sells herself? Yes. And is wanton? And cheap! She rolls on top of you and you see her eyes glinting in the dark before you close your eyes and start calling out. . . .

11

As he lay in Lin's nuptial bed of not long ago, he opened his eyes wide, still finding it hard to believe he was not dreaming. Naked and beautiful, and looking down at him like this, Lin had taught him what it was to be a man. Lin led him from the sitting room down to the very end of the corridor to her bedroom. Thick velvet curtains hung to the floor, and the only light came from under the chrysanthemum-yellow shade over the tall vase-based table lamp. She sat him at the desk and brought out a big photo album with pressed-metal edging. As he turned the pages, he saw that the photos were all of her, either in sleeveless, low-cut dresses revealing her arms, shoulders, and legs, or else in wet bathing suits that clung to her body; her husband had taken these at Beidaihe just after they married. At this point, Lin leaned toward him, and he felt her hair brush his cheeks. He turned to put his arms around her slender waist and, as his face pressed against her breasts, he became aware of the fragrant warmth of her body. He straight away pulled down the zipper at the back of her dress, got her onto the bed, and started wildly kissing her on her lips, face, and neck, then, after removing her bra, her nipples. This was what he had sought in his dreams. He was in such a desperate hurry that he tore her delicate sexy panties that were not available in ordinary shops. But he was not able to get an erection and could not enter her. Again, it was Lin who eased his mind by saying that by this time of the night her parents would be asleep and that they do not come to her room anyway. Also, her husband's hi-tech weapons research institute was far away in the mountains of the western suburbs; army discipline was strict, and he could not come home unless it was a weekend. He suddenly needed to urinate, so Lin put on a dress, went outside in her bare feet, and came back right away with a washbasin. He latched the door, but pissing so noisily into the enamel washbasin made him feel like a thief. Switching off the light, Lin helped him off with his shoes and socks, then got him to lie down naked in the bed. She pulled the bedcover over him just like a big girl in his teenage dreams, or like a kind nurse on the battlefield caring for him, cleaning his bleeding wounds with her gentle, firm hands. It was then that he suddenly had an erection. He turned, bore down on this spritely woman, and carried out his most important act since birth.

He left Lin's room before daybreak. The courtyard was pitch-black, and above the branches of the old persimmon tree was a blue-black square of sky. Lin quietly removed the bolt, and the heavy door creaked open. He slipped out and, glancing back, watched the big ancient metal-studded door close, then wheeled his bicycle into the middle of the *hutong*. Not in a rush to get on his bicycle, he listened to his footsteps as he made his way through the maze of *hutong*. He did not want to go home immediately, and if his room-mate Old Tan started asking questions, he would have to talk his way around things. As he was coming out onto the street, his footsteps were gradually absorbed by the noises and sounds of the city waking up. The first lot of empty electric trolleybuses rumbled by; then in both directions, the number of cyclists and pedestrians gradually increased. He took a few deep breaths, and, as his lungs relaxed, he felt an exhilarating freshness and a sense of quiet self-confidence.

At midday, he saw Lin in the big dining hall. She was wearing a long-sleeved dress and a silk scarf. Her collar was buttoned up. When her colleagues at the long table left, Lin glanced at him and quietly said, "My neck is all purple where you kissed me."

It was hard for him to say if he was in love with Lin, but from that time onward, he lusted for her beautiful body. They arranged other meetings, but he could not go to her home on a regular basis. If her parents were at home, he was forced to listen reverently while they spoke passionately about national events. They were always lecturing him, and he had to put on an act of being good. It was as if he belonged to the generation of successors to the revolution, and, to agree, he had to say many hypocritical things. When the elderly couple started yawning and left the sitting room, Lin would signal with her eyes and they would start talking some nonsense about the office. When it grew quiet in her parents' room, he would get up and say something in a loud voice to indicate that he was leaving. Lin would escort him out of the sitting room and take him into the courtyard where the lights were already out. He would quietly circle back into the corridor, wait by a post as Lin put out the sitting-room lights, then slip into her bedroom to spend the night in utter bliss.

He preferred to meet Lin outdoors: in a park, by the city wall, or among lilac and jasmine bushes. They would spread their overcoats on the ground, or have quick sex standing against a big tree. If Lin's husband had to go away on an assignment to a military site, they would go to the hollows of Badaling and stay until sunset, then at twilight, in the night wind, grope their way down the mountain to catch the last bus back to the city. Sometimes they took a train further off to the Western Hills and got off at Mentouqi, where Peking Man was discovered, or some small station where the train stopped for only one minute. They took food with them, and would climb to the other side of the mountain and find some secluded spot where they would totally abandon themselves in the sun and the howling mountain wind. It was only at such times, lying on the grass in the wilds and looking at the clouds floating in the sky—free of worries, free of danger, and making love—that he felt natural.

Lin, two years older, was a fireball of lust, and she loved with a burning passion. Sometimes she was quite unreasonable, but he needed to exercise self-restraint. Lin dared to play with fire, but he had to consider the consequences. Lin had no intentions of divorcing her husband, and even if she were to raise the matter of marrying him, her parents would not approve of taking into their revolutionary family a son-in-law with an ordinary family background, who was not even a member of the Communist Youth League. Also, Lin's husband had the backing of a military family, and if the matter were taken up at the workplace, Lin would escape punishment. Disaster would fall on him alone. If such a time came, Lin would be level-headed. She would not break with her family and give up her elite status just to spend a life with him as one of the ordinary people. In addition to the marriage laws, a new regulation stipulated that workers of the state had to be twenty-six years of age before they were eligible to register for marriage. In the brand-new society, where unprecedented innovations were occurring every day, the new people loved and married for the sake of the revolution, and that was how the new plays and films of the time promoted it. The state issued tickets for performances, and attendance was compulsory.

One day, bypassing the department and section chiefs, Wang Qi's secretary asked him to report immediately to the bureau chief's office. He therefore knew it was not a work-related matter. Comrade Wang Qi, a wise and kindly middle-aged woman, was seated behind a big desk: the size of the desk denoted a cadre's rank. Comrade Wang Qi rose to her feet and closed the door to her office. This was further indication of the irregularity of the situation. He started getting nervous. However, the bureau chief got him to sit on the long sofa and drew up a leather chair for herself; she was making a deliberate show of being friendly.

"I'm a busy person." That was clearly the case. "I haven't had time to chat with university graduates like you who have recently arrived. How long have you been working here?"

He responded.

"Are you used to working here?"

He nodded.

"I've heard that you are bright, that you have become good at your work very quickly, and also that you even do some writing in your spare time."

The bureau chief knew everything, someone must be reporting to her. She then warned, "Don't let it affect your work here."

He hastened to nod. Luckily, no one knew what he wrote.

"Do you have a girlfriend?"

So this was the problem. His heart started pounding. He said no, and instantly felt his face turn red.

"It's worth thinking about finding a suitable match." The word "suitable" was emphasized. "But it is too soon for marriage. If your revolutionary work is done well, your personal matters can be easily resolved."

The bureau chief said that they were just having a casual chat, and throughout spoke gently, but this conversation, too, was revolutionary work. She was not having an idle chat with him, and, before standing to open the door, she warned, "I have heard comments from the masses about your having too close an association with Lin. If it is just a comrade relationship because you are both working together, then it is all right, but you must be careful about the consequences. The workplace is concerned about the healthy development of young people."

The workplace was of course, the Party, and the bureau chief's asking him in for a talk naturally reflected the concern of the Party. She returned to Lin, "She is a simple woman, she is very friendly, but she lacks wisdom."

If there happened to be an incident, the responsibility would naturally fall on him. The conversation, lasting less than five minutes, ended at that point. It took place before the outbreak of the Cultural Revolution, before the bureau chief's husband was declared an anti-Party black-gang go-getter, before Comrade Wang Qi herself was declared an anti-Party element, and while she still held an important position in the workplace. Whether it was a hint, an alert, or a warning, the message was clear. The heavy palpitations in his heart and the burning sensation on his face took a long time to subside.

He resolved to break up with Lin. After work, he waited downstairs for her, and they walked out of the building together. He knew they were being watched. He needed challenge, but with such a challenge he was keenly aware of his own impotence. They walked along the road, pushing their bicycles, for some time, before he eventually told Lin about this conversation.

"So what?" Lin didn't take it seriously. "Let them say what they like."

He said probably it was nothing for her, but it would not be so in his case.

"Why?" Lin came to a stop.

"It's an unequal relationship!" he blurted.

"Why is it unequal? I don't understand."

"Because you've got everything and I've got nothing."

"But I'm willing!"

He said he did not want favors, that he was not a slave! Actually, what he wanted to say was that under the unbearable circumstances, it was impossible to have an emotionally happy life. However, at the time, he could not make himself clear.

"So, who's treating you as a slave?"

Lin came to a stop under the streetlight and glared at him. People passing by were stopping to look at them. He suggested going to Jingshan Park to talk. The park stopped selling tickets at nine-thirty and closed at ten. He said they would be out quickly, and the gatekeeper let them in. Normally, when they had a date, they would cycle to the park after work, go up the hill, and find a clump of bushes away from the path, where they could see the lights of the whole city. Lin would casually take off her panty hose, and she did this very seductively. Her panty hose were luxury goods at the time and only available in service departments for people traveling overseas; they were not available in ordinary shops. There was not enough time to go up the hill, so they stopped in the shadow of a big tree by the path not far from the gate. His intention had been to make it quite clear that their relationship was henceforth ended, but when Lin started crying, he didn't know what to do. He held her face in his hands and brushed away her tears, but she began to weep and then to sob loudly. He kissed her, and they embraced like a pair of heartbroken lovers. He could not stop himself from kissing her face, lips, neck, breasts, and belly. The siren sounded over the loudspeakers: "Comrades in the park, your attention, please!"

The park had powerful loudspeakers that made a person's eardrums reverberate. At festivals, from morning to night, they were used for broadcasting revolutionary songs; they were also used at normal times to get people out of the park at closing time.

"Comrades in the park, your attention, please. It is closing time, and the park will be immediately locked up for cleaning!"

He ripped her panty hose under her skirt, thinking it was the last time. Lin hugged him tight, she was shaking all over. However, it was not the last time, but they no longer spoke at work. Each time before parting, they had to decide the location for their next date: in the shadows where streetlights did not reach, by which wall, or under which tree. Once on the street, they would get onto their bicycles separately, and cycle ten or twenty meters apart. The greater the secrecy the greater was the feeling that it was an illicit affair, and, more and more, he sensed that the relationship would end sooner or later.

12

The telephone wakes you and you wonder if you should answer it.

"It's probably a woman, have you forgotten a date?" She is sitting propped against the pillow and turns to look down at you.

"More likely it's for some reception," you say.

"Someone was knocking while you were asleep." She sounds tired.

You raise your head to look up. The sun behind the velvet drapes is shining through the gauze curtains onto the back of the sofa, a newspaper had been pushed under the door. You reach out to pick up the phone, but it stops ringing.

"Have you been awake long?" you ask.

"I feel rather hollow. You started snoring as soon as you fell asleep."

"Why didn't you give me a shove and wake me up? Didn't you sleep at all?" You caress the curves of her shoulders; her body is familiar and intimate, even the warm smell of her body.

"You were so fast asleep. Go back to sleep, you haven't had a decent sleep for two nights." Her dull eyes have dark shadows beneath them.

"Isn't it the same for you?" Your hands glide down her shoulders, grab her breasts and squeeze them hard.

"Do you still want to fuck me?" She looks at you with a wretched expression.

"What are you saying! Margarethe. . . ." You can't understand.

"As soon as you had ejaculated, you fell fast asleep right on top of me."

"That's awful, just like an animal!"

"It's really nothing, people are animals. But what a woman needs even more is a feeling of security." She gives a weak smile.

You say you feel very relaxed when you are with her, she is very generous.

"It depends on who it is. Not everyone who wants it, gets it."

"You didn't have to say that!" You say that you are deeply touched by how kind she has been to you.

"But you will forget sooner or later," she says. "The day after tomorrow, no, it should be tomorrow—another day has gone by and it's probably already midday—I'll go back to Germany and you'll go back to Paris. We can't live together."

"We are sure to see each other again!"

"Even if we saw each other again it would only be as friends. I don't want to be your lover."

She takes your hands from her breasts.

"Why, Margarethe?"

You sit up in bed and look at her.

"You already have a woman in France, it's not likely that you don't."

Her voice is harsh and you don't know how to respond. The sun has moved from the back of the sofa to the armrests.

"What time is it?"

"I don't know."

"But surely you also have a boyfriend? You must." This is the only response you can come up with.

"I don't want to keep up this sort of sexual relationship with you, but I think we can be friends, no doubt, good friends. I didn't think it would suddenly become so complicated."

"What do you mean?"

You say that you love her.

"Don't, don't say that, I don't believe it. Men always say that when they make love with women."

"Margarethe, you are very special." You want to reassure her.

"Is it because I am a Jew, and you've never had one before? It was just a whim, you don't understand me at all."

You say you want to understand her, but that she keeps everything to herself. You have told her a great deal about yourself, but she won't open up. You remember how she kept mumbling something while you were making love.

"All you want is my flesh, not me." She shrugs.

But you say that you really want to understand her, her life, her thoughts, you want to know everything about her.

"For something to write about?"

"No, as a good friend, if I don't count as a lover."

You say she has revived many feelings in you, not just sexual feelings. Memories you thought you had forgotten have come back to life because of her.

"You just thought you had forgotten, it's just that you had not thought about them. However, pain can't be obliterated and forgotten."

She is lying on her back and her eyes are wide open. Without eye makeup, her eyes look a deeper gray-blue. Her nipples are pale red, and the aureoles an even paler red. She covers herself with the sheet and says not to look at her like that. She hates her body. She had said this while making love.

"Margarethe, you are truly beautiful and so is your body!"

You say you like the sensuous women in Klimt's paintings and that you want the sun shining on her so that you can see her more clearly.

"Don't open the curtains!" she stops you.

"Don't you like the sunlight?" you ask.

"I don't want my body to be seen in the sunlight."

"You're really unusual. You're not like a Western woman, you're more like a Chinese woman."

"That's because you don't understand me."

You say you really want to understand her, totally, not just her body, or, as she puts it, her flesh.

"That's impossible. A person can't totally understand another person, particularly if it is a man regarding a woman. And when a man thinks he has the woman, he does not need to understand her."

"Of course." You are frustrated and, holding your head in your hands, look at her and heave a sigh. "Would you like to have something to eat? We could get them to bring something to the room or we could go to the coffee shop."

"Thanks, but I don't eat in the morning."

"Are you on a diet?" you ask pointedly. "It's already midday!"

"If you want to, get them to bring something. Don't mind me," she says. "I just want to hear you talk."

This moves you. You kiss her on the forehead, then pull up your pillow, lean back, and sit next to her.

"You're very gentle," she says. "I like you, I've given you what you wanted, but I don't want to fall too deeply, I'm afraid. . . ."

"What are you afraid of?"

"I'm afraid of longing for you."

You feel sad and stop talking. You think you should have a woman like this, maybe you should live with her.

"Go on with your story." She breaks the silence.

You say that, for the time being, you would like to listen to her talk about herself, her life, or anything. She says she does not really have anything to tell. She has not had complicated experiences like you.

"The experiences of every woman, written up, constitute a book."

"Maybe a very ordinary book."

"But with unique feelings."

You say you really want to know, particularly want to know, about her feelings, her life, her private life, and her psychological secrets. You ask her, "Were the things you said while we were making love true?"

"I couldn't have said anything. Maybe." She adds, "One day I'll tell you. I really want to communicate with you, not just sexually. I can't bear loneliness."

You say you are not afraid of loneliness and that it was through loneliness that you were not destroyed. It was this inner loneliness that protected you, but at times you longed to sink, sink, into that hole in a woman.

"That isn't sinking. To regard women as bad is a male prejudice. What is disgusting is that men use but don't love."

You are trying to get her to reveal her secrets.

"You think they love you then you find out it's a fraud. When men want women, they say wonderful things, but once they've finished, that's it. But women need to be deceived like this so that they can deceive themselves," she says. "You still only think of me as a novelty and you haven't had enough, I can tell."

"The Devil is in everyone's heart."

"But you're fairly sincere."

"Not necessarily."

She cackles with laughter.

"Now this is Margarethe!"

You also relax and start laughing.

"A prostitute?" she asks, sitting up.

"It was you who said that!"

"A slut who brought herself to your door?"

Her eyes are looking right at you, but you can't see behind those gray-blue eyes. She suddenly starts laughing so violently that her shoulders shake, and her big, pendulous pearlike breasts tremble. You say you want her again and push her down onto the pillow. The phone rings as she closes her eyes.

"Take your call. Soon you will have a new woman," she says, pushing you away.

You pick up the phone. It's a friend inviting you to Lamma Island for dinner. You say to hold on and put your hand over the mouth-piece to ask if she will come. If not, you will postpone for a day, so you will be able to spend the time with her.

"We can't spend all the time in bed! If we do, you will turn into a skeleton and your friends will blame me for it."

She gets out of bed and goes into the bathroom. The door isn't shut and there is the sound of splashing water. You put down the phone and lie there lazily. It is as if she is your partner, and you can't be away from her. You can't resist calling out loudly, "Margarethe, you're a wonderful woman."

"I offered you a gift, but you didn't take it!" she shouts back above the sound of the splashing water.

You call out loudly that you love her. She also says she wants to love you but that she's afraid. You instantly get out of bed to get into the bath with her, but the door slams shut. You look at your watch lying on the table and open the curtains. It is already after four o'clock.

Coming out of the underground at Sheung Wan station, you see a line of wharves along the coast. The air is crisp and fresh. The boats in the harbor are tinged with the gold of the setting sun and there is a bright glare. A barge with the waterline almost right up the sides is cutting through the waves and churning up white foam. The texture of the concrete and steel buildings on this side of the water can be seen clearly, and the outline of the buildings seems to be shining. You want to have a cigarette to confirm that it is not an illusion, and you tell her everything underfoot seems to be floating. She draws close to you and gives a chuckle.

There is a row of food stalls below a huge Marlboro advertisement, but once through the iron gates, "No Smoking" posters are everywhere, like in America. Work has just finished, and every fifteen or twenty minutes, there is a ferry to each of the islands. Most of those going to Lamma Island are young, and there are quite a few foreigners. The electric buzzer sounds and is followed by the clatter of hurried but orderly footsteps. On board, people doze off or take out a book to read, and it becomes so quiet that only the sound of the motor can be heard. The ferry quickly leaves the noisy town, and the clusters of tall and even taller buildings gradually recede into the distance.

A cold wind starts up, and the boat gently rocks. She's tired. At first she leans on you but then draws up her legs and lies down in your arms. You feel relaxed. She is asleep in an instant, docile and peaceful, and you cannot suppress a feeling of sadness. There are no signs in the cabin apart from the "No Smoking" signs and, with its mixture of races, it does not look like Hong Kong and it does not look like it is soon to be returned to China.

Beyond the deck, the night scene gradually grows hazy, and you become lost in thought. Maybe you should live with her on some island and spend your days listening to the seagulls and writing for pleasure, unencumbered by duties or responsibilities, just pouring out your feelings.

After disembarking and leaving the wharf, some people get onto bicycles. There are no cars on the island. Dim streetlights. It's a small town with narrow streets, shops and restaurants one after another, and it's quite lively.

"If you had a tea room with music, or a bar, it would be easy to make a living here. You could write and paint during the day and open for business at night. What do you think?" Dongping, who comes to meet you, bearded and tall, is an artist who came from the Mainland a year or so ago.

"And if you felt weary, you could go to the beach any time for a swim."

Dongping points to some small fishing boats and rowboats moored in the harbor at the bottom of the stone steps down the slope; he says a foreigner friend of his bought an old fishing boat and lives in it. Margarethe says she's starting to like Hong Kong.

"You can work here; your Chinese is good and English is your mother tongue," Dongping says.

"She's German," you say.

"Jewish," she corrects you.

"Born in Italy," you add.

"You know so many languages! What company would not pay a high salary to employ you? But you wouldn't have to live here; Repulse Bay over on Hong Kong Island has many grand apartments on the mountains by the sea."

"Margarethe doesn't like living with bosses, she likes artists," you say for her.

"Great, we can be neighbors," Dongping says. "Do you paint? We've got a gang of artist friends here."

"I used to paint because I liked it, but not professionally. It's too late to start learning."

You say you didn't know she painted, and she immediately says in French there is a great deal you don't know about her. At this point, she distances herself but still wants to maintain a secret language with you. Dongping says that he didn't study in an art college and was not officially recognized as an artist: that was why he left the Mainland.

"In the West, artists don't need official recognition and don't need to have studied in an art college. Anyone can be an artist. The main thing is whether there is a market, whether one's paintings can sell," Margarethe says.

Dongping says there is no market for his paintings in Hong Kong. What the art entrepreneurs want are copies of impressionistic concoctions with a foreign signature for Western galleries, and these are bought at wholesale prices. He does a different signature each time and can't remember how many names he has signed. Everyone laughs.

On the first floor, where Dongping lives, the sitting room adjoins the studio, and the residents are painters, photographers, poets, and columnists. The only person who is not an artist or writer is a foreigner, a good-looking young American. Dongping formally introduces the man. He is a critic, and the boyfriend of a woman poet from the Mainland.

Everyone has a paper plate and a pair of chopsticks, and they help themselves to the seafood hotpot. The seafood isn't alive but it is very fresh. Dongping says he brought it all home just before you arrived, but now, in the bubbling hotpot, it's curled up and no longer moving. The crowd is very casual. Some are walking about barefoot, and others are sitting on floor cushions. The music is turned on loud, it is a string quartet on big speakers, Vivaldi's vibrant *Four Seasons*. Everyone is eating and drinking, talking all at once and not about anything in particular. Only Margarethe is reserved and dignified. Her fluent Chinese instantly makes the young American's Western accent and intonation sound inferior, so he starts talking to Margarethe in English. He raves on to her and makes the young woman poet jealous. Margarethe later tells you that the guy doesn't know anything, but he was taken by her and kept hovering around her.

One of the artists says that he had been uprooted from East Village or West Village—you don't remember which—in the grounds of the Old Summer Palace. In the name of urban beautification and social security, the place was closed down by the police two years ago. He asks you about the new art trends in Paris, and you say that there are new trends every year. He says that he does art on the human body. You know that he had suffered a great deal in China because of his art, so it is best not to say that his sort of art is now history in the West.

In the course of things, people start talking about 1997. All the hotels have been fully booked for the day of the handover ceremony between Britain and China, the day the People's Liberation Army would move in. There would be hordes of journalists from all over the world congregating here, some say seven thousand, and others eight thousand. On the morning of July 1, the birthday of the Chinese Communist Party, immediately after the handover ceremony, the British governor of Hong Kong would go to the naval base and leave on a ship.

"Why doesn't he take a plane?" It is Margarethe who asks.

"On the day, there will be celebrations all along the road to the airport, and it would be too sad for him," someone says. But no one is laughing.

"What will all of you do?" you ask.

"That day, don't go anywhere else. Just come here to eat seafood with me," Dongping says with a joyless smile. He seems to be very generous, not as rough as he used to be, and he has become wiser.

People stop joking and the music suddenly seems to be louder, and who knows what season Vivaldi has reached.

"It doesn't matter!" the American says in a loud voice.

"What doesn't matter?" his girlfriend retorts. She then rebuffs him, "You can never make yourself understood when you speak Chinese!"

After dinner, the American takes out a piece of opium the size of a fingernail to share around, but the two of you must catch the last boat back. Dongping says there is plenty of room, and the two of you can stay the night, then go for a swim in the morning. Margarethe says she is tired, and also that she will be flying out at midday tomorrow. Dongping escorts the two of you onto the ferry and, when it departs, he is left alone on the wharf, holding both hands high, and waving. You say to Margarethe that you were close friends in Beijing and had suffered together. He is a rare friend. He doesn't know any foreign languages and can't go anywhere. The police raided his home in Beijing. He often had parties with music and dancing, but the neighbors thought that there were indecent activities going on and reported him to the police. Afterward, through various strategies, he got to Hong Kong. This trip to Hong Kong is to say good-bye to him.

"It's hard making a living anywhere," Margarethe says sadly. You lean against one another by the railing on deck. The sea breeze is cool.

"Do you really have to leave tomorrow? Can't you stay one more day?" you ask.

"I'm not as free as you are."

The wind blows spray into your faces. Once again you confront a farewell, maybe this is an important moment for you. It seems that your relationship should not come to an end just like that, but you do not want to make promises, and simply say, "Freedom is in one's own hands."

"It's easy for you to say that, but, unlike you, I have a boss." She has turned cold again, like the sea wind. Above the sea is pitch-black darkness, the specks of bright light on the island have vanished.

"Talk about something interesting." Sensing she has upset you, she adds, "You talk and I'll listen."

"What shall I talk about, the March wind?" You talk nonsense and restore a nonchalance to your voice.

You sense her shrugging her shoulders, and she says it's cold. The two of you go back into the cabin. She says she's tired, and you look at your watch; there is still half an hour before reaching Hong Kong Island. You say she can lean on your shoulder and have a nap. You are also overcome by weariness.

13

March wind. Why March? And why wind? In March, on the North China plains, it is still very cold. Endless stretches of muddy marshlands and alkaline flats on the ancient riverbed of the Yellow River have been reclaimed for farmland by reform-through-labor prisoners. If there was no drought, the millet sown in winter would result in a harvest of the same amount of seed after the beginning of spring. In accordance with the newly promulgated highest instructions of the highest leadership, these prison farms were converted into May Seventh Cadre Schools, and the original prisoners and military police were sent to the desolate uninhabited highlands of Qinghai province. Hence the farms came to be farmed by purged bureaucrats and workers from the Red Capital.

"The May Seventh Cadre School is not a haven from the winds of class struggle!" The army officer from Beijing had come to convey this instruction. This time it was a purge of the May Sixteenth counterrevolutionary group that had infiltrated every nook and cranny right down to mass organizations. Anyone who was investigated would instantly be considered a practicing counterrevolutionary. The very first time he was confronted, soon after the initial period of the movement to sweep away Ox Demons and Snake Spirits, he was so frightened that he made a confession on the spot. But now he had become a fox and was capable of biting back. He, too, could bare his sharp fangs and put on a mean pose. He was not going to wait for a pack of hunting dogs to pounce on him. Life, if this could be called life, had thus taught him to be an animal. At most, he was a fox surrounded by hunters, and, if he made a false move, he would be torn to shreds.

After several years of chaotic warfare over what was right one day and wrong the next, a whole series of crimes could be listed for anyone who had to be purged. As soon as a person was investigated, problems were sure to be found, and if a person had problems he would be declared the enemy. This was known as fighting to the death in the class struggle. As the army officer had named him as the main target of investigation, all that remained was for the masses to get fired up so that they would direct their fire at him. He was fully aware of this process and, before the masses were fired up, he had to bide his time.

Right up to the day before the commanding officer announced that he was to be investigated, the masses were still laughing with him. The masses lived with him and, in the same dining hall, drank the same corn gruel and ate the same unleavened mixed-grain buns with him. They slept together on the cement floor of the granary on a mattress padded with straw. The row upon row of communal mattresses were forty centimeters in width per person—no more, no less—measured with a tape measure, whether one was a high-ranking cadre or an odd-job worker, fat or thin, old or sick. However, the men and the women were separated. Husbands and wives without young children to take care of couldn't stay in the same place. Everything was organized in military formation—squad, platoon, company, battalion—and everyone came under the leadership of the commanding officer. At six o'clock in the morning, the bugle call got people up, and they had twenty minutes to brush their teeth and have a wash. They then stood before the portrait of the Great Leader on the wall to seek "morning instructions," sang songs from Mao's *Sayings* and, holding high the little red book, shouted out "long live" three times before going to the dining room to drink gruel. Assembly followed, and Mao's *Selected Works* were recited for half an hour before people shouldered their hoes and pickaxes to work on the land. Everyone had the same fate. What was the point of all this endless fighting?

The day he was taken off work to write a confession, it was as if he had the plague and everyone was afraid of catching it. No one dared to talk to him. He didn't know what they were investigating, so when he saw a close friend heading for the mud-walled lavatory, he followed him in, undid his trousers and, pretending to urinate, said in a low voice: "Why are they investigating me?"

The friend gave a dry cough and, putting down his head as if he were totally engrossed in shitting, didn't look up. There was nothing for him to do but leave. It turned out that even when he went to the lavatory he was being spied on. The joker who had received the letter to implement the investigation on him was outside the mud wall, pretending to be deep in thought.

A meeting to "help" him was held on the cement drying ground. To help was to use mass pressure to force a person to admit to mistakes, and mistakes were the same as crimes. The masses were like a pack of dogs slinking off to bite as the whip directed, thereby ensuring that they themselves would not be lashed. He was familiar with this infallible key to mobilizing the masses.

The scheduled speeches became more intense and vicious. Each speech was prefaced by quoting from the little red book that was used as a cross-reference for a person's words and actions. He put his notebook on the table and made it clear he was taking notes. This was the signal he wanted to give: he had taken a stance, and he was recording everything. When the day came and things changed, he was not going to forgive anyone. The past years of constantly changing political movements had turned people into revolutionary gamblers and scoundrels. The winner was a hero and the loser was the enemy.

He took notes rapidly and tried not to miss a single sentence. He made it no secret that, right then and there, he was hoping for the day when he would seek a tooth for a tooth. That bald-headed, prematurely senile Tang so-and-so was making a speech, getting himself more and more excited by quoting venerable Mao's exhortations to fight against the enemy. He put down his pen and looked up to glare at this joker. Tang's hand, clutching his little red book, started shaking, probably a habit he couldn't control, and getting more and more flustered, sprayed spittle as he spoke. In fact, Tang's behavior came from fear. With his landlord family background, he could not join any of the people's organizations, and he was merely taking the opportunity to put on an act to score some good points for himself.

He had no choice but to pick on a weakling like this, someone who was terrified and just trying to survive. He swore, put the cap back on his pen, announced he was not taking part in this sort of meeting until his problem was clarified, and forthwith left. Apart from the few company and platoon cadres dispatched by the army officer, most of the hundred or so present were from his old rebel faction and, for the time being, the atmosphere was not right for launching a criticism against him. He had risked taking a stance to allow his faction to steady itself, but, of course, he knew this would not be able to stop him from being charged with a raft of crimes. He had to flee the cadre school before the net closed around him.

At dusk, he went off on his own to a distant village, leaving the precincts of the cadre school within that endless long line of cement posts tied with barbed wire.

Alongside the village was a kiln for slaking lime. He approached the kiln where he saw some peasants douse kerosene on the stack of coal inside and light it. Soon thick smoke was billowing out. They sealed up the opening of the kiln, let off a string of crackers, and left.

He hung around for a while and saw that no one had followed him from the cadre school.

It was gradually getting late, the sun was a ball of orange, and the rows of huts on the farm had already become blurred. He walked toward the setting sun, passed ridges of corn fields that had not yet started to turn green again, and kept going. Some sparse, withered plants grew on the white saline land, and the soil underfoot became loose and soft. Before him were stretches of swamp. Wild geese called in the limp, yellow reeds as the sun turned crimson to set somewhere further off along this ancient watercourse of the Yellow River. In the darkening mist, it was all mud underfoot, and there was nowhere he could sit down. He lit a cigarette and thought about where he could seek refuge.

His feet were sinking into the mud. He had smoked one cigarette. His only option was to have a peasant family take him in. It would mean revoking his city residential permit and having to live the rest of his life as a peasant, and this had to be done before he was declared the enemy. But he did not know anyone living in any village. He thought hard, and suddenly remembered that his classmate at middle school, the orphan Rong, had been among the first batch of urban educated youth to go off to "establish new socialist villages" ten years earlier. Afterward, Rong had settled in a small county town in the mountains. Through this classmate, maybe he would be able to find some place to go.

When he got back to the dormitory, everyone was busy having a wash and getting ready for bed. The old and the weak were worn out and were already lying down. Without bothering to go to the well to fetch water for a wash, he crawled into bed. There was no time to waste. That night he would have to go to the county town to send a telegram to Rong. It was forty kilometers there and back, and it would be impossible to get back before dawn. He would first have to sneak off to a village outside the farm to borrow a bicycle from Huang, a cadre who worked in his platoon. Workers such as Huang, with elderly relatives and children, were settled in the homes of peasants in nearby villages.

After the last person lay down and the lights went out, he waited until there was a rhythmic sound of snoring. In the dark, the old cadre next to him tossed and turned, making the chaff mattress rustle; probably he could not get warm enough and couldn't fall asleep. He quietly told the old man he had diarrhea and was going to the lavatory. The underlying message was that should the night warden ask where he was, that was how to get rid of the man. He didn't think the old man would betray him: prior to the announcement that he was to be investigated, he was the leader of his work squad and he always gave the old man the lightest chores. He had the old man repairing loose hoes and guarding the drying square to make sure neighboring peasants didn't come with a sack to casually fill it with grain, then run off. The old man was a revolutionary from the Yan'an period and had a doctor's certificate for high blood pressure. However, when his faction was targeted in the movement, his military credentials weren't recognized and he, too, was sent here to the cadre school.

Dogs were barking everywhere in the village. Huang opened the door with his padded jacket slung over his shoulders. His wife was on the earthen *kang* under the bedcovers, and his little girl, awakened by the knocking, was crying. He hastily explained his desperate predicament and promised to get the bicycle back before daybreak. He said that he definitely would not implicate them.

Rain had not fallen for a long time on the dirt road into the county town. It was thick with dust and so uneven that the bicycle was shaking all the time. A wind started up, blowing dust and grit right into his face. He was choking and could hardly breathe—oh, the wind and grit that March night in early spring. . . .

While at middle school, he and Rong, this classmate from whom he was seeking help, used to discuss the meaning of life together. This began with a bottle of ink. Rong had been taken in by an elderly widow without any children, and lived nearby. So, after school, Rong often came over to his place and they would do their homework, then listen to music. Rong played the two-stringed *erhu* well, and was crazy about the violin, but there was no question of his buying one. Rong could not even afford to buy one of the very cheap tickets for special student movies during the summer holiday break. He once bought an extra ticket for Rong, but Rong kept making excuses. He couldn't understand, but when he said the ticket would be wasted, Rong finally explained that if he saw one he would want to see another, and he would become addicted. However, Rong did not refuse to come to his house to play his violin.

One day, after finishing their homework, they listened to a record. It was Tchaikovsky's *Violin Quartet in G Major*, and Rong was enraptured. He remembered clearly that they were silent for a long while. Suddenly, he said he wanted Rong to know that the ink in the bottle on the table was not blue. Rong said, to be more accurate, it was ink-blue. But, he argued with Rong, when people saw this color and said it was blue or ink-blue, it established an agreement or a convention that gave it a common name, but, in fact, the color seen by each person was not necessarily the same. Rong disagreed, saying that however either one of them saw it, the color didn't change. The color, of course, did not change, but whether or not the color seen in the eyes of each person was the same, no one could know. Rong said there had to be an explanation. What was communicated was simply the term "blue," or "ink-blue," and, in fact, the visual perception conveyed by the same word was different. Rong asked what was the color of the ink in the bottle? He said who knows? Rong was silent for a while and then said he found it all a bit scary.

The yellow-orange rays of the afternoon sun were shining on the floorboards of the room. Years of washing and scrubbing had made the grain of the wood stand out. Suddenly, he was infected by Rong's terror. With the sun shining on them, even those very real floorboards became odd, and he began to wonder if they were actually so real after all. People could not comprehend the world, and the existence of the world depended on an individual's perception of it. If, when a person died, the world, too, became murky, or perhaps no longer existed, then what definite meaning did being alive have?

Afterward, he went to university while Rong stayed on in the village and worked as a technician in a small hydroelectric plant. They corresponded and continued such discussions for quite some time. This sort of awareness threw into question their entire school education; it was completely at odds with the unwavering certainty of the ideals of serving the people and the construction of a new society. He came to fear that his life was disappearing, it was as if there was no place for his sense of mission or responsibility to life. Now, however, even just being able to stay alive had become a serious problem.

He knocked for more than half an hour on the door of the county post office, and even knocked on all the windows facing the street. Finally, lights came on, and someone opened the door. He explained that he was from the cadre school and had to send an official telegram. Writing the message was not easy, and it had to be written in the fancy jargon prescribed for personnel who had been sent to the countryside. Also, he had to get this schoolmate of his, whom he had not contacted for a long time, to understand the gravity of his predicament so that he would speedily find him a commune to settle in and immediately telegraph an official document accepting him as a peasant. He also had to be sure not to arouse the suspicions of the person in the post office sending the telegram.

The road back went by the railway station. A few cheaply built single-story buildings stood alongside the desolate platform, lit by some weak yellowish lights. Two months earlier, the army officer had assigned him and about ten other sturdy youths to go there to meet a large batch of new arrivals from his Beijing workplace. Office staff, laborers, cadres, and their families were all there. No one had the good fortune of being excluded, not even the old, the sick, and the children. It was a special train with many carriages, and the platform was full of offloaded bedding rolls, suitcases, tables and chairs, furniture like wardrobes, and also big earthenware vats for pickling vegetables in brine. They looked like refugees. The army officer called it "war-preparation deployment." There was the heavy smell of gunpowder in Beijing due to the armed conflicts on the China-Soviet border in Heilongjiang province, and the Number One War Preparation Mobilization Command signed by Deputy Commander-in-Chief Lin Biao had arrived at the cadre school.

In the unloading, a big vat was cracked, and brine seeping out made the whole place stink of rancid fermenting vegetables. Taking advantage of his laborer family background, the old man who used to be gatekeeper in the back courtyard of the workplace building, started to swear loudly. Whom he was swearing at wasn't clear, and no one tried to stop him. Anyway, the man's supply of salted vegetables for a whole winter had been ruined. With their heads pulled into their scarves against the chilly wind, people kept watch on their own little piles of "home" as they sat on bedding rolls or suitcases waiting to be assigned to some villages near the cadre school. Not daring to cry aloud, children with faces red from the cold quietly sobbed by the side of the grown-ups.

Three hundred big carts mobilized from several communes had assembled outside the station, and braying mules, neighing horses, and cracking whips created a greater ruckus than the village market. A small car was stuck among the mules, horses, and carts, and could move neither forward nor backward. Finally, with bright red badges on his collar and cap and his greatcoat draped over his shoulders, Officer Song emerged from the car. He walked to the platform, climbed onto a wooden crate, and started waving his arms about. Officer Song, who was in charge of the cadre school, had an army-bugler background and no significant revolutionary credentials.

While he had played a role in spurring on the troops on frontier bat-tlefields, he couldn't shift these peasants' carts, and the chaos simply got worse.

From noon until dark, cart after cart had finally removed all the people, but the platform was still piled with furniture and crates. He and a few others were told to stay behind and guard these. The oth-ers all went into the waiting room to get out of the wind. However, he stacked some crates and wardrobes into a wind shelter, and bought himself a bottle of liquor as well as two steamed buns. The buns were made of a mixture of corn flour and wheat flour and were frozen solid by the cold. In his little corner that he had covered with a sheet of canvas, he gazed at the weak yellowish lights on the plat-form and thought about finding a wife. With a wife and a child, he would be the same as the others with families and children, and he would be able to get lodgings in a peasant home in one of the vil-lages. He would still be working on the land, but at least he would have a small mud hut and be able to get away from the collective lodgings where people were staring right at one another all the time, and one was afraid of being overheard while having a dream.

He thought back to the previous year, when armed battles were raging, before the army took control of the factories and schools, to that night in the small inn on the embankment of the Yangtze he spent with a university student when there was nowhere else to stay. "We are the generation that fate has decreed should be sacrificed." When the woman had the courage to write this in her letter, he knew that her situation must have been hopeless.

There were no battlefields now, but enemies were everywhere. Defenses were up all over the place, but defense was impossible. He could retreat no further. No longer wildly hoping for anything more, all he wanted was a house in a village, where he could settle down with a wife, but even that possibility was about to vanish.

Before dawn, he got the bicycle back to the village. Huang and his wife had waited for him and didn't go to sleep; they were dressed. The coal stove they had brought with them from Beijing was burning, and the house was warm. Huang's wife had prepared dough and was making soup noodles for him. He didn't decline. Having had no dinner, he had pedaled hard and fast for forty kilometers, there and back, and he was utterly famished. They watched him devour a big bowl of noodles. Before leaving, he waved to them and said that he hadn't been there. They said, of course you haven't, of course you haven't. He had done all he could, the rest was up to fate.

14

"So you weren't declared the enemy?" she asks as she stirs her coffee.

"It was close." But you managed to escape. What else could you say?

"How did you escape?" she asks, still in an offhand manner.

"Do you know what 'to simulate' means?" you ask, forcing yourself to smile. When an animal is in danger, it pretends to be dead or else puts on a fierce look. It does not panic and lose control. But, in your case, you had to be very calm as you waited for a chance to escape.

"So, you're a wily fox?" she laughs softly.

"Yes," you admit. "When dogs were all around hunting you, you had to be more wily than a fox or they would have ripped you to shreds."

"But people *are* animals, you and I are animals." She sounds hurt. "But you aren't a wild animal."

"When everyone had gone crazy, one turned into a wild animal."

"Are you also a wild animal?" she asks.

"What do you mean?" It is your turn to ask.

"Nothing special, I was just asking." Her eyelashes lower.

"To keep a patch of clean soil in one's heart, one had to work out a way of escaping from the arena."

"Did you escape?" she asks, her eyelashes moving up.

"Margarethe!" The smile goes from your face. "Stop talking about Chinese politics. You're leaving tomorrow and there are other things to talk about."

"I'm not talking about China and I'm not talking about politics," she says. "I want to know if you are a wild animal."

You pause to think, then say, "Yes."

She does not respond but looks hostile. After returning to the hotel from Lamma Island, she said in the elevator that she didn't want to go to bed straight away, so you and she came to this coffee shop. The lights are low and the music is soft, in another corner two gays are drinking wine. There is no sugar in the bit of coffee in her cup, but she stirs it with the spoon from time to time. She must have something on her mind that she doesn't want to talk about in bed. The gay lovers call the waiter, pay, and go off hand-in-hand.

"Do you want something else? The man is waiting to close." You are talking about the waiter.

"Are you treating?" She tilts her head back and has a strange look.

"Of course, it's not that much."

She orders a double scotch, then says, "Will you join me?"

"Why not?" You order two double scotches.

The waiter wearing a tie is polite but gives her a look.

"I want to have a good sleep," she explains.

"Then you shouldn't have had coffee just now," you point out.

"I'm tired, tired of living."

"What are you talking about? You're young, so beautiful, in the prime of life, you should enjoy yourself to the full." You tell her that it is she who has again filled you with lust, and you put your hand on hers.

"I hate myself, I hate my body."

Her body again!

"You, too, have used it. Of course, you're not the first and you won't be the last," she says, pushing away your hand.

Your confusion passes and, with a sigh, you withdraw your hand.

"I also want to be a wild animal, but I can't escape. . . ." she says, head bowed.

"Escape from what?" It's your turn to question her, and this is more comfortable. Being interrogated by a woman is stressful.

"I can't escape, I can't escape from fate, I can't escape from this sort of feeling. . . ." She takes a big mouthful of scotch and tosses back her head.

"What feeling?" You go to push back her hair so you can see her eyes, but she brushes it away herself.

"Women, a woman feels . . . you wouldn't understand." She laughs softly again.

It seems probable that this is what is causing her pain, and, looking searchingly at her, you ask, "How old were you at the time?"

"At the time," she pauses, then says, "I was thirteen."

The waiter is standing behind the counter with his head down, probably preparing the bill.

"That's too young," you say. Your throat feels tight, and you gulp down a big mouthful of scotch. "Go on!"

"I don't want to talk about it, I don't want to talk about myself."

"Margarethe, if you want mutual understanding, not just a sexual relationship, then it isn't just a matter of what you want. We should be able to talk about anything," you protest.

She is silent for a while, then says, "It was early winter, a dull day . . . Venice is not always sunny, and there were not many tourists on the streets." Her voice seems to be coming from far away. "From the window, a window that was very low, I could see the sea and the gray sky. Usually, when I sat on the windowsill, I could see the dome of the church. . . ."

She looks out the window at the mass of lights above the pitch-black sea.

"And the dome of the church?" you say, prompting her.

"No, I could only see the gray sky." She continues, "It was below the window, on the stone floor of his studio that he, that artist, raped me. There was a radiator in the room, but the stone was very cold."

You shudder.

"Do you find this upsetting?" Her gray-blue eyes watch you intently from behind her glass, yet she also seems to be staring at the transparent scotch.

"No," you say. But you want to know if she was to some extent fond of the man before and after this.

"At the time I didn't understand anything, I didn't know what he was doing to my body, my eyes were wide open and staring at the gray sky. I only remember that the stone floor was very cold. It wasn't until two years later, when I discovered changes in my body and I'd become a woman, that I understood. So I hated my body."

"But did you go again, did you continue to go to his studio? During those two years?" you ask.

"I can't remember very clearly. At first, I was frightened and couldn't remember anything that had happened during those two years. I only knew that he had used me, and I was frightened all the time, frightened others would find out. He kept asking me to his studio, and I didn't dare tell my mother, because she wasn't well. At the time, we were very poor, my parents had separated and my father had gone back to Germany, and I didn't want to stay at home. At first I went with another girl my age to watch him paint. He said he would teach us to paint, starting off with sketches. . . ."

"Go on." You wait for her to go on, and watch her turning the glass in her hands. The scotch she has been sipping leaves streaks on the inside of the glass.

"Don't look at me like that, I'm not going to tell you everything, and I want to make that quite clear. I don't know, and I can't explain why I went again. . . ."

"Didn't he say he wanted to teach you to paint?" you say, reminding her.

"No. He said he wanted to paint me, he said my curves were gentle. At the time, I was tall and slender, still growing and just starting to fill out. He always got me to comply, he said my body was very beautiful. My breasts were not like they are now. He really wanted to paint me, that's all."

"So, you agreed to it?" You test her, wanting to find out what had happened.

"No—"

"I'm asking whether you agreed to be his model, not about what happened after he raped you," you explain.

"No, I didn't agree, but each time he would take off my clothes. . . ."

"Was this before or after?"

You want to know if she had agreed to model for him before that. That is, had she presented herself naked to him.

"It was like that for two years!" she says decisively, then drinks a mouthful of scotch.

"Like what?" You want to get a better idea.

"What do you mean by 'like what'? Rape is rape, what else is there to it? Surely you know that."

"I've never experienced it."

You have a drink and try hard to think about something else.

"For two whole years," she frowns, turns the glass in her hand, "he raped me!"

That is, she had not resisted. You can't stop yourself from asking, "Then how did it end?"

"I ran into that other girl at his studio. To begin with, I used to go to his studio with her. We had known one another for a long time, and often saw one another. But after the first time he raped me in his studio, I didn't see her again. One day, I had put on my clothes and was about to go out when that girl turned up. I came face to face with her in the passageway by the landing. She tried to avoid me, but her eyes fell upon me and looked me up and down. Then, without a greeting or a good-bye, she turned to leave. I called her name, but she walked faster and, with a toss of the head, was going down the stairs. I turned, saw him standing awkwardly by the door of the studio, and immediately understood!"

"Understood what?" you ask.

"That he was also raping her," she says. "For two years he had been raping me and also her!"

"She, the girl," you say, "maybe she accepted and wanted it, maybe she was jealous of you—"

"No, of course it's impossible for you to understand that look! I'm talking about the way that girl looked me over. I hated myself, not just that girl. It was only through her eyes that I was able to see myself, and I hated him and also my body that had prematurely become a woman's."

Left speechless, you light a cigarette. Outside the big window, the city lights illuminate the night sky, and the gray-white nebula seems to be speeding. The lights in the front section of the lounge have been turned off, only the lights over your table in the rear section are still on.

"Should we leave?" you ask, glancing at the bit of scotch left in her glass.

She drains her glass and smiles at you; you can tell she is a bit tipsy. You raise your glass and empty it, saying that it is to wish her well on her journey.

Back in the room, removing the clasp and loosening her hair, she says, "Do you still want to fuck me?"

You don't quite know how to reply and, somewhat in a daze, sit by the table in the round-backed chair.

"If you really want to. . . ." she murmurs as the corners of her mouth turn down. She takes off her clothes in silence, her bra, her black panty hose and underpants, then lies there on her back staring at you. Her face has a drunken and yet childish look. You don't make a move, you would not be able to fuck her, and somehow you pity her. You must force yourself to be mean, as you coldly question her further.

"Did he ever give you money?"

"Who are you talking about?"

"The artist, weren't you his model?"

"The first few times, but I didn't take it."

"And later?"

"Do you want to know everything?" There is a bitter edge to her voice.

"Of course," you say.

"You know too much already," she says weakly. "I have to keep a bit to myself. . . . Since my mother died I have never returned to Venice."

You have no idea how much of what she has told you is true, or how much she hasn't told you. You say that she is a very intelligent woman, to console and soothe her.

"What's the use of being intelligent?"

She is weaving a net to snare you. What she wants is love, and what you want is freedom. You have paid too high a price for the small freedom of controlling your own freedom, but it is really hard for you to leave her. She compels you, not just to enter her physically, but also to enter deep into the secret recesses of her mind. You look at her voluptuous body, but she gets up and abruptly turns to you.

"Just sit there and don't move! Just sit there and talk."

"Until morning?" you ask.

"As long as you've got something to say, say it, I'm listening!"

Her voice is commanding, yet imploring and radiating loveliness, intangible softness. You say you want to feel her reactions, otherwise you would be talking to a vacuum, you would not know when she had fallen asleep, and would feel let down.

"All right, you take off your clothes, too! Just make love with your eyes!"

Chuckling to herself, she props a pillow behind her back against the headboard and, legs crossed, sits facing you. You take off your clothes but are unsure about going across to her.

"Just sit in the chair, don't come near!" she commands.

You obey, and you confront one another naked.

"I want to look at you and feel you like this," she says.

You say that this is like exposing yourself to her.

"What's wrong with that? A man's body is sexy in the same way, don't feel so aggrieved." At this, her lips curl up and she looks wickedly pleased with herself.

"Revenge? Compensation? Is that what you want?" You say this to mock her, this must be what she wants.

"No, don't think so badly of me. . . ." Her voice suddenly seems to be wrapped in a layer of downy feathers. "You're very gentle," she says with sadness in her voice. "You're an idealist, you're still living in dreams, your own dreams."

You say no. You only live in this instant of time, you no longer believe in lies about the future. You need to be able to live in reality.

"Have you never used violence on a woman?"

You think for a while, then say no. Of course, sex and violence are inevitably linked, but that's another matter. The other party has to be willing and accepting. You have never raped anyone. You ask her whether the men she has had were rough.

"Not necessarily. . . . It's best if you talked about something else."

She turns away and leans on the pillow. You can't see her expression. You say that you have experienced the feeling of being raped, of being raped by the political authorities, and it has clogged up your heart. You can understand her, and can understand the anxiety, frustration, and oppression that she can't rid herself of. Rape is not a sex game. It was the same for you, and it was only long afterward, after obtaining the freedom to speak out, that you realized it had been a form of rape. You had been subjected to the will of others, had to make confessions, had to say what others wanted you to say. It was crucial to protect your inner mind, your faith in your inner mind, otherwise you would have been crushed.

"I'm terribly lonely," she says.

You say you understand her, want to go over to comfort her, but are afraid she might wrongly think that you just want to use her.

"No, you don't understand, it's impossible for a man to understand. . . ." Her voice is tinged with sadness.

You can't help saying that you love her, that, at least at this instant in time, you have really fallen in love with her.

"Don't say that it is love. It's so easy saying it, every man can blurt it out."

"Then what shall I say?"

"Say whatever you like. . . ."

"What if I say you're a prostitute?" you ask.

"Who craves excitement and carnal lust?" she says miserably.

She says she is not a sex object. She hopes she will live in your heart, genuinely communicate with your inner heart, and not simply be used by you. She knows that it's hard, almost futile, but she still hopes that it will be like this.

15

He recalled that, as a youngster, he once read a fairy tale, the author and title of which he had since forgotten. The story went like this: there was this kingdom, where everyone wore a bright mirror on the chest, and the smallest wicked thought would reflect in the mirror. Everything was revealed, and everyone could see it, so no one dared to be even slightly wicked, because there would be nowhere to hide, and the person would be driven from the kingdom. It therefore became a kingdom of pure people. The protagonist entered this kingdom of ultimate purity, maybe he stumbled upon it—he didn't remember too clearly. Anyway, the protagonist also had a mirror on his chest, but in it was a flesh-and-blood heart. An outcry went up among the masses—he was terrified when he read this. He could not remember what happened to the protagonist, but the story left him feeling shocked and uneasy. At the time, he was still a child and did not have any really wicked thoughts, but he couldn't help feeling scared, although of what, he had no idea. As he became an adult, such feelings gradually paled into oblivion; he already had hopes of becoming a new person and, moreover, of living a peaceful life in which he would be able to sleep soundly, without nightmares.

The first to talk to him about women was his schoolmate Luo, a precocious boy who was a few years older. While Luo was a senior in middle school, several of his poems had been published in a magazine, earning him the title of poet among his classmates. He greatly admired Luo. However, after failing the university entrance exams, Luo worked off his frustration by going alone to the school basketball court. There, he would strip to the waist and, sweating all over in the hot summer sun, jump and shoot baskets. Luo didn't seem to be upset about failing and said he was off to fish in the Zhoushan Archipelago. This convinced him that Luo was a born poet.

Some years later, when he went home for the summer vacation, he saw Luo in a white apron selling bean curd at a vegetable market near his home. Luo gave a wan smile when he caught sight of him, and, taking off his apron, got the plump elderly woman who sold vegetables to take care of his bean-curd stall. As they went off together, Luo told him that he had been a fisherman for two years, but when he came back he couldn't find work. Finally, the subdistrict office assigned him to the cooperative vegetable stall to sell bean curd and to look after the accounts.

Luo would count as a genuine slum-dweller. His shanty, a structure of broken bricks and woven bamboo with a coat of mortar, was divided into an inner and an outer room. His mother slept in the inner room, and the outer room served as the main room and kitchen. On one side of the shanty, Luo had extended the roof and put together some sheets of pressed asbestos to build himself another room. In the far corner, where one couldn't stand up straight, stood a collapsible canvas bed and a small desk with a drawer; against the wall on the other side was a rattan bookcase. Everything was meticulously tidy and clean. Although Luo's mother was at work in the factory, Luo took him into this room the size of a chicken coop instead of the main room of the shanty, and got him to sit at the desk while he himself sat on the canvas bed.

"Do you still write poetry?" he asked.

Luo pulled out the drawer and took out a diary. It contained neatly written poems, each clearly dated.

"Are these all love poems?" he asked, leafing through the pages. He had not thought that this big fellow who was always a loner at school wrote lyrical poetry like this. He still remembered the old literature teacher reading out lines from Luo's poems in composition classes, and he said to Luo that these love poems were totally different from those early poems, which were filled with impassioned youthful determination.

"Those poems were like that so that they'd get published, but now even those poems wouldn't get published. These poems here were written for that little slut," Luo said, and started talking about women. "That little slut was just having a bit of fun with me. She had found herself a cadre who was more than ten years her senior and was waiting to get the marriage registered. She used to stay up all night knitting pullovers for that man. I got this book of poems back from her and I don't write anymore."

He thought it was best to get off the topic of women and started talking to Luo about literature. He said that the new life of the new era should have a new literature, but he wasn't sure what exactly this new literature of this new life would be like. However, he didn't think it could be about the good things happening to good people, like in the new folk songs of the Great Leap Forward that filled the pages of all the newspapers and magazines. He also talked about the fiction of Gladkov and Ehrenburg, and the plays of Mayakovski and Brecht. At the time, he wasn't aware of the purges of counterrevolutionaries by Stalin, Ehrenburg's *Thaw,* or the execution of Meyerhold.

"The literature you're talking about is too far away," Luo said. "I don't know where you will find any literature. I spend my time selling vegetables during the day, then, at night, after all the stalls close, I do the accounts. Sometimes I read a bit, but it's all about faraway happenings, and I just read to fritter away time, get rid of the bore-dom. And I don't know where this new life is. The bit of pride I had as a student vanished long ago; I just find myself some girls to have a bit of fun."

He found Luo's decadence sadder than Luo's talk about the little slut. He said he had never touched a woman and this time it was Luo who was surprised. "You're a real bookworm!" Luo said without envy of his apparently better circumstances. Luo was, after all, a few years older and said magnanimously, "I'll get you a girl so you can have a bit of fun. You definitely won't have any problems touching Little Five." Luo said this Little Five was a very easygoing girl, a randy little cunt. He again heard Luo talking disrespectfully about women.

"I'll get her to come. This slip of a girl can play the guitar. She's not like those girls at school, all of them with their airs," he said.

He, of course, wanted to know such a girl, and Luo went off to fetch her. He read through Luo's love poems, some of which were quite explicit. In his view, they surpassed Guo Moruo's "Goddess" in extolling sex, and he was deeply moved. He was even more con-vinced that Luo was indeed a genuine poet, but, at the same time, he knew that these poems definitely could not be published, and he felt sorry for Luo.

Before long, Luo was back. He turned to Luo and said, "Now, this is poetry!"

"Ha, I wrote them for myself to read." Luo gave a bitter laugh.

Little Five arrived wearing clogs. This young girl with intensely black eyes in a sleeveless round-neck floral top had big breasts. She was barely fifteen, but her body was already that of a young woman. She didn't come into the little room but leaned against the doorway.

"He also writes poetry," Luo said, to introduce him to the girl.

In fact, Luo had never read any of his poetry, but this seemed to be an ideal introduction. The girl would have read these erotic poems, and such an introduction would have had an implicit meaning. The girl smiled, and her full lips took on a sultry look; he had never seen a girl with such sexy lips. He closed the book and started talking to Luo about something else. It was he, and not the girl, who felt awkward.

Luo took from behind the door a guitar that had lost most of its varnish and said to the girl, "Little Five, how about singing for us."

He had been saved from his embarrassment. Little Five took the guitar and asked, "What shall I sing?"

"Whatever you like. How about 'Kalinka'?"

This Russian folk song used to be very popular among the youth, but had been replaced by songs extolling the new society, the Party, and the leaders.

Little Five put down her head to pluck the strings. Muted soft notes arose, but she didn't seem to be listening, and looked listless. When she looked at him, he felt utterly confused. Somewhere in the room a cricket quietly chirped, and outside the small window the hot sun glared fiercely. The girl played a tune, stopped, and told Luo she didn't feel like singing. When she turned to him, she seemed to be looking somewhere above his head.

"If you don't want to sing, then don't," Luo said. "But come to see a movie tonight."

The girl smiled without answering, and put the guitar by the door. When she got as far as the main room, she turned and said, "I've got things to do at home!" Then she went off.

"The hell she has. As if I'd believe that crap," Luo said. "You really don't know how to flirt with girls. Don't you want to date her?"

He fell silent. Luo said there wasn't much of a future, so his group of losers often found girls to have a bit of fun, to play the guitar, and to sing together. Sometimes they went to the lake outside the city. They would have a swim or steal a small boat, row out to where the lotus grew in thick clumps, and steal some of the pods. Little Five went with them, and, at night in the middle of the lake, anyone could roam her body and she wouldn't complain. She was a very worldly wench. It was obvious Luo was in love with her, but he said he had a woman. The two of them had grown up together, but she had joined a song-and-dance troupe in a military zone and couldn't marry a vegetable seller like him. Anyway, she got pregnant. That was last winter. Getting an abortion in a hospital required a marriage certificate and a work card, but where could he get hold of these? On top of that, the woman was military personnel, and she had to obtain permission from her superiors to get married. If her workplace found out, she would, of course, be expelled from the army, lose that good job, and end up hating him for the rest of her life! Furthermore, the tiny income from the cooperative vegetable stall was barely enough to feed himself, how would he be able to support a wife and a child? Luckily, one of his maternal uncles was a doctor in a county town, and, thanks to his uncle persuading his associates at the county hospital, Luo was able to take her there, say they were married, and have the abortion performed.

"I went with her early on Sunday morning, and she had to get back to the song-and-dance troupe by ten o'clock that night for roll call. It was army regulation. We had to change buses on the way and were waiting by the bus-stop sign. It had been dark for some time, it was raining, and there wasn't anyone else around. She said she was still bleeding down there, and as I put my arms around her the two of us wept miserably. Afterward, we separated, just like that. Can this be expressed in writing?" Luo asked. "Where is this new life?"

Luo said he couldn't help being decadent. He had womanized in the two years he spent fishing. When the men on the island went out to fish on the high seas, there was no way of knowing if they would be back. He was a young boy just out of school, there was an abundance of sex-crazed women in the fishing village, and that was how it all started. There was nothing romantic to it, and, after he had had his fling, he knew that it was really fucking boring. There was no one he could have a conversation with, so he chose to come back and sell vegetables.

"What gave you the idea of being a fisherman?" he asked Luo.

"I had no choice, I had to find something to do. At the time, like you, I wanted to go to a prestigious university to study literature. Don't you know why I failed?" Luo asked.

"You were the most outstanding in the whole class and acknowledged as a poet by your fellow students. It didn't occur to me that you would fail," he said.

"It was all because of that fuckin' poetry," Luo said. "The year of the university entrance examination was just before the antirightist campaign. Hadn't they called upon people to speak out? The provincial publications got some young writers to take part in a meeting where they were encouraged to speak their minds. I joined with some other young writers and said that there were too many restrictions on topics. Poetry was poetry, why did it have to be divided into industrial themes, agricultural themes, and lives of young people? I also said that they had published my worst poems with the best lines deleted. Because of those comments, they sent in a report to the school. The principal had me in for a talk, and it was only then that I found out I was in trouble. I don't know what happened to the others. I was the youngest, and I had spoken less than the others. At least, I was able to come back to sell vegetables."

Afterward, he bought three tickets to the movies. He waited at the door of the theater until the show was due to start, when Little Five turned up running and out of breath. She said Luo had to go on night duty at the vegetable stall and couldn't come. He wasn't sure if it was Luo's intention to push Little Five onto him, but as soon as they went inside the darkened theater, he took Little Five's hand and they sat down in a couple of seats on the side. He had no idea what the movie was about and only recalled that he was holding the girl's soft hand all the time and that his hot palm was sweating.

He thought that as all the boys had felt the girl, why shouldn't he? Before that, he had never touched a girl. Love for him was something totally different.

At senior middle school, he fell in love with a girl from a lower grade and got to speak with her at the New Year school dance. Right through the night, whether they were playing at solving riddles written on lanterns or some other game, he kept close to that girl in a red pinafore with black flowers. In the hazy light of dawn, or maybe in the reflected light of the streetlights on the snow, he followed the girl as she walked home with some other girls. They were laughing and looking back at him from time to time, and he knew they were talking about him.

He did not think that he, too, could casually touch a girl. When he came out of the theater with Little Five, he deliberately avoided the main street and went into an alley, all the time holding her hand. The girl went along with him, looking at her shoes as she walked, and, now and then, kicking stones on the road. At a corner unlit by the streetlights, he took Little Five's arm and tried to draw her to him. She shook her head and looked at him wide-eyed.

"You men are all bad."

He said he wasn't like that and only wanted to kiss her.

"Why?" she asked with a frown, as the whites of her eyes showed.

He let go of her and said he had never kissed a girl before. Little Five said she'd have to think about it.

His hands fell to his sides, and he hung his head. He did not expect to hear Little Five say, "Then go ahead and kiss me."

He touched her tightly closed lips and immediately withdrew. Little Five closed her eyes, her lips relaxed, and he kissed her again. This time, her lips were thick and soft. He touched her firm breasts through her loose-fitting clothes, and the girl murmured, "Don't hurt me. . . ."

His hand found its way inside her clothes and roamed over her swelling breasts. But he did not dare and had not considered having sex with a girl he did not love. He did not yet know about lust, but he could tell that the girl was really passionate. Afterward, at the university, he received a letter from Little Five. It was a simple letter asking whether he would be back for the summer vacation.

That summer he didn't return. It was the great famine that followed in the wake of the Great Leap Forward. During the summer vacation, university students were required to do voluntary labor, digging holes to plant trees in the Western Hills of Beijing. Everyone was swollen from hunger but nevertheless obliged to donate the whole vacation to carrying out these futile "good deeds." He regretted that he had not been able to sink into total depravity when he was fooling around with Little Five that summer vacation, and he secretly wanted to be totally decadent.

16

In the taxi on the way to the airport, you and Margarethe hardly speak. It seems that everything has already been said, and the taxi is not the place for anything left unsaid.

At the entrance to the immigration barrier, she gives you a gentle hug—as she says you are just friends—her lips touch your cheek, then, without looking back, she goes in.

You had noticed the dark rings around her eyes, and even though she was wearing makeup, you guessed that her face must have been much paler. The two of you had not slept for three days and three nights, no, four days and three nights. From the first night after the play, you were up all night until the next morning, and then from night until the next day, and after that another night. Right now it should be the morning of the fourth day. It had been three days and nights of making love over and over again, striving to dig and suck in the other party, and you, too, were exhausted. It was a bout of sudden frenzied passion, then the temperate farewell of ordinary friends who did not know when they would meet again.

Outside the airport, you come into the brilliant sunshine and steaming heat. There is a long queue at the taxi ramp, and you are extremely tired. When you get into the taxi and the driver asks where you want to go, you hesitate, then simply say "Central," the hub of the bustling city. You do not want to go straight to the hotel, to that empty bed. Her bare body is already linked to the room, the bed, and your thoughts. You have grown used to talking with her, and the words of your inner mind, when you are talking to yourself, always address her, what you say is for her to hear. She has deeply penetrated your feelings and thoughts. When you took possession of her body, she took possession of both your body and mind.

"Where do you want to go in Central?" The driver can tell that you are from the Mainland and he asks you in hesitant Mandarin.

You have dozed off in the taxi, and, opening your eyes, ask, "Is this Central?"

"Yes. What street do you want?"

The taxi pulls over to the curb. In the rearview mirror, you see the driver scowling, he doesn't want to drive around in circles looking for a destination you can't name. You pay the fare and get out. High buildings soar up on both sides of the road, and for a while you can't get your bearings. You follow the road, but, oddly, there aren't many pedestrians, yet Central is usually thronging with crowds and very noisy. Also, there is not the usual traffic congestion, there aren't many cars, and the traffic is moving briskly. Afterward, you find that the shops are all shut, although the windows still have their displays on show. The tall buildings block out most of the sunlight, so it is only the middle of the road that is bright. You can't help feeling that you are daydreaming.

You recall her saying she had to get back to Frankfurt by Monday, that the company she was working for had a business meeting with its Chinese counterpart, and at this you realize that it is Sunday. On the morning of this day of rest, the usual thing is for families or friends to arrange to get together for breakfast in one of the many restaurants. For the nonstop-busy people of Hong Kong, this is a form of entertainment.

For a whole month, there have been rehearsals, performances, dinner receptions, appointments, meetings, and you have never relaxed like this, strolling around on your own in the heart of this lonely town. You are just getting to know the city, but you don't know if you will come back, just like you don't know if you will ever see her again, ever be so close to her again, pouring out your frustrations and abandoning yourself to lust.

On the last night, she got you to rape her. It was not sex play, she really had you tie her up, got you to tie up her hands, got you to beat her with a leather belt, got you to beat the body that she hated. What she wanted to convey to you was the feeling that after rape, the betrayed and alienated physical body no longer belonged to her.

You tied her wrists with her panty hose, and, holding the metal buckle of the belt, lightly struck her with the end. You laughed in the dark to let her know it was a game to give her the sadomasochistic sexual pleasure she wanted, and she also laughed.

But that was not what she wanted, what she wanted was for you to really beat her. You started to hit her harder and harder so that you could hear the sound of the leather against her flesh. Her flesh convulsed and contracted, but she didn't call out to stop. You didn't know how much she could bear, and when she called out in surprise, you immediately threw down the belt and went to caress her. She swore at you for being a fool, struggled to untie her hands and sat up. You apologized. She lay on her back in the bed, and you lay over her. Then as you felt her tears wetting your face, your own tears began to flow. You said you could not rape her and that you no longer had lust.

She said it was impossible for you to understand her suffering, the suffering of a promiscuous woman who had been raped. All you wanted was sexual enjoyment.

You said that you loved her, and, because you loved her, you could not rape her. You said you hated violence.

She also said she wanted you to cry, that when you cry you are more real. She became gentle and loving and kept stroking you, stroking you all over.

A one-hundred-percent woman, you said. No, a wanton woman, she said. You said no, she was a good woman. She said no, you didn't know, after some time you would hate her. It was impossible for her to live the life of a normal woman, because she could never be satisfied. She really wanted to have a life with you, but it was impossible. Furthermore, you would have to forgive her for this psychosis of hers. She did, in fact, want a peaceful and secure life, but no one would be able to provide her with that sort of peace and contentment. And you would not marry a woman like her, you only wanted her body for the enjoyment you wanted but had not yet found.

You said you were afraid of marriage, afraid of being controlled by a woman. You had a wife. You knew what marriage was about. For you, freedom was more precious than anything, but you couldn't help loving her. She said she could not be your lover, you obviously had a woman, and if you didn't have one you would find one. In fact, you were gentle and fairly honest—she said she had said "fairly" and that she was not exaggerating. You said she was a very lovely woman. But was she like this with all men? She said she had given much of herself to you because she liked you, and that you, too, had given her much, it was equal. She also said that she had understood men too early and already had no illusions. People were practical: she was her boss's lover, but he had to go home to his wife and children on weekends. She was his mistress and, apart from the weekends, she accompanied him on work assignments. Also, he needed her for doing business with China.

Her deep throaty voice, her voluptuousness, her frankness, were tangible and, just like her strong body, aroused your lust, inducing memories with the aftertaste of pain, but filling those memories with a sensuousness that made them bearable. Her voice continued to excite you, and it was as if she were chatting softly right next to you, giving you her warmth and the fragrance of her body. Through her, your repressed lust was released, and recounting your memories to her brought both pain and joy. You needed to talk endlessly with her as you searched for those many memories, and, while you were talking, a profusion of small forgotten details kept surfacing with increasing clarity.

The Bank of China Building, glass from top to bottom, reflects, like a mirror, the strands of white clouds in the blue sky. The sharp corner of the triangular building is knife-thin, and Hong Kong people say that it is like a meat cleaver cutting through the heart of the city and destroying the excellent *feng shui* of the island. The building of some finance group alongside has been fitted with some odd metal contraptions, futilely, to resist the baleful influences of the Bank of China Building. This is how Hong Kong people deal with the problem. The palatial Victorian mansion of the Legislative Council, located in the middle of a cluster of tall buildings, is quite insignificant and symbolizes an era that will soon end.

Next to the Legislative Council, crowds are milling in the square with a bronze statue. There are crowds by the fountain, under the covered walkways, the pavements and even the road. You think you have come across some meeting or demonstration. But the people are talking and laughing, food is laid out on the ground, boom boxes are playing pop songs, only dancing is missing.

Amazed at the streets of picnic groups between the tall buildings, you thread your way through them until you come to the closed doors of the Prince's Building where there is a banner with a portrait of Christ on the Cross. A priest is explaining the gospel, and the faithful are repenting in the open air. Eighty to ninety percent of the congregation are women, all with dark complexions. You suddenly realize that this is probably where the Filipino maids of rich Hong Kong families gather for recreation on Sundays. To support their families, these women work in Hong Kong so that they can send money back to the Philippines. There is a buzz of talking and laughing, but you do not understand their language and cannot hear their pain of being away from home.

How long will this situation continue? Will new immigrants from the Mainland replace the Filipino maids? When the whole world is expelling immigrants, can this place be an exception? Of course, you need not worry yourself unnecessarily, the big buildings under the blue sky and white clouds will not crumble, and Hong Kong Island will not turn into a desert. At this instant, as you make a detour and move through the crowds, you are assailed by a profound loneliness, but this is the loneliness that has always been your salvation. In any case, you are not Christ and do not have to sacrifice yourself to enlighten the world. Moreover, there is no chance of your being resurrected, so what is important is for you to live properly in this present world.

Once again, you are plunged into the darkness evoked by the sound of her voice. As if in a dream, with one foot heavy and one light, you stagger about in broad daylight through this noisy crowd while fresh and old memories weave together.

You say Margarethe—speaking to her in your mind—the story of the new people is terrifying, but you no longer need to wash your heart and change your face to cleanse your errors and misdeeds. The pristine kingdom of that brand-new society was nothing but a huge fraud. People who did not understand, were confused, could not explain their own actions—that is, living human beings—were subjected to interrogation about themselves to such an extent that they lost the very basis for their existence.

What you want to say is that Margarethe does not need to purify herself, there is no need for her to repent, and, moreover, rebirth is impossible. She is, she is just like you!

A woman had given you life. Heaven is a woman's womb, whether it is the womb of one's mother or a prostitute. You would prefer to sink into the dark chaos rather than have to pretend being a virtuous man, a new person, or the follower of some religion.

You are on an overhead bridge with an endless stream of cars speeding below. On Sunday, there are few people on this normally busy thoroughfare between the tall buildings and the shops. You lean on the rail and look down on the road below. You are really tired. There are still two more performances of your play and there is more than an hour to the matinee show at two o'clock. The evening show is at seven o'clock, and after that performance there will be photo ops with the actors, and then dinner, which will go on until quite late. You should catch up on some sleep but are reluctant to go back to the hotel. She still pervades your senses, that wild frenzy before parting, the smell of her body with your semen smeared on her heaving breasts.

You go down to the street and come to a movie theater, and, without finding out what is playing, you buy a ticket and go in. You need to be alone in the darkness, to be engrossed in your thoughts about her. It is a Hong Kong slapstick comedy. Your eyes close, you understand little Cantonese, and this is just the thing for taking a nap. The seat is soft and comfortable, and you stretch out your legs. It is your good fortune to have won the freedom to express yourself, there are no taboos, and you can say whatever you want to say and write whatever you want to write. Maybe, as she had suggested, you should write all this down for yourself as a record. You should look with transcendent eyes upon yourself, a man who is an animal with a consciousness, an animal stranded in a human forest.

You have nothing to complain about. To be able to enjoy life, you have paid a price, but, apart from lies and bullshit, what doesn't come at a cost? You should articulate your experiences in writing, leave traces of your life, just like the semen you ejaculate. Surely blaspheming the world will bring you joy! It has oppressed you, and you have the right to seek revenge like this.

There is no hatred. Margarethe, do you hate? You asked her if she hated you, and she shook her head as she laid it on your belly. You stroked her tangled mass of soft hair and let her suck you. She said she was your slave and you were her master, she belonged to you. You were less generous and just kept taking.

You should regain your equilibrium, look at the world, including yourself, with normal eyes. The world is like this, and will continue to be like this. A person is so insignificant, and one can achieve nothing more than making such a gesture.

When you wake up, the lights are on, and people are quickly getting up and leaving. You come out of the theater, hail a cab, and return to the hotel. When the woman at reception hands you the key, there are two telephone messages for you, to return calls. They are probably for dinner appointments, but at night, you have a farewell dinner with the actors and you can't go off somewhere else. Back in your tidy room, there are no items of her clothing on the bed, floor, or desk; it is as if a woman had not stayed here with you. You can't help feeling sad, and lie down fully clothed on the bed. The freshly changed, newly laundered sheets and pillowcases smell clean, and the air conditioner is humming. Not a sign of her or a trace of her smell remains, and, unfortunately, no surveillance camera to prove she had made love with you and that you had not been hallucinating.

Margarethe, you are calling out to a real woman, this is not just the sound of your inner mind. She has aroused your past, and it stands there before your eyes. She is already fused with your memories, and you can't help wanting to retrieve both your fresh and almost forgotten memories.

Right now, she is on a plane, and by tomorrow, this week will have passed. And, as she said, she will again be her boss's lover, and, as she had with you, she will make love with her boss. You have already fallen in love with this sadomasochistic prostitute and can't help thinking of her, her moistness and smell, which arouse your lust. Was she telling the truth when she said she had been raped at thirteen, or was that a strategy of seduction? Should you just treat her as a slut? Or should you let her accompany you in your thoughts, be a companion in your heart, so that you can share with her your loneliness and suffering?

Maybe you should make up your mind to write down the memories and experiences she has summoned up, but is it worth doing? You no longer need to waste your life doing such utterly meaningless things, but then, what is meaningful? Is that play of yours, which is banned on the Mainland but has been staged here and due to go on stage again tonight, meaningful? Was it worth the suffering it brought you? If you had not written that play, wouldn't your life have been much easier? Why, then, do you write?

If it is only through expressing yourself that you exist, then is that the reason for your existence? Does this then mean that you are a book-writing machine, driven by vanity to squander away your life? Perhaps she is right, just sink into carnal lust so that you can savor the pain. Since it is impossible to extricate yourself from it, simply sink into it. What need is there for you to promote morality, and where, in fact, can morality be found? That you are no match for the world and can only take refuge in the written word for a little solace and joy is like Margarethe's telling you about her suffering in order to exorcise it, even though doing this is unbearable.

You take a hot bath, then a cold shower, and feel refreshed. You must return to reality by going to see the final performance of your play. With the young actors, you will eat, drink, joke, make lofty pronouncements about human beings, then leave them with the perplexities of being human.

17

It was a tailor-made new society, brand new and shiny, in which everyone was a glorious worker. People were organized into work units so that they could serve the people, even the barefoot peasants who worked in the fields and the bathhouse workers who pared the calluses from people's feet. Outstanding workers were selected as model workers and commended in the newspapers. There were no idlers, begging and prostitution were banned, and grain was allocated according to the number of mouths to be fed so that not a single bowl of rice would be wasted. The sense of personal gain was eradicated and everyone relied upon a wage or salary. Everything was the shared property of society, including the workers who were rigorously managed so that they would be perfect. There was no escape for the bad, and those not executed were sent to prison or to a farm to be reformed through labor. Red flags fluttered everywhere and, although it was only the first stage, a human ideal of a heavenly kingdom had come into being.

New people were also created. A perfect model, an ordinary soldier called Lei Feng, who grew up as an orphan under the five-star red flag not knowing what it was to be an individual, selflessly saved others and sacrificed his own life. When this hero of few desires first learned to read, he felt boundless gratitude to the Party for being able to read the *Selected Works of Mao Zedong* and to write about it. Lei Feng was willing to be a bright, shiny cog in the machinery of the revolution so that citizens could model themselves on him. And everyone had to do just that. He was dubious about this type of new people, but the confession system at the university required that everyone confess their thoughts to the Party. One's own thoughts and those of others, including one's doubts, all had to be reported at special summing-up meetings. He was tricked and frivolously asked if one could be a hero without having to throw oneself on a bag of explosives and getting blown up, and wasn't the function of the engine more important than that of a cog. This instantly sent his fellow students into an uproar, the women students making the loudest protests. He was criticized, luckily only at a class discussion, so it was not too serious. However, he had been taught a sound lesson: a person had to lie. If one wanted only to tell the truth, then there was no point living. It was fundamentally impossible for a person to be pure, but it was only many years later that he was able to comprehend this. He was able to learn through other people's and his own experiences, but only after having personally verified the experiences of others and suffering as a consequence.

You now do not need to take part in compulsory study meetings to confess your words and actions, and you no longer have to repent. You also distance yourself from any new myths that are similar to those. However, at that time he was frustrated and needed to talk about how he felt, so he arranged a get-together with some old schoolmates who were in Beijing and studying at university. They met at the Purple Bamboo Courtyard Park in the western suburbs. From different universities, luckily, they were not directly linked in an association, but only did a bit of writing when they felt deeply moved. All of them had written things like poetry, and simply wanted to come out of the intellectual shackles of the campus to relax. The park had only recently opened to the public and was fairly deserted. A teahouse by the lake sold cakes, but those poor students could not afford to go inside to sit down. However, on the grass in the shade of the trees, farther off, there were some quiet spots without any people. The fresh smell of wheat wafted on the breeze from the fields above the earth embankment, so probably it was May, because the grain was ripe.

Big Head said he wanted to write a play like Mayakovski's *Bathhouse*. He was nicknamed Big Head, because he had won the first prize in a mathematics competition for all middle-school students in Beijing, and also because the cap he wore in winter was two sizes bigger than that of anyone else. Big Head, fortunately, went back to his mathematics and didn't write about any bathhouses or mud baths. However, as two of his articles had been published, in English, in an international students' mathematics journal just before that anticulture Cultural Revolution broke out, he was sent for eight years to herd cattle on a farm. Big Head's problem was not the result of that get-together in the park but came about after he had graduated. He made a flippant comment in the dormitory of his research institute and was reported by a colleague.

It was the reedy Mandarin Jacket Cheng, who got in trouble on that occasion. His nickname came from middle-school days, when he used to wear his father's old clothes that were several sizes too big for his skinny body. Without his knowledge, a fellow student read Cheng's diary and reported it to the secretary of the Communist Youth League. Mandarin Jacket was the only one of their group who had somehow weaseled membership into the League. The diary had a note on their get-together, but had not recorded what they had talked about. Cheng got in trouble because he had written about women in the diary. It was said to have been pornographic and lewd, but it wasn't clear if the women were figments of his imagination or real. When people from Cheng's university arrived to question him about Cheng, he broke out in cold sweat.

At the get-together, he had talked about Ehrenburg's memoirs, Paris at the beginning of the century, and the bar frequented by that group of surrealist poets and artists. He had also talked about Meyerhold, who was shot for his involvement with formalism. What Big Head talked about was even more frightening. They listened with bated breath as he told them about Khrushchev's secret report on Stalin, which he had read in the English edition of *Moscow News*. At the time, strict controls on foreign-language publications in university libraries were not yet in place. The fourth person at the get-together was studying biology and genetics, and he had raved on about Indian philosophy and said that Tagore's poetry was like a meeting with immortals. The people who came to question him didn't ask about any of this. In other words, Mandarin Jacket was indeed a good friend and had not betrayed them. What they asked was whether women students were present and whether he knew anything about Cheng's off-campus relationships with women. At this he knew they were out of danger. So ended their one and only get-together.

You had been living in Paris for a number of years but had never thought to look for that bar. Once, quite by chance, after dinner at the home of a French writer, you left with a Chinese poet who was also living abroad. It was a lively scene at the Latin Quarter at midnight, and, passing by a bar crowded with people sitting inside and outside the door with a glass panel, you looked up and saw the neon sign LA ROTONDE. It was that bar! The two of you sat down at a small round table that had just been vacated; around you were tourists speaking English or German. On the eve of a new century, the French poets and artists had all gone elsewhere.

All of you refused to take part in any movements, refused to commit to any ideology, and refused to join any groups. Luckily, those of you at the Purple Bamboo Courtyard Park managed to pull the brake in time. No one reported on the others; otherwise, even if you had not been branded counterrevolutionaries, the things you talked about would have been recorded in your files, and you wouldn't be here today. Afterward, all of you learned to wear a mask, and either extinguished your voice or else hid it deep at the bottom of your heart.

On waking, a few clouds are slowly drifting in the night sky outside the window, and, for an instant, you don't know where you are; you are relaxed and lethargic. It has been a long time since your thoughts have meandered like this into the past. You look at your watch and get out of bed. You must get to the theater before the end of the performance, for photo ops with the actors and stagehands, and then go to dinner with them. Parting after the last performance is always somehow sad.

From city to city, country to country, your journey is less secure than a migratory bird's, you simply enjoy these moments of pleasure. As long as you can fly, you persevere, and if your heart and body die, you will just drop down. You are now an unfettered bird, seeking joy in flight, and no longer need to go looking for suffering.

A private room has been reserved at the restaurant, and the group of thirty or forty clink glasses, laugh, talk, and exchange addresses. But most of you will never meet again, the world is just too big. The sturdy young woman with big eyes who played the female lead wants you to write something for her on a poster, so you write next to her name: "A good woman."

Her eyes narrow as she wickedly asks, "Good in what way?"

"Good in being free," you say.

Everyone cheers, so she raises both arms and pirouettes to show off her supple and beautiful figure. Another, a brash guy, asks, "What do you think about marriage?"

You say, "Anyone who hasn't been married should get married."

"What about those who've been through a marriage?" he goes on to ask.

You can only say, "Then try a second time."

Everyone claps and cheers. The brash guy does not let up and goes on to ask, "Do you have lots of girlfriends?"

You say, "Love is like sunshine, air, and wine."

Everyone rushes up to have a drink with you. With young people, there are none of those rules and etiquette, it's rowdy and a lot of fun.

"Then what about art?" It is the shy voice of a young woman standing a couple of people away from you.

"Art is simply a mode of life."

You say that you are living at this time and in this instant, and do not seek immortality. Epitaphs are erected for the living and have nothing to do with the dead. You have had a lot to drink, and it doesn't matter if you rave on. Writing plays is for enjoyment, and when you write them, you enjoy yourself to the full. You say that working with them was a pleasure and thank everyone.

Your associate director is a slim man, cool-headed and experienced, older than the actors. Speaking on their behalf, he says they all really like this play that you had written ten years ago but had not dated. They hope you will return to stage your new plays. You do not want to disappoint them, and say that the world is not big, Hong Kong can be seen at a glance on the map, and there would be opportunities. Of course, you know quite well that once a bird has flown from its cage, it will not want to fly back into it. You think about the parched high plateau of Central France, where you once looked down from the cliff at the little city with its prominent church spire at the foot of the mountain. Some distance from the highway, a Frenchwoman lay on her back sunbathing naked among the bushes. Her voluptuous arms shading her eyes were a dazzling white in the sun, like the rest of her body. The wind brought with it the screeching of eagles and the flapping of their wings as they circled below your feet, halfway down the mountain. French eagles became extinct a long time ago, and these eagles had been purchased in Turkey, then set free here.

You need to distance yourself from suffering, calmly scan those dim memories, and find in them some bright spots, so that you will be able to investigate the road you have traveled.

They are still young, but do they have to go through your experiences? That is their affair, they have their own fates. You do not take on the sufferings of others, are not the savior of the world, you seek only to save yourself.

18

You find retelling that period quite difficult, and for you now, he of that time is hard to comprehend. In order to look back, you must explain the vocabulary of those times, restore special meanings to words. For example, the proper noun "Party" was totally different from the word used in the saying "The morally superior person comes together with others but does not form a party." As a child, he often heard his father proclaim this to assert his own moral superiority, but afterward, his father did not dare say this again. At the mention of the word "Party," his father turned solemn and reverent, and his hand shook so badly that liquor spilled from the cup he was holding. If he had not been so terrified, he would not have tried to kill himself. Such was the greatness and might of the noun "Party." The great and mighty nation, moreover, ranked below the Party and, needless to say, the place where persons worked, were paid, and ate meals—the "work unit"—belonged to the Party. Thus, a person's residential permit, grain allocation, housing, as well as personal freedom, were determined by the Party "work unit." However, this did not apply to the enemy, and hence the word "comrade" assumed extreme importance, and everyone used all means to ensure that that word would remain attached to his or her name. To fail to do so made one an "Ox Demon and Snake Spirit," who had to be "purged" from the "work unit" and forced to undertake "reform through labor."

So, whenever the Party decided to initiate a movement to purify the ranks, the people of every work unit fought with a vengeance. Everyone was afraid of being purged: a person could be classified as "Revolutionary Comrade" (twenty-six grades) or "Ox Demon and Snake Spirit" (divided into five big categories). This classification determined whether one had a city residential permit (for people not required to work in agricultural production and who received fixed monthly coupons to buy goods and grain products), whether one had to undergo reform through labor, or whether one was to live or die. And this classification depended on policies that fluctuated according to the bitter infighting of the twenty or so members of the Party Center (usually the Political Bureau and the Secretariat of the Party Center), on their subsequent transmission, and on internal party documents that were inaccessible to people in general. A person's fate was thus miraculously determined with ten thousand times greater accuracy than the prophecies of the Bible. Failure to comply with regulations constituted an error if minor, and a crime if major, and this was accordingly recorded in a person's file.

What was recorded in the file was, of course, not simply a person's life. Wrong words and actions, general political and moral conduct, a person's written thought-reports and confessions, as well as the verdicts and judgments of the Party organization of the work unit, were collected together and placed under confidential supervision by special personnel. A person was tracked from one work unit to another but did not need to imagine ever being able to see the file.

Also, for example, the word "study" was not the dictionary definition of acquiring knowledge or the learning of a particular skill. No, it referred solely to the eradication of thinking that failed to conform to what had been stipulated by the Party at a particular time. Don't laugh! The word "private" was interpreted as "individual," and, by extension, could also mean psychological evil that had to be ruthlessly eradicated. Moreover, the May Seventh Cadre Schools were definitely not schools as generally known in past and present times, in China or elsewhere. Application for enrollment was not necessary, and, once assigned, attendance was obligatory. In the cadre school, people supervised one another while undergoing intensive physical labor designed to snuff out thinking and to punish anyone with an education or capable of reflective thinking. The Party only permitted one kind of thinking, that is, the thinking of the Supreme Leader. At the time, it was the same for Party cadres and ordinary public personnel, including their family members. If one was sent to a cadre school, it was impossible to protest. Like the work unit, the cadre school controlled a person's grain rations, place of residence, and outside travel. There was no possibility of playing truant, like a child, and, furthermore, where could one hide?

All these terms had their own related vocabulary, enough for compiling a dictionary of words and phrases, but you have no intention of exerting yourself compiling such a dictionary just to benefit historical research.

And, on the subject of history, for example, this so-called Cultural Revolution took place just thirty or so years ago, and yet there were numerous revisions prior to the Party Representative Conference official interpretation of 1981. There were considerable changes of course from Mao's Ninth Congress of the Chinese Communist Party edition to Deng Xiaoping's Third Plenum of the Party Central Committee edition, but investigating these changes is, at present, prohibited. Also, the various popular revisions of the history of the Cultural Revolution are all different. Is it the history of the Cultural Revolution by the Red Guard Danian, the history of the Cultural Revolution by Big Li of the rebel faction, or the memoirs of the Party secretary Comrade Wu Tao who fell from political power? Or is it the subsequent appeal by the son of Old Liu who was beaten to death? Or is it the memorial speeches at the ceremony to compensate and exonerate the old commander who starved to death in the political prison he himself had established during the bloody battles? Or is it the history of the suffering of that abstract notion, "the people"? And do "the people" have a history?

During the Cultural Revolution, people were "rebelling," whereas before that people were "making revolution." However, after the end of the Cultural Revolution, people avoided talking about rebelling, or simply forgot that part of history. Everyone has become a victim of that great catastrophe known as the Cultural Revolution and has forgotten that before disaster fell upon their own heads, they, too, were to some extent the assailants. The history of the Cultural Revolution is thus being continually revised. It is best that you do not try to write a history, but only to look back upon your own experiences.

At the time, he was impulsive and stupid, and the bitterness of having been duped was like swallowing rat poison. If it had been swallowed, then vomiting should have been able to get rid of it. In theory, it was simple, but repeated vomiting still couldn't completely get rid of it.

Righteous indignation and political gambles, tragedy and farce, heroes and clowns, were created through people being manipulated. Blah! Blah! The high-sounding righteous words, discussion, and vilification, all proclaimed the words of the Party. People lost their own voices, became puppets, and could not escape the big hand behind, which controlled them.

Now, when you hear impassioned speeches, you secretly smile. Slogans calling for revolution and rebellion give you goose bumps, and as soon as heroes or fighters appear, you quickly step aside. All that fervor and righteous indignation should be fed to dogs. You should have fled that arena for baiting animals to tear at one another long ago. It is not for you. Your domain lies only between paper and pen, writing not as a tool in the hands of others, but simply to speak to yourself.

You strive to collect memories. The reason he went crazy at that time was probably because the illusions he believed in had been shattered, and the imaginary world of books had become taboo. Also, he was young, had nowhere to dissipate his energy, and couldn't find a woman for his body and soul. Sexually frustrated, he simply stirred the water in mud puddles.

The utopia of the new society, like the new people, was a rewriting of a legend. Now, when you hear people lamenting the destruction of their ideals, you think to yourself that it was a good thing they were destroyed. And whenever you hear anyone loudly proclaiming ideals, you think it is some quack peddling dog-skin bandages again. If someone prattles on and tries to convert you, or preaches to you, you quickly say sure, sure, see you some other time, and, with luck, slip away.

You no longer engage in polemics and prefer to go off to have a beer. Life is irrational; so, must a rationale be formulated for human existence before people can be people? No, you simply narrate, use language to reconstruct the he of that time. From this time and this place you return to that time and that place, using your state of mind at this time and this place to tell of him at that time and that place. Probably this is the significance of this investigation of yours.

He originally had no enemies, so why was it necessary to find them? It is only now that you realize that if there still are enemies, they are dead-and-buried shadows left in your heart by Old Man Mao. And you simply have to walk away from them. There is no need to tilt at shadows, to fritter away the little life that you still have.

Now you are without "isms." A person without "isms" is more like a person. An insect or a plant is without "isms." You, too, have a life and will no longer be manipulated by any "isms," and you prefer to be an onlooker living on the fringes of society. Unavoidably, there will be perspectives, views and tendencies, but, finally, no particular "isms." This is the difference between the you of the present and the he that you are investigating.

19

The first battle between Red Guards broke out in the main courtyard of the workplace. In the middle of the day, when people were coming out of the building to go to the dining room, a Red Guard from outside came and put up a poster on the courtyard wall. He was stopped by a security guard. Some Red Guards from the workplace came and tore down the poster.

The cocky youth with glasses was surrounded on all sides, but he loudly protested, "Why can't I put it up? Putting up posters has been authorized by Chairman Mao!"

"That's Liu Ping's son trying to overturn the verdict on his father, don't let him get up to mischief!"

A security guard motioned to the gathering crowd and said, "Don't crowd around here, go off and eat!"

"My father's innocent! Comrades!" Shoving aside the guard, the youth held his head high to address the crowd. "Your Party committee has changed the general direction of the struggle away from Chairman Mao's revolutionary line, don't let them hoodwink you! If they aren't up to something underhanded, why are they scared of posters?"

Danian squeezed his way out of the crowd of silent onlookers and said to some Red Guards of the workplace, "Don't let this stinker pose as a Red Guard, take off his armband!"

Holding high his arm with the armband and protecting the armband with his other hand, the youth went on to shout, "Comrade Red Guards! Your general direction is wrong! Boot out the Party committee and make revolution, don't be accomplices of the capitalists! All of you comrades who want to make revolution, go look inside the university campuses, they are proletarian rebel territories. You are still under the White Terror out here—"

The youth was pushed back against the wall. He turned to the crowd of onlookers for help but no one dared to come to his rescue.

"Who is *your* comrade? You turtle grandson of the fuckin' landlord class, how dare you pose as a Red Guard? Take it off!" Danian ordered.

A scuffle broke out for the armband. The youth was strong but could not fend off several people tackling him. First his glasses flew to the ground and were instantly trampled, then his armband was pulled off. This self-assured, confident successor to the revolution was now propped against the wall, cowering, his arms protecting his head. Then, falling on his haunches, he began to wail uncontrollably and was instantly transformed into a miserable pup.

Old Liu was also dragged out, tottering and stumbling, from the building and denounced in the courtyard. But he was an old revolutionary who had experienced a lot in life and did not buckle like his son. Holding his head high, he tried to speak, but, immediately, Red Guards pushed his head to the ground so that his face was covered in dirt and he could do nothing but keep his head down.

Squashed in the crowd, he witnessed in silence what had happened, and in his heart he chose to rebel. He slipped out during worktime and went around the university campuses in the western part of the city. At Peking University, which was thronging with peo-

ple, among the posters covering the buildings and walls, he saw one
by Mao Zedong: "Bombard Their Headquarters—My Poster."
When he got back to his workplace office, he was still fired up. Late
that night, when nobody was around, he wrote a poster. He did not
wait for people to come in for work to collect signatures. He was
afraid that by morning, when he was more clear-headed, he might
not have the courage. So he had to put up the poster in the middle
of the night, while he was still fired up. The masses had to heroically
speak out to overturn the verdicts on people branded as anti-Party.

In the empty corridor of the building, some old posters rustled in
a draught; this sense of loneliness was probably necessary to support
heroic action. The impulse for justice sprang from a sense of tragedy,
and he had been thrust into the gambling den, although at the time
it was hard to say whether he wanted to gamble. In any case, he
thought he had seen an opening and there was something of gambling with life in being a hero.

The stalwarts, branded anti-Party at the start of the Cultural Revolution, had not been able to raise their heads, and the activists following the Party committee had not received directives from their
superiors, so when people saw the poster they remained silent. For
two whole days, he came and went alone, drowned in feelings of
tragedy.

The first response to his poster was from the manager of the book
warehouse, Big Li, who phoned to fix a time to see him. Big Li and
a thin youth, a typist called Little Yu, were waiting for him in the
courtyard in front of the kitchen.

"We agree with your poster and we can work together!" Big Li
said, and shook his hand to confirm that he was a comrade-in-arms.

"What's your family background?" To be a rebel also took into
account a person's family background.

"Office worker." He did not explain any further. Such questions
always made him feel awkward.

Big Li looked at Little Yu, as if to ask what he thought. Someone came with a flask to get hot water, and the three stopped talking. They heard the water filling the flask and the person walking off.

"Tell him about it." Little Yu had approved.

Big Li told him, "We're setting up a rebel Red Guard group to fight them. Tomorrow morning, at eight o'clock sharp, we're holding a meeting at the teahouse in Taoranting Park."

Another person came along with a flask, so the three of them parted and went their separate ways. It was a clandestine association and not to attend would be a sign of cowardice.

Sunday morning was very cold, and the pellets of ice on the road crunched underfoot like broken glass. He had arranged to meet with four youths at Taoranting Park in the south of the city. His workplace was far away in the north, so it was not likely that he would meet anyone he knew. The sky was gray and overcast, and no one was in the park, because all forms of enjoyment had been stopped during this abnormal period. As he trudged along the road crunching the ice, he felt as if he had a divine mission to save the world.

The tables by the lake were deserted and inside the teahouse, behind thick cotton door curtains, only two old men were sitting opposite one another by the window. When everyone had arrived, they sat outside around a table, each warming his hands on a mug of hot tea. First of all, each gave his family background as was required for rebellion under the red flag.

Big Li's father was a shop assistant in a grain store, his grandfather used to mend shoes but he was dead. At the start of the Cultural Revolution, Big Li had put up a poster about the Party branch secretary, and for this he had undergone correction. Little Yu, the youngest, had come straight from middle school to the workplace, where he had been working as a typist for less than a year. Both of his parents were workers in a factory, but he had been expelled from the Red Guards for getting to work late and leaving early. Another, Tang, worked as a motorbike traffic officer and before that he used to drive a car in the army. His family background was impeccable but he had a glib tongue and, according to him, the Red Guards had expelled him because he was keen on practicing comic dialogue. Another person wasn't present because he had to take care of his sick mother in hospital. Big Li conveyed the message that the person unconditionally supported rebelling and fighting the restoration faction.

Finally, it was his turn, and he was about to say he lacked the qualifications for being a Red Guard and that it wasn't necessary to include him in their group. However, before the words came out of his mouth, Big Li waved his hand and said, "We all know your stance, we also want to unite with revolutionary intellectuals like you. Those present today are core members of the Red Guard of our Mao Zedong's Thought!"

It was as simple as that, and there was no need for further discussion. They, too, regarded themselves as the successors of the revolution, and it was right for them to safeguard Mao's Thought. It was indeed as Big Li said, "In the universities, the rebel group has already thrashed the old Red Guards, what are we waiting for? Victory will be ours!"

That very night, back in the empty workplace building, they put up the manifesto of their rebel Red Guard group. Big posters targeting the Party committee and the old Red Guards were posted in the corridors of every floor of the building down to the main hall, and out in the main courtyard.

At daybreak, when he returned to his small room, the stove-heater had long since gone out. The room was chilly, and his fervor, too, had subsided. He got into bed to reflect upon the significance and consequences of their actions, but, overcome by exhaustion, fell fast asleep. When he woke up, it was already twilight, but his head was still fuzzy. The accumulated pressure of staying vigilant day and night for months had dispersed, and he went on to sleep for a whole night.

He was up early, and went to work not expecting to see poster responses pasted everywhere upstairs and downstairs. Suddenly, hero or not, he was indeed a fighter who was in the limelight. The tense atmosphere in the office had relaxed, and people who had been avoiding him a few days ago now all greeted him with a smile and spoke to him. Old Mrs. Huang, under investigation at the time, held his hand and would not let go. Tears streaming down her face, she said, "You have spoken the thoughts in the minds of the masses. You people are Mao Zedong's true Red Guards!" She was simpering like the old villagers greeting the Red Army that had come to liberate them, as shown in revolutionary movies, and even the stage words were much the same. Even Old Liu who never revealed his emotions smiled as he looked at him, nodding to indicate his respect. This superior of his, too, was waiting for him to liberate him. No one knew that they were only five hastily assembled youths, and their suddenly becoming an unstoppable force was due to the fact that they also wore red armbands on their sleeves.

Some put signatures to their announcement of withdrawal from the old Red Guards, and Lin was among them. This gave him a ray of hope that maybe they would resume their former liaison, but at noon, when he looked around in the dining hall, he did not see her. He thought that probably, at this time, she was keen to avoid him. In the corridor upstairs, he came face to face with Danian, who pretended not to have seen him and quickly walked past, but he was no longer swaggering with his head arrogantly cocked.

The somber workplace building, with its individual offices, was like a giant beehive, and operating procedures were built up in layers of authority. When the original authority was shaken, the whole hive started buzzing. People deep in discussion stood in groups in the corridors, and wherever he went, people nodded at him or stopped him for a chat whether he knew them or not. They were flocking to talk to him just as they had flocked to talk to the Party secretary or political cadres during the eradication of Ox Demons and Snake Spirits campaign. In a few short days, almost everyone had indicated they were rebelling, and every section had discarded Party and administrative structures and formed combat teams. He, a low-level editor, had, in fact, become a prominent figure in this workplace building with its huge hierarchy of grades, and it was as if he was the leader. The masses needed a leader like a flock of sheep needed to stay near the sheep with a bell, but the lead sheep was itself driven by the loud crack of a whip and didn't know where it was going. Anyway, he did not have to sit in the office all day, and he could come and go without anyone questioning him. People took the work from his desk, did his editing for him, and he was not allocated other work.

He had gone home early, and, entering the courtyard, saw a grubby person with messy hair sitting on his stone doorstep. He gave a start when he saw it was Baozi, from the family next door. They were friends as children, but had not seen one another for many years.

"You devil, what brings you here?" he asked.

"It's really great that I've found you, but it's impossible to give you a one-word answer!" Baozi, king of the urchins in the alleys and lanes in those days, had now learned to sigh.

He unlocked the padlock and opened the door to his room. The retired old man next door also had his door open and poked out his head.

"He's a schoolmate from my old home down south."

Now that he, too, wore a red armband, he took no notice of the old bugger and stopped him with one sentence. The old man's face wrinkled up into a smile that exposed his sparse teeth as he chuckled approvingly before retreating into his room and closing the door.

"I escaped without a towel or toothbrush and have been posing as one of the hordes of students who have come to Beijing. Do you have something for me to eat? I haven't eaten properly for four days and nights. I've only got a handful of loose change and don't dare spend any of it. By pretending to be a student, I've been able to get a couple of steamed buns and a bit of thin gruel in hostels."

As soon as he came into the room, Baozi slapped on the table a few Mao-head banknotes and some coins he had taken out of his pockets. He went on to say, "I escaped through the window the day before I was to be denounced by the whole school. A sports teacher, denounced for feeling a student's breasts during gymnastics, was dragged out as a bad element and beaten to death by Red Guards."

Baozi's forehead was creased with anxiety and he looked utterly wretched. Where was that mischief-making devil that went around stripped to the waist in summer as a child? Baozi could tread water, swim under water, and stand upside down like a dragonfly with his feet sticking up above the surface. When he went off to the lake to learn to swim without telling his mother, he had this companion to bolster his courage. Baozi was two years older, more than a head taller, and when it came to fighting he was really tough, so if he ran into boys looking for a fight, as long as Baozi was there, he was not afraid. It was unthinkable that this intrepid desperado would today travel so far to seek him out for protection. Baozi said that after graduating from teachers' college he was sent to teach language at a county school. At the start of the Cultural Revolution, the Party secretary used him as a scapegoat.

"I didn't compile the teaching material, so how could I know which essay was problematical? I'd told some anecdotes and stories to liven up the teaching and I was attacked for doing most of the talking in the classroom. Could language classes be taught without talking? I was locked in a classroom and guarded day and night by Red Guards. I've got a wife and a child, and if there was a tragic outcome, even if I wasn't killed but just maimed, how would my wife bring up a baby that was not even one month old? I got out through a window on the first floor and scaled down a drainpipe without any

trouble. I did not go home, because I didn't want my wife implicated. The train was crammed with students all the way here and it
was impossible for tickets to be inspected. I've come to lodge a
grievance, you've got to help me find out whether a low-level
teacher like me with the significance of a sesame seed, and not even
a Party member, could possibly be a member of the black gang
within the Party."

After dinner, he took Baozi to the reception office for the masses
located on the street to the right of the west gate of Zhongnanhai.
The gate was wide open and the whole place lit up. The main courtyard was teeming with people who were pushing and shoving, and
they were moved along slowly by the crowd. In a shed in the middle
of the courtyard, military officials with cap and lapel badges were sitting at rows of desks, listening and taking notes, as people from all
over the country lodged complaints. Baozi stood on his toes as he
strained to hear in between people's heads about the "thinking of
the Party Center," but it was too noisy. As soon as people got to the
desks, they started shouting to be heard as they struggled to ask
questions. The receptionists gave brief, discreet, standard responses,
and in some cases simply took notes and answered without even
looking up. The two of them were pushed away before they got anywhere near the desks, and were pushed, helpless, all the way into the
corridor downstairs.

Posters protesting against persecution and extracts of speeches by
important officials covered the walls. The speeches of these Party
Center leaders who had been newly appointed or had not yet fallen
from power were full of malice and hidden meanings, and also con-
tradicted one another. Baozi started to panic and asked if he had pen
and paper with him. He told Baozi not to worry about copying it all
down because he had collected lots of these notices as well as stenciled copies of speeches. When they got home, they could go
through them carefully.

All the offices in the building were open and officials here were also dealing with complaints. It was not as crowded, but there were queues outside the doors. In one of the offices, a youth, holding an old army cap that was white from washing, wept loudly as he related his grievance; tears streamed down as he spoke in thick, almost incomprehensible Jiangxi or Hunan dialect. He was telling about a local massacre. Men and women, old people and even babies, had been herded onto the threshing square and, group after group, beaten to death with hoes, meat cleavers, and metal-tipped carrying poles. The corpses were thrown into the river, and there was a terrible stench. The youth, almost certainly a descendant of one of the Five Black Categories, clutched the old army cap as his credential, otherwise he would not have dared come to the capital to report this grievance. The people crammed inside and outside the door of the office listened in silence as an official took notes.

After leaving the reception office and coming onto Chang'an Avenue, Baozi wanted to go to the Ministry of Education to see if there were directives for middle-school teachers. The Ministry of Education was located in the west of the city, just a few stops away, but blocking the road at the bus stop were schoolchildren from out of town, each carrying a school bag with an embroidered five-point red star. When the bus arrived, even before it came to a stop, they started surging on. The bus had already been full, so those getting off and those getting on had to grapple with one another. The doors unable to close, the bus started to move off with people caught in the doors. Although Baozi could scale drainpipes and jump out of buildings, he could not squeeze past these children who were as agile as monkeys.

They made their way by foot to the Ministry of Education. The whole of the building had been converted into a hostel for students from out of town. From the main hall downstairs to the corridors of every floor, all the offices had been vacated, and everywhere there were wheat stalks, grass mats, gray blankets, plastic sheeting, and disorderly rows of bedding. Enamel basins, bowls, chopsticks, and spoons were strewn all over the floors, and there was an all-pervasive stench of sweat, preserved radishes, shoes, and unwashed socks. Boisterous students with nowhere to go in the harsh winter cold had fallen fast asleep from exhaustion as soon as they lay down. They were all waiting for the Commander-in-Chief's seventh or eighth review the following day or the day after. There were around two million at each review, and youngsters started assembling in the middle of the night, first filling Tiananmen Square and then both sides of the square for ten kilometers from east to west along Chang'an Avenue. The Commander-in-Chief, accompanied by Deputy Commander-in-Chief Lin Biao holding his little red book of Mao's *Sayings,* would drive in an open jeep past walls of frozen students, many layers deep on both sides. These youngsters, waving the precious little red book, hot tears streaming down their faces, screamed themselves hoarse, wildly shouting "long live" to wish a long life to Chairman Mao. Then, fired with revolutionary zeal, they all went home to smash up everything that was old—wrecking schools, destroying temples, and attacking workplaces.

When he and Baozi got back to his room, it was very late and everyone was asleep. He opened the door of the coal stove, and the two of them warmed their frozen hands. As the wind blew through the cracks of the door and window, their faces glowed from time to time, reflecting the flames. Their meeting was unexpected, and neither of them had any intention of recalling childhood memories of what seemed to be another world.

20

"There's a rock there," the joker in front of you points out.

You couldn't fail to see a rock that size and are on the point of going around it, when you hear the joker say, "Try moving it!"

Why waste the energy, you wouldn't be able to move it anyway.

"So, you think an insensate rock can't be moved?" the joker says triumphantly.

You prefer to believe that is so.

"There's no harm trying," the joker's baiting you, and his face is all smiles.

You shake your head, not wanting to try something stupid like that.

"It's flawless and more solid than granite, a magnificent boulder!" The joker circles the rock, clucking his tongue.

Even if it's a boulder, it's got nothing to do with you.

"What a solid foundation it would make, such a pity not to make use of it!" The joker can't stop himself from giving a big sigh.

You're not erecting a monument and you're not building a tomb, what would you want it for?

"Go on, try to move it!" The joker puts his arms around the rock and holds onto it.

You wouldn't be strong enough anyway.

"It wouldn't move even if you kicked it."

You're quite sure that is so, but still touch it with your foot.

This gets the joker all excited and he goes on baiting you, "Stand on it and have a go!"

Have a go at what? But succumbing to his egging you on, you stand on it.

"Don't move!" The joker circling the rock is, of course, also circling you. You don't know if he's watching the rock or watching you. You can't help following his eyes and, in so doing, you also turn a circle while standing on top of the rock.

At this point, the joker looks you squarely in the face, his eyes narrowing as he smiles, and says in a friendly tone, "So, it can't be moved!"

Naturally, he's talking about the rock and not you. You smile back at him and go to get down, but the joker puts up a hand and stops you, "Not so fast!"

He sticks out the index finger of his raised hand and, watching his finger, you let him talk on.

"Look, you've got to admit that this rock is solid and can't be moved, don't you?"

You have no choice but to agree.

"Feel it!"

The joker's pointing to the rock at your feet. You don't know what he wants you to feel, but, in any case, your feet are standing on the rock.

"Do you feel it?"

Does the joker want you to look at the rock or at your feet?

The joker's finger suddenly moves upward; he's pointing above your head, and you can't help looking up to the sky.

"The brightness and purity, transparency and boundlessness of the sky opens up the heart!"

You hear the joker talking, but the sun is hurting your eyes.

"What do you see?" the joker asks. "Try saying what you see, just say whatever you see!"

You try to look at the sky but see nothing and only get dizzy.

"Have a good look!"

"What do I actually have to look at?" you find you have to ask.

"The unblemished sky, the sky with its authentic, true light!"

You say the sun is hurting your eyes.

"That's right."

"What's right?" You close your eyes and there are gold stars inside your eyelids. Your feet are unsteady, and you go to get down off the rock again, but hear him next to you, reminding you: "What is right is that you are dizzy and not the rock."

"Of course. . . ." You're getting confused.

"You are not the rock!" the joker says decisively.

"Of course I'm not the rock," you acknowledge. "Is it all right to come down?"

"You are far from being as solid as this rock! I'm talking about you!"

"Right, so I may as well—" You give him the answer he wants and go to step down.

"Don't be in such a hurry. But standing on the rock you can see farther than if you came down, right?"

"Of course." You again give him the answer he wants, without even thinking.

"In the distance right in front of you—don't look at your feet, I said, look in front of you—what do you see?"

"The horizon?"

"What's the horizon? There's always a horizon! I'm talking about above the horizon, have a good look—"

"At what?"

"Surely you see it?"

"Isn't it just sky?"

"Look again carefully!"

"It's no good," you say, blinded, "there are all sorts of bright colors. . . ."

"That's right, you can have any color you want. What a brilliant, beautiful sky, everything to be hoped for is right before your eyes, and you may be considered as having opened your eyes."

"Surely it's all right to get down now, isn't it?" You close your eyes.

"Look at the sun again! This time look again at the sun in its golden brilliance, its magnificence! You will discover, listen to me, you will discover miracles! Unimaginable miracles, the most beautiful miracles!"

"What miracles?" you ask as you cover your eyes with a hand.

The joker takes your other hand, and you feel there is a bit of support as you hear wind pouring into your ears. The joker gives a clue, "The world has such brilliance!"

The joker removes the hand you have over your eyes. You see in the sky an ink-blue-black bottomless pit and start worrying.

"You're worried, aren't you?" This joker is experienced. "When people see miracles they always get worried, otherwise why would they be called miracles?"

You say you want to sit down.

"Hold on a bit longer!" he commands you.

You say you really can't hold on any longer.

"Even if you can't, you have to. If others can hold on, why can't you?" he reprimands you.

Your legs give way, and, doubling over, you sprawl on the rock seeking his help and wanting to vomit.

"Open your mouth! If you want to shout then shout, if you want to call out then call out!"

So, following his instructions, you give a mighty roar but can't stop your nausea and chuck up a lot of bile.

Whether the cause is justice, an ideal, virtue, the most scientific ideology, or a heavenly endowed mission, it will cause a person mental and physical anguish, endless revolutions and repeated sacrifices. And God or savior, or heroes on a lesser scale, or exemplars on an even lesser scale, and the nation on a grand scale, and the Party above the nation, are all built on such a rock.

As soon as you open your mouth to shout, you fall into this joker's trap. The justice you seek is this joker, and you slaughter for this joker. So you must shout this joker's slogans and, losing your own voice, learn to parrot words; hence you are recreated, your memories erased. Having lost your head, you become this joker's follower and, even while not believing, you are forced to believe. Having become this joker's foot soldier and henchman, you sacrifice yourself for this joker, then, after he has done with you, you are discarded on the joker's altar to be buried alive with him or set on fire to enhance this joker's brilliant image. Your ashes must flutter along with the joker's in the wind until the joker is thoroughly dead, and, when the dust settles, you, like dust, too, will vanish.

21

Lin had her head down as she pushed her bicycle from the shed near the main entrance of the building. She had been avoiding him for some time. He blocked the exit and playfully bumped her bicycle with his front wheel. Lin looked up and forced a wry, apologetic sort of smile, as if to say it was she who had bumped into his bicycle.

"Let's ride together!" he said.

Lin did not get on her bicycle as in the past to take the cue and head off, cycling some distance in front, to a secret rendezvous. In any case, the Cultural Revolution had closed down all the parks at night. They walked for a while, pushing their bicycles, without saying anything. The walls along the road were now covered with university rebel Red Guard slogans naming members of the Political Bureau of the Party Center, and the Deputy Premier. These new slogans blotted out the old slogans by blood-lineage Red Guards that had called for the sweeping away of Ox Demons and Snake Spirits.

YU QIULI MUST BOW HIS HEAD TO ACKNOWLEDGE HIS CRIMES BEFORE THE REVOLUTIONARY MASSES!

TAN ZHENLIN, YOUR FUNERAL BELL IS TOLLING!

Lin had removed her red armband and wrapped her head and face with a long gray scarf. She tried her best to cover herself, to make herself inconspicuous, and, mingling with pedestrians wearing gray and blue padded coats on the street, her graceful figure was no longer prominent. All restaurants had closed for the day, so there was nowhere to go; anyway, it seemed, there was nothing to talk about. The two of them walked with their bicycles in the cold wind, with a clear distance in between. Thrown up by gusts of wind and grit, fragments of posters drifted about under the streetlights.

He was stirred by the solemnity of the impending all-out fight for justice, but could not help feeling miserable, because his love affair with Lin was on the brink of ending. He wanted to restore his relationship with Lin but how could he broach the topic and how could he make it a relationship between equals so that he was not simply the recipient of Lin's love? He asked about Lin's parents, expressing his concern, but Lin walked on in silence without answering. He could not find the words to get through to her.

"There seems to be a problem with your father's history." It was Lin who first spoke.

"What problem?" he said, alarmed.

"I'm just alerting you," Lin said flatly.

"He's never taken part in a political party or group!" he protested immediately, out of a basic instinct for self-preservation.

"It seems as if . . ." she cut herself short.

"It seems as if what?" he asked, stopping in his tracks.

"That's all I've heard."

Lin kept pushing her bicycle without looking at him. She thought of herself as being superior, she was alerting him, showing concern for him, she was concerned that he might do something crazy. She was protecting him, but he could tell that it was no longer love. It was as if he had concealed his family background from her, and her concern was spoiled by her doubts. He tried to explain: "Before Liberation, my father was section chief in a bank and a steamship company, then he was a journalist with a private commercial newspaper. What's wrong with that?"

What instantly came to his mind was the small cloth-covered booklet of Mao's *On New Democracy*, which his father hid with the silver coins in the shoebox under the five-drawer chest when he was a child, but he said nothing, it was useless. He felt wronged, primarily because his father was not him.

"They say your father was senior staff—"

"So what? He was still hired staff and lost his job before Liberation. He has never been a capitalist and has never represented the capitalists!"

He was furious, but instantly he felt weak. He knew he would not be able to regain Lin's trust.

Lin made no response.

He put his foot on the bicycle-stop in front of a poster freshly pasted up, stood there, and asked, "What else is there? Who's saying this?"

Lin steadied her bicycle and, averting her eyes, looked down to say, "Don't ask, just be aware of it."

The youngsters in front of them collected their buckets of paste and ink, got on their bicycles, and left. The posters they had just written were still dripping with ink.

"So you've been avoiding me because of this?" he asked loudly.

"Of course not." Lin still did not look at him but quietly added, "It was you who wanted to break off the relationship."

"I miss you, I really miss you!"

He spoke loudly but felt weak and helpless.

"Forget it, it's impossible. . . ." Lin said softly, avoiding his eyes. She turned, pushing her bicycle to go off.

He grabbed the handlebars of her bicycle, but Lin put her head down and said, "Don't be like that, let me go, I'm just telling you that there is a problem with your father's history—"

"Who said this? People in the political section? Or was it Danian?" he kept asking, unable to contain his fury.

Lin straightened up and turned away to look at the cars on the road and the endless stream of bicycles on both sides.

"My father wasn't declared a rightist—" He wanted to argue, but that, too, was something he wanted to forget. He remembered his mother saying that it was all over and in the past. That was when his mother was alive, he was still at university and had gone home for the New Year.

"No, not that problem. . . ." Lin turned her handlebars and put a foot on the pedal.

"Then what problem is it?" He grabbed her handlebars again.

"They say he had hidden a gun. . . ." She bit her lip, got on her bicycle, and pedaled away hard.

There was an explosion in his brain and he seemed to see Lin speed by with tears in her eyes; maybe he was seeing things or maybe he was just feeling sorry for himself. Cycling away with her head wrapped in the scarf, Lin merged with the others on bicycles and, as scraps of paper and dust flew into the air beneath the streetlights, soon it was impossible to make her out. It was probably at that point that he reeled and stumbled against the poster that had just been pasted on the wall, and got ink and paste on his sleeve, and, as a result, he firmly remembered how it was when he and Lin parted.

His mind had seized up and he was in a quandary. He did not get on his bicycle right away because the weight of the words "hidden a gun" had made his head spin. When he came to his senses and thought about the implications of these words, he knew he had no option but to go all the way with rebelling.

Their band of twenty or so charged into the *hutong* at the side of Zhongnanhai. At the red gate bristling with sentries, they demanded that the senior cadre representing the Party Center come to their workplace both to acknowledge culpability and to exonerate cadres and masses declared anti-Party. When they entered the office, the old revolutionary who held the rank of general before taking command of this important position actually received them, unlike the noncommittal and reticent senior cadres of their workplace who just hid away in their offices. The man had an extraordinary presence, and remained seated, majestic and dignified, on the high-backed leather chair behind the desk in that very spacious office.

"I won't get up to greet you, I've had too many meetings with the masses. When I was taking part in the revolution and mass campaigns, who knows where you lot of youngsters were? Of course, I am not promoting seniority simply because I am much older than all of you." The senior cadre was the first to speak. His voice was loud without being pompous, but his attitude and tone sounded as if he was speaking at a meeting.

"You young people want to rebel, and that's excellent! But I have had a little more experience. I have rebelled and carried out revolution against others, and others have done the same to me, and I have committed errors. Errors in what I said has upset some comrades and made them angry. I have already apologized to my comrades, what else do you want? Are you incapable of committing errors? Are you always correct? I would never dare say that of myself. It is only Chairman Mao who is always correct! And there can be no doubts about that! Who among you is not capable of committing errors? Ha-ha!"

This motley group had been fired with righteous indignation and ready to fight, but now everyone was docile and, in fact, respectfully receiving a reprimand without a sound of protest. He had detected both resentment and a veiled threat in what the old man said; nevertheless, it was his own fault for being the leader of this motley group and he was obliged to go forward. He asked, "Are you aware that following your order to collect reports, that very night every single person was interrogated? Over a hundred people were branded anti-Party and many more now have records in their files. Would it be possible for you to direct the Party committee to declare a reversal of those cases and to have those records destroyed in public?"

"People have their own jobs to look after, your Party committee's problems are its own. Don't the masses also have problems? I can't say for sure what your Party committee will do, but I have spoken to them about it. I have already retracted what I said, the very words I myself had spoken!"

The senior cadre was getting bored and had risen to his feet.

"Then would it be possible for you to say all this again when you make your report at another such meeting?" He couldn't back down now.

"That would have to be approved by the Party Center. You see, I work for the Party and have to observe Party discipline. I am not free to say anything I like."

"In that case, who approved your speech ordering the collection of reports?"

This was prohibited territory, and he was aware of the weight of his words. The senior cadre fixed his eyes upon him, his eyebrows thick and graying, and said coldly, "I am responsible for whatever I say. Chairman Mao is still using me; I have not been dismissed! Of course, I am personally responsible for whatever I say!"

"Then may we quote what you said on a poster so that everyone can read it? We have been delegated by the masses and this would help when we report back."

Having said this, he looked at the masses by his side, but none of them had anything to say. The senior cadre was staring at him. He knew that this was a power struggle between unequal parties, but there was no way out for him, so he said, "We will write up what you said, then invite you to check if it is all right."

"Young man, I admire your courage!"

The senior cadre remained dignified. Having said this, he turned, opened a door behind his desk, and went out. The door, which earlier had not even been noticed, immediately shut; all that remained was the leather swivel chair and the motley crowd looking vacantly at him. However, that menacing and scornful sentence lingered in his mind.

The paunchy Party secretary stood up to make his report at the meeting. He was mumbling and no longer held his back straight or his head high, as he did a few months ago sitting alongside the senior cadre of the Party Center. Instead, he was wearing reading glasses and held his notes in both hands farther away than the microphone as he read out a word at a time. He was struggling to make out the words: "I now understand that I had misinterpreted . . . the spirit of the Party Center. I gave . . . wrong instructions. I harmed . . . the revolutionary fervor of comrades and hereby earnestly—" At this point, Comrade Wu Tao paused, then raised his voice to continue, "Very earnestly apologize to all comrades present—"

He lowered his big head in a token bow. He seemed to be senile, but sincere and humble.

"What wrong instructions? Be more specific!" someone in the meeting asked loudly.

Wu left his notes and, head bowed, looked over the top of his glasses at the people in the meeting. At the same time, those present started looking around at one another. Wu immediately returned to his notes and went on reading methodically. He read even more slowly, enunciating each of his words with greater clarity. "When old revolutionaries encounter new problems, we deal with them according to old paradigms based on our experiences. But, under the new circumstances of today, this absolutely—will not—do!"

It was all empty bureaucratic talk, and there was a stir in the meeting again. Probably thinking he was about to be interrupted again, Wu suddenly left his notes to say loudly and emphatically, "I gave wrong instructions, I committed an error!"

"What old paradigms? You make it sound as if it's nothing! Do these old paradigms of yours refer to opposing rightists?" This time, it was a section head, a Party member, who had stood up. It was a woman nearing middle age, who had been labeled anti-Party. Not knowing how to respond immediately, Wu looked at the woman through his reading glasses, which had slipped down his nose.

"What do those old paradigms of yours refer to? Do they refer to opposing rightists by luring snakes out of their lairs?" The woman was agitated and her voice was trembling.

"Yes, yes." Wu hastened to nod.

"Whose instructions were these? What were the instructions? Make yourself clear!" the woman followed up.

"Comrades of the Party Center leadership, our Party Center—" Wu took off his glasses to try to see who the woman was.

The woman was not intimidated, and, raising her head, asked loudly, "Which Party Center are you referring to? Which leader do you mean? How did you receive your instructions? Speak up!"

The people at the meeting all knew that the sacrosanct Party Center had already split, and that even the Political Bureau of the Party Center was in the process of being replaced by Mao Zedong's Central Cultural Revolution Proletariat Command Group. Comrade Wu Tao's headquarters had lost control of the meeting, and a buzz of voices arose. However, as Party secretary, Wu Tao rigidly kept to Party rules. Without replying, and assuming an injured tone, he loudly silenced the meeting, "I represent the Party committee in apologizing to those comrades who have been subjected to criticism!"

He again lowered his head, but this time he bent the whole of his body forward and this seemed to be quite an effort for him.

"Hand over your blacklist of names!" The middle-aged man who shouted out was a Party cadre who had been subjected to criticism.

"What blacklist?" Wu, alarmed, immediately asked back.

"The blacklist based on your investigations to decide who was to undergo reform through labor!" It was the woman section head shouting again. She was pale, agitated, and her hair was in a mess.

"There's no list!" Wu reached over and seized the microphone to immediately deny this. "Don't believe rumors! Comrades, don't worry, our Party committee does not have a blacklist! I guarantee in the spirit of the Party that a blacklist does not exist! I admit that some comrades have suffered, and that our Party committee has inappropriately attacked some comrades. We have committed errors, but a blacklist of names definitely does not—"

Before Wu had finished, there was a disturbance in the left corner of the meeting. Someone had left his seat and was heading for the dais.

"I want to speak! Why can't I speak? If it really doesn't exist, why are you worried if people speak out!"

It was Old Liu, pushing aside the security officers barring him from getting onto the dais.

"Let Comrade Liu Ping speak! Why can't people speak? Let Comrade Liu Ping speak!"

During the shouting, Old Liu pushed his way through, mounted the dais, and turned to the meeting. Shaking his fist at Wu Tao, also on the dais, he said, "He's lying! When the Cultural Revolution started and the first poster went up, the Party committee held an emergency meeting. The branch Party secretaries of departments were then instructed to carry out personnel rankings, so the political department has had these name lists from way back! Needless to say, when people were investigated—"

The meeting exploded and, up front and at the back, people had stood up at the same time and were shouting and yelling.

"Get the people of the political department to come forward!"

"Get the people of the political department to come forward to testify!"

"Hand over the blacklist of people targeted for criticism!"

"Only allow leftists to rebel! Don't allow rightists to overturn things!" The person who had shouted this was already charging up to the dais. It was Danian.

"Revolution is not a crime! It is right to rebel!" It was Big Li shouting this slogan, his face red, and he was standing on his seat. He, too, stood up. The meeting had turned into a riot and everyone was standing up.

"I have had thirty-six years in the Party, I have never been anti-Party, and the Party and the people can investigate my history—"

Before Old Liu finished, Danian had jumped onto the dais and seized him.

"Get the hell down! An anti-Party careerist like you, with a land-lord father hidden away, has no right to speak!"

Danian had grabbed Old Liu by the shoulders and was pushing him off the dais.

"Comrades! My father is not a landlord. During the War of Resistance he supported the Party and the Party has a policy toward enlightened gentry. This can be checked in the archives—"

The Red Guards who had torn off the armband from the arm of Old Liu's son were on the dais and Old Liu, shoved off the dais, fell to the floor.

"Beating up people is not allowed! It is futile to repress revolutionary mass movements!" He was worked up and could not help shouting out.

"Let's go!" Big Li waved an arm as he gave a yell and, leaping over the backs of seats, charged up to the dais. Their group had also surged onto the dais.

The two groups confronted one another, each shouting slogans and on the brink of fighting. The meeting was a total shambles.

"Comrades, Red Guard comrades, Red Guard comrades on both sides, please go back to your seats—"

Wu was tapping the microphone but nobody took notice, and the cadres of the political department were too afraid to intervene. Everyone at the meeting was standing up and feverish with excitement. He was on the dais and somehow had grabbed the microphone from Wu's hand and was shouting into it, "If Wu Tao won't capitulate then let him be destroyed!"

The meeting instantly responded in agreement, and he took the opportunity to declare, "The Party committee no longer has authority to hold such meetings to intimidate the masses; if meetings are to be held, they must be convened by us, the revolutionary masses!"

Below the dais everyone was clapping. He had ended the stalemate in the confrontation between the Red Guards and seemed to have become the leader needed by the unruly masses.

The Party secretary who had been deprived of his power to terrorize had become the target of the masses. To protect himself, the senior cadre of the Party Center had dissociated himself from Wu Tao and could not be contacted by telephone. Comrade Wu Tao who had given "wrong instructions," too, had thus become a pawn in the gamble at a higher level of politics.

22

And how is Margarethe? She had dragged you into a quagmire with writing this damn book. It is hard going forward or backward, but there is no stopping. People are no longer interested in those worn-out stories, and you yourself are fed up with being tormented. Each of her letters to you is signed with a yellow star of David. She never forgets that she is a Jew, but you want to erase the imprints of your suffering.

You phoned her seven, eight, or even ten times but the tape always repeated the same string of long convoluted sentences. You could only make out one German word, *bitte* . . . no doubt it was asking you to leave a message, but she didn't ever phone back. In her last letter, she said find yourself a happy woman, she can't live with you. It would be too painful, doubly painful, because she wants a secure family, a child, to be a mother. Can a Jewish child of a Chinese father be happy? The Chinese in her letters was odd, and the characters with strokes missing gave an unfamiliar feeling that was unlike her fluent spoken Chinese, which was intimate and sensual, even in the choice of words. When she talked about the body and sex, she was so natural you could feel her warmth, her moistness.

However, her letters were cold and pushed you away from her flesh and her feelings; they were sarcastic and you couldn't help feeling hurt. As far as you could understand, she was over thirty and couldn't drift through the world not knowing if you would meet next in Paris or in New York, while you, an eternal Ulysses, were on your modern odyssey. Just treat it as a beautiful chance encounter, a beautiful encounter among many. She had given you everything you wanted, so let it stop there, she can not be your woman. Like friends, you simply parted, and maybe it's possible for you to remain friends for a long time, but she doesn't want to be your lover. So, find yourself a French filly to play sex games that will gratify your fantasies, someone who will give you inspiration without adding to your suffering. It won't be hard for you to find such a woman, a prostitute, who takes your fancy. But what she wants is peace and security, a home that can give her warmth and love. She is not searching for suffering, but she can't get rid of it, because she lacks security, and it is this, which you can't provide for her.

But you can't find a woman like her, who will listen to you talk about the hells of the world. People don't want to listen to those rotten old truths and would prefer watching made-up disaster and horror films produced in Hollywood. If you were writing a story about sadistic sex, the lovemaking would excite, and you would enjoy a climax, even if there were no one to talk to and you were just talking to yourself. So you may as well continue by yourself in this observation, analysis, reminiscence, or dialogue.

You must find a detached voice, scrape off the thick residue of resentment and anger deep in your heart, then unhurriedly and calmly proceed to articulate your various impressions, your flood of confused memories, and your tangled thoughts. But you find this is very difficult.

What you seek is a pure form of narration. You are striving to describe in simple language the terrible contamination of life by politics, but it is very difficult. You want to expunge the pervasive politics that penetrated every pore, clung to daily life, became fused in speech and action, and from which no one at that time could escape. You want to tell about an individual who was contaminated by politics, without having to discuss the sordid politics itself. Nevertheless, you must return to his state of mind at that time, and to describe this accurately is even more difficult. The many layers of accreted, intersecting happenings in memory can be easily made to capture the attention of readers, but you want to avoid impurities, because it is not your intention to write stories of suffering. You seek only to narrate your impressions and psychological state of that time, and to do this, you must carefully excise the insights that you possess at this instant and in this place, as well as put aside your present thoughts.

His experiences have silted up in the creases of your memory. How can they be stripped off in layers, coherently arranged and scanned, so that a pair of detached eyes can observe what he had experienced? You are you and he is he. It is difficult for you to return to how it was in his mind in those times, he has already become so unfamiliar. Don't repaint him with your present arrogance and complacency, but ensure that you maintain a distance that will allow for sober observation and examination. You must not confuse his fervor with his vanity and stupidity, or hide his fear and cowardice, and to do this is excruciatingly difficult. Also, you must not become debauched by his self-love and his self-mutilation, you are merely observing and listening, and are not there to relish his sensory experiences.

It is he that you must allow to emerge from your memory, that child, that youth, that immature man, that daydreaming survivor, that arrogant fellow, and that scoundrel who gradually became crafty. That you of the past had a conscience, and, while vestiges of kindness remained, he was wicked, and you must not make excuses or repent for him. As you observe and listen to him, you naturally feel an irrepressible sorrow, but you must not let this emotion lead to vagueness or a drifting off into sentimentalism. While observing and examining him unmasked, you must turn him into fiction, a character that is unrelated to you and has qualities yet to be discovered. It is then that writing is interesting and creative, and can stimulate curiosity and the desire to explore.

You do not play the role of judge, and you should not regard him as a victim. In this way, the fervor and the suffering that are destructive to art make way for observation and examination. Of interest is not your judgment or his righteous indignation, your sorrow or his suffering, but, rather, the process of this inquiry.

23

During the Cultural Revolution, big posters and slogans covered all walls and filled the streets. Slogans covered all the lampposts and were even written on roadways. With more fanfare than at the grand ceremonies for National Day, from early morning to late at night, pamphlets fluttered in the air, as cars with big loudspeakers shuttled back and forth broadcasting songs to extoll Mao's *Sayings*. Party leaders of various ranks, who previously stood on the viewing platform to review the people, now wore paper hats as they were escorted by the rebelling masses onto open trucks and paraded in public. Some wore tall paper hats that would blow off in the wind, so that both hands were needed to hold them down, while others simply wore an overturned wastepaper basket from the office. But, in all cases, the person wore a placard on the chest bearing his or her name in black characters with a big red "X" through it. When the Cultural Revolution began in the early summer of 1966, middle-school children criticized and attacked principals and teachers like this. Then, by early autumn, Red Guards were hauling out people belonging to the Five Black Categories and attacking them in the same way. By midwinter that year, the old revolutionaries of the

Party, whose very profession was class struggle, were targeted for attack by the Red Guards. All this followed Mao's blueprint for mobilizing peasant movements, and had been devised by the Great Leader when, starting out from Hunan province, he had absolutely nothing.

Wu Tao was on the dais in the auditorium. Big Li was trying to push his head down, but he was quite stubborn. He had his dignity and, angry about being unjustly treated, refused to lower his head. Big Li punched him, right in his fat belly, and Wu Tao doubled over with pain, his face purple, but he did not raise his head again.

Sitting in the place formerly occupied by Wu Tao, on the dais covered with red tablecloths, he presided over all the denunciation meetings convened by the joint mass organizations. He was confronted by increasingly violent behavior, and he seemed to be sitting on top of a volcano. If he tried to exercise any restraint, he would be forced off the dais in exactly the same way. At the meeting, people's emotions ran high. One by one, each Party committee member was called to stand at the front of the dais, learned how to bow his head, and reported on Wu Tao's words and actions. All their instructions had been from higher up, each admitted errors, and each admitted the same things, but not a single sentence was their own. Chen, the tall, slim deputy secretary of the Party committee, whose stooped gaunt figure made him look like a dried shrimp, had a bright idea and added in his report that Wu Tao had recently told core members of the Party committee: "Chairman Mao doesn't need us anymore."

Emotions at the meeting boiled over again and everyone started shouting, "Destruction to anyone who opposes Chairman Mao!"

He detected grief in the shouting of the slogans "Down with Wu Tao" and "Long live Chairman Mao." It was coming from the inner depths of Wu Tao; it sounded familiar, and he remembered that the senior cadre at Zhongnanhai had been resentful like this before he had discarded Wu Tao. However, coming from Wu Tao's own lips, that resentment had turned to grief.

As chair of the meeting, he had to appear harsh, even while knowing that this slight amount of grief and resentment could hardly be defined as opposing the Great Leader. The scoundrel had to be thoroughly crushed. If restored to power, Wu would have no qualms about having him branded a counterrevolutionary for chairing the meeting.

The meeting passed a resolution, and Wu Tao was ordered to hand over the Party meeting minutes and his work notes. After the meeting, he, Tang, and Little Yu got into the black Jimu limousine reserved for the exclusive use of the Party secretary, and set off immediately to carry out a search of Wu Tao's house, taking Wu Tao himself along with them.

He wanted this to be less traumatic, so, without using strong-arm tactics, he got the old man to open each of the drawers and the bookcase containing stacks of documents. Tang and Yu were rummaging through a wardrobe and ordered the old man to hand over the keys to the suitcases.

"They are only old clothes," the old man grumbled in protest.

"Then why are you afraid of having them searched? What if they contain black documents on the masses?" Tang, hands on his hips and looking very cocky, obviously enjoyed carrying out the search.

The old man went into the dining room to get his wife to fetch the keys. It was dinnertime, food was on the table, and the door was open. Wu's wife was there with a small child, their granddaughter, and she stayed inside throughout, deliberately chatting with the little granddaughter. The thought crossed his mind that maybe something important was hidden in the dining room, but he immediately banished the thought. To avoid having to face them, he did not enter the dining room.

Only two months earlier, Red Guards had searched his own room. One Sunday soon after, someone knocked on his door, and, standing outside, was a pretty girl with a fair complexion. The sun shining at that angle made her eyes sparkle and the hair around her ears shine. She said she was the landlord's daughter from the adjoining courtyard, and had come to collect the rent for her family. He had never gone there but knew that Old Tan and the landlord were old friends.

The girl stood at the doorway, took the money he handed her, frowned, and, glancing inside, said, "The furniture inside, the table and that old sofa, belongs to my family and will be removed in due time."

He said he could help her shift the furniture right away. She made no response, but, before she turned and went down the steps, her bright eyes swept coldly across him with obvious hostility. He thought the girl must have wrongly assumed that he had reported on Old Tan so that he could take over his lodgings. A few weeks passed, but the girl did not come to collect rent or to remove the furniture. It was only when the old man from next door came to collect rent for the housing department of the street committee that he found out all private real estate had become public property. He did not bother to find out what had happened to the landlord, but the cold look the girl had given him remained fixed in his mind.

He avoided seeing Wu's wife and the little granddaughter. Even though the child was small, she would remember and would continue hating him for a long time.

Tang brought out one suitcase at a time. Unlocking them, Wu Tao said they contained his daughter's and her child's clothing. When he saw the bras and dresses, he suddenly felt embarrassed, recalling how it was when the Red Guards found condoms while searching through Old Tan's things in the room they shared. He waved them to stop. Tang was searching the sofa, pulling up the cushions, feeling down between the armrests, and demonstrating the expertise of someone who suddenly had been delegated the responsibility of carrying out a search. However, he was anxious to end the search and had parceled up bundles of letters, documents, and notebooks.

"Those are my private letters and have nothing to do with my work," Wu said.

"We're going to examine them. They will be recorded, and if there are no problems they will be returned," he retorted.

What he wanted to say, but did not, was that they had actually been very polite.

"This is . . . the second time in my life!" Wu hesitated as he said this.

"Have Red Guards already been here?" he asked.

"I am referring to forty years ago. When I was an underground agent for the Party . . ." Wu's eyelids wrinkled as he gave a bitter smile.

"But didn't your people also search homes when you tyrannized the masses? I doubt that your people were as polite as us," he said with a grin.

"That was the doing of Red Guards in your workplace. Our Party committee did not decide all that!" Wu insisted.

"But the name lists were supplied by the political department! Otherwise, how would they have known whose homes to search? Why didn't they search your home?" he asked, staring at Wu.

Wu kept quiet. He was, after all, experienced in the ways of the world and he even silently escorted them to the gate of the court-yard. But he knew Wu Tao hated him and that, if reinstated, the old scoundrel would have him sent to hell straight away. He had to find enough evidence to get Wu branded as the enemy.

After returning to the workplace building, he spent the whole night going through Wu's letters and found a family letter referring to Wu as his elder cousin. The letter said, "The People's Government is magnanimous and has been lenient in meting out punishment. However, it is hard for me, because I am sick and have old folks and young children at home. I hope that you, Elder Cousin, will be able to speak on my behalf to the local government authorities." Clearly, this relative had problems with his political history and was seeking Wu's help, but he put the letter into a document envelope and wrote on it "examined." Something had psychologically prevented him from taking the matter further.

In those times, he hardly went home, and just slept in the office that served as the headquarters of their rebel group. Day and night, there were big and small meetings, liaising with, then breaking off with various people's organizations, and endless internal squabbles within their rebel group. Everyone seemed to be like ants in a hot frying pan, frantically running around and advocating rebellion. The old Red Guards announced they had rebelled against the Party committee and were now known as the Red Revolutionary Rebel Column, and even the political cadres had established their own Battle Corps. However, as people scrambled to find some way out, they were all much the same in their switching of loyalties, betrayal, opportunism, revolution, and rebellion. Once the original network of order and authority had been thrown into disarray, restructuring occurred in all parts of this beehive-like workplace building, and countless secret plots were not confined to this one floor.

At all the denunciation meetings of the various people's organizations, Wu Tao would, without fail, be hauled out for criticism. Danian's crowd was savage. Not satisfied with Wu Tao just having to wear a placard, bowing, and hanging his head, they pulled back his arms, forcing him to his knees until he fell flat on the ground—just as they had dealt with Ox Demons and Snake Spirits a few months earlier. Robbed of their political authority by the rebel group, they were reduced to asserting their authority on the person of Wu Tao, this old Party secretary who, discarded by the Party, had become a useless old dog whose bad odor, people feared, might rub off onto them.

One day, after a snowfall, he saw Wu Tao at the back of the workplace building. He was digging up snow that had become packed solid from people walking on it. Wu heard someone coming and quickly moved out of the way. He stopped and asked, "How are you?"

The old man held onto his hoe, and, panting for breath, repeated, "Fine, fine. You don't use physical violence, but they do."

Wu had put on a miserable look just to get on good terms with him, he thought at the time. It was a year later that he began to pity this old man for whom nobody dared to show any concern. The old man swept the yard with a big bamboo broom every morning, always head bowed and wearing a dirty, old, blue jacket with patches. Nobody who went by even so much as glanced at him. Obviously, he had aged a great deal, his shoulders drooped and the skin around his eyes and on his cheeks had become flaccid. It was only then that he began to feel sorry for Wu Tao, although he didn't ever speak to him again.

The struggles that allowed for only one survivor turned everyone into enemies, and hostility blanketed people like an avalanche. Waves of intensifying winds pushed him to confront one party bureaucrat after another. He did not hate them as individuals, but he wanted to have them branded as the enemy. Were they all enemies? He could not decide.

"You are being too soft on them! They showed no mercy when they oppressed the masses. Why don't you have the whole lot of those accomplices hauled onto the dais?" Big Li was reprimanding him at an internal meeting of the rebel group.

"Can you overthrow all of them?" He paused, then retorted, "Can one totally reverse things so that every person who had unjustly denounced others is branded the enemy? People have to be allowed to correct their errors. To win over the masses, some thought has to be given to a strategy for differentiating how people are to be treated."

"Strategy, strategy, you're just an intellectual!" Big Li, bad-tempered and pushy, said this with derision.

"Why are we joining up with and taking in just about anyone who comes along? The rebel group isn't a plate of stir-fried vegetables!

That's the rightist opportunist line, and it will snuff out the revolution!" This older sister, a Party member, had recently joined their command department and she was challenging him. She had studied the history of the Party and was quite radical. The "correct line" struggle had started within the rebel group. "The revolutionary leadership authority must be firmly controlled by authentic leftists and not by opportunist elements!" This Party-member older sister of the rebel group was all worked up and her face was like a red rag.

"What are you getting up to!" He banged the table. Being in this motley group had made him tough, but he was worried.

He could not remember how he got through those days and nights of so much endless argument, righteous anger, inflammatory revolutionary words, lust for personal power, stratagems, plotting, collusion and compromise, indignation with ulterior motives, unthinking recklessness, and wasted emotions. Unable to resist, he allowed himself to be manipulated into arguments to challenge the conservative forces and also into endless quarrels within the rebel group.

"Political power is vital for the revolution. If we don't seize power, our rebelling will be so much wasted effort!" Big Li, enraged, also banged the table.

"Can you hold onto power if you don't unite with the majority?" he retorted.

"Unity will only last if it is unity created by struggle!" Little Yu held up Mao's little red book of *Sayings* to shore up his own weak class origins. "We can't listen to you, because at critical times the intellectuals will always waver!"

They all regarded themselves as blood-lineage proletariat and believed that this red country should belong to them. Revolution or rebellion, it finally came down to seizing power. This fact was so simple that it surprised him. But, at the time, he did not know what he wanted, and even his rebelling was a path he had strayed onto by mistake.

"Comrades, Chen Duxiu failed to seize political power at a critical point of the revolution! He was a rightist opportunist!" The Party-member older sister dismissed him with this reference to Party history, then began shouting slogans to the people at the meeting.

"All of you who are not for the revolution can get the hell out of here!" the more radical among them shouted along with her. As a late-comer, she was trying to maneuver herself into a leadership position.

"If you want to be the leader, then go for it!"

He rose to his feet angrily and left the smoke-filled meeting room where forty or fifty people had been puffing on cigarettes the whole night. In the office next door, he pulled together three chairs and went to sleep. He was upset and confused. If he wasn't a fellow traveler of the revolution, was he then an opportunist rebel? Probably he was, and this was unsettling.

On the night of that New Year's Eve, the meeting thus unhappily dispersed. In the New Year, sporadic war began between Big Li's crowd and the most radical members of the Battle Corps that had announced a takeover of the paralyzed Party committee and political department.

"Smash the Party committee! Smash the political department! Revolutionary comrades, do you support or oppose the New Red Political Authority? There is a clear line of demarcation between being revolutionary or not!"

Little Yu was shouting into the broadcast system. Offices had been fitted with speakers, and the announcement of the political coup blared through all the corridors and rooms. Escorted by Big Li, Tang, and some service personnel, a group of old cadres and some young Party branch secretaries all wearing placards on their chests were paraded through the corridors of the entire building. In the lead was Wu Tao, beating on a gong.

What were they up to? Probably this was precisely how revolutions began. Those once dignified leading cadres who were the embodiment of the Party now filed past, one after the other, heads bowed, abject and wretched. The Party-member older sister led the rebel group with her fist raised and, shaking it, she loudly shouted, "Down with the capitalist road elements in positions of power! Long live the New Red Political Authority! Long live the victory of Chairman Mao's revolutionary line!"

In imitation of the national leaders at reviews, Tang waved at the people squeezed in the corridors and blocking office doorways. This made some laugh, but made others look grim.

"We know you are opposed to their seizing power—" the former field officer said.

"I don't, but I oppose their method of seizing power," he replied.

The person who approached him had transferred from the army to work as a political cadre. He was only a deputy department chief, and, in the chaos, was eager to advance himself. All smiles, he said, "You've got much more influence with the people than that mob. If you put yourself forward, we will back you. We hope that you will rally a contingent to work with us."

This conversation took place in the confidential documents room of the political department, a room he had not previously entered. The workplace documents and personnel files, including his own file with a record of his father's problem, were all kept in this place. When Big Li's crowd seized power, they pasted paper seals on the metal security cupboards as well as the locked document cupboards. The seals could be torn off at any time but nobody would dare to destroy the files.

The former field officer had sought him out in the main dining hall and said he wanted to exchange ideas with him. However, his arranging to meet in this room indicated another motive and, entering the room, he somehow sensed this. He knew who was behind the former field officer, because a few days earlier, the Party-committee deputy secretary, Chen, had given him a signal by putting a big bony hand on his shoulder. Chen formerly headed the workplace political department and seldom spoke or laughed; after being denounced, he had turned stony and cold. Chen had come up to him from behind and, as no one was around, had actually called his name and even addressed him as "comrade." Chen put his hand on his shoulder for one or two seconds, gave a nod, and walked past. This seemingly casual act, however, intimated extraordinary closeness, a pretense of having forgotten that it was he who had denounced Chen at a big meeting. This man far outstripped that motley crowd of rebels in political experience and meanness, yet here he was, stretching out a hand to him. He was by no means an old hand at playing politics, and was not as cunning as this man, but he knew he could not stand in their ranks. He reaffirmed his position, "I don't condone how they have seized power, but that doesn't mean that I am opposed to the general direction of those who have seized power. I definitely support rebelling against the Party committee."

This pleased the former field officer, who was silent for a while before saying with a nod, "We're also rebelling."

It sounded as if the man were saying "We're also drinking tea." He laughed, but said nothing.

"We were just having a casual chat, treat our conversation just now as having never occurred." Having said this, the former field officer stood up.

He left the confidential documents room, declined their deal, and severed links with them.

Less than ten days later, in February, after the New Year, the old Red Guards and some political cadres again organized a corps to oppose the seizure of power and smashed the workplace broadcasting station that was controlled by the rebels. The first armed conflict broke out between the two sides, and there were some injuries, but he was not present at the time.

24

Is it worth writing pure literature, that pure literary form where style, language, word games, linguistic structures, patterns simply follow their own course, but which is unrelated to your experiences, your life, the dilemmas of life, the quagmire of reality, or you, who are a part of the filth? Pure literature is a subterfuge, a shield, a limitation, and there is no need for you to crawl into a cage demarcated by others or yourself.

Your writing is not in the cause of pure literature, but neither are you a fighter using your pen as a weapon to promote truth. You don't know what truth is, but you don't need someone else to tell you what is. You know you are certainly not the embodiment of truth, and you write simply to indicate that a sort of life, worse than a quagmire, more real than an imaginary hell, more terrifying than Judgment Day, has, in fact, existed. Furthermore, it is very likely that when people have forgotten about it, it will make a comeback, and people who have never gone crazy will go crazy, and people who have never been oppressed will oppress or be oppressed. This is because madness has existed since the birth of humanity, and it is simply a question of when it will flare up again. Then are you trying to play the role of a teacher? Many have worn themselves out as teachers and preachers, but have people become any better?

It is best not to strive to make yourself despair, so why go on relating all this misery? You are distressed, but even if you wanted to, you can't stop. You must have this release, it has become an affliction, and the reason, you suspect, is because you yourself have this need.

You vomit up the folly of politics, yet, at the same time, you manufacture another sort of lie in literature, for literature is a lie that hides the writer's ulterior motive for profit or fame. However, what guides or stops the pen are not utilitarianism and vanity, but a deep, instinctual, animal drive, and differences within the species are due to the persistence of this drive, which is not affected by temperature changes, whether one is hungry or not, or the seasons. It is just like shit; if there is the need to, it is discharged. But it is unlike shit in that it is discharged in different places, and what is discharged must be endowed with sensuality and aesthetic beauty—for example, linking grief to your enjoyment of language. While exposing the land of your ancestors, the Party, the leaders, the ideals, the new people, and also that modern superstition and fraud—revolution—you use literature to create a gauze curtain, so that, viewed through it, that trash can at least be looked at. Hidden on this side of the curtain, in the dark with the audience, you derive pleasure; so doesn't this provide satisfaction?

Lies are everywhere in the world, and you are similarly creating lies in literature. Animals do not tell lies but exist in the world no matter how it is, whereas humans need to use lies to adorn this forest of humanity, and it is this that distinguishes animals from humans. More cunning than animals, humans need to use lies to conceal their own ugliness in order to seek a reason for living: to articulate pain in order to alleviate pain seems to make pain bearable. In ancient times, the dirges at funerals in the villages had the effect of drugging the senses, and, like the singing of Mass in churches, the singing of these could be addictive.

Pasolini adapted for cinema Sade's exposés of the evil of political power and human nature; by using only the screen to separate the audience from reality, he made people feel that they were viewing the violence and evil from the outside. That there can be a tantalizing quality in violence and evil is probably the wonder of art and literature.

Sincerity is the same for the poet and the novelist. The writer hides like a photographer behind the camera, affecting impartiality and detachment behind an objective camera, but what is projected on the negative is still self-love and self-pity, masturbation and sadism. That eye with its pretense of neutrality is driven by all sorts of desires, and what is manifested is tinged with aesthetic taste while claiming to look with indifference upon the world. It is best that you acknowledge that your writing strives for reality but that it is separated from reality by a layer of language. It is by cloaking naked reality with a gauze curtain, ordering language and weaving into it feelings and aesthetics that you are able to derive pleasure from looking back at it, and are interested in continuing to write.

You articulate in language your feelings, experiences, dreams, memories, fantasies, thoughts, assessments, premonitions, sensations, as well as providing the music and rhythms for linking these to the existences of real people. In the process of linguistic actualization, the present and past history, time and space, concepts and knowledge, all become fused and leave behind magical illusions created by language.

The magic of literature lies in willingness on the part of the author and the reader. Unlike political frauds that even the unwilling are forced to accept, literature may either be read or not, there is no coercion. You do not choose literature because of a belief in its purity; for you, it is simply a means of release.

Also, you are not polemical. You do not extend or amputate according to the other person's height, do not tailor yourself to the framework of theories, do not restrict what you say to what interests others. Your writing is only to bring pleasure and happiness to your life.

And you are not a superman. Since Nietzsche, there has been a glut of both supermen and common herds in the world. You are, in fact, very ordinary, the epitome of ordinariness and practicality. You are relaxed and at ease, have a smile like Buddha's, although you are not Buddha.

You absolutely refuse to be a sacrifice, refuse to be a plaything or a sacrificial object for others, refuse to seek compassion from others, refuse to repent, refuse to go mad and trample everyone else to death. You look upon the world with a mind that is the epitome of ordinariness, and in exactly the same way you look at yourself. Nothing inspires fear, amazement, disappointment, or wild expectation, hence, you avoid frustration. If you want to enjoy being upset, you get upset, then revert to this supremely ordinary, smiling, and contented you.

You do not detest the world and its ordinary ways that will always be fashionable. By not exaggerating your challenge to those in power, you have survived to enjoy freedom of speech. You have also received kindness from others and, as far as you are concerned, the principle "I don't want others to owe me anything and I don't want to owe others anything" is wrong. You are indebted to others, and others are indebted to you, but adding together all the kindness you have received from others, you have certainly received much more than you have given. Indeed, you are very lucky, so why are you complaining?

You are not a dragon, not an insect, not this, not that, so, "are not" is thus you, but rather than negation, "are not" is a sort of reality, a trace, a cost, or a result. At the end point, that is, at the brink of death, you are merely an indication of life—expression and speech that confronts "are not."

You have written this book for yourself, this book of fleeing, your *One Man's Bible*, you are your own God and follower, you do not sacrifice yourself for others, so you do not expect others to sacrifice themselves for you, and this is the epitome of fairness. Everyone wants happiness, so why should it all belong to you? However, what should be acknowledged is that there is actually very little happiness in the world.

25

He saw no future in the total chaos of the times, so it was best for him to get out of danger. He wanted to retrieve that lost world, the startling beauty he had seen in the person of the landlord's daughter, the beautiful contour of her face and her slim figure. As the girl stood sideways outside his door, her pink fleshy earlobe was outlined in detail by the sunlight in the courtyard and her hair, eyebrows, and lips seemed to radiate light. Her beauty had entranced him, but the hatred in the girl's eyes was daunting. He wanted to dispel the girl's misunderstanding of him, so he went to the neighboring courtyard. He had imagined it to be a quiet courtyard complex with just the one family, which would be an isolated little paradise cut off from the chaotic world. The old man from next door had not come to collect rent for the street committee, so he went to pay his rent in the neighboring courtyard as an excuse to see the girl.

The small door on the street opened when he touched it, and the little courtyard inside the wall gave him a shock: it was a shambles, a clutter of odds and ends piled by the wall and under the eaves. An old woman was washing bedcovers in an aluminum basin at the top of the steps right in front of the main door, and there was a small child inside the house crying and making a racket. He thought he had come through the wrong door and was about to retreat when the old woman looked up and asked, "Who are you looking for?"

"I've come to pay the rent. . . ."

"What?"

"I live in the courtyard next door, and I'm looking for the landlord. No one has collected the rent for months." He had come prepared with an explanation.

The old woman shook the soapsuds off her hands and pointed to the apartment at the side with a lock hanging on the door, took no more notice of him, and went back to washing the bedding in the basin.

He could only guess that something had happened to the landlord's family. It seemed that the whole place had been confiscated as public property and that the family had been relegated to occupying a side apartment. The hatred in the girl's eyes would now be even harder to erase, but he lacked the courage to return to the courtyard to look for her again.

In the early spring, in March, he went to Xiehejian in the Western Hills on the outer fringe of Beijing. He got on a train at Xizhimen, a station mainly for freight trains. It was a slow train to the outer suburbs in the mountain area of the northwest, and two hard-seat carriages had been coupled at the rear. The high tide of endless streams of students had passed, and the empty carriages were left with just a few passengers at the front and back. He sat down by the window of an unoccupied compartment. The train went through a series of tunnels and then began to wend its way through valleys. Out the window, he could see the old steam engine at the front puffing smoke and steam as it pulled a string of freight cars and this empty hard-seat carriage swaying at the back.

At a small stop called Goose Wings, where there was no platform, he jumped off and watched the long-distance train continue around the side of the mountain. The stationmaster waved the flag and blew the whistle, then went into the small hut by the shoulder of the road, leaving just him standing on the gravel by the side of the railway tracks.

While at university, he had come here as a volunteer laborer to dig holes and plant trees on the mountain. It was also in early spring, and the ground was still frozen. Each time he swung his pickax, he would not bring up two inches of soil, so, in a few days, his palms were covered in blood blisters. Once he was almost killed when he jumped into the bone-chilling river to recover the hemp bag containing the saplings he was to plant. He had it soaking in the river and it was swept away by the fast-flowing current. For this, he was commended, but the Communist Youth League still did not want him. He and some fellow students, all of whom had been refused membership, called one another "Old Reject." They formed a theater group and had just put on two plays when cadres of the student association at the university sought them out and spoke with them separately. They were not ordered to stop, but the theater group could no longer function, and, as a matter of course, disbanded.

They had performed Chekhov's *Uncle Vanya*. It had old-fashioned charm, with a sweet and kindly country girl from a small farm saying nostalgically that everything should be beautiful, with beautiful people in beautiful clothes and also with beautiful hearts; it grieved for a past that was like the old photographs he had burned.

He walked along the railway sleepers for a while, but, seeing a train coming from the distance, he went down the shoulder of the road and headed for the rock-covered riverbed. The water in the Yongding River was clear, unless it was swollen with rain or the sluices of the government dam upstream had been shut off.

He had brought Lin here and taken photographs. Lin had a beautiful figure, and she stood barefoot in the water with her skirt scooped up in her arms. Afterward, among the bushes on the mountain, they picnicked, kissed, and made love. He regretted not having photographed her nude as she lay in the grass, but all that was now beyond his reach.

What else could he do? What else was there to do? There was no need for him to go back to his office desk to arrange those virtually identical propaganda documents as he was meant to, as no one was in charge of him. Also, there was no need for him to rebel: that strange righteous indignation, too, had passed. For several months, he had headed the assault on the opposition, but now the thrill and excitement had completely vanished, or, rather, he had tired, had had enough of it. He should bravely retreat while he still could; there was no need for him to play the role of a hero.

He took off his shoes and socks, and walked barefoot in the clear icy current. As the water gently trickled in shining broken ripples and sparkled in the sunlight, he suddenly started thinking clearly. He should go to see his father because he had not received a letter from home for a long time, and he should also take the opportunity, when no one would notice, to travel south to clarify this business in his file about his father having "hidden a gun."

He rushed back to the city by early afternoon, went home to get his bankbook, cycled to withdraw money before the bank closed, then went to Qianmen Railway Station to buy a ticket for that night. He returned home to lock his bicycle in his room, and, carrying the satchel he normally took to work, he boarded the express train south at eleven o'clock.

Father and son had not seen one another for two years, and, when he suddenly turned up, his father was overjoyed. His father went off to the free market and bought fresh fish and live shrimp, and went to the kitchen to gut the fish. When his mother died, his father became morose and seldom spoke, but now he was a different person, doing the cooking, cheerful and talking a lot. Then came his father's concerns about politics, and he kept asking questions about the Party and the national leaders who had vanished from the papers. Not wanting to upset his father straight away, he sat at the table, drinking, and talked about things that couldn't be read in the newspapers. He told his father there was an internal struggle going on in the highest echelons of the Party, but that it was something about which ordinary people would not be able to find out anything. His father said he knew, he knew; in the provinces and the cities, it was the same. His father also said that he had joined the rebels and that the head of the personnel department, who had denounced a string of people, had been overthrown. He held back for a while but felt he had to warn his father.

"Father, you mustn't forget the lesson of the anti-rightist period—"

"I did not oppose the Party! I only raised some views about a particular person's work!"

His father became agitated. His hand began to shake, and he spilled the liquor from his cup onto the table.

"You're not young, and you have problems with your personal history, you can't join such groups! You don't have the right to take part in such campaigns!" He was also very agitated. He had never spoken in that tone of voice to his father before.

"Why can't I?" His father slammed his cup on the table. "There's nothing wrong with my history, I didn't join with reactionaries, I have no political problems! That year, the Party called upon people to speak out, and I simply said that the wall between the masses should be torn down. I was referring to that person's work style. I did not say a word against the Party. It was his revenge! I said this at the meeting, and many people were present, they all heard and can testify to this! That blackboard document of mine with more than a hundred characters had been requested by their Party branch!"

"Father, you're too naive—" he went to argue, but his father cut him short.

"I don't need you to lecture to me! Just because you've done a bit of study! Your mother overindulged you, she spoiled you rotten!"

After his father had calmed down, he had to ask him. "Father, did you ever have any guns?"

His father was stunned. It was as if he had been struck on the head. Slowly his head drooped, and he stopped talking.

"Someone has divulged that my file has this problem," he explained. "I made this trip to see if you were all right. Is there any truth in the matter?"

"Your mother was too honest. . . ." his father mumbled.

In other words, it was true. His heart went cold.

"It was a year or two after Liberation. Census forms were issued for people to fill out, and there was a column for weapons. It was your mother's fault, she was asking for trouble, she insisted that I honestly write down that I had sold a gun to a friend. . . ."

"What year was this?" he asked, glaring. His father had become the object of his interrogation.

"It was a long time ago, during the War of Resistance. It was still the Republican Period, before you were even born. . . ."

People all testified like this, they had to, he thought. However, the matter of the gun was already an incontestable fact, and he had to struggle to pull himself together and to curb his anger. He could not interrogate his father, so he said quietly, "Father, I'm not blaming you, but where is this gun?"

"I passed it on to a colleague at the bank. Your mother said she couldn't understand why I was keeping the thing, but I had it for protection, because of the social unrest in those times. She said I wouldn't know where to aim it, and what if it went off by accident? So, I sold it to a colleague at the bank!" His father laughed.

But this was not a laughing matter, and he said sternly, "But it is recorded in my file that you had hidden a gun."

These were Lin's exact words, and he could not have heard them wrongly.

His father shook and almost shouted, "That's impossible! It happened more than thirty years ago!"

Father and son looked at one another. He believed his father more than the file, but he had to say, "Father, they are sure to investigate."

"In other words . . ." His father was wretched.

"In other words, who would now admit to having bought the gun?" He, too, despaired.

His father covered his face with both hands. He had finally realized the implications, and was weeping. The food on the table, hardly touched, had gone cold.

He said he did not blame his father, and, whatever happened, he was still his son, there was no question of his not acknowledging him as his father. During the great famine in the aftermath of the Great Leap Forward period, his mother had also been naive. She responded to the call of the Party and went to a farm to be reformed through labor; excessive fatigue led to her drowning in the river. He and his father were left to depend upon each other, and he knew his father loved him very much. When he came home from university swollen from malnutrition, his father used two months of meat-ration coupons to buy pork fat to make lard for him to take back with him. His father said it was cold up north and impossible to get hold of anything nutritious, whereas here carrots could be bought from the peasants. He could never forget his father pouring the boiling fat into a plastic jar, which immediately shriveled up and melted; the fat ran from the table to the floor. In silence, they got on their haunches to scrape up the solidified lard, bit by bit, with a spoon from the floor.

He went on to say, "Father, I've come back to clear up this business about the gun, for your sake and for mine."

It was only then that his father said, "I sold the gun to an old colleague at the bank more than thirty years ago. After Liberation, I have only had one letter from him. If he is still alive, he will be working at the bank. Do you remember him? You used to call him Uncle Fang. He was very fond of you and would never betray you. He didn't have any children and said he wanted to have you as his god-child, but your mother refused."

There was an old photograph at home, if he hadn't burned it, he recalled. This Uncle Fang was bald and had a fat round face. He was like a Buddha, but in a suit and tie. The child in a knitted pullover who sat on the lap of this living Buddha in a suit was holding a gold Parker fountain pen and wouldn't let go of it. The pen was later given to him, and he treasured it as a child.

After spending a day at home, he continued south by train another day and night. When he found the local bank and made inquiries, the youth at reception turned out to be a member of a rebel group. Then, after asking the cadre in charge of personnel, he found out that a certain Fang had been transferred twenty years earlier to a savings office in the suburbs. This was probably because old personnel who had been retained were not trusted.

He rented a bicycle and found the savings office. They told him that Fang had retired, and gave him his address.

At the end of a passageway of a simple two-story building, was an old woman in an apron washing vegetables at the communal tub. She gave a start at his inquiry, and asked instead, "What do you want him for?"

"I was passing through on a business trip and came to pay a visit," he said.

Hedging, the old woman wiped her hands incessantly on her apron, then finally said that he was not in. He suspected that she was Fang's wife, so, with a smile, he explained that he was the son of Fang's old friend so-and-so, and that he had come to visit his old uncle. The old woman quietly exclaimed, then took him to a door. She opened it to let him in, then brought tea and invited him to sit down. She told him her husband was working in the vegetable garden and that she would fetch him right away.

The old man came in with a hoe and placed it behind the door.

His one droopy eyelid was twitching, and a few sparse strands of white hair sprouted from the sides of his shiny head. Addressing him as Uncle Fang, he again explained that he was the son of such-and-such a person, and conveyed his father's regards.

The old man nodded, his droopy eyelid twitching, as he looked at him for a long time before slowly saying, "I remember, I remember, I remember. . . . My old colleague, my old friend. . . . How is your father?"

"He's all right."

"Ah, it's good to know he's all right, it's good to know he's all right!"

After chatting awhile, he said he was in trouble, or, rather, that he might be in trouble. It had to do with his father's having sold a gun.

The old man lowered his head to look for something, then took his cup in his trembling hands. He said he didn't want the old man to testify, but only wanted him to tell him what had happened. "Did my father ever get you to sell a gun for him?"

He stressed the word "sell" and said nothing about the old man having bought it. The old man put down his cup. His hands stopped shaking, and he went on to say, "This did take place, but it was decades ago, during the War of Resistance, when we were refugees; there was chaos and fighting in those times, and we had to protect ourselves from bandits. We had worked many years in the bank and had some savings, but, as banknotes depreciated, we converted our savings into gold and silver jewelry. We wore this on our persons, and carried a gun just in case."

He said his father had told him all this, but that was not the problem. The problem was that what had happened to the gun was never resolved, and it had been entered into his file that his father had hidden a gun. He said this as calmly as he could.

"This is hard to believe!" The old man sighed. "People from your father's work unit also came to investigate. It's hard to believe that it's also causing trouble for you."

"It hasn't yet, but it could, and I have to think of how to cope if something does flare up."

He explained again that he had not come to investigate, and put on a smile to put the old man at ease.

"It was I who bought the gun," the old man finally said.

"But my father said he got you to sell it for him—"

"But who did I sell it to?" the old man asked.

"My father didn't say," he said.

"No, it was I who bought the gun," the old man said.

"Does he know?"

"Of course he knows. Later on, I threw it into the river."

"Does he know?"

"How could he have known? By then, it was after Liberation, and there was no social unrest, so why would a person keep something like that? I secretly threw it into the river one night. . . ."

There was nothing he could say to this.

"But why did your father have to bring it up? He's a trouble-maker!" The old man was blaming his father.

"If he knew that you had thrown it into the river . . ." he tried to defend his father.

"The problem is, he's just too naive!"

"He could also have thought the gun was still around and was afraid that if it was found and the owner traced—"

He wanted to defend his father, but his father had, in fact, made the report and had also implicated this old man. It was his father who was to blame.

"It's hard to believe, it's hard to believe. . . ." The old man sighed, again and again. "Who would have thought something that happened over thirty years ago—before you were even born—would go from your father's file into your file!"

This gun at the bottom of the river must have rusted away to nothing and no longer existed, but undoubtedly remained on this retired old man's file, he thought but did not say. Changing the topic, he said, "Uncle Fang, you don't have any children, do you?"

"No." The old man sighed but said nothing.

The old man had forgotten that he had wanted him as a godchild. Luckily; otherwise he would have been as heavy-hearted as his own father.

"If you want to come and investigate further—" the old man said.

"That won't be necessary," he cut the old man short. He no longer felt the same as he did prior to this visit: there was no sense in blaming either this old man or his father.

"I'm already nearing the end of my life. Just finish listening to me," the old man insisted.

"The thing no longer exists, does it? Surely it has totally rusted away?" He stared at the old man.

The old man's mouth opened wide, showing a few sparse teeth, as he burst into loud laughter. A tear fell from his droopy eyelid.

The old man and his wife began preparing food and suggested that he stay for a meal. But, saying he had to get back to the city to return his bicycle then catch the night train, he firmly declined.

Uncle Fang saw him out of the building to the main road. Waving him off, he said to convey regards to his father, then said, "Take care! Take care!"

He got on his bicycle. When he looked back and could no longer see the old man, he suddenly thought: I've gone to all this trouble, but what fuckin' use is it going to be?

26

So you can, in fact, turn back to look at him, that unfilial son of a doomed family, a family that was not destitute but by no means rich, a family that was in-between being proletarian and capitalist. Born in the old world but growing up in the new society, he somewhat superstitiously believed in revolution, then from half-believing and half-doubting, he rebelled. However, he grew weary of the futility of rebelling, then discovered that it was nothing more than a toy cooked up by politics, so he refused to be a foot soldier or make any more sacrifices. But escape was not an option. He was forced to don a mask and somehow got along by losing himself in the crowd.

Thus he became a member of the two-faced faction, and wore a mask that he put on when he went out, like putting up an umbrella when it rained. Back home, behind the closed door, where he wouldn't be seen, he took off the mask to have a break. Worn too long, the mask would stick to the face, fuse with the flesh and the nerves, and he would not be able to remove it. It should be noted that this condition was prevalent everywhere around him.

His real face only came into existence later on, when, finally, he was able to take off the mask. But taking it off was not an easy matter, because the face and the facial nerves had become stiff from wearing the mask, and it took much effort to laugh with joy or to grimace with pain.

He was probably born a rebel; not a rebel with a clear objective, direction, or ideology, but simply one with a basic instinct for self-preservation. Later on, when he realized that his act of rebellion was being orchestrated, it was already too late.

From then on, he was devoid of ideals, but he did not want others to spend time thinking them up for him. He would not be able to pay for them, and he was afraid of being duped again. He no longer daydreamed, so he did not need to use fancy words to deceive others or himself. He no longer entertained any illusions whatsoever about people and the world.

He did not want comrades, and did not want to make plans with anyone to achieve goals, so there was no need to seize power. All that was too painful, and the endless struggles were psychologically draining. It was a blessing to be able to avoid big families and organized groups.

He refused to smash the old order but he was not a reactionary. If someone wanted a revolution, then let them go ahead, so long as it was not a revolution that made life impossible for him. To sum up, he could not be a fighter. He preferred to be away from revolution and rebellion, in a place where he could eke out a living and look on from a distance.

In fact, he had no enemies. It was the Party that was intent on making an enemy of him, and he couldn't do anything about it. The Party gave him no choice and was intent on making him conform to a pattern, and his failure to conform meant that he was the enemy of the Party. Moreover, in order to lead, the Party needed to make a target of people like him to arouse the will and spirit of the people, to whip up the masses into displays of righteous indignation. So he was made an enemy of the people. But he had no quarrel with the people, he only wanted to be able to live his own insignificant life without having to depend for his livelihood on being used as a practice target.

He was this sort of a loner, and had always wanted to be like this. It may now be said that he had no colleagues, no one above or below him, no leader, no employer; he led and hired himself, and everything he did he did cheerfully.

But he was not a misanthrope. He continued to eat at the hearth of human society and was fond of the food of his ancestral land, a taste he had acquired as a child because of his mother's wonderful cooking. Naturally, he also liked Western food, French *haute cuisine*, of course, and also Italian pasta, supposedly brought by Marco Polo from the Tang Empire, but sprinkled with Parmesan cheese that didn't exist in China. Japanese raw fish laced with hot raw mustard was excellent, and so was Russian caviar, especially the black variety. Also, if Korean barbecued beef and *kimchi* were served with Indian *rhoti*, it was a perfect dish. Kentucky fried chicken was the only thing he couldn't eat; for him it was bland and tasteless. He was fussy about food because he had gone through some good times in his childhood.

And he was also fond of women. As a youth, he had sneaked a look at his mother's youthful body while she was having a bath. From then on, he deeply appreciated beautiful women. In those times, when he was without a woman, he would write about them, and what he wrote contained a lot of sex; in this respect, he was not a virtuous gentleman. Furthermore, he had great admiration for Tang Yin and Casanova, but he was never as lucky, so all he could do was to consign his sexual fantasies to his writings.

This is the report you have written for him to replace his file in China, which, no doubt, still exists, but which he will never see.

27

He looked at the cracks in the papered ceiling. The rats running around and fighting all night had widened the cracks, and had left his bedding covered in strips of black dirt. He had never been so idle, there was nothing to do, he did not have to get up early to get to work on time, and he no longer had to busy himself with rebelling. He did not read, because all the books that were readable had been put into wooden boxes or cardboard cartons, and he did not commit anything to writing. He had to stay awake so that he would not slip back into a nightmare. The old retired worker in the next room was up early and had his radio turned on full blast, tuned to the revolutionary opera *Red Lantern*. It was really irritating, and even while he masturbated under the bedcovers with his eyes closed, striving again to enjoy Lin's hot naked body, he was not able to block out the solemn, virtuous words of that high-pitched singing. He was left feeling miserable.

He thought about getting a ladder to mend the cracks in the ceiling. But if he were to make a mistake, that brittle sagging paper shell could collapse, and it would be impossible to clean up the filthy mess of years of accumulated dust. It would take an expert to paper a ceiling. Instead, he moved the things piled on Old Tan's bed into a corner of the room, moved his own bedding there, then dismantled his own bed. Old Tan definitely would not be coming back.

If he wanted to go for a walk, there was nowhere he could go but to buy one of the bulletins put out by the people's organizations. These, in fact, contained much revealing information, and back home he would cook dinner and read as he ate. From the leaders' speeches to various people's organizations, he detected different views, hidden meanings. The many vehement pronouncements changed continually, like pictures in a magic lantern. A day earlier, a leader could be interpreting Mao's newest directive, then, tomorrow or the day after, sure enough, the secret killing machine would fall on that leader, who would suddenly be transformed into an anti-Party criminal. His righteous indignation had cooled, and doubts kept springing up in his mind, although he did not dare to acknowledge this.

However, he had to make an appearance at the workplace from time to time, to drop in at the rebels' headquarters that had formed after various splintering and regrouping. As people came and went, he would smoke a few cigarettes and chat. He simply showed his face, listened to a bit of news, then slipped away when nobody was watching. There were endless struggles and regroupings, then new struggles, and he was not interested.

Chang'an Avenue was where things were happening and where there was the most news, so whenever he went to the workplace, he always made a detour. Tents and bamboo-matting shelters were up everywhere outside the red-brown walls of Zhongnanhai. There were the red flags of the university rebel groups and a huge red horizontal banner displaying the words: BEIJING BATTLE-LINE LIAISON POINT OF THE PROLETARIAN REVOLUTIONARY GROUP TO HAUL OUT LIU SHAOQI FOR CRITICISM. Several hundred big loudspeakers, day and night, blared out war songs nonstop, and the nation's president was denounced in the name of the Supreme Leader, the Red Sun. However, even this sight failed to excite him.

"Newest material on Liu Shaoqi's daughter exposing her father! Read all about it! Former wife exposes Liu Shaoqi's misappropriation of revolutionary funds to buy gold shoehorns!"

Among the circle of people around the newspaper seller, he saw Big Head, his classmate from middle-school times, and clapped him on the shoulder from behind. Big Head got a fright, but was relieved, and smiled when he turned and saw who it was. Big Head was carrying an artificial-leather satchel and had bought a bag of newspapers and other publications.

"Let's get out of here, come to my place!" He felt a pang of nostalgia, for Big Head had become the last link with the life he had lost.

"I'll get a bottle of liquor!" Big Head was also excited.

The pair of them got on their bicycles and went off to Dongdan Market, where they squabbled over paying for the cooked food and liquor, then went back to his room. The afternoon sun was shining through the curtains, it was warm inside, and, after a few cups of liquor, their faces were flushed, and their ears were burning. Big Head said he was hauled out at the beginning of the movement. After he had made some careless comments in his dormitory, they searched and found his two small notebooks blaspheming Mao's philosophy. However, people were aiming higher nowadays, and could no longer be bothered with his petty reactionary words. He also said he had never put up a poster, that the movement had not involved him; nevertheless, he could not work at his mathematics and was simply collecting newspapers and secretly doing a bit of reading.

"What books?" he asked.

"*A Mirror for Good Government,* I brought it with me from home." A smile congealed on Big Head's round face that was flushed from alcohol.

He had never been interested in the art of empire, and couldn't fathom Big Head's smile.

"Haven't you read Wu Han's *Biography of Zhu Yuanzhang*?" Big Head asked, testing him, putting out a feeler.

The Cultural Revolution had started with criticisms of Wu Han, the deputy mayor of Beijing. A specialist in Ming history, Wu Han had written books on how the first Ming emperor, Zhu Yuanzhang, had assassinated the meritorious officials who had helped establish his empire. Wu Han committed suicide at the beginning of the movement and set a precedent for countless subsequent suicides. He understood what Big Head was implying, it confirmed his own suspicions, and, tapping his fingers on the table, he shouted, "You devil!"

Big Head's eyes shone enigmatically behind his glasses, he was no longer the bookworm he had been as a youth.

"I scanned it, but took it all to be history, old imperial history. It didn't occur to me that . . . Could things have gone a full circle?" he asked, testing Big Head.

"A boomerang. . . ." Big Head took him on, chuckling.

"But isn't that dialectics?"

"Only it's not clear whether it's high- or low-level dialectics. . . ."

What was implied and hinted at, what could be articulated neither directly nor obliquely, was whether it was imperial control strategies with an ideology or political power strategies with the trappings of ideology. History is big on ideology, but what was the reality?

Big Head stopped smiling. The radio on the other side of the wall was still on, and now it was another of the revolutionary operas directed by Madam Mao, *Red Detachment of Women*: "Advance, advance, the burden of revolution is heavy and the resentment of women is deep!" Madam Mao, Comrade Jiang Qing, who had been prohibited from taking part in politics by the Party elders, was now resolutely in the process of realizing her political ambitions.

"Why is the soundproofing so poor?"

"It's better with the radio on over there."

"Don't you have a radio?"

"My roommate Old Tan had a transistor, but it was confiscated, and he's in solitary confinement at the workplace."

The two of them fell silent for a while and could clearly hear the singing on the radio in the room next door.

"Do you have a set of chess? Let's have a game!" Big Head said.

He fished out a carved-bone chess set from one of the cardboard cartons of Old Tan's belongings piled against the wall, moved the liquor and food, and began setting up a game on the table.

"What made you think of reading this book?" He returned to their discussion as he moved a chess piece.

"When the newspapers had just started criticizing Wu Han, my old man got me to make a trip home, he said he had applied to retire. . . ."

Big Head moved a chess piece, lowered his voice, and deliberately mumbled. His father was a history professor and also had a Democratic Personage title to his name.

"Do you have that book by Wu? Is it still available?" He moved another chess piece.

"We had one at home, my old man got me to read it, but it was burned a long time ago. Who would dare to keep the book? He only got me to take an old hand-sewn copy of *A Mirror for Good Government,* a Ming woodblock edition, and it counts as his legacy to me. Old Mao used to get senior cadres to read it, otherwise I wouldn't still have it." Big Head said the word "Mao" very softly, as part of a casual comment, then made another move.

"Your old man is really smart!" He wasn't sure if he was praising Big Head's father or lamenting that he didn't have such a wise head of the family. His own father was so muddle-headed.

"But he was too late. They wouldn't let him retire and, with the problem of his personal history, they still had him hauled out for criticism." Big Head took off his glasses, peered close to the chessboard with his dull, nearsighted eyes, and said, "What's this shit game you're playing?"

Suddenly, he scrambled the game and said to Big Head, "I've had enough of this crap game, they're a whole lot of stinking cunts!"

Big Head gave a start at his coarse language, but suddenly burst out laughing. The pair of them then laughed loudly until tears came to their eyes.

You must both be careful! If someone reports your discussion, it will be enough to get the pair of you executed. Terror lies hidden in everyone's hearts, but people don't dare articulate it, can't bring it into the open.

When it was dark, he first went into the courtyard to put out the rubbish, a bucketful of chicken bones and coal cinders from the stove. When he saw that the neighbors all had their doors shut, Big Head quickly got on his bicycle and left. Big Head was living in a collective dormitory and was still being investigated. His father had kept an eye on him, but when the army moved in to implement and supervise the purification of class ranks, Big Head's carelessness while chatting in the dormitory meant that one sentence became a heinous crime: he was sent to be reformed through labor, to herd cattle for eight years on a farm.

The fear generated by that conversation caused them to avoid one another. They didn't dare make any further contact, and it was only fourteen years later that they met again. Big Head's father was dead, and an uncle in America had helped him to liaise with a university for further study. When Big Head had his passport and American visa, he came to say good-bye and mentioned that evening when, happy with alcohol, ears burning, they cracked the mystery of Old Mao's unleashing of the Cultural Revolution.

Big Head said, "If what you and I said that day had been exposed, I wouldn't have been herding cattle and would be somewhere else!" He also added that if he could get a teaching position in a university in America, he would probably never return.

That night, fourteen years earlier, after Big Head left, he opened wide the door to his room to let out the smell of alcohol. Afterward, he locked the door, allowed himself to calm down from the excitement and fear, and stretched out on the bed to look at the black cracks in the ceiling. It was as if he had pried open an ants' nest, and inside was a pitch-black, wriggling chaos. The ceiling could collapse on him any time, and this made him feel numb all over.

28

It was winter again. The stove door was shut, and he was sitting in bed, propped up against the headboard. The only light came from the table lamp, and the metal shade clamped to the bulb cut down the light that illuminated the floral bedcover and left the upper part of his body in darkness as he gazed at the circle of light on the bedcover. On the gigantic chessboard without borders, winning or losing was not decided by the chess pieces but by the chess players in the dark manipulating them. So, if a chess piece wanted to have its own way and stupidly refused to let itself be taken, surely it was crazy? You are less than insignificant, nothing but an ant that can be squashed underfoot any time, any place. But you can't leave this ants' nest, and can only mingle with the swarms of ants. Whether it was a matter of philosophical impoverishment or impoverished philosophy, from Marx down to those revolutionary sages, who could have foreseen the calamities and spiritual impoverishment this Cultural Revolution would bring?

There was a tapping on his window. At first, he thought it was the wind, but the glass was pasted with paper on the inside, and the curtains were drawn. Again, there were two soft taps.

"Who is it?" he sat up and asked. There was no response, so he got out of bed and walked barefoot to the window.

"It's me." A woman's voice came from outside, softly.

He could not make out who it was, but he unlatched the door and opened it a crack. In a gust of cold wind, Xiao Xiao pushed open the door and came in. He was surprised by this middle-school student coming so late at night and, as he was only in his underpants, quickly got back into bed and left it to the girl to close the door. She had almost got the door to close, when it blew open again and the chilly wind howled as it poured into the room. Xiao Xiao put her back against the door to stop it from blowing open.

"Latch it." He said this without thinking, but when he saw the girl hesitate before turning and gently pushing in the metal latch, his heart thumped. The girl unraveled the long woolen scarf wrapped tightly around her head to reveal her pale but refined features. Her head was bowed, and she seemed to be catching her breath.

"Xiao Xiao, what's the problem?" he asked, sitting up in bed.

"Nothing." The girl looked up but remained standing by the door.

"You must be frozen, open the stove door."

The girl took off her knitted woolen gloves. With a sigh, she took the iron hook lying by the stove, and opened both the stove door and the iron cover on top. It was as if she was expected to do this. Clearly, this thin, ungainly girl was not spoiled at home and was used to domestic chores.

Xiao Xiao had come with a crowd of middle-school students to his workplace to take part in the movement that soon split into two factions. This girl and a few other female students leaned toward their faction, but they were fickle and moved from faction to faction; they were enthusiastic for a few days and would then disappear. It was only Xiao Xiao who came regularly to their headquarters. She didn't yell and shout, and she was not keen on arguing, like the other girls, but always remained quietly on the side, reading newspapers or helping to copy out posters. Her calligraphy with a brush was passable, and she was patient. One afternoon, there was an urgent job to write out a batch of posters to attack the opposition, and by the time they had all been written and pasted up, it was already after nine o'clock at night. Xiao Xiao said her home was at the Drum Tower, and, as it was on the way, he offered her a lift. He got her to sit behind him on the bicycle rack. When they passed by the entrance of his courtyard, he suggested having something to eat before going on. Xiao Xiao came into his room, and it was she who went ahead and made noodles. After eating, they got on the bicycle and he took her to a *hutong*, where, insisting there was no need for him to go in, Xiao Xiao jumped off the bicycle and disappeared like smoke.

"Have you eaten?" he asked her out of habit.

Xiao Xiao nodded as she rubbed her hands. The heat radiating from the stove made her face instantly turn red. He had not seen the girl for a while, and was waiting to hear why she had come. Xiao Xiao remained seated on the chair by the stove, pressing her lovely face in her warmed hands.

"What have you been doing lately?" This was the only thing he could think to ask as he sat in bed.

"I haven't been doing anything." Xiao Xiao gazed at the fire with her hands on her cheeks.

He waited for her to continue, but the girl said nothing.

So, he went on to ask, "What's happening in your school?"

"All the windows of the school have been smashed, and it's too cold, so no one goes. My schoolmates have scattered everywhere, they don't know what they will be doing either."

"That's great. You don't have to go to school and can stay at home."

The girl did not answer. He leaned across, pulled his trousers off the shelf at the foot of the bed, then started to get out of bed.

"You can just lie there. It's all right. I've just come to talk with you." At this, Xiao Xiao turned and looked at him.

"Then make yourself some tea!" he said.

Xiao Xiao just sat there without moving. He guessed why she had come. Her face was flushed, and there was a glint in her bright eyes.

"It's a bit hot, shall I take off my padded coat?" Xiao Xiao said. She seemed to be asking both herself and him at the same time.

"Take it off if you're hot," he said.

The girl stood up and removed her padded coat. She was not wearing a jacket and had on a dark-red, knitted sweater that clung to her upper body. He saw her protruding breasts and said awkwardly, "I'd best get up."

"There's no need, there's really no need," Xiao Xiao said.

"It's very late, it won't be good if you are seen by the neighbors." He was worried about her being there.

"It's pitch-black in the courtyard, and the only glimmer of light was from your window. Nobody saw me come in." Xiao Xiao's voice had turned gentle, and, instantly, this girl who was a stranger was on intimate terms with him.

He nodded to indicate that she could come to him. Xiao Xiao walked to his bed, and, as her legs touched the bed, his heart began to pound. He heard a rustle as Xiao Xiao pulled up her sweater and the faded, pink, cotton shirt tucked in her trousers to reveal her slim, lustrous body and part of her breasts. He instinctively reached out to touch her, and the girl put her hand on his, but he was not sure if she wanted to guide or to stop him. He looked up at Xiao Xiao, but could not see the expression in her eyes. Her smooth body gleamed in the circle of light, and, at the lower part of the breast he was pressing on, was the raised line of a tender, red scar. The girl's delicate fingers were squeezing his hand tightly, so, not bothering about the scar, he thrust his hand into the girl's tight-fitting shirt and seized the breast that no longer seemed to be small but was firm and had swelled up. Xiao Xiao was mumbling something, but he did not have time to work out what she was saying. He swept her into his arms, and the next moment she was in his bed.

He could not remember how the girl got under his quilt, or how she had undone the tight buttons at the waist of her trousers. The smooth, moist part between her thighs had no hair yet, but he did not know whether or not she was a virgin. He only remembered that she didn't squirm, didn't resist, didn't kiss him, and didn't take off her thick padded trousers, but only pulled them down to the knees so he could fondle her. Then, she pulled up her sweater and shirt again, but, under the quilt, the soft part between her legs was all wet. What he did remember was that, as the girl snuggled against him with her eyes closed, the light under the shade shining on her slightly parted, full, red lips, he felt a tenderness for this girl whom he thought unattractive and not yet grown up. This incident was unexpected, and, not being prepared, he was afraid of getting her pregnant. He did not dare go any further, he did not dare to enjoy her. He didn't know if this was why she had come, and didn't know what she meant by showing him the scar on her breast. He didn't know what would happen the next day, didn't know his tomorrow or the girl's, or whether they still had a tomorrow.

He lay there quietly, listening to the ticking of the clock on the table in the all-pervading silence. He wanted to ask about the scar. The girl had clearly come because of it, and would have thought about things before resolving to act. Afraid of shattering the suffocating silence, he turned on his side and looked at her for a long time. The ticking of the second hand alerted him that time was passing. It was when he raised himself to look at the clock that Xiao Xiao opened her eyes and, under the quilt, pulled together her clothes, buttoned her trousers at the waist, and sat up.

"Are you leaving?" he asked.

Xiao Xiao nodded and, still with her purplish-red socks on, crawled out from under the quilt. She got out of the bed and bent down to put on her shoes. All this time, he lay there, watching in silence as she put on her padded coat and wrapped the long scarf around her head. Then, as he saw her take her knitted gloves from the table, he asked her, "Are you in some sort of trouble?" He thought to himself that he sounded harsh.

"No," Xiao Xiao said, looking down. She took her gloves and slipped them on, a finger at a time.

"If you're in some sort of trouble, then speak up!" He felt he had to say this.

"It's nothing." Still looking down, Xiao Xiao suddenly turned and started to unlatch the door.

He quickly got up and went barefoot across the icy-cold brick floor, thinking to stop the girl, but not knowing what to do.

"Go back, you'll catch a chill," Xiao Xiao said.

"Will you come again?" he asked.

Xiao Xiao gave a nod and went out, slowly pulling the door shut behind her.

But Xiao Xiao did not come again, nor did she reappear at the workplace headquarters of their rebel faction. However, he did not have Xiao Xiao's address. Of that gang of middle-school students, the girl had stayed the longest in their rebel group, but he had no way of finding out what had happened to her. He only knew that she was called Xiao Xiao, which could even have been a nickname used by her schoolmates. But what he clearly knew was that on this Xiao Xiao's breast—below the left breast, no, the right breast, it was his left hand and the girl's right breast—there was almost an inch-long, still raw, blood-red scar. He recalled that the girl was yielding and didn't squirm, but that she wanted to show him the scar. Was it to win his sympathy or to seduce him? She was probably seventeen or eighteen, and still had no hair between her legs, but her body was beautiful, beautiful enough to arouse him. Maybe it was only because the girl was too young, too frail, that he was afraid of shouldering such a responsibility. He didn't know if Xiao Xiao's parents had been attacked, and there was no way of knowing how she had been wounded. Had the girl come to him because of the scar? Was she seeking his protection, someone to turn to? Maybe she was afraid and confused? Maybe she got into his bed hoping to be comforted? But he didn't dare accept her, and didn't dare ask her to stay.

For some time after, whenever he took his bicycle out, he would make a detour past the *hutong* where Xiao Xiao had got off, but he never saw her again. It was only then that he regretted not having got Xiao Xiao to stay. He hadn't said anything kind or comforting to the girl. He was so careful, so overly cautious, and so spineless.

29

"Why were you arrested?"

"I was sold out by a traitor."

"Were you a traitor? Speak up!"

"The Party examined my history and came to a decision long ago."

"Should I read this document to you?"

The old scoundrel started to panic, and the bags under his eyes twitched a couple of times.

" 'At a critical juncture in the fight against the Communists, to stamp out disorder in order to save the nation, I was not vigilant, careless about whom I befriended, and was led astray.' *Do you remember those words?*"

"I don't recall having said them!" The old man was adamant in his denial, and the sides of his nose began to sweat.

"That's nothing, just the first sentence to prompt you, should I read on?"

"I really can't remember, it was many decades ago." The old man's tone had softened, and his prominent Adam's apple bobbed up and down as he swallowed saliva.

He picked up the document from the table and waved it. He was acting out a repulsive role, but it was better to be the judge than being judged by others.

"This is a copy, the original bears a signature and a thumbprint. Of course, it's the name you had at the time. You had to change your name and surname, surely you can't have forgotten that?"

The old man was silenced.

"I'll read some more sentences to help jog your memory." He read on, " 'I earnestly beg the government for a lenient acquittal and hereby sign this guarantee that should there be any suspicious persons ingratiating and aligning themselves with the Communist bandits, I will forthwith report them.' *Doesn't this count as being a traitor to the Party? Do you know how the underground Party dealt with traitors?*" he asked.

"Yes, yes." The old man nodded repeatedly.

"Then what about you?"

"I didn't ever betray anyone. . . ." Beads of sweat began to ooze from his bald forehead.

"I'm asking you, were you a traitor to the Party?" he asked.

"Stand up!"

"Stand up when you speak!"

"Make an honest confession!"

Several members of the rebel faction were all shouting rowdily.

"I . . . I had to sign the guarantee so that they would let me out. . . ." The old man stood there, trembling. His voice, low in his throat, was barely audible.

"I didn't ask how you were released. If you hadn't capitulated, would they have let you out? Speak up! Isn't that being a traitor?"

"But I . . . But, afterwards, I reestablished links with the Party—"

He cut him short. "That was because, at the time, the underground Party didn't know you had capitulated."

"The Party forgave, pardoned me. . . ." The old man bowed his head.

"You were pardoned? You were brutal with punishing other people. When you punished the masses, you went into a rage and didn't let people off even after they had written a confession. 'Instruct the branches under your supervision to make sure the evidence sticks so that the verdict can't ever be reversed.' *Did you say this?*"

"Speak up! Did you say this?" someone roared.

"Yes, yes, I made an error. It was the same as having betrayed the Party," the old man quickly admitted.

"How can it be just an error? You make it sound like it's nothing! You had people jumping out of the building to commit suicide!" Someone banged on the table.

"That . . . That wasn't me, that was how it was carried out—"

"This was your instruction, you yourself gave the instruction: 'Historical problems have to be linked to actual behavior and need to be thoroughly investigated.' *Did you or did you not say this?*" this comrade kept at him relentlessly.

"Yes, yes." The old man was learning to be clever.

"Who is anti-Party? It is you who have betrayed the Party! Write all that down!" this comrade shouted harshly at him.

"What do you want me to write?" the old man asked, looking forlorn.

"Do you need a secretary to write it?" another comrade asked scornfully.

Everyone started laughing and talking all at once. They were excited, it was as if they had caught a big fish. The old man looked up a little, his face ashen. His slack, colorless lower lip began to tremble as he spoke.

"I . . . I've got a heart problem. . . . Could I have a drink of water?"

He shoved a glass of water on the table to him. The old man took a small medicine bottle out of his pocket, tipped out a pill with his shaking hands, and swallowed it with a gulp of water.

It flashed through his mind that the old scoundrel was older than his own father. . . . Hey! Don't you have a heart attack and drop dead here. He said, "Sit down and drink up all the water. If you need to, you can lie down on the sofa for a while."

The old man didn't dare go to the sofa where people were sitting, and looked miserably at him.

He gave up the idea and made a decision, "Now listen, first thing in the morning, bring a detailed account of your capitulation, and of your betrayal of the Party. Outline, clearly and in full, how you were arrested, how you got out of prison, who were the witnesses, and what confessions you made in prison."

"Ai, ai." The old scoundrel immediately bowed and nodded.

"You may leave now."

As soon as the old man went out the door, his comrades, who were all fired up for action, turned on him.

However, he was a slick talker, and just as mean. "Do you think he can get away with all this evidence against him? The heavenly net of the dictatorship of the proletariat won't let him escape! Don't let the old bastard have a heart attack and drop dead right in front of us."

"What if he goes home and commits suicide?" someone asked.

"I doubt that he would have the courage. If he wasn't afraid of dying, he would not have capitulated back then. He'll deliver his confession tomorrow without fail. What do all of you think?"

His comrades were speechless. He thoroughly detested the old bastard who spouted the Party line every time he spoke. But he felt sorry for him now that his own faith in revolution had been destroyed and he had dispensed with the myths that the perfect new people and the glorious revolution had created. The old scoundrel had concealed the matter of his capitulation by using a former pen name as his real name. By doing this, he had evaded successive investigations, yet he must have spent all these years in trepidation, he thought.

Can't a person's faith change? Once aboard the Party ship, does it have to be for the whole of a person's life? Is it possible not to be a loyal subject of the Party? Then what if one has no faith? By jumping out of the rigid choice of being either one or the other, you will be without an ideology, but will you be allowed to exist? When your mother gave birth to you, you did not have an ideology. You, the last in a generation of a doomed family, can't you live outside ideology? Is not to be revolutionary the same as counterrevolutionary? Is not to be a hatchet man for the revolution the same as being a victim of the revolution? If you don't die for the revolution, will you still have the right to exist? And how will you be able to escape from the shadow of revolution?

Amen. You were born with sin and unqualified to be a judge, but, cynically and for your own self-protection, you infiltrated the rebel ranks. At this very time, you are even more certain of this. It is also to find a refuge that, on the pretext of investigating Party cadres, you get a wad of letters of introduction stamped with official seals, draw a sum of money for expenses, and go off wandering everywhere. There's no harm in getting to learn a bit about this inexplicable world and seeing if there's anywhere to escape this catastrophic revolution.

On the southern bank of the Yellow River, in the city of Ji'nan, he found a small workshop on an ancient street. The person he was investigating had been released from a prison farm. The middle-aged woman supervisor wearing sleeve protectors was pasting up paper boxes. She replied, "The person's been gone a long time."

"Is he dead?" he said.

"If he's gone, of course he's dead."

"How did he die?"

"Go and ask his family!"

"Is his family still here? Who are they?"

"Who, in fact, are you investigating?" the woman asked back.

He couldn't say to some woman worker in a workshop that opened onto the street that the dead person and the cadre under investigation had been classmates at university and had joined the student movement of the underground Party organization, and afterward they had been in a Nationalist prison together. Also, there was no point in wearing himself out trying to explain all this cast-iron revolutionary logic. But he did have to get hold of a document saying that the person was dead, so that he could claim his travel expenses.

"Would you be able to put your seal on it?" he asked.

"Put my seal on what?"

"A testimony that the person's dead."

"You'll have to go to the public security supply office. We don't issue death certificates."

"All right. Which way do I have to go to get to the Yellow River?" he asked, imitating the woman's Shandong accent.

"What Yellow River?" the woman asked.

"Our China has only one Yellow River. Isn't your Ji'nan city on the bank of the Yellow River?"

"What are you talking about! What's to see there? I've never been there."

The woman went back to pasting her paper boxes and ignored him.

There was a saying that a person should not give up before reaching the Yellow River, and he suddenly thought of going to see it. The Yellow River had been eulogized from ancient times, and he had passed over it many times, but always in a train, and its greatness could not be seen as it flashed by through the metal framework of the bridge. A passer-by on the street told him that the Yellow River was a long way off, he would have to take a bus to Luokouzhen, then walk up the high embankment. It was only from the top of the embankment that the river could be seen.

When he climbed to the top of the high embankment of bare loess, there was no sign of anything green. On the other shore was a dusty flood area without any villages and not a single shrub. A rolling sludge lay below the fractures and slopes formed by silting at different water levels. The riverbed was high above the town. Was this fast-flowing, brown, muddy river the Yellow River that had been praised in songs over the ages? Did the ancient civilization of China originate here?

Below the horizon, as far as the eye could see, was the muddy river speckled with dazzling sunlight. But for the black shadow of a boat floating in the distance under the sun, there was absolutely no sign of life. Had the people who had sung its praises ever actually come to the Yellow River? Or had they simply made it all up?

That distant shadow against the sky, the sailing boat with a wooden mast, swayed as it neared. The gray-white sail had big patches, and a man, stripped to the waist, was holding the rudder. A woman in a gray jacket was also on the deck, throwing something overboard. The rocks in the cabin, which filled half of the boat, were probably used for mending breaks in the embankment during seasonal flooding.

He went down to the shore. It gradually became slushy mud, so he took off his shoes and socks and held them as he walked barefoot in the slippery quagmire. He bent down and scooped a handful of mud that dried in the sun into the shape of a shell. A revolutionary poet once sang: "I drink the water of the Yellow River." But this muddy soup was not for humans, and even fish and shrimp would find it hard to survive in it. It would seem that dire poverty and disaster can be eulogized. This great muddy river, which was virtually dead, shocked him and filled him with desolation. Some years later, an important member of the Party Center said he wanted to erect a great statue to honor the spirit of the nation in the upper reaches of the Yellow River, and probably it has already been erected.

The train south made an unscheduled stop during the night at a small station on the northern bank of the Yangtze River, and people were shut in the unbearably hot and stuffy carriages. The ceiling fans were whirring, but the rank odor of sweat made it even harder to breathe. Several hours passed like this. The explanation over the broadcast system was that there was armed fighting at a station up

ahead. The tracks were piled with rocks, and they didn't know when
the train would be able to go through. It was only after passengers
surrounded the train guard to protest that the doors were opened
and everyone got out. He went to a pond by a paddy field, washed
himself, then lay on the embankment to look at the stars in the sky.
The sound of angry voices died down, and, as the croaking of frogs
filled the air, he began to doze off. He thought back to when he was
a child and lay on a bamboo bed in the courtyard to stay cool, and
had also looked at the sky like this. But those childhood memories
were more remote than the bright morning star in the sky.

30

Bags of cement had been stacked waist-high across the road, with gaps left to poke rifles through. In front of the barricade was a mass of road construction equipment: roadblocks, cement mixers, and bitumen boilers. Concrete blocks strung with barbed wire had been put up to make a passage on the road just wide enough for a person to get through. Traffic had been cut, and a line of seven or eight empty electric trolleybuses with their cable rods removed stood on one side of the intersection. The footpaths, however, were crowded with pedestrians and nearby residents: young adolescents squeezing in and out, women with babies, and old men in singlets and slippers waving rattan fans. They were all standing against the iron railing of the footpath waiting to watch something happen. Were they waiting for an armed battle? There was much talk in the crowd, some were talking about the Red Command and others about the Revolutionary Command. Anyway, the two factions had mobilized their forces and there was going to be a fight. He couldn't work out which faction was in control of the road to the railway station, but, making his way through the crowd, he crossed the intersection and started walking toward the roadblock.

Blocking the exit, at the end of the passageway of concrete blocks strung with barbed wire, were workers wearing red armbands and woven-willow safety helmets: they were armed with sharpened steel drills. He took out his work permit. The guard opened it, took one look, and waved him through. He was not from the area and had nothing to do with the dispute between the two rival factions. There were no vehicles on the road, and it was lonely and deserted, so he walked in the middle of the road where the bitumen radiated the heat of the glaring sun. People tend not to go crazy in broad day-light, he thought.

Bang! A loud noise cut the hot drowsy loneliness. At first, he didn't know that it was a rifle shot, and he looked around at the two sides of the street. The wall of a big factory had a slogan written on it in characters the size of a person's head: FIGHT WITH YOUR LIFE TO DEFEND CHAIRMAN MAO'S PROLETARIAN REVOLUTIONARY LINE! At this, he realized that the sound he had heard was a rifle shot. He started running, but immediately stopped. He mustn't show that he was panicking, because it would make the sniper even more suspicious of him. However, he immediately got onto the footpath and walked at a brisk pace.

It was impossible to say where the shot had come from. Was it warning off pedestrians? Or was it aimed at him? They wouldn't indiscriminately kill someone, would they? He was passing through, and had nothing to do with their dispute. But supposing someone shot and killed him, who would come forward as a witness? He sud-denly realized that he could have been killed by the sniper, that his life was in danger, and he immediately turned down the very first lane. The lane, too, was lonely and deserted, and it seemed as if all the residents had evacuated the area. Terror sprang up in his heart. Only then did he believe that the whole city could easily turn into a battlefield, that people could suddenly become enemies because of an invisible line, and that both sides could go into bloody battle because of it.

As expected, the square in front of the railway station was crowded with people, and there was a line of travelers snaking from the tightly closed ticket window. He asked someone in front what time they would start selling tickets, but the person didn't know and simply shrugged. He got into the line, and, before long, people from out of nowhere had lined up behind him. None of the people in the line had big pieces of luggage, and there were no old people or children. They were all strong young men, apart from a young woman with two short plaits, farther ahead in the line. From time to time, she looked around, but as soon as she made eye contact with someone, she averted her eyes. She seemed to be on edge, probably afraid of being recognized. It was his guess that many of the people in the ticket line were on the run, but the large numbers gathered in the square put his mind at ease, so he sat on the ground and lit a cigarette.

There was a stir, and the line instantly broke up. Something had happened. He stopped someone to ask, and was told that the river had been sealed off. He asked what that meant. There would be no ferries and trains operating! There was also talk that there would be a bloodbath. Whose blood and who was it going to wash? He couldn't get an answer. The people in the square had suddenly dispersed, and the ten or so, who, like him, had nowhere to go, gradually came together and formed a new line at the tightly shut ticket window. It was as if they had to do this to get the support of the others. By this time, the sun was setting, the clock at the station was pointing at five o'clock, and no one else was turning up.

The ten or so people left had been cut off from any source of information. Sensibly, they no longer stupidly lined up in the sun but found some shade to chat or smoke. Now and then, people made comments: the two factions were making their final decision, the military would soon intervene, boat and rail transport services couldn't be stopped for long and, at the latest, would be running again the next day. It was all positive thinking. He no longer asked questions. The young woman was still there but kept some distance from everyone. She stayed in a corner with her head down and her arms hugging her knees.

He was hungry and thought of buying something to eat so that he would be able to last until morning. Sleeping with his backpack as a pillow on concrete meant nothing more than looking at the stars all night, and somehow he would be able to get through this summer night. He left the ticket window and went around to the nearby shops, but they were all closed and shuttered for the night. There were no eating places open, and the streets and lanes on either side were empty and deserted. No vehicles had passed by for several hours. At this point, he sensed the air becoming thick, and he became tense, and, not daring to venture farther, he turned back. The shadow of the clock tower had already extended to the center of the square, and there were fewer people in front of the ticket window. The young woman was still huddled in the same spot and the talkative person was no longer talking.

The shadow of the clock tower now stretched over most of the square, and the outline of the dark shadow became more distinct with the sun directly behind. All strangers to one another, they were at a station, waiting for a train, but they didn't know when it would arrive. What if the tracks had been cut? Were they really waiting for a civil war?

Bang-bang-bang! A burst of muffled gunfire reverberated in everyone's hearts, and they all got to their feet. Following this was a continuous volley of gunfire, also muffled, but this time it was machine-gun fire, and it was somewhere not far away. Everyone scattered like animals, and he, too, ran for his life. This was war, he thought.

It was a blind alley, a narrow corridor with a wall on the one side and hemp bags stacked higher than a person on the other. He had escaped into a warehouse. When he stopped to catch his breath, he heard a noise, and, turning around, he saw the young woman slumped against a pile of hemp bags, also trying to catch her breath.

"What happened to the others?" he asked.

"I don't know."

"Where are you going?"

The woman did not answer.

"I'm going to Beijing."

"I . . . am too," the woman said after a pause.

"You're not a local, are you?" he asked, but the woman didn't answer.

"University student?" he asked, but again she didn't answer.

It gradually grew dark, and a cool breeze started blowing. He felt his sweat-soaked shirt clinging to his back.

"We'll have to find a place to spend the night, it's not safe here," he said, walking out of the warehouse. He looked back and saw the woman quietly following but keeping a few paces away. He asked, "Know of anywhere to stay?"

"Near the station, but it's too dangerous to go back. There are places along the river, close to the wharf, but it's a very long walk," the woman said quietly. She was clearly a local, so he insisted that she lead the way.

Sure enough, below the big embankment, along the river, in a little street of old houses, youths were standing outside or sitting in doorways, chatting with one another across the road and asking about the battle. Until the bullets hit them in the head, they couldn't help being curious, even excited, by it all. The shops and little eating places were all closed, but two places with lights on the doors were old-style inns, where traveling traders and craftsmen used to stay. One of them was full, but the other one had a small room with a single bed.

"Do you want it or not?" asked the fat woman behind the counter, waving a fan.

He immediately said yes and took out his identity card. The woman took it and made an entry in the register.

"What's your relationship?" the woman asked as she wrote out the entry.

"Husband and wife." He winked at the woman beside him.

"Surname and name?"

"Xu—Ying," she answered after a pause.

"Work unit?"

"She hasn't got work yet, we're going back to Beijing," he answered for her.

"There's a five-*yuan* deposit. It's one *yuan* per day, and the account is settled when you vacate the room."

He paid the money. The woman kept his identity card and came out from behind the counter with a bunch of keys. She opened a small door by the stairs and pulled the light cord inside. A light bulb hung from the sloping ceiling. Having squeezed into this little nook, a storage space under the stairs that had been converted into a small room with a single bed, they couldn't straighten up. At the other end of the room was a washbasin stand and nothing else, not even a chair. The fat woman shuffled off in her slippers, waving her bunch of keys.

He shut the door. He and this woman, Xu Ying, looked at one another.

"I'll go out soon," he said.

"There's no need," the woman said, sitting down on the bed. "It's all right."

It was only then that he took a good look at the woman. She was very pale, so he asked, "Are you very tired? You can lie down and rest."

The woman remained seated and didn't move. Footsteps clattered overhead. Someone came down the stairs, then, outside, there was the sound of splashing water, most likely the person was having a wash in the courtyard. The little room had no window for ventilation, and it was unbearably hot and stuffy.

"Would you like the door open?" he asked.

"No," the woman said.

"Would you like me to get you a basin of water? I'll wash outside," he said.

The woman nodded.

When he came back later on, the woman had washed and combed her hair. She had changed into a round-neck sleeveless top with little yellow flowers, and, shoes off, was sitting on the bed. She had replaited her hair tightly, and the color had returned to her face; she had a girlish look. She bent her knees to leave half the bed clear, and said, "Sit down, there's room here!"

For the first time, the woman smiled. He also smiled, relaxed, and said, "I had to say that." He was, of course, referring to when they registered and he had put them down as husband and wife.

"I understood, of course." The woman's lips scrunched up into a smile.

He then bolted the door, took off his shoes, sat cross-legged at the other end of the bed, and said, "I can't believe it!"

"What?" the woman asked, tilting her head to one side.

"Do you need to ask?"

This woman called Xu Ying again scrunched up her lips into a smile.

Afterward, many years later, when he thought back to that night, there was also flirting, seduction, lust, passion, and love. It was not just a night of terror.

"Was that really your name?" he asked.

"I can't tell you right now."

"Then when will you?"

"You'll know when the time comes. Wait and see."

"See what?"

"Isn't it clear to you yet?"

He stopped talking and felt cozy and comfortable. The footsteps on the stairs had stopped, and there was no more splashing out in the courtyard. A sort of tension began to coalesce, and it was as if something was about to happen. It was only some years later, when he thought back to that time, that he again experienced such a feeling.

"Is it all right to put out the light?" he asked.

"It is a bit too bright," she said.

When he felt his way back to the bed after putting out the light, he bumped her leg, and she immediately moved away but let him lie beside her. He was very careful, and lay on his back very straight on the outside part of the bed. However, in the single bed, their bodies inevitably touched, and, if she didn't move away, he didn't try too hard, either. The woman's clammy warmth and the stifling heat in the room made him sweat all over. In the dark, he could vaguely make out the sloping ceiling that seemed to press down on him and made the heat feel even more oppressive.

"Would it be all right if I took off my clothes?" he asked.

The woman didn't respond, but didn't indicate that she objected. When their bodies touched after he'd removed his shirt and trousers, she didn't move away, but she was obviously not asleep.

"Why are you going to Beijing?" he asked.

"To see my maternal aunt."

Surely this wasn't the time to be visiting relatives? He didn't believe her.

"My aunt works in the Ministry of Health," the woman added.

He said he also worked in a state workplace.

"I know."

"How do you know?"

"When you took out your identity card."

"And do you also know my name?"

"Of course, didn't you register just now?"

In the darkness, he seemed to see, or, rather, sense that the woman had her lips scrunched up in a smile.

"Otherwise, I wouldn't. . . ."

"Be sleeping with me, right?" he said it for her.

"As long as you know!"

He detected something gentle in her voice, and when he unavoidably put his hand on her thigh, she didn't try to move away. But then he thought she trusted him and he didn't dare do anything else.

"Which university are you at?" he asked.

"I've already graduated, I'm waiting to be assigned work," she said, evading his question.

"What did you study?"

"Biology."

"Have you dissected corpses?"

"Of course."

"Including human corpses?"

"I'm not a doctor, my studies are theoretical, but, of course, I've done practical work in hospital laboratories. I'm just waiting to be assigned to a work unit. The project was set up, if it hadn't . . ."

"If it hadn't what? This Cultural Revolution?"

"It had already been settled that I would go to a research institute in Beijing."

"Are your parents cadres?"

"No."

"Then your maternal aunt is a high-ranking official?"

"You want to know everything."

"I don't even know if your name is real or not."

The woman was smiling again; this time, her whole body was shaking, and he could feel it with his hand. He grasped her thigh and could feel her flesh through her trousers.

"I'll tell you," she put her hand on his and shifted it from her thigh as she murmured, "I'll tell you everything. . . ."

He took her hand in his, and it gradually became relaxed, soft.

Banging on the door! It was the front door of the inn.

The two of them went stiff, and, listening with bated breath, tightly clutched one another's hands. There was a commotion, and the front door opened; it was either a night search or a special investigation. A group of people loudly questioned the woman in charge, then went around knocking at each of the downstairs rooms. Some of them went upstairs, and their footsteps resounded above on the wooden steps. A door-to-door search was taking place on both floors. Suddenly, there was a loud thumping noise on the floorboards, someone was running. Shouting and swearing immediately followed, then total chaos. There was a dull thud, like a heavy burlap bag falling to the ground, a man howling, and then a confusion of footsteps. The howling abruptly turned into a piercing scream then gradually faded.

They sat on the bed, their hearts pounding wildly, as they waited for someone to knock on the door. There was another period of agony as the search was repeated upstairs and downstairs. However, no one came to their door, either they had overlooked this small room under the stairs, or the details he gave upon registering meant that he was of no interest to their investigation. The front door was locked, the woman grumbled for a while, then silence prevailed again.

In the darkness, she was suddenly shivering. He swept her trembling body into his arms and kissed her sweaty cheeks and soft lips. Their perspiration and tears mingled as they lay in the bed. He ran his hand over her sweat-covered breasts, unbuttoned her trousers, and put his hand between her legs, she was wet, couldn't move, and let him do whatever he wanted. When he entered her body, the two of them were naked. . . .

Afterward, she said he had taken advantage of her momentary weakness to possess her, it wasn't love. But, he said, she had not resisted. Silent, when they had finished, he touched the sticky fluid between her legs and became anxious. At the time, university students were not permitted to marry, and becoming pregnant and having to get an abortion would bring disaster upon her. However, she put his mind at ease by saying, "I've got my period."

At this, he made love to her again. This time, she held nothing back, and he could feel her thrust herself forward to accept him. He realized that he had changed her from a virgin into a woman: he had had experience with women. However, if she only resented him and did not have tender feelings for him, as the morning sunlight came through the cracks of the door, she would not have let him wash the blood from her thighs with a wet towel, then, afterward, been so loving to him. He remembered, when he knelt on the brick floor and began kissing her erect nipples, that it was she who tightly embraced him and murmured "Don't make them go big" but she lay there on the bed with her eyes closed and again gave herself to him.

At the time, neither could have known what awaited them, or could predict what would follow. It was irrepressible wild passion, he kissed every part of her, and she did not try to stop him. His pent-up tensions violently discharged, and the two of them were covered in blood, but she didn't rebuke him. Afterward, when he came back with a basin of clean water, she asked him to turn around until she had tidied herself up.

She was stopped at the wharf on the river just as he got onto the ferry. They heard at the inn that trains were running but that people were only being allowed out of the station, not into the station. Those wanting to board the train had to take the ferry to the other side of the river, so a huge number of passengers had amassed at the wharf. A heavy morning mist clung to the river, and the sun was a red ball in the sky. It was like a painting of the Judgment Day. On the ferry, a sailor with a round-neck shirt and a badge on his chest shouted through a hand-held loudspeaker, "Let the nonlocal travelers get on first! Nonlocals should present their work identity cards and get on first!"

The crowd squeezing onto the wharf was not in a line, and, suddenly, there was chaos. The two of them became separated, and when he called out her name, the name she had used to register at the inn, she didn't answer to it. He still had her bag, which she had pushed into his hand. Maybe she wanted to get rid of the bag, for it contained her student card and that dossier of requests for help printed by her workplace. He was shoved onto the deck, but anyone who couldn't produce nonlocal identification was stopped on the wharf. She, with her two short plaits, was squashed in the jostling crowd. He looked down from the railing of the deck and shouted out to her again. It was still her made-up name, and she seemed not to have heard and just stood there in a daze, maybe she didn't understand in time that he was calling to her. The ferry drew away from the wharf.

31

A vast quagmire, reeds growing here and there, you're in a quagmire, you reek of stinking mud and want to crawl somewhere dry so you can stand up, you wash yourself, even your face, with the water lying on top of the mud, clearly knowing you won't be able to wash yourself clean, somehow you've got to get out of this swamp, you jump as hard as you can but still land in swampy water, you somersault and get yourself into a worse mess, muddy and wet, you have to crawl on. . . .

A faint glow in the distance, there seems to be a light, you head for it, that is, you crawl toward it, light is coming through a crack, it's a house, there's a door, you crawl to the threshold, reach for the door, it suddenly opens, you hear wind but there's no wind, the large hall has a circle of light, you crawl into the circle of light, you finally stand up, it's a solid timber floor, then you find—fuck!—not a thing at all, you can't see a thing. . . .

You need to adopt a posture, so you don't move, turn into a statue.

You need to be like a thread of gossamer, drift in the air, gradually disappear like clouds.

You need to be like a thorny branch on a jujube tree, like leaves frozen purple on a tallow tree in early winter.

You need to wade across a stream, need to hear bare feet squelching on cobblestones.

You need to drag heavy memories out of a vat of dye, make the floor wet.

You need a stark, white stage with bright lights, so that he and a woman, both naked, can roll about as everyone looks on.

You need to look down at them from high up, show your gaping eye sockets, two black holes.

You need to see the dark shadows of the bright, round moon in the lonely sky behind this door.

You need to couple with a she-wolf, put your heads up together and howl.

You need to take light quick steps, di-di-da, di-di-da, and pirouette right here.

You hope your dancer, he, will thrash and leap about like a fish out of water.

You hope a cruel hand will seize that big, slippery, thrashing fish, slash it open with a knife, yet you don't want it to die just like that.

You need a soprano voice using the highest pitch to narrate a forgotten story, like your childhood.

You need to be in darkness, like a sinking ship slowly entering the seabed, and you want to see a profusion of bubbles rising serenely and soundlessly.

You need to turn into a fish with a big head and swim about in the reeds, swishing your tail and moving your head.

You want to be a sorrowful eye, penetrating and grieving, an eye observing the world as it turns this way and that, and this eye is in the palm of your hand.

You want to be a multitude of sounds, a velvety alto teased out from its midst and set against a wall of sounds.

You want to be a piece of jazz, flowing but unpredictable, passionate and yet so smooth. Then you abruptly strike an odd posture, adopt a scary expression with an ambiguous smile, an enigmatic smile that solidifies, then turns wooden and stiff. Afterward, you calmly slide out, turn into a mud fish, and leave that odd smile on that atrophied face. The mouth opens and reveals two tobacco-stained front teeth, or, maybe, they are two fitted front teeth that are shining with a golden glow on that joyful, smiling, atrophied face. All this will also be a lot of fun.

You want to be the little boy pissing in a small square in the center of Brussels. Young boys and girls, taking turns, crane their necks so that the spring water he pisses collects in their mouths. Some other girls stand on the side, cackling with laughter. However, you are an old man sitting in a café, watching them, a very old man whose deeply wrinkled face looks the same whether he is laughing or not. You take a sip of the sweet ale that is as dark as soy sauce.

You want to weep and wail in front of everyone, but don't make a sound. People won't know what you are weeping about, won't know whether you are really weeping or whether you are acting, but you want to have a good cry in front of this playacting world. Not making a sound, of course, you mime that you are weeping, and get the honorable members of the audience to look on helplessly. Next, you rip open your shirt and take out a plastic red heart. Then, from it, you take out a handful of straw or toilet paper and throw it to those willing to applaud. You strut about with an elegant gait, and then, then slip and fall and can't get up. You have had a heart attack on stage. Really, you don't need to be saved. It's just theater to show suffering, joy, grief, and lust. And then, with a crafty smile that could be a laugh or a grimace, you quietly slip off with a young woman. You have just met, but she has won your heart, and you make love standing up in the lavatory. People can only see your legs, her legs are around your waist. Then you noisily flush the toilet. You want to flush yourself like this, to cleanse yourself, so that the world will weep, so that the windows of the world will be washed with rain, so that the world will turn all hazy, so hazy that it could either be rain or mist. You then stand at the window and watch snowflakes falling soundlessly outside. Snow covers the whole city like a huge white shroud wrapping corpses, and you, by the window, mourn his loss of his self. . . .

Or, for a different perspective, it is you in the audience, watching him crawl onto the stage, a deserted stage. He is standing naked in the bright light, and it will take a little time for him to get used to it, to see past the stage lights, and to see you sitting in the red velvet seat in the last row of the empty theater.

32

The bag the girl left with him had a student card in it. Xu was, in fact, her surname, but her given name was Qian. There were also some pamphlets and reports on the crisis. She could have been heading for Beijing to file a complaint, but all this was public printed matter, so maybe she was just going to Beijing to get out of danger and had given him her bag because she was afraid of being identified.

He had no way of knowing what had happened to Xu Qian and all he could do was search for news about the city from posters and pamphlets posted in the streets. He rode his bicycle along Chang'an Avenue from Dongdan to Xidan, to the railway station at Qianmenwai, and then to the gate at the back of Beihai, and he read through each of the crisis notices about armed battles in the provinces that were posted everywhere. There were reports about massacres, shootings, and brutal tortures, even photographs of corpses, and these all seemed somehow related to Xu Qian. He was certain that disaster had already befallen her, and could not help feeling an acute sense of pain.

The bag, also containing Xu Qian's sleeveless round-neck top with little yellow flowers, which still smelled of her, and the blood-stained underpants she had rolled into a ball, seemed to have become a relic that gave him twinges of pain deep in his heart. It was as if he had developed some sort of fetish, and he kept shifting about the contents of the bag. He even took off the red plastic cover from the copy of Mao's *Sayings*, where he found a slip of paper with an old address on it. The name Boundless Great Men Hutong had already been changed to Red Star Hutong, and it probably was the home of her maternal aunt. He charged out the door but, thinking he would appear too presumptuous, returned to his room, stuffed all the things on the table back into the bag, and took it with him, leaving behind only the top and underpants she had worn that night.

At ten o'clock at night, he knocked on the gate of a house with a courtyard and got them to open up. A sturdy young fellow who stood blocking the entrance gruffly asked, "Who are you looking for?"

He said that he wanted to see the maternal aunt of Xu Qian. The young fellow scowled and was clearly hostile. He thought of mentioning his Red Guard lineage, but that strong impulse vanished, and he said coldly, "I've come to convey a message and to deliver something to her aunt."

At this, the other party said to wait, and closed the gate. After a while, the young fellow came back and opened the door. He was with an elderly woman. The woman looked him over and politely asked what could he have to tell her. He took out Xu Qian's student card and said he had something to hand over to her.

"Please come in," the woman said.

The northern room directly facing the courtyard was in disarray but retained the style of a senior cadre's reception hall.

"Are you her maternal aunt?" he asked.

The only response seemed to be a nod, as she got him to sit down on the sofa.

He said that her niece—presumably, it was her niece—was stopped on the wharf and couldn't get on the ferry. The aunt looked through the pile of pamphlets. He said it was very tense in the city, machine guns were being used, and there were night searches. Xu Qian clearly belonged to the faction they were searching for.

"Why are they rebelling!" the aunt exclaimed, or, maybe, asked, as she put the pamphlets on a low table.

He explained he was worried that something might have happened to Xu Qian.

"Are you her boyfriend?"

"No." He wanted to say that he was.

There was a lapse of silence, so he got up and said, "I just came to let you know. Of course, I hope nothing has happened and she is safe."

"I'll get in touch with her parents."

"I don't have her home address," he mustered the courage to say.

"I will write to her family."

The aunt clearly didn't intend to give him the address, so he could only say, "I can leave the address and telephone number of my work unit."

The old woman gave him a piece of paper to write on, then escorted him to the gate. As she locked it on the other side, she said, "You know this place, you're welcome to come again."

She was just being polite in response to his unnecessary act of kindness.

Back in his room, he lay on his bed and tried to remember every detail of what had happened that night, every word Xu Qian had spoken. Her voice in the dark and the responsiveness of her body were now etched in his mind.

There was knocking on his door. It was a cadre from his faction. Huang came in and asked, "When did you get back? I've been here several times, looking for you. You haven't shown up at the workplace, what have you been up to? You can't keep on being so carefree! They are beating up the cadres one at a time, and are breaking up our meetings!"

"When did this start?" he asked.

"This afternoon. They have already started fighting!"

"Has anyone been hurt?"

Huang said Danian's gang beat up the section chief in charge of accounts in the finance office and broke the man's ribs when they kicked him. It was because he had a capitalist family background. The cadres who showed support for his faction have all been threatened. Huang's background as a petty trader was also bad, even though he had been a Party member for almost twenty years.

"If you can't protect the cadres who are supporting you, your faction will be crushed!" Huang was agitated.

"I withdrew from the command unit a long time ago and only do survey work," he said.

"But everyone wants you to come and take charge. Big Li and the others don't realize that they have to protect the cadres. Everyone is from the old society. Whose family or relatives don't have some problem? They have announced a big meeting to haul out and denounce Old Liu and Comrade Wang Qi. If your crowd doesn't stop them, none of the cadres will dare to join forces with your crowd. I'm not the only one who thinks this, and Old Liu and a number of middle-ranking cadres have sent me to find you. We all have faith in you and support you. You must come forward to hold them off!"

The cadres were also forming their alliances behind the scenes, and the struggle for power had resulted in everyone forming gangs and factions just to survive. He had been chosen by the cadres behind his faction, and was again being pushed center stage.

"My wife also asked me to talk to you. We've got a small child, and, if we're branded as something or other, what will happen to our child?" Huang looked hopefully at him.

He knew Huang's wife. She worked in the same department, and it was hard not to be sympathetic. Maybe he was upset about having lost Xu Qian. Her being intercepted, and the humiliation he imagined she would have to suffer, had again triggered off his feelings of righteous indignation. His innate feeling of sympathy and compassion for the powerless or threatened generated an impulse that drew on his lingering heroism. Probably because his spine hadn't been broken, he refused to allow himself to be defeated. That night, he sought out Little Yu and persuaded him that the cadres supporting them had to be protected. Yu immediately went off to see Big Li. That night, he didn't sleep, but went out to enlist several other youths.

Early the next morning, at five o'clock, he went to the *hutong* where Wang Qi lived, and checked out the number of the house. The nail-studded old-style gate was shut tight. It was quiet in the *hutong*, and no one was around, although the breakfast vendor at the entrance to the *hutong* was already open for business. He drank a bowl of very hot soy milk and ate a fried bun, fresh out of the oil, but still didn't see a familiar face. It was only after he had bought his second bowl of soy milk and eaten another fried bun, that Big Li arrived on his bicycle. He waved and called out to him. Big Li got off his bicycle and shook his hand like an old friend.

"You're back? We really need you," Big Li said, then went up close and said quietly, "Old Liu's been relocated, he's been hidden. When they get there, they won't find anyone."

Looking quite haggard, Big Li was obviously sincere; their former rivalry had suddenly vanished. Their relationship was very much like that of the children's gangs in the lanes and alleys, but with an additional element of loyalty. However, the hypocrisy that existed in comrade relationships was absent. In this chaotic world, gangs and groups had to be formed so that there was something for people to rely on.

Big Li added, "I've contacted a fire-fighting detachment, the chief is a good friend, if there's a fight, I'll only have to make a phone call, and a whole bunch of firefighters will be there in their fire engine.

They'll turn their hoses on what goes hard between the legs of those guys!"

At about six o'clock, Little Yu and six or seven youths from the workplace arrived at the entrance of the *hutong*, and they went up together to Wang Qi's gate where they stood leaning on their bikes and dangling cigarettes in their lips. Two small cars entered the *hutong* and stopped more than thirty meters away, they were cars from the workplace but no one got out. They confronted one another like this for four or five minutes, then the cars reversed, turned around, and drove off.

"Let's go in and see Comrade Wang Qi," he said.

Big Li hesitated and said, "Her husband's a reactionary."

"It's not her husband we're coming to see." He led them in.

The former bureau chief came out to greet them and said over and over, "Thank you for coming, comrades. Come in and sit down, come in and sit down!"

Wang Qi's husband, former theorist for the Party and now an anti-Party reactionary rejected by the Party, a small, thin, old man, acknowledged them with a nod. The doors of the two adjoining rooms had seals pasted on them, and there was nowhere for him to go, so he just paced back and forth, chain-smoking and coughing.

"Comrades, you probably haven't eaten. I'll go and make some breakfast," Wang Qi said.

"There's no need, we've just eaten at the entrance to the *hutong*. Comrade Wang Qi, we've only dropped in for a visit. Their cars have gone, and they won't be coming back," he said.

"Then let me make some tea for all of you. . . ." She was a woman, after all; this former bureau chief held back tears as she quickly turned away.

Just like that, things inexplicably changed, and he was protecting the wife of an "anti-Party reactionary." When Wang Qi was in her job, she had cautioned him for having too close a relationship with

Lin, but that pressure had dissipated long ago, and, compared with the string of events that had happened since, hardly counted as anything. Nevertheless, he was grateful to her for being lenient and not following up on his affair with Lin. Now, it could be said, he had repaid her.

While he, Big Li and the others drank tea made by the revolutionary cadre Wang Qi, the wife of a reactionary, they held a meeting on the spot and resolved to establish a dare-to-die group with those present forming the core members. If Danian's crowd tried to haul out and denounce their cadres, they would go forth and protect them.

Nevertheless, when armed fighting broke out, Wang Qi was hauled out by Danian's mob, and was to be denounced in the office. The corridors were crammed, and the office turned into a battlefield, with people jumping onto the desks and shattering the plate-glass covers on them. He couldn't retreat and was pushed inside, so he also stood on a desk to confront Danian.

"Drag him down, that fuckin' offspring of a bitch!" Danian ordered his mob of old Red Guards, not attempting to disguise their genealogical enmity.

He knew that if he showed any sign of weakness, they would set upon him and beat him up until they had maimed him. They would then dig up everything in his father's unsettled case to trump up a charge of class revenge against him. The people in his faction, inside and outside the office, were mostly gentle, frail, elderly bureaucrats and intellectuals, and most of the cadres were also from literary backgrounds. All of their families had problems, like his own. They certainly wouldn't be able to save him and moreover, wanted young people like him to come forward to oppose Danian's faction.

"Hey, listen! Danian, I'm warning you, we've got a gang, too, and the guys in our gang aren't short of fuel to burn. Any of you dare to make a move, and we'll serve up the whole lot of you on a platter tonight! You can believe us or not!" he, too, roared out.

When people become animals, their primitive instincts return;

wolves and dogs both bare their teeth. He had to be menacing, his eyes had to look fierce, and he had to make this quite clear to the other party. He was a desperado who was capable of anything, and, at that time, he probably looked very much like a bandit.

There was the sound of fire-engine sirens down below. Big Li had got help just in time. The helmeted fire-fighting detachment, followed by the brother rebel group from the print factory in a truck, had arrived. They entered the building with a big flag in a show of might. Each faction had its own strategies, and this was how armed battles flared up in the universities, factories, and workplaces. If they were backed by the army then guns and cannons were deployed.

33

He first read it in a stenciled pamphlet. Mao had received the rebel-faction heads of the five universities of Beijing in the Great Hall of the People, and said, "You, little generals, have now committed errors." It was like the emperor saying to his generals that it was now time for them to step down. The "little general" Kuai Dafu, who had distinguished himself in purging old revolutionary warriors on behalf of the Commander-in-Chief, proving himself as a student leader, immediately understood the implications and broke into tears. The old man had used a poster at Peking University to ignite the flames of the Cultural Revolution, and now, to extinguish that mass movement he had initiated, he again started on a university campus. Half a million workers directed by Mao's security corps drove onto the campus of Tsinghua University.

That afternoon, on hearing this news, he rushed there and was witness to workers, led by army personnel, taking the solitary building opposite the gymnasium, the last stronghold of the earliest university rebel group, the Jinggang Mountain Militia. Worker propaganda teams, wearing red armbands, sat on the ground side by side, in circle upon circle around the building and the sports field, for a considerable distance. In the last rays of the setting sun, two big red banners were lowered from the windows of the top floor. Written on them in black were the words: "Plum blossoms flower in the snow unvanquished, Jinggang Mountain people are brave enough to ascend the scaffold!" Each of the words was larger than a window, and the banners stretching several floors down swayed in the wind. A group of forty or fifty army personnel and workers crossed the space in front of the building, went up the steps to the main door, then, after a while, finally went in and cut off the water and electricity. He mingled with the crowd of thousands of workers and onlookers watching in silence, and he could hear the two banners flapping in the wind.

After almost an hour, the big red banner on the right dropped from the top of the building and slowly floated down. As it fell on the stairs at the front of the building, the other banner also dropped. Instantly, shouts of "long live" went up from the crowds. Then the loudspeakers, drums, and cymbals of the worker propaganda teams started up in full force. The students who had also shouted "long live" when they were rebelling, now held a white flag as they filed out like surrendering prisoners of war with their hands raised and head bowed. An even larger number of workers entered the building, dragging out several heavy machine guns, as well as wheeling out a flat trajectory gun that didn't seem to have any ammunition.

It was a simple takeover, although on the previous night, when the worker propaganda team drove onto the campus, students had thrown a homemade hand grenade in the dark and injured several workers. This was probably an act of frustration. The Great Leader they were protecting had finished using them and had discarded them. Children discovering an adult has tricked them throw tantrums; it was nothing more than that.

He realized that the chaos would soon come to an end, and could see that his own fate would not be any better. So, on the pretext of doing a survey, he immediately left Beijing again.

"Go back!"

When he visited his maternal uncle on his way through Shanghai, he received his first warning.

"Go back where?" he asked. He told his uncle about his problem, the unsettled case of his father's hidden gun. "Even if I had a home, I wouldn't be able to go back!"

Hearing this, his uncle started coughing, and, taking out his inhaler, sprayed it down his throat.

"Go back to your workplace and just get on with your job!"

"The whole workplace is paralyzed and there's nothing to do. So, by saying that I was conducting an investigation, I was able to leave Beijing and do a bit of traveling."

"What investigation?"

"Aren't they investigating old cadres? I've investigated the histories of some old cadres and have discovered that it's not at all so—"

"What do you know? This is no game, you're not a child anymore, don't lose your head without knowing how you lost it!"

His uncle wanted to cough again, and sprayed his inhaler down his throat again.

"It's impossible to read anything, and there's nothing to do."

"Observe, can't you observe?" His uncle said, "I'm an observer. I close my door and don't go out. I don't join any faction and just watch the circular enactment of people rising to power and falling from power."

"But I have to go to work. I'm not like you, Uncle, you can stay at home because you have to convalesce," he said.

"You can keep your mouth shut, can't you?" his uncle retorted. "Your mouth is on your own head!"

"Uncle, you've been convalescing at home for a long time. You don't know that once a campaign starts, you have to take a stance. It's impossible not to get swept up in it!"

This old revolutionary uncle of his, of course, knew very well, and gave a long sigh. "These are chaotic times. In the past, people could hide in the old forests on remote mountains or go to a monastery and become monks. . . ."

Only then was his uncle quite frank with him: it was the first time they discussed politics together. No longer treating him as a child, his uncle said, "I've had to use my illness to escape the winds of political change. Following the Great Leap Forward, antirightist tendencies in the inner Party became entrenched, and since then, I have stood aside. I've not involved myself with what has been happening for seven or eight years, and only through this have I been able to prolong my feeble life."

His uncle also spoke about his former commander, Yuan, who was in the upper echelons of the Party. During the Civil War, he and Yuan were willing to die for one another. On the eve of the Cultural Revolution, Yuan paid him a visit when passing through. He sent the guard outside and told his uncle, "Something big is about to happen in the Party Center, and it is unlikely that we will meet again." He left behind a brocaded bedcover and said it was to commemorate their final farewell.

"Tell your father that no one can save anyone; get him to do whatever he can to protect himself!"

These were the last words his uncle said to him as he escorted him to the door. Not too long afterward, this uncle, who was not very old, came down with influenza and was admitted to the army hospital where he had an injection. A few hours later, he was wheeled into the morgue. His former commander, that revolutionary Yuan Xun, who had been incarcerated, also died a year later in the army hospital. But it was many years later that he read about this in a memorial article exonerating Yuan. As revolutionaries in those very early days, they could not have imagined that, even without making a bid to seize power, they, too, would see themselves staring death in the face because of the revolution. It was impossible to know whether or not they had regrets.

*   *   *

Then why did you rebel? Did you go up to the grinding machine to ensure that there would be plenty of mincemeat filling for pancakes? Looking back on those times, you can't help asking him.

He says he had no choice, circumstances did not allow a person to be a dispassionate observer, and he knew he was just a pawn in the movement. He suffered terribly, not because he was fighting for the Commander-in-Chief, but simply in order to exist.

Then couldn't you have found some other means for just surviving? For example, by simply being an obedient citizen, going with the flow, living for today and not being concerned about tomorrow, changing with the political climate, saying what people wanted to hear, pledging allegiance to whoever was in power? you ask.

He says that was even harder, it needed much more effort than being a rebel. It needed much more thinking; one needed to be constantly working out the unpredictable weather, and could a person accurately predict heaven's temperament and mood? His father was one of the common people and he did just that, and when it came to the crunch, he ended up swallowing a bottle of sleeping pills. His father's demise was not very different from his old revolutionary maternal uncle's. There was no clear goal to his rebelling. It was simply due to his instinct to live, but he was like a praying mantis putting up a foreleg to stop a cart.

Then, perhaps, you were born a rebel, or at least born with a rebellious streak?

No, he says, he was gentle by nature, like his father. It was just that he was young, at an impressionable age, and very inexperienced. He couldn't follow the road of his father's generation, but didn't know what road to take.

Couldn't you have escaped?

Where could he escape to, he asks you instead. He couldn't escape from this huge country, and he couldn't leave that big beehive-like workplace where he got his salary. That beehive allocated his city residence permit, his monthly grain coupons (fourteen kilos), oil coupons (half a kilo), sugar coupons (quarter of a kilo), meat coupons (half a kilo). It also issued his annual fabric coupons (nine meters), his salary scale–based industrial certificates (2.05 certificates) for buying a watch, a bicycle, or everyday commodities such as wool, and even determined his citizen status. If he, this worker-bee, left the beehive, where could he fly? He says there was no other option, he was just a bee whose refuge was this hive. As the hive was infected with madness, what else was there to do except wildly buzz around, attacking one another?

But did wildly buzzing around save your life? you ask.

He was already buzzing around. If he'd known all this earlier, he wouldn't have been an insect. He smiles sardonically.

An insect that can smile is somehow grotesque. You go right up to take a good look at him.

It's the world that is grotesque, not the insect that has taken refuge in the hive, the insect says.

34

Beyond the pass at Shanhaiguan it got cold early, and he had run into chilly winds blowing down from the northwest. The bicycle, hired in the county town, was impossible to ride against the wind, and even pushing it was hard. At four o'clock in the afternoon it was already dark, when he reached the place where the commune was located, but the village he was going to was a further ten kilometers away. He decided to stay the night in the cart station, where the peasants stopped for a break with their donkey- and horse-carts. He forced himself to eat a bowl of hard sorghum along with the two strips of salted turnip that had gone bitter, then stretched out on the woven rush mat on the earthen *kang*. In weather like this, the villagers didn't take their carts out, so he had to himself a communal *kang* that could accommodate seven or eight people. His letter of introduction from the nation's capital seemed to have made an impression, because a special effort had been made to heat the *kang* for him. However, as the night wore on, it got so hot that the lice on him were probably oozing oil. Even after he had taken off everything except his underpants, he was still sweating, so he got up, sat on the edge of the *kang*, and smoked, as he pondered the real possibility of seeking refuge somewhere in a village during these chaotic times.

He was up early. There was still a strong north wind, so, leaving the clumsy, heavy-duty bicycle at the cart station, he set off on foot against the wind, and, after three hours, arrived at the village. He asked from house to house whether there was an elderly woman with such-and-such a surname who was a primary school teacher. People all shook their heads. There was a primary school in the village with one teacher, a man, but his wife had given birth and he had gone home to look after her.

"Who else is at the school?" he asked.

"There hasn't been a class for more than two years. It wasn't really a school, so the production brigade converted it into a storehouse. It's piled high with sweet potatoes!" the villagers said.

At this point, he asked for the Party secretary of the production brigade, to get someone in charge.

"The old one or the young one?"

He said he wanted a villager who was in charge, so, naturally, the old one was better, he would be sure to know about things. He was taken there. The old man, a bamboo pipe clamped in his teeth, was weaving a rattan basket. Without letting him explain why he had come, the old man mumbled, "I'm not in charge, I'm not in charge!"

It was only after he said that he had come specially from Beijing to carry out an investigation, that the old man became respectful and put down his work. Holding the bronze bowl of his pipe and exposing his brown-black teeth, his eyes narrowed as he listened to him explain the situation.

"Oh, yes, there is such a person, the wife of old man Liang. She taught at the primary school, but she retired because of illness, a long time ago. People have been here to investigate her, but her husband is a shadow-play singer with a poor-peasant family background, so there weren't any problems!"

He explained that he was looking for this old man's wife because he was doing an investigation on another person, that it didn't actually concern the woman herself. At this, the old man took him to a house on the outskirts of the village. At the front door, he shouted out, "Old man Liang, your wife!"

There was no answer. The old man pushed open the door. No one was there, so, turning to the village children who had followed behind, he said, "Go quickly and fetch her, a comrade from Beijing is waiting for her in the house!"

The children dashed off, shouting as they ran. The old man also left.

The walls of the main room were gray-black from smoke, just like the square table and two wooden benches, the only furniture in the room. The kitchen adjoined, but the fire was not burning, so, feeling extremely cold, he sat down. It was gloomy outside, although the wind had died down. He stamped his feet trying to get warm, but, after a long wait, there was still no sign of anyone.

He thought about his waiting in this destitute, faraway village for the former wife of a high official. What could have made her settle in this village? Why had she become the wife of a poor peasant, a shadow-play singer? But what did this have to do with him? It was simply to delay his return to Beijing.

After almost two hours, an old woman appeared. Seeing him inside the house, she hesitated, stopped, but finally came in. The old woman wore a gray scarf around her head, a dark-gray padded jacket, an old pair of padded crotchless overtrousers that puffed out because they were tied at the ankles, and a pair of grimy black padded shoes. Could this genuine old peasant woman be the revolutionary hero of those times, who had been educated at a prestigious university and had worked in intelligence? He got to his feet and asked if she was Comrade Such-and-Such.

"No such person!" the old woman instantly said with a dismissive wave.

This gave him a shock, but he went on to ask, "Are you also known as . . . ?" He repeated the name.

"My surname is the same as my husband's, Liang!"

"Is your husband a shadow-play singer?" he asked.

"He's very old and stopped singing a long time ago."

"Is he here?" he asked cautiously.

"He's out. Who, in fact, are you looking for?" the old woman retorted, as she took off her scarf and put it on the table.

"Forty years ago, did you stay in Sichuan? Did you know someone called . . . ?" He said the name of the high official.

The woman's eyes lit up, but her sagging eyelids immediately drooped again. Those were not the eyes of an ignorant village woman.

"You even had a child by him!" Having blurted this out, he had to calm the woman.

"The child died a long time ago," the woman said, as she rested her hands on the table and sat down on the bench.

It was her. He felt he should try to console her, "You did much work for the Party, but old revolutionaries—"

The woman cut him short, "I didn't do anything, I just cared for my husband and gave birth to a daughter."

"Your husband of that time was secretary of a special zone of the underground Party, surely you were aware of this?"

"I wasn't a member of the Communist Party!"

"But your husband, your husband at the time, was involved in the secret activities of the Party. Surely you knew about this?"

"I didn't," she insisted.

"It was you who covered his escape and, by giving a secret signal, also helped his contact to escape and not get arrested. You were very brave!"

"I don't know anything about this, I didn't do anything," she adamantly denied.

"Do I need to provide you with details to help you remember?

You lived on the first floor, and there was a rattan fan hanging at the window overlooking the street. At the time, you went to the window and took down the fan, you were holding a baby in your arms. . . ." He waited for her response.

"I don't remember any of that." The old woman closed her eyes and ignored him.

He went on coaxing her, "There are testimonies from the people involved, written documents. Your husband, your former husband, escaped by climbing from the clothes-drying porch at the back. He has written a statement on this, it was a meritorious act that you carried out for the revolution."

The woman snorted and gave a little laugh.

"You covered your husband's escape, but you yourself were arrested by undercover spies lying in ambush!" he exclaimed with a sigh. This was a ploy often used in investigations.

Her eyes wide-open, the woman suddenly asked in a loud voice, "If you know everything, why are you carrying out this investigation?"

At this he explained, "Don't get upset, you're not under investigation and neither is your former husband. You covered his escape, so he wasn't arrested, all that is clearly documented. What I want to find out about is the other underground Party member. He was later arrested, had nothing to do with you, but was put in the same prison. How did he get out? According to his statement, the Party organization saved him. Could you tell me something about the situation?"

"I've already told you, I was not a Party member, so don't ask me whether or not the Party saved him."

"I'm asking about the situation in the prison. For example, when a person was released, were certain procedures adopted?"

"Why don't you go and ask the guards at the prison? Go and ask the Nationalist Party! I was a woman locked in a big prison while still nursing a baby at my breast!"

The woman lost her temper and started banging the table like an old village woman in a fit of rage.

Of course, he, too, could have lost his temper. At the time, the relationship between an investigator and a person being investigated was like an interrogation: like between a judge and the accused, or even between a warden and the prisoner. However, he forced himself to say calmly that he had not come to investigate how she came to be released. He was asking her to provide information on general procedures at the prison. For example, were there special procedures for the release of political prisoners?

"I was not a political prisoner!" the woman said categorically.

He said he was willing to believe that she was not a member of the Party and that she had been implicated because of her husband, he believed all this. But he did not want to, and there was no need for him to, have difficulties with her. However, since he had come to carry out an investigation, he asked her to make a statement.

"If you don't know anything about it, then just write that you don't know. I'm sorry I've disturbed you, and the investigation will finish here." He first made this quite clear.

"I can't write anything," the woman said.

"Weren't you a teacher? And, it seems, that you also went to university."

"There's nothing to write." She refused.

In other words, she was not willing to leave any documentation about that part of her life. It was because she did not want people to know her background that she had hidden herself in this village to spend the rest of her days with a peasant shadow-play singer, he thought.

"Have you ever tried to see him?" He was asking about her former husband, the high official.

The woman declined to comment.

"Does he know you're still alive?"

The woman remained silent and made no response. He could do nothing more, so he capped his pen and put it into his pocket.

"When did your child die?" he asked as a matter of course, as he got up.

"In prison, it was just one month old. . . ." The old woman abruptly stopped and also got up from the bench.

He did not pursue the matter, and put on his padded gloves. The old woman silently escorted him out the door. He nodded his head to her in farewell.

When he got to the dirt road with two deep wheel ruts and looked back, the old woman was still standing at the door, without her scarf. Seeing him turn, she went back inside the house.

On his way back, the wind changed; this time it blew in from the northeast. It began snowing more and more heavily, so that, with the grain harvested, everything became a vast bare plain. The snowflakes filling the sky came straight at him, and it was hard to keep his eyes open, but he got back to the cart station before dark and collected the rented bicycle he had left there. Although he didn't have to get back to the county town that night, for some reason, he quickly got on the bicycle. The dirt road and the fields were blanketed in thick snow, and he could barely make out the road. The wind blew from behind, sweeping the snow in all directions, but, at least, it was blowing in the right direction. Gripping the handlebars tightly, he bounced up and down in the snow-covered ruts of the road. From time to time, the bicycle and the rider would fall into the snow, but he would pick himself up and get back on the bicycle to continue on, unsteadily. Lashed up by the wind, it was all swirling snow before him, everything was a vast expanse of gray. . . .

35

"You clown!" the former lieutenant colonel rebuked him, but he was now the favorite of the Army Control Commission. He was also the deputy leader of the team in charge of purifying class ranks, although, of course, army personnel were actually in charge.

You really were a clown. You were a bean made to jump helplessly in the all-embracing sieve of the totalitarian dictatorship, but you didn't jump out of the sieve, because you didn't want to get smashed up.

You had to welcome being controlled by army personnel, just like you had to take part in the parades to cheer each of Mao's latest string of directives released on the radio news at night. As soon as the slogans had been written, people assembled, formed ranks, and began marching on the streets, usually until midnight. To gongs and drums and the shouting of slogans, one contingent after another marched across Chang'an Avenue from the west, as one contingent after another marched across from the east, each on parade for the other. You had also to be enthusiastic and not let others see that you were worried.

You certainly were a clown, otherwise you would have been "dog shit, less than human." Those were Old Man Mao's own words of warning, to draw a line of demarcation between the people and the enemy. Faced with choosing between being dog shit and being a clown, you chose to be a clown. You loudly sang the army song, "Three Main Rules of Discipline and Eight Points for Attention." Like a soldier, you stood to attention before the portrait of the Commander-in-Chief that hung in the middle of the main wall of every office, and, holding high a red plastic-covered copy of Mao's *Sayings*, you shouted "long live" three times. After the implementation of army control, all this was compulsory daily ritual at the start and finish of work. It was called "seeking instructions in the morning" and "reporting at night."

At such times, you had to be careful not to laugh! Otherwise there would have been dire consequences, unless you were prepared to be a counterrevolutionary and hoped that at some future date you'd become a martyr. The former lieutenant colonel was absolutely correct, he was a clown, but he didn't dare to laugh. It is only you of the present, who recalling those times, can laugh, although you find that you can't.

He was the representative of a group of people's organizations in a ferret-out team controlled by army personnel. When that group of masses and cadres chose him, he knew that his judgment day had come. However, the masses and cadres of the group that looked to him for support did not know that that single item in his file, his father's having "hidden a gun," could see him purged from that one big revolutionary family.

At the meeting of the ferret-out team, Officer Zhang read aloud an "internal control" list—that is, a list of persons on whom internal control was to be carried out. This was the first time he had heard the term, and it gave him a shock. The "internal control" was not directed only at ordinary workers, but included certain Party cadres. The ferreting-out was to start with "bad people" who had infiltrated people's organizations. This was no longer the Red Guard violence of two years ago, or the armed fighting between factions of people's organizations. It was now leisurely, and directed by army personnel, and, like a strategic plan of war, it was planned, coordinated, and fought in stages. The Army Control Commission had removed the seals from the personnel files, and in front of Officer Zhang were piles of materials on people with "problems."

"All of you here are representatives of people's organizations. Comrades, I hope all of you will rid yourselves of any capitalist-class factional feelings, and purge any bad elements who have infiltrated your organizations. We can have only one standpoint, and that is the standpoint of the proletariat. Factional standpoints are not allowed! We will discuss each of these cases, decide whom to put in the first list and whom to put in the second list. Of course, there is also a third list, and whether they are dealt with leniently or harshly depends on whether those persons take the initiative to admit their crimes, and on how they conduct themselves in confessions and disclosures!"

Officer Zhang had a wide face and a square jaw. His eyes swept over the representatives of the various people's organizations as he jabbed a thick finger at the big pile of documents. Then, removing the cover on his cup, he began to drink his tea and to smoke.

He cautiously raised some questions, but only because Officer Zhang had said discussions were allowed. He asked what problems Liu, his former superior and department chief, had apart from a landlord family background? Also, there was a woman bureau chief who, back in those times, had been an underground Party member and organizer of student movements. According to the findings of his group, she had never been arrested, and there were no suspicions of her having been anti-Party or having capitulated to the enemy. Why had she also been listed for special investigation? Officer Zhang turned to him, raised the hand holding the cigarette, and gave him a look. That was when the former lieutenant colonel had rebuked him: "You clown!"

Several decades later, you were able to read a number of memoirs that gradually shed light on the internal struggles within the Chinese Communist Party. At the Political Bureau meetings, Mao Zedong probably gave his generals a look like this if they so much as offered the slightest dissent, then went on smoking and drinking his tea. Other generals would come forth to rebuke them. It was not necessary for the old man to say anything.

You, of course, were not a general. The former lieutenant colonel also yelled at him, "You insect!" Quite right, you were a very small insect. What was your ant's life worth anyway?

After work, he went to get his bicycle from the shed downstairs and ran into Liang Qin, who worked in his office. When he had rebelled two years earlier, it was Liang Qin who had taken over his work. But his life as a rebel had ended. Seeing no one around, he said to Liang, "Go on ahead, but after the intersection slow down. There's something I want to talk to you about."

Liang went off on his bicycle and, afterwards, he caught up.

"Come to my home for a drink," Liang said.

"Who else will be there?" he asked.

"My wife and son!"

"No, it wouldn't be convenient. Let's just cycle and talk like this."

"What is it?" Liang had immediately sensed that something was wrong.

"Do you have any problems in your background?" He didn't look at Liang and asked the question as if it was nothing of importance.

"No!" Liang almost fell off his bicycle.

"Have you ever contacted anyone abroad?"

"I don't have any relatives abroad!"

"Have you ever written letters to anyone abroad?"

"Wait! Let me think. . . ."

There was another red light, and they each put a foot on the ground and stopped their bicycles.

"Yes, I have. People at the workplace asked me about it, it was many years ago. . . ." Liang was on the verge of tears as he said this.

"Don't cry, don't cry! You're out on the road. . . ." he said.

At that point, the green light came on, and the tide of bicycles started surging ahead.

"Tell me what else there is to this, I won't implicate you!" Liang had pulled himself together.

"There is talk that you could be a spy, you will need to be careful."

"Where did you hear this?"

He said he didn't know.

"I did, in fact, write a letter to Hong Kong, to a neighbor of mine. We had grown up together, but, later on, one of his paternal aunts got him to go to Hong Kong. I did, in fact, write him a letter asking him to get me a dictionary of English idioms, that was all, and it was many lifetimes ago! It was during the war in Korea, when I had just graduated, I was in the army as an interpreter in a prisoner-of-war camp. . . ."

"Did you receive the dictionary?" he asked.

"No! You're saying . . . the letter was never sent? Was it intercepted?" Liang went on to ask.

"Who knows?"

"I'm suspected . . . of having communicated with a foreign country?"

"It was you who said this."

"And do you suspect me?" Liang turned to ask him.

"I'm not going into that with you. Just be careful!"

As a long, two-carriage, electric trolleybus passed close by, Liang swerved and almost collided with it.

"No wonder they transferred me out of the army. . . ." For Liang, everything had suddenly become clear.

"All this is not so important."

"What else is there? Tell me everything, I won't bring you into it, even if they beat me to death!" Liang's bicycle swerved again.

"Don't get yourself killed in the process!" he warned.

"I won't stupidly kill myself! I've got a wife and a son!"

"Just be careful!"

He cycled around the corner. What he didn't say was that Liang's name was on the second list.

Some years later . . . How many years was it? Ten . . . no, twenty-eight years later, in Hong Kong, you answered a telephone call in your hotel. It was Liang Qin, who had read in the papers about your play. You didn't instantly recognize the name, and thought it was someone you had once met, and that the person wanted to see your play but couldn't get tickets, so you quickly apologized that it had already closed. He said he was your old colleague and wanted to take you out for a meal. You said you were flying out the next morning and that there wasn't time, maybe next time. He said, in that case, he would drive over right away to the hotel to see you. It was awkward to put him off, and it was only after putting down the receiver that you remembered him and your last conversation on your bicycles.

Half an hour later, he came into your room. He was dressed in a suit, leather shoes, linen shirt, and a dark-gray tie, but he was not flashy like the new rich from the Mainland. When you shook his hand, there was no gold Rolex watch, thick gold bracelet, or heavy gold ring. However, his hair was black, and, at his age, it would have been dyed. He said he had settled in Hong Kong many years ago. That neighbor from his youth, to whom he had written for the dictionary, found out how much he had suffered because of that letter, and felt so bad that he arranged for him to come out. He now had his own company, and his wife and son had moved to Canada on visas they had purchased. He told you frankly, "During these years, I have earned some money. I'm not wealthy, but I have enough to live out my old age in relative comfort. My son has a Ph.D. from a Canadian university, so I don't have anything to worry about. I commute, and if I can't stay in Hong Kong, I can pull out anytime." He also said he was grateful for the words you said to him back then.

"What words?" You couldn't remember.

" 'Don't get yourself killed in the process!' But for those words of yours, I wouldn't have been able to keep watching what was happening."

"My father couldn't keep watching," you said.

"He killed himself?" he asked.

"Luckily, he was discovered by an old neighbor who called an ambulance, and he was rushed to a hospital and saved. He was sent to a reform-through-labor farm for several years. Then, less than three months after being exonerated, he became ill and died."

"Why didn't you alert him at the time?" Liang asked.

"How could I dare write at that time? If they found out, my own life would also have been in jeopardy."

"That's right, but what sort of problem did he have?"

"Talk about yours, what sort of problem did you have?"

"Hey, let's not talk about all that!" He sighed, and, after a pause, asked, "How's your life?"

"What are you referring to?"

"I'm just asking, I know you're a writer, I'm asking how you are financially. You understand . . . what I mean, don't you?" Liang was unsure how to put it.

"I understand," you said. "I'm managing."

"I know that it's hard to make a living as a writer in the West, especially for Chinese. It's not like in business."

"Freedom," you said. What you want is freedom, the freedom to write the things you want to write.

He nodded, then again worked up the courage to say, "If you . . . Look, I'll be frank. For a time, I was financially constrained and didn't have the money, but you need only to say. I'm not some big tycoon but . . ."

"If you were a big tycoon you wouldn't be talking like this." You laughed. "A big tycoon would donate the money to carry out some fancy bit of engineering that would enable him to do more trade with the homeland."

Liang Qin took out a business card from his suit pocket, added an address and telephone number, and gave it to you, saying, "That's my mobile number. I've bought the house, so that address in Canada won't be changing."

You thanked him, said you didn't have a problem, and that if you had to rely on writing for a living, you would have stopped writing a long time ago.

He was deeply moved and blurted, "You're really writing for the people of China!"

You said you were writing only for yourself.

"I know, I know, write all about it!" he said. "I hope you'll write all about it, really write all about those times that were not fit for human beings!"

Write about all that suffering? you asked yourself after he had left. But you were already weary of all that.

However, you did think about your father. When he was exonerated and came back from the reform-through-labor farm, he was restored to both his former job and salary, but he insisted on retiring and came to Beijing to see you, this son of his. He planned to do some traveling after that, to drive away his cares and to spend his last years peacefully. You couldn't have known that the very night after you had spent the day with him at the Summer Palace, he was to cough blood. The next day, he went for a hospital examination and they found a shadow on his lung. It was diagnosed as full-blown lung cancer in its final stage. One night, his illness suddenly got worse, and he was admitted to a hospital. Early the next morning, he was dead. When he was alive, you asked him why he had attempted suicide. He simply said he really no longer wanted to live at the time. However, when he had just been able to live again, and, moreover, wanted to live, he suddenly died.

When those who had been exonerated died, their work units had to hold memorial services to offer some sort of commiseration to the families. At the memorial service, the son, who was a writer, of course, had to say something. Not to do so would have been disrespectful to his deceased father and also to the leadership of the comrades at the workplace, who had arranged the memorial service. He had been pushed to the microphone in the memorial hall and could not refuse before his father's ashes. He could not say that his father had been a revolutionary, although he had never opposed the revolution, and it was not appropriate to call him a comrade. All he could say was this: "My father was a weak man. May his soul be at peace in Heaven." That is, if there was a Heaven.

36

"Haul out before the people that evil scum of the Nationalist Party, the reactionary soldier-hooligan Zhao Baozhong!" the former lieutenant colonel loudly announced into the microphone on the dais. Officer Zhang, head of the Army Control Commission, wearing badges on his collar and cap, sat majestically alongside, showing no signs of emotion.

"Long live Chairman Mao!" The meeting suddenly erupted into a unified shout.

A fat old man in the back row of seats was dragged to his feet by two youths. The old man pulled his arms free and put up one arm to frantically shout, "Long live Chairman—Mao! Chairman—Chairman. . . ."

The old man's voice was hoarse, but he struggled on. Two retired army personnel came forward. They had learned how to make an arrest in the army: they twisted the man's arm behind his back and immediately forced him to his knees, so that his shouts were stifled in his throat. Four burly youths then seized the fat old man and proceeded to drag him, but, like a pig refusing to be trussed up for slaughter, he pushed and stamped his feet against the floor as everyone watched in silence. While the old man was dragged along the passageway from his seat to the dais, a placard strung with barbed wire was forced around his neck, but even with his ears pinned back, he kept trying to shout. His face was swollen and had turned purple, and mucus ran from his eyes and nose. This old worker looked after the book warehouse and was once a soldier who had given his loyalty to the Liberation Army after escaping three times when conscripted by the Nationalists. He was eventually forced to bow his head and kneel on the ground. He was the last of the Ox Demons and Snake Spirits to be dragged out.

"If the enemy refuses to capitulate, it must be destroyed!" This slogan resounded through the meeting hall. However, the old man had capitulated to the Party over thirty years ago.

"Fight resolutely to the end, there's just one road to death!"

It was also at this venue, four years earlier, that former Party secretary Wu Tao (now among those lined up, head bowed, bent at the waist) had designated this old man to serve as a model for studying Mao's *Selected Works*. As representative of the working class that had suffered in the past, the old man had railed against his hardships under the old society and sung sweet praises to the new society. The old man also wept and sniveled back then while educating the literary men of the workplace who were not reforming themselves.

"Haul out that dog of a spy Zhang Weiliang who has been communicating with foreign countries!"

Another person was pulled from his seat and dragged before the dais.

"Down with Zhang Weiliang!"

Without being struck, the man collapsed, and, paralyzed with fear, could not stand up. Every person at the meeting kept shouting, for any single person could suddenly become the enemy and could also be struck down.

"Confess all and be treated leniently, resist and be treated harshly!"

These were all Old Man Mao's illustrious policies.

"Long live—Chairman—Mao!"

At the time, there were so many denunciation meetings and so many slogans to shout, but one had to be careful not to make mistakes when shouting the slogans. The meetings were usually at night, when people were weary and tense. However, making a mistake in shouting a slogan instantly made a person an active counterrevolutionary. Parents had to repeatedly instruct their children not to draw anything carelessly, and not to tear up newspapers. The front page of newspapers always had the Leader's portrait on it, so it couldn't get torn, soiled, trodden on, or be hastily grabbed to wipe one's bottom if one was in a hurry to take a shit. You didn't have any children, and it was best that people did not. You only had to control your own mouth, ensure that what you said was always perfectly clear. And, especially when shouting slogans, you had to be vigilant and under no circumstances stumble over the words.

In the very early hours of the morning, on his way home, he cycled past the north gate of Zhongnanhai. Going up the white, arched, stone bridge, he held his breath as he glanced down at the mass of shadows cast by the trees in the hazy streetlights inside Zhongnanhai. Then, coming down the other side of the bridge, he released the gears and coasted down as he breathed out. He had managed to get through today. But what would happen tomorrow?

He got up early and went to work. At the bottom of the big workplace building was a corpse. It had been covered with an old straw mat taken from one of the beds in the living quarters of the building security personnel. The foot of the building and the cement ground were splattered with gray-white brain matter and purplish-black blood from the corpse.

"Who is it?"

"Probably someone from the editorial office. . . ."

The head was covered with the mat. Was there a face?

"Which floor was it?"

"Who can tell what window it was?"

Up to a thousand people worked in the building, and there were several hundred windows; it could have been from any of the windows.

"When did it happen?"

"It must have been just before daybreak."

They couldn't say that it was late at night after the ferret-out meeting.

"Didn't anyone hear it?"

"Stop your babbling."

People paused for a moment but went straight into the building to start work on time. In each of their offices, they looked at the wall with the portrait of the Leader, or else looked at the backs of the heads of the people who had arrived before them. Exactly at eight o'clock, loudspeakers in all the rooms sounded, and the whole building reverberated with the loud singing of "Sailing the Seas Depends on the Helmsman." This big beehive was more disciplined than it used to be.

On his desk was an envelope with his name on it. He gave a start. It had been a long time since he had received any correspondence, and nothing was ever sent to his workplace. He stuffed it into his pocket without reading it, but spent the whole morning trying to work out who had written the letter. Was it from someone who didn't know his address? The handwriting was unfamiliar, could it be a warning? If someone wanted to expose him, it wasn't necessary to send him a letter, could it be an anonymous letter of warning? But there was an eighty-*fen* stamp on it, and local postage was only forty *fen*, so it had to be from somewhere farther off. Of course, the eighty-*fen* stamp could be a camouflage. The person must be very kind, maybe it was someone from his own work unit who couldn't contact him directly and had thought up this way of doing it. He thought of Old Tan from whom he had not heard for a long time. But would Old Tan be allowed to write letters? Maybe it was a trap, a snare set for him by someone in an opposition faction, and his actions were being observed right then. He felt he was being spied on, for sure he would be on that third list, still without names, that the army officer had spoken about at the meeting of the ferret-out teams. He became disoriented and started wondering if the people walking in the corridor were watching for abnormal behavior in hidden enemies after that big ferret-out meeting. That was exactly what the army officer had ordered at the meeting the previous night to rally people into battle: "Make sweeping accusations, make sweeping exposures, dig out every single one of those active counterrevolutionaries who are still operating!"

He became aware of the window behind him. Suddenly, realizing how someone could jump just like that, he broke into a cold sweat. He struggled to calm down and to look unperturbed. Those in the office, who had not jumped, all looked unperturbed. Surely, they were also pretending? Those who were not able to pretend, lost control, and had jumped out of windows.

He held out until it was time for lunch. Even people more revolutionary than him had to eat, he thought. Instantly, he realized he had just had a reactionary thought. He had to obliterate such reactionary thoughts, and it was not a question of a single sentence. All that accumulated anger in his heart could foment disaster for him. Indeed: "Disaster springs from the mouth." This famous saying, the epitome of rationality, was the essence of human intelligence in ancient times. What truth do you still want? This truth is absolute, don't think about anything else! Don't even try thinking. But you are a spontaneous being, your affliction is precisely that you always want to be the initiator of your actions, and this is at the root of your endless disasters.

All right, now let's go back to him. That spontaneous being lingered about until everyone had left the office, then went to the lavatory. It was quite normal to relieve oneself before going to eat. He latched the door of the lavatory cubicle and took out the letter. It turned out that the letter was from Xu Qian. "We of this generation that has been sacrificed do not deserve any other fate. . . ." As soon as his eyes fell on these words, he immediately tore up the letter, but, changing his mind, he put the pieces back into the envelope. He noisily flushed the toilet, inspected the cubicle for any stray pieces of the letter, came out, washed his hands, scrubbed his face with water to steady his nerves, then went to the dining room.

Back in his room at night, he latched the door and pieced together the letter. He read it over and over. It was a voice of grief that spoke of despair, but said nothing of the night they had spent in the little inn, or of what had happened after she was intercepted at the wharf. In the letter, she said that this was her only and last letter to him, and that he would never see her again. It was a suicide letter. "We of this generation that has been sacrificed do not deserve any other fate" was how the letter began. She said she'd been assigned work as a primary-school teacher in some remote place in the big mountains of northern Shanxi province, but had refused to go and would not budge from the hostel in the county town. Before her, an overseas Chinese student had been sent to a school in the big mountains, where she was the only teacher. The woman had taken with her by donkey six boxes of trousseau prepared for her in advance by her parents in Singapore. Within a week, she was dead, and no one was able to give the cause of death. If she went, he would never see her again. Qian was crying for help. He was her last link to a bit of hope. It seemed that her parents and her aunt had not been able to do anything to save her.

In the middle of the night, he rode his bicycle to the post and telecommunications building in Xidan. There was a telephone number printed on the county hostel letterhead, and he asked to make an urgent telephone call. An unfriendly woman's voice speaking in a drawl asked for the name of the person he wanted. He explained that he was making a long-distance call from Beijing and that he wanted to speak to Xu Qian, the university student waiting to be assigned work. He was put on hold. The receiver buzzed for a long time before an equally unfriendly voice asked, "Who is it?" He repeated the name of the person he wanted to talk to, and the other party said, "That's me." He couldn't recognize her voice, because that night they spent together, neither dared speak aloud. Hearing this unfamiliar voice, he didn't know how to respond. The receiver kept giving a hollow buzz, and he mumbled, "It's good to know you're alive." Qian said, "You gave me a terrible fright! I'm in shock from being woken in the middle of the night!" He wanted to say that he loved her, that she must go on living no matter what, but he found it impossible to say all the things he had thought up while he was cycling. The switchboard operator in this small county town would certainly be listening to the urgent long-distance call from Beijing so late at night. The telephone was still making a hollow buzz, and he told her he'd received her letter. The telephone was buzzing again, and he didn't know what to say. She said coldly, "If you have to, phone during the day." He said, "I'm sorry, go back to bed." She hung up.

37

A young woman is lying on top of you. You're in bed, not fully
awake. She's giggling and the two of you are messing around.
You're really enjoying yourself and hope you are not dreaming.
You're squashed under her, and, down her open collar, you touch
her smooth skin, feel her firm breasts. She doesn't resist, and goes
on having fun with you. You're delighted by this unexpected
encounter, but can't say her name. You vaguely know it, but are
afraid of getting it wrong. You sift through your memories. In such-
and-such a situation, there was this girl, you often saw her on your
travels but were never able to get close to her. She is now pressing
against you and you say you didn't think you would meet her like
this. You're really so very happy! She says that she is here just to see
you. On her way through the city, she heard that you were here for
a conference, so she came to see you. You say don't leave! She says of
course not, but she does have to fix up her luggage and go through
registration procedures. You don't immediately make love with her,
thinking to yourself there will be plenty of time, she has come from
far away specially to see you, so it's not likely that she will leave right
away. You get out of bed and ask where her luggage is. She says over

there, in the adjoining room. You turn and see that the two rooms indeed adjoin, in fact there is nothing separating them, and, moreover, the other room has two beds in it. You're worried someone else will take the room, so you say you will have to quickly get a hotel attendant to get you a double room. But it happens to be the lunch break, so you go to the dining room together to have something to eat. She follows closely, snuggles against you, and says it was very hard, finding you. You keep trying to remember her name, steal glances at her familiar face, but you can't be sure. She's more like a woman than a young girl, an older teenager or a young woman, so there shouldn't be any problem making love with her. Moreover, she has come to see you. She says shouldn't you first introduce her to the person in charge of the conference? You say you are now a free man and can stay with anyone you want to. You don't have to get anyone's approval, and you take her with you to the service desk of the hotel to change to a double room. The man behind the desk hands you a key and a slip of paper. There's a number on the key tag, and you ask where the room is. The man says he is only in charge of registration, and, to find that out, you would have to phone up, the phone number is on the slip of paper. You ask if you can use the phone on his desk, and he says you will need coins. You can't find any coins in your pocket, and talk to the man again. Is it all right to call first and pay later? He doesn't say either yes or no, so you make a call and are told that the room is on the third floor. You get in the elevator, and it takes you to the top floor, and you come out onto a parking lot. The two of you get back into the elevator, go down, but still can't find the room. You stop a maid with a trolley, who is cleaning rooms, and she tells you to go down one floor. The two of you finally arrive on the ground floor and find an elegant dining room, so you think you may as well eat first. The maître d' in a tie politely apologizes and says reservations are needed, and that they are fully booked. You tell him you are taking part in the conference, and he says special arrangements have been made for conference participants in another dining room. You and she get into the elevator again, to look for the room. You scrutinize the number on the key and find something odd about it. The number is 11 GY, and you've found rooms with numbers 14, 15, and 16, but there isn't a number 11. You ask the fat woman sitting on a high stool at the bar by the passageway, thinking she is a hotel guest and will know about the number. The swivel stool spins around as the woman points behind you, saying, right there, it's that hole! You don't understand why it's a hole. Written on the brass plate on the doorframe is number 11 G, the second letter isn't clear but it could be Y. You part the glass-bead curtain, and inside is a huge row of joined mattresses. You look around the big room. Above, to the right of the joined mattresses, there is yet another layer of bedding, which stretches inside the wall. Access is only by crawling in, but the four double mattresses all have pillows. You think that if you want to make love with her, you will put her luggage in the farthest corner. You come out of the room and think to yourself that somehow you will have to find another room. However, she says she is traveling with another woman and they have to stay together. Luckily, they know people in the city and will be able to find somewhere to stay. But, you say, as she has come to see you . . . She says next time, there will be opportunities. She turns to leave, and you wake up, full of regret. You try to recall the memory, to clutch at some clues, so that you will know how you came to have this dream. You discover you are in a single bed in a small room, and there is a bird chirping outside the window.

For a while, you can't remember how you came to be sleeping here, your head is throbbing, and you aren't fully awake. Last night, you drank too much. You haven't drunk to excess like this for a long time. You drank scotch, five-grain liquor, and red wine, then, to quench your thirst, also beer. A full case of beer had been opened, but some cans are still left. Someone brought the scotch from England, and the five-grain liquor was from China. You remember now: a group of Chinese writers and poets have come for a conference here, in the southern outskirts of Stockholm, at the international center named after the assassinated Swedish president Olaf Palme.

You open your eyes and sit up. Outside the window is the lake with clouds hanging low over it. Lush shrubs and trees grow on the flat stretches of parkland, and there is only the singing of birds, no one is around, and it's very peaceful.

You recall the fragrant warmth of the woman in the dream and can't help feeling disappointed. Why did you have such a dream? It must have been because last night everyone was talking about China again, and you had a lot to drink. China always gives you a headache. But that is the purpose of the conference, to discuss contemporary Chinese literature. The Swedes had sponsored the visit of a group of Chinese writers from China and elsewhere, providing the plane tickets, and food and accommodation for a few days. This was an ideal place for a vacation. There was plenty of beer, but because liquor was heavily taxed, the conference participants brought it along with them. There was heavy drinking until dawn. In July, it was summer, and it was a white night; the sky did not become dark, and at midnight it was like dawn. The other side of the lake was a continuous hazy forest with a streak of bright-red dawn above, the birds and insects were sleeping, but these old friends went on talking loudly on the wooden jetty next to the lakeside sauna hut. They engaged in lofty discussions, and their voices resonated into the distance. Ripples stirred on the mirror-smooth surface, spreading in circles to the middle of the lake and making the weeds and the reflections tremble. And this was not a dream.

One of the friends insisted on talking about a whole lot of bizarre happenings in China that had nothing to do with literature. He said that this person who fed the animals in a zoo went to work early one morning, before they started selling tickets. He had just gone in through the side gate for zoo personnel, when he heard the roaring of the tiger he normally fed. He wondered why it was roaring if it wasn't feeding time, and went to take a look. The tiger was lying in the cage in a pool of blood, with its front paws missing. A rescue attempt was made, the wounds bandaged, but the tiger had lost too much blood, and there was no tiger blood for a transfusion, so they couldn't save it.

"Why had the tiger's paws been chopped off?" someone asked.

"Surely everyone here has heard stories about Chinese people eating bear paws?"

"But I've never heard about tiger paws being eaten."

"It's for making tiger-bone liquor, which has been a cure for rheumatism from ancient times! Where else could you hunt for a tiger these days, except at a zoo?"

Everyone broke out laughing and said, "You scoundrel, you're anti-Chinese right through. You've made it all up, haven't you?"

This friend, however, was quite serious and said he had read it in an official Mainland newspaper. "A friend sent me a newspaper clipping from China, it was just a two-line item. In Sweden, it would have made front-page headlines! And, for sure, the environmentalists would have marched in the streets. Hey, does Sweden have a Green Party?"

You didn't go to the dining room for breakfast. From your window, you watched the limousines downstairs drive off to take the others sightseeing in Stockholm.

Afterward, you went for a walk along the gravel path around the lake. On the surrounding fields, here and there, stood big, white, plastic bags that probably contained grass fodder. At the edge of the dark-green forest, these white bags looked surreal, and you again seemed to be entering a dream.

As you follow a track into the forest, the light around the lake vanishes, and, deeper into the forest, the trees seem to get taller, the tallest and straightest being the Korean pines. Suddenly, you hear the shouting of children, and you can't help feeling emotional. It's as if you have returned to your childhood, even though you know those times no longer exist. You stop to listen, to prove you're not hearing things, then hurry on. The track turns, and right ahead, between the trees, is a clearing where two girls are dragging sacks of, most likely, pine cones. The taller of the two is wearing jean shorts, cut off so the frayed edges come above the knee. Farther off, a boy is running about with a butterfly net. The two girls stop from time to time, and, as you don't want to disturb them, you slow down. The boy is in front, running and shouting. The girls call out to him, but he takes no notice and keeps running, so the girls follow, dragging their sacks. The sound of the children gradually fades into the distance, and, by the time you can no longer see them, the dirt track has started to disappear into the grass, and the place looks quite desolate. You still seem to faintly hear the shouting of the children, and you stop to listen, but it is only the rustle of the waves of pines as the wind passes through the tops of the trees.

You keep trying to recall that dream, to recall the tactile sensation of fondling her smooth firm breasts and to recall that indistinct but familiar face. Instead, you recall another dream you have had. The odd thing is that you have had this dream so many times that it has turned into a memory, so it seems that there really was such a girl. After school, she and her girl classmates were a happy lot and were always together. You seem to have been in the same class, but it was not easy to get on friendly terms with her. Those girls also made friends with boys, in fact, they only made friends with boys, but you could never get into their circle. You then remember a big courtyard complex where you once lived. Your home was in a back courtyard, and it was hard getting there through the front courtyard where a lot of people were living. The girl, it seems, lived in the front courtyard. Just like that, another dream is summoned up. The girl lived in a little dead-end street, an old courtyard complex that was very deep, with one entrance after another. Her family lived in the first courtyard, in the left wing after entering the gate, and a classmate of yours from middle school also lived in that courtyard. You went to see this classmate to see if the girl's family still lived there, but, when

you got there, you didn't see your classmate. This summons up
other dreams that are more like vague memories, and it's hard differentiating the dreams from the memories. You recall that when
you were four or five years old, during the chaos of war, you and
your parents were refugees and had lived in such a big courtyard
complex. But you are searching for a big girl with full breasts, and
your memories and dreams are all confused.

Your childhood years are dim and hazy, and only some points of
light appear before your eyes. How is it possible to retrieve past happenings that have become submerged in what has been forgotten?
It's hard to confirm what gradually appears, and it's hard to decide
in the end whether it is memory or something you have imagined.
Moreover, are memories accurate? They are fragmented and jump
backward and forward, and, when you try to track them, the flashing
points of light become dim and turn into words, but you can only
link up a few of them. Can memories be retold? You doubt it, and
you also doubt the capacity of language to do this. One retells memories or dreams, because some wonderful things that give you
warmth, fragrance, longing, and impulses flash up. But can this be
said of words?

You remember clearly that there was such a girl, and that you sat
at the same desk, on the same wooden bench, and that she had a fair
complexion. He once broke his pencil during a test, and when the
girl noticed, she pushed the pencil box full of sharpened pencils she
had on the desk to him. From then on, he began to take an interest
in the girl, and would look out for her on his way to and from
school. He once picked up a perfumed card that had dropped out of
her textbook, and, after school, the girl gave it to him. When the
boys from the class saw this, they started chanting, "The two of
them are in love! The two of them are in love!" It made him blush,
and, probably because of that, thereafter, warmth, fragrance, and
femininity all came to be associated for him.

You also remember a dream from your teenage years. It was in a garden with long uncut grass, and among the clumps of grass lay the pure, white, naked body of a woman, a cold statue of carved marble. This was a dream he had after reading Mérimée's novel *The Venus of Ille*. He slept close to the statue, and how he had sex with it was unclear, but there was a cold puddle around his thighs. It was a winter's night, and he woke up terrified.

You think about Bergman's old black-and-white film *Wild Strawberries*, which captures in detail an old man's anxiety about death; probably you've gradually moved into the phase of old age. In another of his films, *Cries and Whispers*, you feel sympathy for the three sisters and their buxom maid, who are all tortured by loneliness, sexual desire, illness, and fear of death. Can literature and art communicate? It is, in fact, pointless discussing this, but there are people who do believe that this is impossible. And can Chinese literature communicate? Communicate with whom, the West? Or communicate with the Chinese on the Mainland, or with the Chinese living abroad? And what is Chinese literature? Does literature have national boundaries? And do Chinese writers belong to a specific location? Do people living on the Mainland, Hong Kong, Taiwan, and the Chinese-Americans all count as Chinese people? This, again, brings in politics, so let's talk just about pure literature. But does pure literature really exist? Then let's talk about literature. But what is literature? These issues are all of relevance to the conference and are all endlessly contested.

You're tired of the debate over literature and politics. China is already so remote from you; moreover, you were expelled from the country long ago, and you do not need to bear that country's label. You simply write in the Chinese language, and that's all.

38

Buses were parked in front of the building from which five persons had jumped to their deaths less than a month ago. The first batch of about a hundred people to go to the countryside had assembled for final instructions from the army officer. As ordered by Officer Zhang, pinned on each person's chest was a red paper flower hurriedly made by office personnel before the buses were to be boarded.

This detachment of fighters was mostly elderly. There were also women, people of retirement age who hadn't been permitted to retire, as well as people on sick leave with high blood pressure. Among their numbers were old cadres from the Yan'an base area and old guerrilla fighters who had fought local battles on the plains of central Hebei province. In accordance with Mao's newly promulgated May Seventh Directive, these people were all off to cultivate the land, and wearing this paper flower on the chest signified that reform through labor was glorious.

Officer Zhang came out of the building, touched the brim of his cap with his fingers in a salute, then stood at attention before everyone, "Comrades, from now on you are glorious May Seventh fighters! You are the advance detachment and have the important mission of establishing the Communist university called for by our Great Leader, Chairman Mao. I wish all of you a rich harvest in both your labor and thinking!"

He was regular army personnel and didn't waste time talking. Having said this, he raised his arm and signaled for the buses to be boarded. In front of the building were family members, as well as colleagues who had come to see them off. People were waving from all the windows of every floor of the building. There had been enough fighting between factions, and those leaving all counted as comrades. It was an emotional situation, some of the women were wiping tears from their eyes, but on the whole, there was a cheery atmosphere.

He was secretly pleased. He had organized his belongings, even scrubbed the enamel chamber pot in his room, and packed everything into the wooden boxes they had provided him. People sent to the country were provided with two boxes at no cost, but additional ones were charged. All this came from documents issued by the May Seventh Office, which the State Council had newly established. He nailed up his boxes of books. Just when he would be able to open the books again, he didn't know, but they would accompany him in life, they were his last bit of mental sustenance.

When he delivered his application to be sent to the country, Officer Zhang was hesitant and said, "The ferret-out work hasn't been completed, then there will be many difficult tasks—"

Without waiting for the officer to finish talking, he started a barrage of prattle, explaining in a single breath his resolve and his need to undertake labor and reform. He added, "Officer Zhang, I want to report that my girlfriend was allocated work in the country after graduating from university. When the cadre school is fully established, I can get my girlfriend to come, then I will be able to carry out a lifetime of revolution in the countryside!"

He had made it clear that he was not hiding anything and that he had given thought to practical matters. Officer Zhang rolled his eyes. His fate had been decided.

"All right!" Officer Zhang took his application.

He heaved a sigh of relief.

Only one person said, "You shouldn't go!"

It was Big Li, and he knew that he was reproaching him. Comrade Wang Qi, whom he had protected, also came to see him off, her eyes were red and she looked away. Big Li had turned up to say good-bye and shook hands with him. His puffy eyes made him look even more sincere, yet somehow the two of them had found it hard to become friends. He detected Big Li's loneliness. Among the disbanded rebel faction, there had been fighting companions, but no real friends. And now he was abandoning all of them.

Before going downstairs to assemble, he went to the room of his former superior Old Liu and shook hands with him. Old Liu tightly clasped his hand, as if he was clutching a piece of straw to save himself, but this piece of straw wanted to escape sinking. They each held the other's hand for a while without saying anything, but both knew that clinging together meant sinking together, and Old Liu was the first to let go. He had finally succeeded in escaping from this beehive of insanity, this building that manufactured death.

At Qianmenwai, the railway station was as usual crowded with milling people, and on the platform and in the carriages, only the heads of those leaving and those seeing them off could be seen moving around. University students had already been sent to the country and border areas earlier on. This time, those being sent to the country to work were mostly middle-school students, who were being sent to settle permanently, as well as workplace staff and cadres. Boys and girls on board the train crammed around the windows, and their parents stood outside the windows, giving numerous instructions. On the platform, there was a loud burst of gongs and drums as a worker propaganda team, leading a band of children who were too young to be sent, transformed the farewell scene into a festive occasion.

The stationmaster in a blue uniform blew his whistle a few times, and people retreated behind the white line, but, for a long time, the train showed no sign of moving. Suddenly, there was a commotion, as armed military police ran up and formed a single row. Then came a long contingent of prisoners, heads shaved, each humping a bedroll on their backs and holding an enamel bowl. They were marching in time, softly chanting in a clear rhythm the slogan: "Strive hard to remake yourself, to resist means death!"

It was a soft chant with the solemnity of a hymn, repeated over and over, and the children stopped beating on their gongs and drums. The line of prisoners crossed the platform diagonally, and, to the sound of the repeated slogan, entered several stifling windowless carriages that had been added to the tail end of the train. Ten minutes later, there was an eerie quiet as the train slowly moved off. At that point, a few irrepressible sobs came from the platform, and, instantly, the inside and outside of the train filled with the sound of weeping children and adults. Of course, some people waved and put on smiles, but the artificially happy atmosphere had completely vanished.

Outside the train window, cement telephone poles, red brick houses, gray concrete buildings, chimneys, and bare branches on trees rapidly receded. However, this was what he wanted: he had finally fled that city of terror. The winds would be colder and harsher, but at least he would be able to breathe freely for a while without having to be on guard all the time. He was young and strong, without a wife or children, without responsibilities, and had only to work the soil. While he was at university, he had worked in the villages. Farmwork was exhausting, but the mental stress would not be as great. He wanted to hum a song, but what old song was there to sing? All right, then he wouldn't sing anything.

39

That soul mate of yours, Louis Armstrong, you think of as a brother. He has been dead a long time, but those old black-and-white movies raining with white lines, that old black soul mate's singing, still have you rolling on the floor.

Gossamer floating in the wind . . .

You must live happily and fully. Oh, Margarethe! You're thinking of her again, it was she who got you to write this damn book that has made you so wretched and miserable. That slut has caused you excruciating pain, and you want to fuck her really hard, so that you will make her hurt like she wants to, that masochist. But even if you were to hurt her much more, you would still not be able to cry.

And you really want to cry, to roll on the floor like a spoiled brat and to cry as hard as you can. But there are no tears, no tears, none at all. Hey, man, you're just getting old!

So what if you're a worm or a dragon! You're more like a homeless dog without an owner, so you don't have to please anyone and don't have to try to get anyone to like you. You, you're a mole that bores holes in the ground. You like the dark, you can't see a thing in the dark, you can't see the hunting rifles. You no longer have goals and what use are goals anyway?

Now that you have a new life, you want to use it as you want to, and you want what's left of your life to be lived more meaningfully. Most important of all, living has to bring happiness, and you must derive happiness from living for yourself. What others think is of no relevance whatsoever.

To be self-activated and to exist for yourself is a freedom that is not external to you. It is within you, and it depends on whether you are aware of it and consciously exercise it.

Freedom is a look in the eyes, a tone of voice, and it can be actualized by you, so you are not destitute. Affirming this freedom is like affirming the existence of a thing, like a tree, a plant, or a dewdrop, and for you to exercise this freedom in life is just as authentic and irrefutable.

Freedom is ephemeral; the instant of that look in your eyes and that tone of your voice springs from a psychological state, and it is that flash of freedom that you want to capture. To express this in language is to affirm freedom, even if what you write can't last forever. In the process of writing, freedom is visible and audible, and, at the instant of writing, reading, and listening, freedom exists in your mode of expression. To be able to obtain that small luxury of freedom of expression and expressive freedom is what it takes to make you happy.

Freedom is not conferred, nor can it be bought, it is your own awareness of life. Such is the beauty of life, and, surely, you savor this freedom just as you savor the ecstasy of sexual love with a wonderful woman.

This freedom can tolerate neither God nor a dictator. To be either of these is not your goal, nor would such a goal be attainable, so rather than wasting the effort you may as well simply want this bit of freedom.

Instead of saying Buddha is in your heart, it would be better to say that freedom is in your heart. Freedom castigates others. To take into account the approval or appreciation of others, and, worse still, to pander to the masses, is to live according to the dictates of others. Thus it is they who are happy, but not you yourself, and that would be the end of this freedom of yours.

Freedom takes no account of others and has no need for acceptance by others. It can only be won by transcending restrictions that are imposed on you by others. Freedom of expression is also like this.

Freedom can be manifested in suffering and grief, as long as one does not allow oneself to be crushed by it. Even while immersed in suffering and grief, one can still observe, so there can also be freedom in suffering and grief. You need the freedom to suffer and the freedom to grieve, so that life will be worth living. It is this freedom that brings you happiness and peace.

40

"Don't think peace will reign once old counterrevolutionaries have been purged. Rub your eyes hard and be vigilant, those practicing counterrevolutionaries are dangerous enemies! They are carefully hidden and crafty, they have accepted our proletarian revolutionary slogans but are secretly instigating capitalist factionalism and blurring our class demarcations. We cannot allow ourselves to be hoodwinked by them, think hard about the people who were sneaking around during the movement. Those two-faced counterrevolutionaries that hold up the red flag while opposing the red flag are sleeping right next to you!"

The deputy chairman of the Army Control Commission, Officer Pang, was political commissar in the army and had come especially from Beijing to visit the farm. Wearing glasses with thick black frames, he stood on the stone mill in the drying square and waved a document in his hand as he made his rallying call: "The May Seventh Cadre School is not a haven from the class war!"

A purge of the practicing counterrevolutionary group designated "May Sixteenth" was under way, and leaders and activists of rebel factions from the beginning of the movement were all marked for investigation. He was instantly relieved of his position as squad leader, and told to stop work to write a full report on those years, detailing the dates and places when and where which people had what secret meetings and had engaged in what shady activities.

At the time, he didn't know that, in Beijing, Big Li had been interrogated for days and nights on end, and that, after being beaten and kicked, confessed to being a May Sixteenth element. Of course, Big Li also named him. Big Li further confessed that the meeting in Wang Qi's home was part of a secret counterrevolutionary plot, which allowed them to collude with members of the counterrevolutionary gang and receive instructions for the ultimate goal of overthrowing the dictatorship of the proletariat. Big Li ended up in a mental institution. Wang Qi had also been interrogated. Old Liu had been beaten to death during an interrogation in the underground room of the workplace building, then taken upstairs and thrown out of a window. It was construed that he had committed suicide to avoid punishment.

Luckily, he got wind of the hunting dogs closing in on the horizon. By this time, he already knew how the political hunt operated. Based on the Number One War Preparation Mobilization Command authorized by Deputy Commander-in-Chief Lin Biao, large numbers of personnel and their families had been sent to the countryside, and this was the sign of an even more thorough purge. The peaceful mood, despite the hard physical labor people were subjected to, swiftly vanished. With the arrival of the newcomers, hostility was reignited and replaced that bit of friendly solidarity that had developed. The old company, platoon, squad units, were dismantled and reorganized, and a branch of the Party was reestablished with cadres appointed by the Army Control Commission in Beijing. He had to watch for a chance to break through their siege and escape before the hunt closed in. In the middle of the night, he sneaked into the county town to send a telegram to his middle-school classmate Rong.

It is said that Heaven never cuts off the road for people. In his case, it was more like Heaven took pity and gave him a road out. In the afternoon, while everyone was working in the fields, he was in the empty dormitory, writing his confession. Someone was outside, so he put on an act and wrote down a few of Mao's sayings. The postal worker from the commune was on his bicycle in the square outside the door, shouting, "Telegram! Telegram!"

He ran outside; it was from Rong. He was smart: for "sender" Rong had written only the telegraphic registration number of the farm technology promotion station of the county where he worked. The message read: "In the spirit of the Party Center document on war preparation, it is agreed that such-and-such a comrade may settle down and work in the agricultural commune of our county. He must report immediately, before the end of the month, after which he will not be accommodated."

While everyone was still working in the fields, he rushed to the cadre-school office that was more than five kilometers away. No one was in the big room with a telephone and typewriter. The small inner room was where Officer Song worked and slept. The door was shut, and there was a rustling noise inside.

"Reporting to Officer Song!"

This was military practice, and he had learned well. After a while, Officer Song emerged in his army uniform, looking immaculate except for an undone hook-and-eye on his collar.

"I count as having graduated from this cadre school, but I am waiting for you to issue me with a certificate!"

He had thought this up on the way, and he said this in a casual manner and with a happy look on his face.

"What do you mean, you've graduated?" Officer Song had an unfriendly look on his face.

With a smile firmly fixed to his face, he presented the telegram in both hands. Officer Song took it with one hand. The man was barely literate and pondered over each word before finally looking up. But, no longer frowning, he said, "Quite right, it does accord with the spirit of the document. Do you have relatives there?"

"I'll be joining relatives and friends to make a living." He quoted verbatim from the war mobilization document transmitted by Officer Song, then hastened to add, "A friend there has arranged it. I'm going to a farming village to settle down permanently! I'll receive a thorough reeducation from the poor and lower-middle-class peasants and then marry a village girl. I can't stay a bachelor all my life!"

"Have you already found a girl?" Officer Song asked.

He detected friendliness, or, maybe, it was sympathy or understanding. Song was a farm villager when he joined the army, and, starting off as an army bugler, he would have had to tough it out before becoming the deputy operations staff officer of a regiment. His wife and children still lived in the village, and he only had two weeks of annual leave to visit his family, so, of course, he missed having a woman. The Army Control Commission had assigned him the hard task of supervising the work of this very large group of people. It was, indeed, a case of Heaven's will in the dark unknown that the deputy chairman of the Army Control Commission, Officer Pang, who was in charge of the purge, had finalized arrangements with the company Party branch secretaries and had hurried back to Beijing two days earlier.

"A friend has set up a girl for me, and, if I don't show up, the whole thing will fizzle out. People are doing hard labor everywhere, so, if I get myself a wife, I'll just set up a home!"

He had to say something that would appeal to Officer Song's village background.

"Quite right. But think about it properly, because, once you go, your Beijing resident permit will be revoked!"

Officer Song had stopped talking as a bureaucrat. He took a book of forms from his drawer, told him to fill it out, then shouted toward the inside room, "Little Liu, he needs a letter with an official stamp! Hurry up and type the letter!"

The young telephone operator and typist emerged gracefully. The rubber bands tight against the back of her head made her freshly combed hair stand out in two bunches. She unlocked a drawer and took out the stamp, then, sitting on the stool in front of the type-writer, began striking one character at a time on the heavy keyboard. As Officer Song checked the letter, he hastened to ingratiate himself, "I'm the first person to graduate under Officer Song!"

"This damn place is all alkaline soil, and nothing will grow except wind and sand. It's not like my old home, where whatever you plant grows, so, it's not, in fact, a matter of it being hard labor everywhere!"

Officer Song eventually put a red stamp on the official letter. Many years later, he met a person who had worked with him in the cadre school and learned that, not long after he fled the place, this kindly Officer Song was caught without his trousers. They happened to shine a torch into the wheat field, and there he was, doing it with the telephone operator. They sent him back to the army. It was Offi-cer Song's fate that his career in the army would be stunted, just like the wheat growing in that poor soil.

On the way back, he heard in the distance the chugging of a trac-tor plowing the soil and shouted out, "Hey, Tang!"

Tang, who used to ride a motorbike as a traffic officer in Beijing, had lost his job and now worked on the farm in the machinery squad, riding a tractor. He ran across the soft, loose soil and caught up with the tractor.

"Hey!" Tang raised an arm to greet him.

"I need your help." He was running alongside the tractor.

"In these turbulent times, when the clay Buddha statue is crossing the river, it's hard even for Buddha to protect himself. What is it? Be quick and don't let anyone see me talking to you, I've heard you're being investigated in your company."

"It's all right now! I've graduated!"

Tang stopped the motor. He climbed up onto the driver's platform and flashed his official letter with a red stamp in front of Tang.

"Right, let's have a smoke!"

"It's all thanks to the kindness of Officer Song," he said.

"You've managed to escape from the sea of suffering, so hurry up and get away."

"Can you help get my luggage to the county railway station at five o'clock tomorrow morning?"

"I'll get a truck. After all, you do have Officer Song's permission."

"Don't mention it to anyone, who knows what dangers are still lurking."

"I'll definitely be there with a truck. If there are any questions, I'll tell them to see Officer Song!"

"Remember, tomorrow morning, at five o'clock sharp!" He jumped down from the driver's platform.

"I'll sound the horn on the road near your dormitory, and you can get on board. Leave it to me, I won't let you down!" Tang said, beating his chest.

The tractor chug-chug-chugged into the distance. He took his time walking the remaining two or so kilometers as he worked out how to deal with this last night, and how to move his luggage and those heavy boxes of books with utmost speed from the dormitory onto the truck at dawn. He waited until dark, dawdled through the dinner period, and only showed up in the dormitory when people had started crowding around the well to draw water for a wash. He also had a wash, and, at the same time, collected all of his things. Before the lights went out and people had to be in bed, he called on the company Party secretary to present his documents for settling permanently in a farming village. The secretary, who had been newly appointed by the Army Control Commission, was sitting on a bench with his shoes off, washing his feet. Once again with an air of jest, he reverently announced to the room full of people, "Officer Song has approved my graduation, so I have come to bid farewell to all you comrades. This does not mean we will not meet again, but just that I am one step ahead. I'm going to be a real peasant, so that I can thoroughly reform myself!"

He also put on a dejected look, as if he had a heavy heart, to show that the road ahead was not, in fact, wonderful. That joker really didn't have time to react and couldn't make out whether or not it was a special punishment he had been given, so he simply said let's see about it tomorrow.

Tomorrow? he thought. By the time that joker goes to the cadre-school headquarters, and by the time they make telephone contact with the Army Control Commission in Beijing, he'll have fled.

When he got back to the dormitory, the lights were out. He made his way through the dark and lay down on his bed, fully clothed. In the middle of the night, he put on a night-light, and, from time to time, glanced at the barely visible hands of his watch. He guessed it was almost daybreak and got up, keeping close to the wall as he put on his shoes. He did not immediately roll up his bedding, because it would wake everyone too soon, and that dog in charge of spying on his movements would probably report to the company Party secretary.

No one knew he was leaving before dawn, and, holding his breath, he waited in the dark, listening intently for the sound of the truck horn. It was fifty or sixty meters from the dormitory to the road, and it would not be very loud. He felt ringing in his ears and opened his eyes wide, so that he would be able to hear with better precision. As soon as he heard the horn, he would have to bundle up his bedding and wake up a couple of people to help him carry those wooden boxes next to the wall.

Just before daybreak, a horn sounded clearly two times. He sprang to his feet, quietly opened the door, and raced up to the road.

"Tang, you can really be counted on!"

Tang had the truck lights on, and raised an arm to signal him. He immediately ran back and woke the two men who slept on either side of him in the communal bed.

"Are you leaving right now?" They crawled to their feet, not fully awake.

"Yes, I've got a train to catch," he quickly rolled up his bedding.

A few minutes later, he leaped into the truck and waved to the vague forms of the two men who had helped him. Good-bye to the May Seventh Cadre School, this labor farm.

41

His head was a total blank. Outside the train window was a vast and desolate gray-yellow plain, trees with bare branches flashed past. He had not slept all night, but was tired, not sleepy. Looking mindlessly out of the window, he still did not dare to believe that he had escaped, just like that. The train passed the big bridge over the Yellow River, and the fields began to show signs of grayish-green: the wheat, after the winter, was starting to turn green. Two or three hours on, after stopping at several stations, the trees flashing past had turned green-gray, and, in the branches of a bare tree, some tender green leaves had appeared. Then lush green new willow leaves could be seen trembling in the wind, bringing tidings of early spring. The thought "You have been saved" welled up in his heart.

The fields turned green after crossing the Yangtze, and bright sunlight sparkled between the seedlings of the paddy fields. This world was real. Only then did he relax and fall into a deep sleep.

Following a change of trains, he got on a long-distance bus that bounced him up and down on the winding mountain road. The old bus rattled, shaking so badly that it felt as if it would fall to pieces. But, outside the window, as far as the eye could see, were luxuriant green mountains with clumps of bright pink azaleas among the bushes on the slopes. He was wild with excitement.

In the small county town, at the end of an old cobblestone street, he found Rong's house, a mud hut with a thatch roof. Not being a local, Rong was not doing particularly well here, but the hut, which he did not have to share, with its vegetable garden enclosed by a bamboo fence, filled him with envy. Rong's wife was a local and worked as a shop assistant in a local store, and their small son, just a few months old, was sleeping in a cradle in the hall. In the courtyard, in the warm sun, a hen with a flock of fluffy yellow chicks was pecking the ground. This scene moved him.

While Rong's wife was in the kitchen, cooking for them, Rong asked about what was happening in Beijing and about his own situation. So, he talked a bit about it. Rong said, "What are all these criticism meetings about? Here, far from Beijing, the county cadres have also had their criticism meetings, although these didn't involve the ordinary people."

"Rong, do you remember when we used to have philosophical discussions in our letters and would ask searching questions to try and find out what was the ultimate meaning of life?" He wanted to joke a bit.

"Don't talk about philosophy, that's all just to frighten people," Rong coldly interrupted. "I spend my days looking after my family. When it rains hard, the thatch roof leaks. This winter, I had to change the thatch. I can't afford a tile roof."

Rong's calm indifference to seeking fame and wealth had allowed him to return to real life. He thought he should be like Rong, pass his days in this real way, and so he said, "I'd best go into the big mountains and find a village to settle in for good!"

However, Rong said, "You'd better think about that properly. You can get into those big mountains all right, but you won't be able to get out. You, you're always fantasizing; be a bit more realistic!"

Rong helped him work out that he should go to a village with electricity, one that could be reached in a single bus trip, so that if he got seriously ill he would be able to get to the county hospital the same day.

"If you want to settle down here, you'll have to get on good terms with the village cadres, the local tyrants. When you go to the county town to report your arrival, don't mention anything about those damn happenings in Beijing!" Rong warned him.

"I know, I won't fantasize anymore," he said. "I've come here to seek a refuge and to find myself a sexy village girl who will bear me sons and daughters."

"My only fear is that you're not going to be able to cope," Rong laughed.

Rong's wife asked him, "Are you serious? I can arrange it for you, it'll be easy!"

Rong turned and said to his wife, "Hey, you can't believe everything he says!"

He found a free-standing mud hut by the primary school of a small farm town. The production team had just built it, and the rafters and tiles had only gone up that winter. The walls, made by compacting mud and stones between wooden separators, had not been whitewashed, and, as there was no ceiling, when there was heavy rain, a fine spray of water would drift in between the tiles. No one had lived in the hut before. He used mortar to fill the gaps between the walls and the wooden door and window frames, pasted white paper on the glass windows for a bit of privacy, and used some planks to make a bed. He lined a part of the earthen floor with bricks, to stack up his boxes of books, which he covered with a piece of plastic and put his bowls, chopsticks, and daily utensils on top. Afterward, he put a big earthenware water vat inside the hut, so that he could ladle water when needed, and, later still, had a desk made at the timber cooperative in the little town. He was quite satisfied.

When he got back from weeding in the paddy fields, he would wash the mud from his feet and calves in the pond floating with duckweed, and then make himself a cup of green tea. Sitting in a bamboo chair, he would look at the distant layers of mountain ranges in the mist before him. The line "Plucking chrysanthemums by the eastern fence, I suddenly see the Southern Mountains," from Tao Yuanming's poem would come to his mind, but his was not the leisurely life of that scholar-official of ancient times who lived as a recluse. Each day, when it was barely light, as soon as he heard the singing on the village loudspeakers—"The east is red and the sun rises, in China there emerges Mao. . . ."—he would go with the peasants to the paddy fields to plant seedlings. However, he no longer had to make a pretense of chanting Mao's *Sayings*. Weary after toiling all day, just to be unsupervised, drinking a cup of green tea, resting in the bamboo chair with his legs stretched out, was all he needed. And, at night, to be able to lie down alone on the big plank bed and no longer have to be on guard about talking in his sleep was really something to be thankful for.

From now on, he was a peasant, relying on his strength to feed himself. He had to learn everything about farm life—plowing, building paddy embankments, planting seedlings, harvesting grain, shoveling manure, using a carrying pole—and he no longer expected that they would still issue him a salary. He had to mingle with the villagers, not give them any reason to be suspicious of him, settle down, and no doubt grow old and die here. He had to make a home for himself here.

In a few months, he was working almost as fast as the villagers, and he was not like the county cadres who, if they were sent there to work, would find excuses to return to the county town every couple of days. For the peasants, the local cadres were aristocrats who worked in the fields purely for show, but for him there was universal praise. He thought he had managed to win the trust of both the peasants and the village cadres, and so he opened those nailed-up boxes of books.

Tolstoy's play *The Forces of Darkness* lay at the top of a box; water seeping through the cracks had added yellow streaks to old Tolstoy's beard on the cover. The play was about a peasant killing a baby, and its dark intense psychology had once shaken him; it was totally different from the early aristocratic feel of *War and Peace,* written in Tolstoy's early years. Afraid it would disturb the inner peace he had only just achieved, he didn't open the book.

He felt like reading some books that were remote from the environment he lived in, some faraway stories that were pure imagination, something puzzling, like *Wild Duck* in *The Collected Plays of Ibsen.* Also, there was the first volume of Hegel's *Aesthetics*, which he had bought years ago but hadn't even opened. Doing some reading would help relieve his physical weariness. He put all his copies of Marx and Lenin on the desk, and, before going to bed, took out of the box the book he wanted to read, and, sitting up in bed with the light on, leisurely flipped through the pages. The light globe hung from the rafter, and, without a shade, lit the window. The peasant homes near and far were in complete darkness at night. People were frugal in their use of electricity and went to bed right after the evening meal. Only his solitary hut had a light on, but he thought that to try to conceal it was pointless and would be sure to arouse suspicions.

He was not reading seriously, but was lost in thought and just turning the pages. He couldn't understand the characters in *Wild Duck*, because old man Hegel would always materialize out of nothing and turn aesthetic feelings into a morass of intellectual analysis. The characters lived in some fictitious village, but if they were to see this real world of his, they would not be able to understand or believe it either. He lay there, listening to the patter of the rain on the tiles above him. In the rainy season, it was wet everywhere, and the grass along the road and the seedlings in the paddy fields grew madly at night, becoming taller and greener by the day. He was to spend his life in the paddy fields, growing and harvesting, year after year. Generations of life would be like paddy rice. People would be like plants, they would not need a brain, wouldn't that be more natural? And the total collected strivings of humankind—that is, culture—would, in fact, be so much wasted effort.

Where was the new life? He recalled these words of his classmate Luo, who had come to this realization much earlier. Maybe he should just find himself a peasant girl and raise children. This would be his home forever.

Before the harvest, there were a few free days, and all the men of the village went up the mountains for firewood, so he also went along, a hacking knife on his belt. He went to the county town once a month, to collect his salary along with other cadres who had been sent to the countryside, and often bought a load of charcoal that would last a few months. Nevertheless, he went up the mountains with the men for firewood just to get to know the situation in the four villages of the commune.

In the gully, before going into the mountains, was a small village of just a few families, which was the commune's most far-flung production team. There he saw an old man with metal-rimmed glasses, sitting in the sun outside his home, squinting at a hand-sewn book riddled with wormholes. He was holding the book in both hands, away from himself, his arms stretched right out.

"Venerable elder, do you still read?" he asked.

The old man took off his glasses, looked up, saw that he was not one of the local peasants, grunted, and put the book down on his lap.

"May I see your book?" he asked.

"It's a medical book," the old man explained immediately.

"What sort of medical book?" he went on to ask.

"*Treatise on Chills*. Do you think you'd understand it?" There was derision in the man's voice.

"Venerable elder, are you a doctor of traditional medicine?" He changed the topic to show his respect.

It was only then that the old man let him take the book. This ancient medical book printed on smooth gray-yellowish bamboo paper, was most certainly a Qing Dynasty edition. Between the wormholes were punctuation circles and commentaries in red cinnabar, written in script the size of a fly's eye. These notations could have been made by his ancestors, but, more likely, had been made long ago by the old man himself. Holding the precious book in both hands, he carefully returned it to the old man. It was, perhaps, his respectful attitude that moved the old man, who called to the woman inside the house, "Fetch a stool and a bowl of tea for this comrade!"

The old man's voice was still loud and clear, because of his many years of physical labor; moreover, his knowledge of traditional medicine, no doubt, kept him in good health.

"There's no need to go to any trouble." He sat down on the stump for chopping firewood.

A sturdy woman getting on in years, who could have been the old man's daughter-in-law or a second wife, emerged from the main hall with a stool, then, from a big earthenware pot, she poured him a bowl of hot tea with big leaves floating on top. He thanked her and took the bowl in both hands. There were green mountains all around, and the tops of the firs moved silently in the wind.

"Comrade, where do you come from?"

"The county town, from the commune," he replied.

"You're a cadre who has been sent to the country, aren't you?"

He nodded and said with a smile, "Is it obvious?"

"You're not a local, anyway. Are you from the provincial capital or from somewhere else?" the old man went on to ask.

"I am from Beijing," he said succinctly.

At this, the old man nodded and asked nothing more. "Then don't leave, just settle here!"

He normally adopted a joking tone when the peasants questioned him during the rest breaks, and he did this without fail, so that he wouldn't need to explain himself. At most, he would add that the mountains were green, and the rivers clear, and how wonderful it all was! But this old man was clearly educated, and it wasn't necessary to say this to him.

"Venerable elder, are you a local?" he asked.

"For many generations. No matter how splendid it is elsewhere in the world, it can't surpass one's home village," the old man said passionately. "I've been to Beijing."

He was not surprised, and went on to ask, "What year was it?"

"Oh, that was many years ago, during the Republican period. I was at university, it was the seventeenth year of the Republic."

"Is that so." He made a calculation. According to the Gregorian calendar, it was forty years ago.

"At that time, the trendy professors wore Western suits and top hats, carried canes, and came to classes in rickshaws!"

Nowadays the professors were either sweeping the streets or washing out lavatories, he thought but didn't say.

The old man said he won a government scholarship to study in Japan, and he had a degree from Tokyo Imperial University.

He fully believed this, but what he wanted to know was why the old man had returned to the mountains. However, he couldn't ask him this directly, so he approached from another angle, "Venerable elder, did you study medicine?"

The old man didn't reply. His half-closed eyes looked across to the forests swaying in the mountain wind, and he seemed to be dozing in the sun. He thought, this was the old man's refuge, and he had studied traditional medicine so that he could treat the villagers if they were sick, it was a means of survival. He had married a village woman to have children so that he would have someone to look after him in his old age, and, now that he was too old to work in the fields, he just sits in the sun reading medical books to pass time.

At night, he wrote a letter to Qian, telling her that he was in a village, that he had settled down more or less for good, and that he had a house. If she wanted to live with him, they would have their own home. He was still receiving his salary, and, being a university graduate, she would also receive a salary. With their joint incomes, they would be able to live comfortably in this village, spend their days peacefully as human beings. He filled the squares on the top and bottom of the letter paper with the word "human," written big and very neatly. He was hoping that she would seriously consider his proposal and give him a positive answer. He also wrote that the primary school was preparing to start classes again, and the plan was to convert it into a middle school. When the children started school again after a break of these few years, they would already be of middle-school age, and one or two middle-school teachers would be needed, she could come and teach. The school would have to reopen sooner or later. The only thing he didn't mention was love, but when he wrote all this, he had a lucky feeling. He again experienced the feeling of hope; it was a hope that needed only Qian's consent. This hope was realistic, and it required only the two of them to realize it. He was even moved by the fact that, in this chaotic world, a refuge could be found. All it needed was for her to be willing to enjoy it with him.

42

The old date tree outside the window had lost all of its leaves, and the bare thorny branches were poking into the leaden sky. Another tree, a tallow tree, had a few trembling purple leaves left on its slender branches. It was early winter when he received a reply from Qian; she said she would come to see him as soon as the village primary school went on winter vacation. It was a simple letter with spare sentences, written in neat characters amounting to just over half a page. There was nothing in the letter about coming to live with him, but she had finally decided to come, so he presumed that she had considered his proposal. Seeing some hope, he went on to turn it into concrete plans.

The late crop of rice had been harvested, dried, threshed, and stored in the production team granary, and the paddy fields had been drained and sown with grass seeds for green fertilizer so that in spring it could be ploughed into the soil to nourish the rice seedlings. Work in the paddy fields had finished for the year, and the peasants were attending to their own affairs, going into the mountains to chop wood and mending their pig enclosures. If earthen walls were put up or houses built, usually it meant there was a marriage or brothers were establishing separate households. He, too, needed to get some things done to prepare for Qian's arrival. He had to wait until after summer for the mud walls to dry right through before he could whitewash them, so, apart from filling in any gaps around the door, windows, and rafters, there was nothing else he could do. When Qian came, she, of course, would sleep in the same bed with him, and to the villagers that would mean they were married. He would have to spread the news in advance, so that the villagers would know that he was going to get married. It would be simple if Qian agreed. They would only need to go to the commune office for a marriage certificate, and there was no need for a banquet, as was the custom in the village. In any case, old customs had all been abolished. The only problem was that Qian's letter did not actually say if she was coming to get married.

The bus station was at the edge of the village, two buildings on the site of the old monastery that had burned down some years ago, and every day a bus came from the county town and immediately went back. He could not remember very clearly what Qian looked like, but, when the bus pulled in, he instantly recognized her, because unlike the locals getting off, she was carrying a travel bag. She had her hair in two short plaits, and her face was tanned. It seemed as if she had put on weight, but it could have been that she was wearing a lot, because it was winter. He went up, took the bag from her, and asked, "Did everything go well on the trip?"

Qian said that from such-and-such a place to such-and-such a place, she had to change long-distance buses, then get on a train, then change trains, before getting the long-distance bus here. Luckily, Rong had bought her a bus ticket and was waiting for her at the bus station, so she was able to get on the bus from the county town right away. Qian heaved a sigh as she said, "This is my fourth day on the road!"

Qian was nonetheless in good spirits and appeared relaxed. On the embankment between the paddy fields into the village, she walked leaning close to him, as if they had been sweethearts for many years, as if she were his wife. The young woman would soon be living with him, be his wife, they would rely on one another for life, were any other explanations needed?

Qian sat on the straw mattress on the plank bed, the most comfortable place in the house. He sat facing her on the only chair in the house, and said, "Take off your shoes, if you're tired you can prop yourself up on the bedding and have a rest."

He made Qian a cup of new-season green tea, the best local produce in this mountain village.

Qian looked at the lumpy walls and the roof tiles without a ceiling. He said he would whitewash the walls after summer and he could buy some timber for a ceiling, he could also get a carpenter to make some furniture, and she could arrange it however she liked. Qian said her cave dwelling also had earthen walls, but it was very dry. Her village was much poorer than this village, it was an expanse of brown loess with scarcely a tree. That season, even corn stalks were chopped up and burnt for firewood, there was not a patch of green anywhere. The primary school she was at was not too bad and there were three teachers altogether; the other two were locals. Village cadres of the production brigade administered the school, and it wasn't easy getting a position in such a school in a big village with over two hundred families. However, the school was one hundred and fifty kilometers from the county town, and buses didn't go there. To get to the county town, she had to get one of the peasants to give her a lift in a mule cart. He said the primary school in town was starting classes again, and he could speak to the commune and county cadres about getting her relocated. Qian was agreeable, she had no illusions and was very practical.

They went to an old teahouse, the only all-day restaurant in the county town, and ordered two sautéed dishes. During the big market festivals on the first and fifteenth day of every month, there was a rowdy din upstairs and downstairs, as peasants from the four villages filled the ten or so square tables to rest their feet, drink tea, and eat. However, usually—and on this particular afternoon—the place was empty. There were only the two of them, and they walked across the creaking floor upstairs to look down from the window onto the small narrow street paved with black cobblestones. The upstairs windows faced the windows on the opposite side, and downstairs there were shops. There was a meat shop, a bean curd shop, and a haberdashery shop; a general store that sold rope, lime, enamel ware, oil, salt, soy sauce, and vinegar; and an oil-and-grain store that also served as a factory for pressing oil and milling rice. There was a wood, bamboo, and metal cooperative that also sold bath soap, buckets, and hoes. And there was a traditional medicine shop that also sold Western medicines. The commune block was located here, too, and had a veterinary clinic, health clinic, savings bank, and a police station with one policeman in charge of the surrounding villages of the commune. Daily necessities were available in the commune block, as well as the most basic level of political authority, which issued marriage certificates stamped with the portrait of the Great Leader.

After eating, they walked the length of the little street in two minutes. He asked Qian if she wanted to buy anything, but she didn't say either yes or no. Anyway, he took her back to the haberdashery shop and bought her a round mirror with a nickel-plated wire stand. He also bought a double-bed sheet that required cotton fabric coupons, and a pair of nylon-and-cotton blend pillowcases that were expensive but did not require coupons. Qian didn't object and helped him to choose these. The few sheets in the shop had big red flowers on them, and the pillowcases all had the word for wedded bliss, "double happiness," embroidered on them; these items were bought by the villagers only for trousseaus, and there was nothing else to choose from. Qian let him buy these without objecting.

When they got back to his mud hut in the village, he closed the back window. There was a pond outside, with duckweed floating on it. Alongside the pond were smooth flagstones, where, morning and night, the village women did their washing, pounding it with wooden rods. In the summer the men also washed their feet and scrubbed down here. It was early winter, and there was no croaking of frogs to be heard.

Qian said she was tired, so he made up the bed with the sheet he had just bought, and Qian helped him. He also took out the pair of "double-happiness" pillowcases. He only had one pillow, so he stuffed a woolen pullover into the other one. Qian took some clothes from her bag and also stuffed them in.

Qian lay down first, while he sat on the bed and took her hand. Qian suggested putting out the light.

He remembered only her body. Everything else was unfamiliar, she was a woman about whom he knew nothing. There were only those few letters, in which she had either appealed to him for help or expressed her grief. The two of them were alike in having been exiled to some remote place, and, sharing the same hardships, sympathized with one another. Did he love her? He thought he did, but what about Qian? He had no way of knowing, but she had traveled thousands of kilometers to see him. Surely she had come to find someone to rely on? She gave herself to him, let him do what he wanted to her, but without any excitement or resistance, and without saying anything. Then she fell asleep, or, at least, he thought she had fallen asleep. He had a woman, a real woman who belonged to him, a wife he could establish a shared life with. Later on, they would come to have a shared language and rely on one another. In any case, he could never marry a village girl. In the village, the women bared their breasts to nurse their babies in the summer, and when they had rest breaks, they would start fights with the young men. He couldn't stand all the crude sexuality, coarse language, and total irreverence. He had, of course, learned to engage in verbal banter with the village women, but he always kept his distance. He didn't get embroiled in fighting with the women like the local village men did. The men would brawl so that they could enjoy themselves fondling the women, but when several women charged at a man and groped in his trousers, there would be noisy swearing and laughing as he sneaked away holding his trousers up. In the village, the farm work was never ending, year in and year out, and there was nothing else to do for fun. This was one of their few joys. The married women said to him, "Hey, why don't you like our local girls? The city girls aren't as juicy as our girls are here. Take a look at Maomei's skin, she's a peach that will ooze with a poke! And, what's more, she's good at any farm work. She's not clumsy like you, and she will save you all the hassle of finding yourself a sexy girl!" This talk had Maomei pouting, and she grabbed someone by the shirt and hid behind the person. He certainly liked this sexy girl, but, having seen these village women in action, he knew what she would be like later on. This was not the life he wanted.

Early in the morning, when Qian opened her eyes, the color had returned to her face and she was smiling. And he was definitely very happy. Qian was not beautiful, but she was cute. She snuggled against him, saw him looking at her, and closed her eyes again. He took her breasts in his hands and began fondling them. Qian was yielding and let his fingers wander over her body, her bent legs parted. He wanted her again but stopped himself. He shouldn't be in such a hurry to satisfy his lust, they were going to live together and there was plenty of time. He kissed her, and Qian's soft parted lips responded, so did her tongue. For the first time, he felt she was trying to make him happy. He thought Qian loved him, and had not simply come to him because of her own predicament.

"Should we go and register?" he asked Qian.

Qian's soft body snuggled right into his arms, and he was deeply moved when she nodded.

"Get up! We're going to the commune right now!"

He wanted to have a home with her, to establish their love as husband and wife. He wanted to show that he loved her by immediately registering their marriage, then thinking of how to get her transferred. They would settle down in peace and security in this mountain village, not worry about what was happening elsewhere, and simply live out their own insignificant lives.

Qian had brought with her a certificate issued by her commune, stating that she was not married, so, before coming, she must have given the matter some thought. The cadres at the commune all knew him, and he did not need to produce any documents. The two of them signed their names on the form, filled in their dates of birth, had it stamped by the secretary, and paid for the cost of the sheet of paper. This procedure took one minute.

Passing a meat stall with half a carcass hanging on a metal hook, he bought a whole leg of pork. Meat coupons were not needed in the village, production was good, and normally no one would starve to death. However, during the years of the Great Leap Forward, because of a single command from the Party, even grain rations were handed over to the commune and there were cases of whole villages starving to death. The villagers had learned from that experience. Every household had a vegetable garden where they grew sesame or rape, so that the seeds could be pressed for oil, and every household kept pigs, so that the villagers were able to eat the meat they themselves had salted. They lacked only money. He said later on they could also raise pigs. Qian glared at him, not understanding his joke.

Their first day as newlyweds was very happy. He lit the charcoal stove and, when the hot charcoals had stopped smoking, took it inside the house and put a big pot of pork on to stew. Qian started to sing softly, it was an old song from before the Cultural Revolution. He urged Qian to sing it loudly, and he sang along with her. Qian sang well, and her voice resonated. This was a discovery for him. Qian laughed and said, "I've had training, I'm a soprano."

"Really?" He got quite excited.

"What's so special about that?" Qian spoke without enthusiasm, but her voice was sweet and lovely.

"It's very important. We will be able to get through the days with you singing like this!"

This was something they had in common. He said, "Sing something for me!"

"What do you want to hear? You choose." Qian was pleased, and, with her head tilted to one side, she looked very beautiful.

"How about singing the Italian folk song 'Come Back to Sorrento'!"

"That's for a tenor."

"Sing 'The Drinking Song' from *La Traviata!*"

"It would be bad if people heard the words," Qian was hesitant.

"It won't matter in this village. Who would understand? You could sing it without the words," he said.

Qian stood up, took a deep breath, but then stopped and said, "It would be best for me not to sing foreign songs."

For a while he couldn't think of what was all right for her to sing.

"I'll sing 'Thirty *Li* Inn,' that old folk song!" Qian said.

As the sound of her singing spread, Qian's eyes shone. Outside the window a crowd of children appeared, and, afterward, a few women. The singing stopped and there was an exclamation outside the window, "What wonderful singing!"

Maomei had said this; she was there among them. The women started chattering.

"Where does the bride come from?"

"She'll be staying for a while, won't she?"

"She should just stay!"

"Where was she born?"

He opened the door and, inviting everyone inside, introduced her, "This is my wife!"

However, they all stayed crowded outside the door, and wouldn't come in. He took out a big bag of hard fruit-candies that he had bought in town and handed them out, saying, "Everything's been revolutionized. Marriage is now done in a new way, I'm married!"

At this point, he took Qian to visit in turn the homes of the Party secretary, then the head and the accountant of the production team. They were followed all the way by a troupe of children with sweets in their mouths. One woman said, "Quick, go and catch an old hen for them!"

People wanted to give them eggs, and a few old folks said, "If you want vegetables, come and get some from my garden!"

"It all sounds great, but when you offer to pay, they say no, no. After they refuse and you offer several times, they then accept. I can't owe them anything for their friendship, but I do have their friendship, I'm not an outsider here!" he said to Qian, feeling quite pleased. He added, "With your wonderful voice, all the schools in the village will want you. When you come here, you won't need to stand soaking in the mud of the paddy fields in rain or scorching sun all year long. And, of course, you will sing your songs for me."

With such a life they should be happy and contented. That night was sheer pleasure for him. Qian was not as passionate, as engaging, as lustful, or as beautiful as Lin, but he was embracing his own lawful wife. Indulging in this basic human pleasure, he no longer needed to be anxious or worried that the walls had ears, or be afraid of being spied on through the window. Listening to the sound of the wind and rain on the roof, he thought, in the morning when the rain stopped, he would take Qian into the mountains for an outing.

43

"You're just using me, this isn't love." Qian lay on the bed, expressionless, but she had said this quite clearly.

He was sitting at his desk by the window and put down his pen to turn to her. For years, he had written nothing, apart from copying Mao's *Sayings* for the investigation, but that was before he had fled the cadre school. They had spent most of the day walking in the mountains, but on the way back got completely soaked when it started raining. The charcoal fire was burning, and steam was coming from their wet clothes that were drying on a bamboo basket.

He got up and went over to sit on the edge of the bed. Qian was lying under the bedcovers, her eyes staring.

"What are you saying?" he said without touching her.

"You've killed me," Qian said. She remained lying on her back, not looking at him.

What she said hurt him. He didn't know how to respond and just sat there.

In the gully by the mountain, Qian was fine, she was in good spirits and started singing. They went up the slope to where the bushes were withered and no one was in sight, so he got Qian to sing as loudly as she wanted. Her clear voice swept through the gully and faint echoes were borne on the wind. The lower part of the slope was a tangled growth of grass and shrubs, and the clumps of rice stalks in the terraced paddies, still to be plowed in after harvest, made it look even more desolate. In spring, the slope would be covered in bright red azaleas, and the flowering rape in the fields would have turned into an expanse of golden yellow. But he preferred this early autumn scene of decay and desolation.

On the way back, it had started raining. By a creek, she picked some daisies that were still flowering and some dark-red branches of little-leaf box, and these were now in a bamboo penholder on the desk.

Qian was weeping wretchedly, but he couldn't work out why. When he tried to put his arms around her, she resolutely pushed him away.

In the rain, Qian's hair got wet, and rain was running down her face, but she had just put down her head and kept walking. He now wondered if she had been crying then. He had simply said don't worry, I'll light the fire when we get home, and you can warm up. He had never lived with a woman before and couldn't work out why she was throwing a tantrum like this just because she had got wet in the rain. He didn't know what to do. He thought he loved her and had done everything he possibly could for her, but maybe that was the extent of human happiness in the world.

He went out and headed for Maomei's home. Why had he gone to her house and not anywhere else? Because it was the second house into the town, it was still raining, and also because Maomei's mother said if he wanted to eat chicken she would catch one for him. Maomei's mother was in front of the house, getting some vegetables, and said she would get him an old hen right away, kill it, and have it sent over. He said there was no hurry, and that tomorrow would be fine.

When he returned home and pushed open the door, he got a

shock. The wet clothes that had been drying on the basket were strewn all over the floor, and the basket had been trampled and flattened. Qian was lying in the bed, her face to the wall. He held back his anger and forced himself to sit at the desk. The rain outside the window kept falling.

With nowhere to dissipate his frustration, he immersed himself in writing and kept writing until he could no longer see and put down his pen. Maomei was at the door, calling out to him. He got to his feet and opened the door. She was holding a plucked chicken and a bowl of innards. Not wanting her to see the clothes strewn on the floor, he took the chicken and quickly went to shut the door. But Maomei had seen it and looked at him in surprise. He avoided Maomei's startled eyes, closed the door and latched it, then sat quietly by the overturned stove, looking at the glowing charcoals on the floor.

"You don't believe in God, don't believe in Buddha, don't believe in Solomon, don't believe in Allah. The totems of precivilization peoples, the religions of civilized peoples, and the even larger number of contemporary creations, like all the idols put up everywhere and the fabulous utopias in heaven, all mysteriously make people go crazy. . . ." This filled several pages, all written on thin letter paper purchased in the little town. Qian had read this after she had started throwing her tantrum, and it was too late to burn it.

"You are the enemy!" The woman who had slept with him in the same bed angrily spat out this sentence. The woman in front of him, hair disheveled, clad only in her underpants, stood there in her bare feet, petrified with fear.

"What are you shouting for? People will hear, have you gone mad?" He went up to her.

The woman retreated step by step. Huddled close to the wall and brushing so hard against it that bits of sand started falling off, she yelled, "You're a counterrevolutionary, a stinking counterrevolutionary!"

He felt that her last sentence was less rabid, so he said, "I'm a counterrevolutionary, a genuine counterrevolutionary! So what!" He had to keep on the attack in order to control the woman's madness.

"You deceived me, took advantage of my momentary weakness, I've fallen into your trap!"

"What trap? Talk sense. That night by the Yangtze? Or this marriage?"

He had to turn the topic to their sexual relationship to hide his inner terror, and, trying hard to sound calm, he forced himself to say, "Qian, you're talking nonsense!"

"I'm quite clear-headed, I couldn't be more so. You can't hoodwink me!"

"What are you making all this fuss about?" He suddenly got angry and went up to her.

"Do you want to kill me?" Qian asked in a strange sort of way. Probably she had seen the anger flashing in his eyes.

"Why would I want to kill you?" he asked.

"You yourself know best," the woman said quietly, holding her breath, frightened.

If the woman had again shouted he was the enemy, probably he would have killed her right then. He couldn't let her come out with those words again, he had to make the woman feel secure, trick her into bed, make a pretense of being a caring husband. He went up to her and slowly said, "Qian, what is troubling you?"

"No! Don't come near me!"

Qian picked up the chamber pot in the corner and hurled it at him. He raised his arms to fend it off, but he was soaked. The acrid smell was worse than the humiliation. He gritted his teeth and brushed off the urine streaming down his face. His lips were salty and bitter, and he spat out with unconcealed derision, "You've gone crazy!"

"You want me certified as mad, but it's not that simple!" the woman said with a smirk. "I'm not going to let you off lightly!"

He understood what she was threatening, and, before things erupted, he had to burn up those sheets of paper on his desk. He had to bide his time and he had to restrain himself from charging at her. At that point, the urine in his hair had again reached his lips, and he spat it out in disgust but without making a move.

The woman squatted on the floor and started wailing loudly. He could not let the villagers hear her, and could not let anyone see this sight. He dragged her to her feet, twisted her arm to stop her from stamping her feet, and pushed her onto the bed. She struggled, weeping and yelling, so he grabbed a pillow and pressed it over her mouth. He thought he was in hell. This was his life, yet he was seeking to live in this hell.

"Make a noise and I *will* kill you!"

He made this threat as he moved away from her, took off his clothes, and wiped the urine off his face. The woman was afraid of being killed, and convulsed as she quietly sobbed. The fat plucked hen, innards removed and feetless legs sticking up, looked just like a woman's corpse. It thoroughly disgusted him.

For a long time afterward, he found women disgusting. He had to use disgust to bury his pity for this woman in order to save himself. Maybe Qian was right, he didn't love her, he had simply enjoyed her, he had for some time needed a woman and needed her flesh. What Qian said was right, too, he had not shown her tenderness, it was contrived, he had been trying to manufacture a make-believe happiness. The expression in his eyes when he ejaculated during intercourse must have betrayed that he didn't love her. However, under the circumstances of those times, terror had induced lust from both parties, which afterward did not become love but, instead, simply left behind the hatred that grew out of carnal release.

Qian sobbed and kept repeating, "You've killed me, I've been killed by you. . . ." Through her sobbing and mumbling, he made out that Qian's father had been chief engineer in a factory during the Nationalist period, and that during the period of purifying class ranks, he had been classified as a historical counterrevolutionary by the Army Control Commission. Qian didn't dare curse the injustice against her father, didn't dare curse the revolution, so she could only curse counterrevolutionaries and she could only curse him. But she was also terrified of him.

"It is this era that has killed you," he retaliated. Qian herself had said something like that in her letter. "The reality is that there is no escape for anyone, and it's our fate to care for one another, so don't talk about love!"

"Then why did you pick me? You could have picked that randy little slut. Why did you have to marry me?"

"Who? Who are you talking about?" he asked.

"That Maomei of yours!"

"I don't have anything to do with that village girl!"

"You're in love with the randy little slut, so why are you using me instead?" Qian sobbed.

"I can't make any sense of all this! We can get divorced right away, we can go to the commune tomorrow and announce we had fraudulently signed our names, say it was all a joke, an abominable farce to give the village cadres and the villagers a good laugh!"

Qian, however, said as she sobbed, "I won't make any more trouble. . . ."

"Then go to sleep!"

He got her to get up, and pulled off the urine-soaked sheet and covers from their nuptial bed. Qian, pathetically, stood out of the way. When he had remade the bed, he threw her some clean clothes from her bag, and told her to get changed and lie down. He got water from the water vat, washed himself all over, and sat on the stool by the fire all night.

Would he go on forever like this, caring for her? Wasn't he just a piece of straw to save her? He had to wait for her to fall asleep so that he could get those sheets of paper from the desk and burn them all. If she had a fit again, he would just have to say that she was psychologically disturbed. He would never write anything down again, he would just rot in this stench.

Qian said she hoped that she would die soon. She would never go with him again to desolate places, along cliffs or riverbanks. He would push her down. He could stop thinking about tricking her to go out the door, she would just stay in the house and not go anywhere!

As for him, he wished that she would drop dead, disappear forever, but he didn't say this. He regretted not having got himself a village girl who was physically and mentally healthy and who had not been educated. She would simply sleep with him, cook, and bear his children, she would never invade his inner mind. No, he hated women.

When Qian left, he took her to the bus stop at the end of town. Qian said, "You don't have to wait for the bus to leave, go home."

He said nothing, but hoped that the bus would move off soon.

44

It was winter again, and he was sitting by the brazier made by one of the locals, which he'd bought for two *yuan*. The brazier had an earthenware inset, which kept the hot coals and ashes warm, and to this he added a wire cover on top for his cup of tea. The winter nights were long, and it had already been dark for some time. In the off season in the countryside, the villagers would do their private work during the day, and at night it was pitch-black everywhere, only his house still had a light on. The incident of his quarrelling with his new wife had the villagers talking for ten to fifteen days, then no one asked about it and everything became peaceful again.

People now came to his house, and, without calling out, just pushed open the door and came in to look around, chat, smoke, and drink tea. That was how he received guests, and if people came, he would offer them a cigarette. He had got to know the village cadres well and established a pattern of life that would let others familiarize themselves with this scholar who did not meddle in village affairs. There were always copies of books by Marx and Lenin on his desk, so the village cadres who could read a little had a certain respect for him. Maomei once knocked at his door and asked if he had something good to read; he gave her a copy of *Nation and Revolution*. She took one look and said, "That's scary, how would I ever manage to read it?"

Maomei had a primary-school education but didn't dare take the book. Another time, his door was open, and having boiled a kettle of water, he was busy washing his sheets. Maomei came to the door and, leaning against the frame, said she could take them to the pond and pound them with a washing rod. She said they would be cleaner, but he declined her kind offer.

The girl stood there for a while, then asked, "Aren't you going away?"

He asked, "Where?"

Maomei pouted and, with an incredulous look, asked, "Then why did that person in your house go away?"

She was asking about Qian, but had avoided saying "your woman" or "your wife." Her bright, beautiful eyes looked seductively at him as she twisted the hem of her shirt and looked down at her shoes. But he couldn't have a sexual relationship with the girl, he no longer trusted women and wouldn't let himself be seduced again, so he said nothing and concentrated on washing the sheets in the tub. Maomei finally got bored and went off.

It was only through writing, and so engaging in a dialogue with himself, that he was able to dispel his loneliness. However before he could start writing, he had to plan things in advance. The thin letter paper could be rolled up and stuffed into the bamboo handle of the broom he kept behind the door: he had removed the inside membranes at the joints of the bamboo handle with a metal spike. When the pages accumulated, they would be put into an earthenware jar for preserving salted vegetables, with a layer of lime on the bottom, and sealed with a piece of plastic tied over the top. He dug a hole to store the jar in the earthen floor of the hut and covered the hole with the big water vat. He wasn't intending to write a book to hide in some famous mountain so that it could be read by later generations. He had not given the matter any thought because it was impossible to think about the future. He did not entertain any wild hopes.

Dogs were barking in the distance, then all the village dogs started barking. Afterward, it gradually became quiet. The dark night was long, but, as he was writing alone under the lamp, the excitement of pouring out his feelings made his heart palpitate. He felt vaguely worried that there were eyes in the dark at the front and back windows. He thought that maybe cracks in the door had not been properly sealed, and yet he had carefully examined the door many times. Still, he could sense footsteps outside the window. He sat stiffly by the brazier, holding his breath to listen, but there was no further movement.

Hazy moonlight came through the glass window pasted with paper on the inside. The moon had appeared in the middle of the night. He again detected movement outside the window and, holding his breath, quietly tugged the light cord looped over the bed headboard. A hazy figure silhouetted on the window disappeared in the next instant. He clearly heard noises in the bushes outside the window. Without putting on the light again, carefully and without a sound, he put away his manuscript, got into bed, and stared in the dark at the moonlit window pasted with white paper.

In the bright moonlight, there are eyes everywhere, spying, observing, surrounding, and watching you. In the hazy moonlight, there are traps everywhere, waiting for you to do the wrong thing. You don't dare open the door or the window, don't dare make a sound. Don't let yourself be tricked by the tranquility of this moonlit night when everyone is asleep. If you panic and lose control, those lying in ambush all around will for sure charge forward to arrest you and bring you to trial.

You mustn't think, mustn't feel, mustn't pour out your feelings and mustn't be solitary! You must either be doing hard physical labor or else snoring when you sleep, or else copulating and producing sperm so that children can be bred and a labor force nurtured. Why are you crazily writing? Have you forgotten the surroundings in which you are living? What is it, are you thinking of being a rebel again? Do you want to be a hero or a martyr? This stuff you're writing will have you eating bullets! You've probably forgotten how counterrevolutionary criminals were executed when revolutionary committees were established in the counties, haven't you? Those only count as minor events compared with today's public denunciations. Hands tied behind their backs, the prisoners are paraded with placards on their chests: written in black are the person's surname and crime, the surname crossed out in red. Wire is tied around their necks so tightly that their eyes bulge. This is the latest red authority's new idea for stifling any protests before executions, so that even in the netherworld those executed needn't think they might become martyrs. Two trucks with military police shouldering loaded rifles escort them as they are paraded through the villages of the commune. The loudspeaker on top blaring slogans, a jeep at the front leads, sending up a cloud of dust and driving chickens and dogs into a wild frenzy. Old women and grown-up girls come to the road at the entrance of the village, and children rush about and run after the trucks. Families wanting to collect a corpse have first to pay a fifty-*fen* bullet fee. But there will be nobody to collect your corpse. By then, your wife will have exposed you as the enemy, and your father is in the countryside undergoing reform through labor. And now you also have an old counterrevolutionary father-in-law, so on the evidence of all this, it won't be a miscarriage of justice to have you shot. Moreover, you have no miscarriage of justice to complain about, so stop writing before it's too late!

But you say you're not demented, that you have a brain, and it's impossible for you not to think. How about it, if you're not a revolutionary, and not a hero or a martyr, but are also not a counterrevolutionary? All you do is let your thoughts and imagination roam beyond the regulations of this society. You're crazy! It's clearly you who are crazy, and not Qian. Look, this person actually wants to let his thoughts and imagination roam! What a preposterous joke! All the women, the old people and the youngsters, will all come out to watch this lunatic eating bullets!

You say you seek a reality in literature? Stop joking! What reality does this person seek? What sort of toy is reality? A very cheap bullet! All right, so does that reality demand that you risk your life to write? But don't worry about that bit of moldy reality buried in the ground rotting, you'll be finished well before that happens!

You say what you want is a transparent reality, like a heap of garbage captured through the lens of a camera. The garbage is still garbage, but through the lens it has the imprint of your grief. What is real is your grief. As you are photographing, you will pity yourself, and you must find a state of mind that will allow you to endure the pain so that you can go on living to create a realm that is purely yours, that is beyond this pig's pen of a reality. Or, one might say, it is contemporary myth. By locating present reality in myth, pleasure can be derived from writing, so that it is possible to achieve existential and psychological balance.

He copied a myth he had written into the notebook left to him by his mother. He attributed the work to "Alipeides," a foreigner he'd invented, who could have been from Greece or some other place, and he attributed the translation to the poet Guo Moruo. At the outbreak of the Cultural Revolution, that old poet announced in the newspapers that all his past writings should be destroyed. For this, he received special favors from Mao and was able to survive. He could say it was a translation Guo made half a century ago and that he had copied it down while at university. Who would be able to check it out in this mountain village, or even in the county town?

Less than half of the notebook was the diary his mother had kept while doing farm labor before she drowned. Seven or eight years earlier, in the years of famine wreaked by the Great Leap Forward, his mother had gone to work on a farm to be reeducated, just as he had gone to the May Seventh Cadre School. She worked hard and had saved up several months of meat and egg coupons to supplement her son's food supplies when he came home. She looked after a chicken farm but was bloated from starvation. At dawn, after working a night shift, she went to the riverside to wash herself and fell into the river; it was not clear whether she was overfatigued or weak from malnutrition. At daybreak some peasants herding ducks to the river discovered her corpse in the water. The hospital autopsy listed the cause of death as cerebral ischemia. He wasn't able to see his mother's corpse. All he had was this diary, which recorded impressions of her reform through labor, as well as a mention that she wanted to accumulate leave so that she could spend a few extra days with her son when he came home for the summer vacation. After he had copied out the myth written under the pseudonym of Alipeides, he placed it in the pot for salting vegetables with a layer of lime on the bottom, and buried it in the earth under the water vat in his house.

45

On the market days of the four villages of the commune, the small street of the county town was lined with carrying poles and big baskets. There were sweet potatoes, dried red dates, chestnuts, pine kindling, fresh mushrooms, unwashed lotus roots, fine white rice noodles, bundles of tobacco leaves, strips of dried bamboo shoots, live fish and shrimp, pairs of hemp shoes all strung together, bamboo chairs, and ladles. And there were women, children, young men and old men, all shouting and calling out to one another, and bargaining. Do you want it or not? No! There was haggling, joking, quarreling. When the small mountain town was not making revolution, life was bearable.

He ran into Secretary Lu, who had been transferred from the provincial capital to work at the grass roots. Lu was with his entourage of commune cadres, some clearing the way and others following behind, it was as if he were a leader on a tour of inspection. However, this old revolutionary, a former local guerrilla fighter whom villagers called Secretary Lu, had not done well in the bureaucracy. Demoted, a grade at a time, during successive political movements in the provincial capital, he had ended up back in his home village. Nevertheless, this still counted as a cadre being transferred to work at the grass roots, so the local village tyrants revered him as some sort of deity. And, of course, he didn't have to do manual labor.

"Secretary Lu," he reverently addressed this mountain-village big boss.

"Are you the person from Beijing?" Secretary Lu obviously knew about him.

"Yes, I've been here a year or so," he said, nodding.

"Are you getting used to being here?" Secretary Lu asked as he came to a stop. He was tall and thin, and had a slight stoop.

"Yes, I was born in the South. The scenery is pleasant, and there is an abundance of produce." He was on the point of praising it as a paradise but stopped himself.

"Generally, people don't starve to death here," Secretary Lu said.

He detected another meaning behind these words and thought Lu must be unhappy about having been transferred to the country-side.

"I can't bear to leave, Secretary Lu, so I would appreciate your taking care of me!"

He seemed to be saying that he was entrusting himself to Secretary Lu, and he really needed someone's protection. He respectfully nodded again and had just started to walk away when, unexpectedly, this Secretary Lu started taking care of him right away. Lu said, "Come for a walk with me!"

So, he followed behind. Lu held back to walk alongside him and continued to talk with him, ignoring the chatter of the commune cadres. He was obviously being especially kind to him. He walked to the end of the little street with Lu and from the shops and houses all the way they were greeted with friendly smiles. He knew he had won the favor of Secretary Lu, and that his status had instantly changed with the townspeople.

"Let's have a look at where you live!"

This wasn't an order, but Lu taking care of him even more. Lu motioned the cadres, to send them away.

He led the way along the raised path between the paddy fields, and they entered his house on the edge of the village. Lu sat down at the desk. He had just made tea, when children started arriving. He went to close the door, but Lu motioned to him, saying, "There's no need, there's no need."

The news quickly spread through the village, and, before long, villagers and village cadres began arriving at his door so that there was an endless stream of hello Secretary Lu, hello Secretary Lu. Lu responded with something of a nod, then, holding his cup, blew on the leaves floating in his tea and started drinking.

There were, in fact, good people in the world. Or, maybe, people were basically good. Or, maybe, Secretary Lu had seen the outside world and had a good understanding of people. Or, maybe Lu also had been born at the wrong time, and was being kind to him because he needed someone he could talk with to alleviate his loneliness.

Lu did not touch the Marx and Lenin books on his desk, he knew they were a camouflage, and, when he got up to leave, he said, "If there are any problems, come and see me."

He escorted Lu to the path between the paddy fields, then his eyes followed his thin, slightly stooped back. This man had strength in his stride, and he was not like an elderly person. It was in this way that he came to be taken care of by this mountain big boss. But, at the time, he didn't understand why Lu had wanted to visit his house.

One night, he was at his desk, completely engrossed in writing, when suddenly someone shouting outside the door gave him a start. He got up right away, quickly stuffed the paper inside his straw mattress, and opened the door.

"You're not in bed yet, are you? Secretary Lu wants you to do some drinking at the Revolutionary Committee Office!"

The man was a worker from the commune, and, having delivered the message, promptly left. At this, he relaxed.

The commune's Revolutionary Committee Office was located on the stone embankment by the river. It was the former residence of a powerful landlord, and had a veranda and a large cobblestone courtyard. The owner was shot during the period when landlords were denounced and their land divided up. The village government took over the building, and, afterward, it became the site of the people's commune. The newly established Revolutionary Committee also carried out its business here. The courtyard and main hall were crowded with people, and indoors there was a strong smell of tobacco and sweat; he had not imagined that it would be so lively at night.

In a room right inside, Director Liu, the new appointee to the Revolutionary Committee, and Old Tao, who was in charge of arming the militias, were drinking with Secretary Lu behind closed doors. Lu got him to sit with them. On the table were peanuts spread out on a newspaper wrapping, a bowl of fried anchovies, and a plate of dried bean curd, presumably brought from the homes of the commune cadres. Some of the men merely put the liquor to their lips, then put it back down on the table; it was for show, and they were not actually drinking. A village youth with a rifle pushed open the door, poked in his head, bowed to those present, then stood his rifle by the door.

"Who told you to bring a rifle?" Old Tao asked crossly.

"Wasn't an emergency assembly called?"

"An emergency assembly is an emergency assembly. Nothing was said about it being an armed action!"

The youth, who couldn't see the difference, explained, "Then what do you want me to do? All the militia brigades have brought their rifles along. . . ."

"Don't go swaggering everywhere with your rifles! Put them all in the weapons department office and wait in the courtyard for the order!"

At that point, it dawned on him that the militias of the entire county would engage in a concerted action at midnight. From the county town to each of the villages, there were "large-scale monitoring and large-scale searching" assaults as soon as the county Revolutionary Committee gave the emergency assembly order. People from the Five Black Categories—landlord, rich, counterrevolutionary, bad element, rightist—were the main targets monitored. If unusual activities were discovered, there were immediate searches. When it was almost midnight, Director Liu and Old Tao went into the courtyard. They spoke about directions in the class struggle, then assigned missions. As the militia brigades set off, the courtyard grew quiet. The dogs nearby started barking first, and dogs in the distance gradually joined in.

Shoes off and sitting legs-crossed on the plank bed, Lu started asking him about his family. He simply said his father was also doing labor in the countryside, but didn't say anything about the unsuccessful suicide attempt. He said he had a maternal uncle who had been a guerrilla fighter, but, at the time, he didn't know that this old revolutionary elder had been admitted to the military hospital with influenza and was dead within hours of receiving an injection. Of course, he also said that as he was not familiar with the people and the locality, he greatly appreciated Secretary Lu's taking care of him.

Lu was silent for a while and then said, "The primary school in town will be reopening, but as a junior middle school. It's important that they learn to read and get some basic education. Go to the school and teach there!"

Lu said that when he was a child, his family was poor, and he was able to get the little education, which had served him to the present, only because of the kind old village teacher who didn't charge him a tuition fee.

After two or three hours, the courtyard started getting noisy again, as the militia brigades returned with their booty. They hadn't captured any counterrevolutionaries, but, in their searches, they had uncovered hidden cash and ration coupons in the homes of Five

Black Categories people. They had also captured a pair of illicit lovers. The man was a metal worker in the town handicraft cooperative, and the woman was the wife of Droopy Mouth in the Chinese medicine shop. The woman's husband had gone to the county town, yet there was this thrashing about in the dark inside the house. The militiamen who caught the illicit lovers said they had listened for a long time, and laughed as they talked about it.

"Where are they?" Old Tao, who was outside, asked.

"They're squatting in the courtyard."

"Are they wearing clothes?"

"The woman is, but the metal worker is naked."

"Get him to put on his trousers!"

"He's got his trousers on, but he didn't have time to put on a shirt. Weren't we told to catch them in the act? Otherwise they wouldn't own up to it!"

Lu called out to them from the room, "Get them to write confessions and let them go!"

Before long, the same militiaman shouted from outside, "Reporting to Secretary Lu, the man says he can't write!"

"Take down what he says and get his thumbprint on it!" This was Old Tao talking.

"Let's go and get some sleep," Lu said, putting on his shoes, then coming out of the room with him. Lu said to Old Tao, "Let them go, we can't worry ourselves with these sorts of things, let them go."

In the courtyard, the woman was cringing by the wall, with her head down. The metal worker, bare to the waist, came forward to kowtow to Lu, saying, "Secretary Lu, you are a kind man, a kind man, I won't forget you as long as I live!"

"Go home, the pair of you, and stop making fools of yourselves! In future, don't do it again!"

Having said this, Lu and he left the courtyard.

It was before dawn and the air was moist, laden with heavy dew. He thought to himself, Secretary Lu's magnanimity was like a mountain, and had given him an escape route. Life would be bearable as long as it was in the domain of this mountain boss.

From then on, he was greeted whenever he ran into commune cadres on the small street of the county town, and even the policeman from the local police station greeted him. They would pat one another on the shoulder, or give one another a cigarette. The middle school subsequently opened, and those big children who had not completed primary school were enrolled for two more years of study but counted as junior-middle-school students. He moved from the village into the town primary school, which had been idle for several years. The villagers all addressed him as "Teacher," and doubts and suspicions about his background vanished.

46

If you can use the smiling face of Buddha to look upon the world, you will be happy, your heart will be at peace, and you will be in nirvana.

You eat and drink with the village cadres, listen to them raving about nothing, bullshitting, and talking about women. "Have you ever touched Maomei?"—"Don't fuckin' talk nonsense, she's a pristine virgin!"—"Come on, have you ever touched her?"—"Hey, hold on, how do you know she's a pristine virgin?"—"Don't keep spouting rubbish, she's been promoted in the militia!"—"So what? You're just bullshitting, come on, out with it!"—"She's a successor to the revolution with the right genealogical background. How about saying something decent!"—"It's you who fuckin' never says anything decent!"—"That's crap, you've had too much to drink!"—"Hey, do you want to have a fight?"—"Come on, just drink up!"

This is life, and you have to drink like this to be happy! And you have to talk about how you managed to get a fir log and had two cupboards made from it. You tell people you are collecting cheap timber at the state price. You've settled here and, sooner or later, you will have to build a house, and building a house requires long-term planning. You will get a vegetable garden going, then build a pig pen, because for a person to get by, he has to keep a pig. Your meaningless chatter and gossip gradually makes you into a normal person, and your existence is no longer conspicuous.

You look at what is on the table. Virtually nothing is left of the big bowls of food, and the group has finished off nine and a half bottles of fiery sweet-potato liquor. You move away from the drunk who has slid under the table and is resting his head on your thigh, push the wooden bench, and stand up. The drunk falls to the floor and starts snoring. Everyone in the room, above the table or on the floor, is a rotten drunken mess with an idiotic smile on his face. It is only the host, Hunchback Zhao, who is sitting upright at the top end of the table, loudly slurping chicken soup. He rightly deserves to be Party secretary of the production brigade, because he can drink a lot but knows how to manage his liquor.

Over the past five days, there had been concerted training for seventy or eighty militia personnel from the villages. On the morning of the first day, they assembled in the commune courtyard, sitting on their bundled bedding, as they listened to instructions from the director of the Revolutionary Committee. Afterward, led by Old Tao, they did target practice on the threshing square, then they laid detonators, let off dynamite, and practiced with explosives under the cliff by the river. Also, on the harvested, drained paddy fields, they practiced squad and platoon assaults, scattering ranks like lightning, as they threw hand grenades, which noisily exploded and sent dirt flying into the air. They had been engaged in heavy action for days, and, on the last night, they were brought to this village. Hunchback Zhao, Party secretary for twenty years, had the credentials and the status for giving a really good feast to these brave stalwarts. Apart from the military-training food subsidy from the commune, there were also ten or so live chickens presented by the villagers. Hunchback's wife wasn't stingy either, contributing an old hen that was still laying, so there were meat and fish dishes, as well as salted vegetables and bean curd.

The heads of the militias were seated at the table in Hunchback's dining hall, the rest were looked after in the granary by the family of the brigade accountant. Those able to dine at Hunchback Zhao's table, naturally, had some standing, and he had been designated by Secretary Lu, as the school representative, to take part in the military training.

"Teacher, you've come from being at the side of Chairman Mao in the capital, you're willing to suffer hardship here, and you're one of our Secretary Lu's people, so don't stand on ceremony. Come and sit in the place of honor at the table!" Hunchback Zhao said.

The women customarily did not sit at the banquet table. Hunchback's wife was in the kitchen cooking, and young Maomei, who was just eighteen and had been promoted to company leader in the militia, was serving the food and running to and from the kitchen. The eight men at the table drank and ate from dusk till midnight. A bottle of liquor just filled a big soup bowl, and this was passed around, for each person to ladle out one scoop. Everyone was given the same amount, no more and no less. After a few rounds, when bottle after bottle had been emptied, he said he couldn't drink as much as everyone else, and, having refused several times, got away without drinking any more.

"That you, a distinguished person from the capital, will consent to drink liquor from the same bowl as us, country bumpkins with mud caked on our legs, is a great honor. Bring Teacher some rice!" Zhao said.

Maomei served him from behind a very big bowl of rice.

Flushed with alcohol, everyone became very talkative, and there was much laughing and joking. From revolutionary rhetoric they turned to talking about women, and started getting crude, so Maomei fled to the kitchen and didn't reappear.

"Where's Maomei? Where's Maomei?"

The men, all with red faces and thick necks, giggled and kept clamoring. Hunchback's wife came out to mediate, "Why do you want Maomei? Don't start getting reckless with your arms and legs just because you're full of alcohol, she's a pristine virgin!"

"Don't pristine virgins think of men?"

"Hmph! Her flesh is not for your lips!"

Everyone then turned to praising Hunchback's wife, saying this and that about her. "She knows how to manage the household and knows how to care for people. Old Zhao is really lucky!"

A local from the village then said, "There isn't anyone who hasn't enjoyed her favors!"

"Get rid of that filthy mouth of yours!" The teasing put Zhao's wife in high spirits. Straightening her apron, she put her hands on her hips and told everyone off, "All of you are gluttons, go get your-selves stuffed on green-feed slops!"

There was no end to the coarse talk, and there was the stench of alcohol all over the place. He could tell from the banter that not one of them had a bad pedigree. Otherwise, how else would they have managed to become village cadres?

"If it wasn't for the kindness of Chairman Mao, would the poor and lower-middle-class peasants enjoy what they do today? How else would we have girl students coming from the city to settle in our villages?"

"Stop all this indecent thinking!"

"It's only you who's fuckin' decent. Have you ever had it off with them? Come on, out with it!"

"There's a teacher present, surely he's disgusted by all this talk!"

"The teacher's not an outsider, he respects us, we people with mud on our legs. Didn't he sleep on the ground with us?"

You had, indeed. You slept with them on paddy-rice hay spread on the floor of a granary, and every day after military training you watched them compete in strength, wrestling, and tumbling, after which the loser had to let the winner grope in his trousers. When the village women watched, they joined in the cheering, some would even go up to tug at the loser's belt, and it would all end up with the men and women getting into a huddle. At such times, Maomei would stand aside, cover her mouth, and just laugh. Everyone was jolly until the whistle signaled for the lights to be put out.

You came out of the main hall; a cool breeze was blowing gently. There was no nauseating stench of alcohol, and the pure fragrance of paddy grass wafted in gusts through the air. In the moonlight, the villages became fused with the shadows of the undulating mountains. You sat down on the stone mill by the house and lit a cigarette.

You rejoiced that you had won their trust. There were no more suspicious noises outside, and no longer figures silhouetted on the windows in the moonlight. You were no longer being spied on. It seemed that you had settled permanently here, and that, from now on, you would mix with these men. They have lived like this for generations. They rolled in the mud and on women's bodies, when they were tired or drunk they fell fast asleep, they did not have nightmares. You could smell the moist air of the mud and felt relaxed, drowsy.

"Teacher, are you still up?"

You turned and saw Maomei come out the back door of the kitchen and stop by the pile of firewood. The hazy moonlight perfectly revealed her feminine charm.

"Teacher, you're really relaxed. Are you looking at the moon?"

She smiled at you. She had a sweet voice with a lilt. She was a sexy girl, her pointed breasts were firm, and you thought they had been touched by men. She was radiant and healthy, without worries or fears. This was the soil that had given birth to her. She would receive you, and seemed to be saying this, but did you want her? She was waiting for your response. In the darkness, her glinting eyes were fixed upon you without embarrassment or fear, once again arousing your lust for women. She was boldly confronting you, late at night, as she leaned against the pile of wood, but, unlike those men, those bandits, you didn't dare flirt with her or approach her, you didn't dare be frivolous, you lacked the courage.

47

A day of rain and another day of rain, fine continuous drizzle. School finished some time ago, after the two afternoon classes, because students must go home to work. Your room near the teachers' office is made of brick, and there is a timber ceiling, so you do not need to worry about rain leaking in. Your mind is at peace, you like rainy days, and you no longer have to put on a big bamboo hat to work with your legs soaking in the paddy fields. With your door shut, there is the sound of the wind, the sound of the rain, as well as the sound of your reading. But not all of these sounds are audible, because you are only silently reading or writing in your mind. However, you are finally living the life of a normal human being, even if you do not have a family. You no longer want a woman to share your roof, you would prefer to live alone rather than run the risk of being exposed. If you feel the urge, you just write about it. By doing this, you win freedom for your imagination, and any woman you want can come to you via your pen.

"Teacher, Secretary Lu wants to see you!" a girl student was calling from outside his room.

He had fitted a spring lock so that people couldn't just walk into his room. If he had to talk to his students, he went to the teachers' office next door, especially in the case of girl students. The headmaster, who lived on the other side of the basketball field, was always watching his door. He had been headmaster of the primary school for twenty years, but now that it had suddenly been converted into a middle school, he was afraid of being replaced by this outsider under the protection of Secretary Lu. He wanted to catch this outsider in some act of impropriety with a girl student, so that he could be made to roll up his bedding and go away. However, he could not convince the headmaster that all he wanted was a place to stay in peace.

This student, Sun Huirong, was a pretty and lively girl. Her father had died of some illness a long time ago, and her mother sold vegetables at the cooperative in town in order to somehow bring up three daughters, Huirong being the eldest. Huirong was always trying to be nice to him: "Teacher, I'll wash your dirty clothes for you!" "Teacher, I've brought you some amaranth fresh from our vegetable garden!" Whenever he passed by the Sun house, if the girl saw him, she would always run out and greet him, "Teacher, come in and have some tea!" He knew almost every family in the small street, and had visited their homes, either sitting for a while in the main hall or else having a cigarette on the doorstep. He had made this town his hometown and was now a local, but he had never been into this girl's home. The girl said to him, "Our home is a women's domain." Probably she wanted a father and didn't necessarily want a man.

The girl had come in from the rain, and her hair was all wet. He got an umbrella and told her to take it home with her, but when he went back inside to get a bamboo hat, the girl had run off. When he had almost caught up with her, he called out. She turned around in the rain and shook her head. The front of her shirt clung to her, revealing her small, developing breasts. She was happy and laughing as she ran off, probably pleased she had delivered such an important message to her teacher.

Lu lived in a rear-courtyard compound of the commune complex, and he went in through the side gate opposite the river embankment. The yard was clean, paved with cobblestones, and there was a small well. At the time when that powerful landlord was executed, the man's mistress was living in this small, secluded, peaceful compound. Lu was lounging on a bamboo couch cushioned with a piece of deerskin. A pot of meat with a delicious pungent aroma was stewing on the brazier that stood on the brick floor.

"It's dog meat with chili. Old Zhang at the police station brought it, he said he had trapped a wild dog. Who can tell if it's a wild dog or a domestic dog, anyway, that's what he told me." Lu didn't get up. "Get a bowl and a pair of chopsticks, and pour some liquor. My back is no good, it's an old gunshot wound and it gives me trouble whenever it rains. At the time, we were fighting a war, and no doctors were around, so just to stay alive counted as being lucky."

He poured himself some liquor, then sat on the little stool by the brazier to eat and drink. Lu talked a lot as he lay on the bamboo couch.

"I've killed people, shot them dead myself, it was war, but I won't go into all that. More people died at my hands than can be counted, and not all of them deserved to die. Instead, those who deserved to die didn't."

Lu suddenly reverted to his normal silence and indifference. He didn't know what Lu was getting at, and this intrigued him.

"That old bastard, Lin Biao, plunged to his death, it's been reported, hasn't it?"

He nodded. The deputy chairman of the Party was trying to flee the country, and his plane had crashed in Mongolia. Well, that was how it was reported in official documents. The villagers were not particularly surprised, and they all said that by looking at Lin Biao's monkey face, one could tell he would come to a nasty end. What if he had been handsome? In that case, the villagers would have thought he should be emperor.

"There are some people who didn't plunge to death." Lu came

out with this statement, then put down his drink. He could tell, Lu was angry and frustrated, but this statement was non-committal. Lu was experienced, and had been through political upheavals; it was not likely that he would tell him what was really on his mind. As for him, it would be unwise to jeopardize their relationship, because as long as Secretary Lu kept out of trouble, he, too, would be able to survive under his protective umbrella. Come on, drink some liquor to go with the dog meat. And stop worrying about whether it's wild or domestic.

Lu got up and gave him a sheet of paper with a classical poem written on it. It followed the *lüshi* pattern for five-character lines, and expressed Lu's joy over a certain person, Lin, plunging to his death. "Could you check if I've chosen words with the correct tones?"

This was probably why he had been asked to come. He thought about it for a while, suggested changing one or two words, then said he could find no other problems. He said he had a book on the patterns for *lüshi* poems and that he would have it sent over, so that Lu could use it as a reference.

"I grew up herding calves," Lu said. "My family was poor and couldn't afford to send me to school. I used to climb the tree by the village teacher's window to listen to the young students reading their lessons aloud, and that was how I learned to recite Tang poetry. The old teacher saw that I was eager to learn, so he didn't charge me tuition fees. From time to time, I would bring him a load of firewood, and whenever I had free time, I attended classes and learned to read. When I was fifteen, I shouldered a musket and went off to join the guerrillas."

This whole stretch of mountains used to be the territory of Lu's guerrilla band in those times, and, although now it was where he had been sent, without his being appointed, he was regarded as the secretary of all the newly reinstated Party secretaries by the communes all around. Lu lived here as a recluse. Lu told him he had enemies—

of course, not the local armies belonging to landlords, rich peasants, and local tyrants; they were all suppressed a long time ago. They were "some people up there." He did not know where "up there" was, or who the "some people" he referred to were, but, clearly, the cadres in the county town wouldn't be able to get rid of Lu. Lu could defend himself any time, the grass matting under his pillow concealed a bayonet, and, in a wooden box under the bed, was a light machine gun, which was in good condition and polished to a shine. There was also an unopened crate of ammunition. All this was commune militia equipment, yet he was storing it in his room with impunity.

Was Lu waiting for an opportunity to win back political power? Whether he had taken these precautions in case troubles should erupt, it was hard to tell.

"In times of peace, the people who live on these mountains cultivate the land, but in times of chaos, they are bandits. Beheadings used to be common, and I grew up watching them. Back in those times, the bandits were bound, but they held their heads high as they stood waiting for the ax, and they wouldn't so much as flinch. It's done differently nowadays. Those to be shot have to kneel, and their necks are tied. The guerrillas were bandits!" Another startling statement came from Lu's lips: "But we had the political objective of overthrowing the powerful tyrants and dividing up the land."

Lu did not say that the land divided up now all belonged to the state, and that, while a small amount of grain was allocated to each person, any surplus had to be handed over to the state.

"What the guerrillas wanted was money and grain. They kidnapped for ransom and tore their victims apart. If, at the designated time and place, a ransom was not delivered, they carried out the same acts of cruelty as the bandits. Two young bamboo saplings, the size of a rice bowl in girth, were held down, as a leg of the victim was tied to each sapling. With a cheer, they would let go of the saplings, and the victim would be catapulted up and torn apart!"

Lu had never done this, but he had obviously seen it done, and he was educating this bookish person, him.

"You're a bookish outsider. Don't make the mistake of thinking that it's easy to get by and that it's peaceful here, in these mountains! If you don't put down roots, you won't survive!"

Lu didn't talk the bureaucratic talk of the petty cadres who were doing their best to get promoted, and he completely swept away any lingering childhood fantasies he had about the revolution. Could it be that Lu would someday need him, and had to make him equally cruel and ruthless so that he could serve as a helper when this mountain king made his comeback to power? Lu also talked about the pale-complexioned intellectuals from town, who joined the guerrillas.

"What do students know about revolution? What the old man said was right." The "old man" he was referring to was Mao. "Political power comes from the barrel of a gun! Which of those generals and political commissars doesn't have blood on his hands?"

He told Lu he could never be a general, he was terrified of fighting. He wanted to make this quite clear in advance.

Lu said, "If that was not the case, why else would you have fled to these mountains? But you must be on guard against being butchered."

This was the law of survival and this was based on Lu's experiences in life.

"Go to the town and do a social survey, say that I sent you. You won't need an official letter, just say it's a job I've given you. I want you to write up historical materials on the class struggle in this town. Just listen to what people say, but, of course, don't completely believe what anyone tells you. You don't need to ask about what's currently happening because you won't get any answers. Let people prattle on, it will be just like listening to a story, and everything will become clear to you. Earlier on, there was no motor-vehicle access into this area, it was a bandits' hideout. Don't think that because the metal worker kowtowed to you he will obey you. He was let off and he was grateful, but, put under pressure, he would chop you down in the dark from behind! That old woman with the limp, operating the hot-water urn on the street, did you think she had bound feet? Having bound feet was never the done thing in these mountains. After being kidnapped by guerrillas, the woman had her shoes stolen in the middle of winter, so all her toes froze off. But she was a woman, and, at least, her life was spared. This house belonged to her family. Her father was executed, and her eldest brother died on a prison farm. They say that her other sibling escaped overseas."

He thus instructed you, and life, too, thus instructed you. As a result, the moral indignation and righteous anger imperceptibly rising from your residual feelings of sympathy and sense of justice were completely snuffed out.

"We've had too much to drink!" Lu said. "Tomorrow, when you wake up, come for a walk with me up to Nanshan. There used to be a temple on the mountain, but it was razed to the ground by Japanese bombs. The Japanese didn't get there, they only got as far as the county town. The guerrillas had hidden on the mountain, so the Japanese could only bomb the temple on top. A monk had built the temple after the defeat of the Heavenly Kingdom of the Taipings, the Long Hairs. Hadn't the bandits provided just the right environment for the rebellion of the Long Hairs? Still, the Long Hairs couldn't compete with the imperial forces, and, when they lost, they fled to this mountain and became monks. There's a broken tablet on the mountain. Some of the words are missing, but come and have a look at it."

48

If one views the world through a lens, the world instantly changes, and even the ugliest things can become beautiful. You had an old camera, and, during those years in the countryside, it always went with you into the mountains. For you, it was another eye. You photographed scenes of the mountains, a mountain of bamboo swaying in the wind, green waves like a mass of feathers fixed on the negative as the shutter clicked. At night, you developed the film in your room, and, even though the color was lost, the brilliance of light in the contrasting of black and white was intriguing, as if it were a dream world. You were using expired movie film, a big two-hundred-meter spool, bought through a friend from a film studio before you left Beijing. For thirty *yuan*, it was virtually a gift. Back in those times, film studios only made news documentaries celebrating the revolution, and it was always with a jubilant fanfare of gongs and drums: the Great Leader inspects the Red Guards, the hydrogen bomb is successfully exploded, and acupuncture is used for anesthesia. Mao's Thought brought victory after victory. By studying Mao's Thought, patients underwent operations on their chests or stomachs, or Mount Everest was climbed and red flags fluttered on the rooftop of the world. The film studios had all gone over to using the overly reddish color film they had started producing in China, but you preferred black-and-white photographs, and could look at them endlessly, without tiring of them.

You looked at the colorless houses of the village, a gray-black roof and a pond in drizzling rain, a log bridge with a hen on it. You were especially fond of the hen. This black creature in front of your camera was pecking on the ground and had cocked its head to look around. Not knowing what a camera was, it stared right at it. Those shiny beady eyes were amazing, and you saw endless meanings in its cocked head and stare.

There was also a photograph of ruins. The insides of the buildings were overgrown with weeds, and the roofs had collapsed. It was a village that had died, and no one since had settled there; it had fallen into total decay and not a trace of the Great Leap Forward of that year remained. That year, all the grain harvested was handed over to the state, and the whole village, including the village Party secretary, was reduced to starving corpses. But the Party was dismissive, and had people put on guard at the county-town bus stop to prevent anyone sneaking in to beg for food. Anyway, the people in the town also had fixed grain rations, and the villagers would not have found anything to beg for. On this mountain, the bigger children all remembered digging up the roots of kudzu vines to fend off hunger; then, when they wanted to shit, having to bend over with their trousers off and getting smaller children to help them dig it out with twigs. The kudzu formed shit pellets that were as hard as rocks, and it was agony to take a shit. All this has been related by the students, and, of course, couldn't be seen in the photograph, but the desolation that could be seen was beautiful. Viewed through the lens of a camera, even disasters could possess aesthetic qualities.

You also captured on camera two lovely young women, the older one eighteen years old, and the younger one fifteen. The older one's photograph was a profile of her deep in thought. Her father was a teacher in the middle school of the county town, and the father of her father, that is, her paternal grandfather, was a landlord. Before she completed middle school, she was sent to this remote mountain. The younger one had been a junior-middle-school student. Her father was a technician in an optometrist's shop in the provincial capital, and, when his daughter decided she wanted to work in the countryside, he couldn't stop her. In the photograph, this younger woman's head was tilted, and she was laughing silly, as if she were being tickled. The two had been working on the mountain for a year, when the primary school reopened and teachers were needed. They were lucky; they no longer had to do manual labor, they became teachers. The two were happy and excited when you told them you wanted to bring your students on a tea-picking excursion. They said to stay at their school, it would be perfect, they had two classrooms so the boys could sleep in one and the girls in the other. The room in the middle was partitioned. The front part was for preparing class work and grading papers. Behind the partition, there was a plank bed—their bedroom; they said you could stay there and they would stay in the village. Before they came to the countryside, while they were at school, they would certainly have denounced their teachers. Yet seeing you, a teacher from the middle school in town, was for them just like meeting a member of their family. They were extremely hospitable, treated you to a meal of steamed salted pork, sautéed eggs, and bamboo-shoot soup, and they talked and chattered nonstop. It was on that occasion that you took the photograph. They were not like the village girls who would hide as soon as you held up the camera, they were self-assured and even posed for you. It was right when the younger woman burst into silly laughter that you pressed the shutter. After you developed and printed the photo, you saw that the older woman had turned her eyes from the camera and looked very sad, and that in the silly laugh of the younger woman was wantonness seldom seen in so young a woman. It was under the thick black branches of an ancient torreya tree by a steep cliff that you took the photograph.

It was April, spring, it was green everywhere, and the tea-picking season was soon to begin. He went in by the hollow in the mountain, and, after crossing á big mountain and a log bridge over a deep river of roaring water that sparkled in the bright sun, arrived at this production brigade specializing mainly in growing tea and bamboo. Halfway up a mountain slope, he found the brigade leader digging holes and planting corn, and they came to an agreement that he would bring thirty students from town to spend ten days picking tea. The students would sleep on the floor in the primary school and would bring their own rice from home. The brigade would provide firewood, vegetables, oil, salt, and bean curd, and the cost for these would later be reimbursed by the school. It was four o'clock in the afternoon, but, as it was not advisable for him to spend the night in the mountains halfway back to town, the two teachers got him to stay the night at the school.

In the mountains, it got dark early, and, when the sun receded to the back of the cliff, the school sports field was already in darkness. The village stockade was shrouded in mist rising from the river, and the men and women on the mountain had stopped work, shouldered their hoes, and gone home. The village started to bustle with activity, dogs were barking, people were talking, and smoke started curling above the rooftops.

Outdoors, the air was heavy with moisture. The older woman got the charcoal fire going, and boiled a pot of water for him to soak his feet. After traveling a whole day on the mountain road, soaking his feet in the hot water relieved his fatigue and was very enjoyable. The other woman brought him her soap. They were grading student assignments by the kerosene lamp, when villagers started arriving after their evening meal. There were men, youths, and young girls. The men mostly sat around the fire, but the youths crowded around the lamp on the table and started playing poker. The two women stacked up the exercise books and put them away. There were a few unmarried village women, but the married women with babies were probably busy at home. Children ran in and out and made an awful racket, while the men flirted and wrangled with the village women. The village women had sharp tongues, and, by comparison, the two women from the city had softer voices and spoke less. However, the student demeanor they had adopted when talking with him earlier had changed. Dirty words occasionally came from their lips, and they would tell anyone off. At night, the primary school served as a community club, and everyone was in high spirits.

"We're putting out the lamps, we're putting out the lamps! The teacher is worn out from walking all day and has to sleep!" The older woman started herding everyone out. People grumbled, but reluctantly went off. The two women also said good night and went off with the last of the crowd.

The remaining embers in the charcoal burner died, and the room suddenly turned cold. A chilly draught was streaming in from the classroom, so he got up and shut the door. It blew open again straight away. When he shut it again, he found there was no bolt. The door and doorframe was pitted with nail holes, but the bolt had been removed. He steadied himself, then went to the classroom to shut the main door, but, in the darkness, could not find the cross bar. The metal holders on the two parts of the door were there, but the cross bar was nowhere to be found. He got a desk and rammed it against the two parts of the door, returned for the lamp, then went into the inner room behind the wooden partition. On the far side, there was a small door that opened to the classroom. The bolt to the door had also been removed, and only the metal bolt-holder remained. Fortunately, the doorframe was tight, so the door was jammed shut. He didn't go out again to see if the door of the other classroom could be bolted. Nothing here was worth stealing, apart from the two helpless young women from the city who usually slept here.

He blew out the lamp, took off his shoes, socks, and clothes, and lay down to listen to the mountain wind groaning like the deep growl of a wild animal. When the wind had passed, he again heard the sound of the water from the deep river. That night he slept badly. A nagging feeling that some wild thing was going to charge in any moment seemed to have kept him half-awake all night. In the morning, when he got up and pulled aside the blankets, he saw stains all over the gray sheet. The same stains were also all over the two pillows. He felt sick.

On the way back, his mind turned to what had happened with his student Sun Huirong, and he came to the realization that he had gradually become weak and cowardly after living these years in the countryside. He had hidden himself away securely, but, while he had peace of mind and could spend long periods of time in front of the mountain looking at the rushing river, not thinking about anything, he was, in fact, no better than a maggot.

49

She wants to look at ancient forests. You say where will you find ancient forests in Sydney, it will take days driving to some uninhabited place on this continent, Australia. Anyway, you've seen everything from the plane. It's an expanse of red-brown dry land with some jagged, fishbone-like mountain ridges poking up out of it. It was like that for hours on the plane. Where will you find primeval forests?

She unfolds a tourist map, and, pointing at a green patch, says, "Right there!"

"That's a park," you say.

"A national park is a nature preserve," she insists. "Animal and plant life there are kept in their original habitat!"

"Are there kangaroos?" you ask.

"Of course!" she replies. "You don't have to go to a zoo to see them. This isn't France where your wolves are purchased from all parts of the world, then fenced off somewhere so they can poke out their heads for tourists to look at."

Unable to change her mind, you mumble, "I'll have to see friends at the Performance Studies Centre about a car."

You also say that, although they had invited you here to put on one of your plays, you had only just met them and don't want to impose on them. She says that the trains go right there, and, pointing on the map to Central Railway Station, draws a line down to the patch of green at the Royal National Park.

"There's a station at Sutherland. See, it's easy to get there!"

She, Sylvie, hair cropped short, boyish like a middle-school student, looks much younger than she actually is, but her ample buttocks indicate that she is already a mature woman. You toast a slice of bread and add milk to your coffee. She drinks her coffee black, never with sugar, and eats her bread without butter. It's all to keep her figure.

The two of you come out of the small building where you are staying. Suddenly, she runs back inside, remembering to get a towel and her bathing suit. She says that just across the nature preserve, the Royal National Park, is the beach, and she will be able to have a swim and lie in the sun.

The train goes from Central Railway Station right through to Sutherland, a small station, and only a few people get off. Outside the station, there is a small town, but it's not clear where the forest is. You say you will have to ask someone, and return to the exit to ask the ticket seller, "Which way is it to the ancient forest? The park, the Royal National Park!"

"You need to go to the next station, Loftus," the ticket seller at the little window says.

So you get tickets and go back into the station. Twenty minutes later, a train comes, but it doesn't go to Loftus. That will be the next train.

Half an hour later, there is an announcement over the loudspeaker that the next train is running late, and the passengers should go to the platform on the other side. She asks the fat stationmaster what the problem is. The man replies, "Just wait, just wait, it'll be here." The door of the guardroom promptly shuts.

You remind her that the day the two of you arrived in Australia, people said it took two to three days, or even a week, by train from Sydney to Melbourne, and that they themselves would never make the trip by train. If they didn't go by plane, they would go by car. You say it's likely you will both be waiting until dark. But Sylvie paces back and forth and is all worked up. You tell her to sit down, but she can't stay seated.

"Go to the vending machine and buy a packet of peanuts, or those oily Australian nuts, the round ones, what are they called?" You're teasing her, and she ignores you.

An hour later, the train finally comes.

Loftus. Outside the station is an even smaller town, also gray and drab, and on the overhead bridge above the railway tracks is a horizontal banner: VISIT THE TRAM MUSEUM.

"Do you want to go?" you ask.

She ignores you, runs back to the ticket window, then signals to you. You start toward the exit, and the ticket seller motions the two of you to go back into the station. You ask her, "Is the ancient forest on the platform?"

"You don't understand his English!" she says.

As you return into the station, you thank the ticket seller in English. She gives you a look, and laughs. She is no longer angry, and explains that the man said it was closer, going via the platform. All right, you follow her across the tracks, walking on the gravel heaped there for repairing the road. A man on duty, in a uniform, is watching the pair of you, and you shout out to him, "The park? Where is the Royal National Park?"

You know this much English. He points to an exit where the fence is broken.

The two of you get to the highway, where there are lots of speeding cars but no pedestrians. A big sign on the fence around the railway station reads TRAM MUSEUM; there is an arrow on it. There is no option but to go there to ask the way. Inside a high gateway is a small, toy-sized wooden hut, and, nailed to it, is a sign with the admission price clearly written on it, the price is different for adults and children, but there is no one inside selling tickets. A large open space has been laid with small metal tracks, and a carriage of an old tram with neatly painted paneling stands there. A woman with ten or so children surround an old man wearing a cap with embroidered sides and a sunshade. He is explaining the history of the tram. The old man finally finishes talking, and the woman and the children get on board the tram. He now turns to them, and touches his cap to salute. Sylvie tells him why she is here, and the old man spreads out his hands and says, "This is the National Park. It's all around us, the two of you and me. This museum of ours is a part of the park!"

He points out the area of the museum, the space from the gateway to where the old tram carriage is stopped.

"But what about the forest, the ancient forest?" Sylvie, her hair short like a boy's, asks.

"It's all forest—" He turns and points at the eucalypt forest by the highway.

You can't help laughing aloud. Sylvie glares at you, then asks the old man, "Which is the way into it?"

"You can go in anywhere, and you can also get on board. It's five Australian dollars for each of you, you're both adults."

"There's no question about that." You then ask, "Does this tram also go into the forest?"

"Of course. These are return tickets, and you don't have to pay me now, pay me if you're satisfied. If you're not satisfied, you can walk back, it's not very far."

With a clang, the old tram moves off. The bell doesn't sound old, and has a clear ring. You are happy, just like the children on the tram, but Sylvie pulls a face and starts to sulk. The tram goes into the forest. There are eucalypts and more eucalypts, all sorts of eucalypts that you can't tell apart. The trunks are brownish-red, brownish-yellow, or greenish-yellow, and the bark is peeling off in strips on some of them. There is also a patch of black, charred trees, and the tips of the contorted branches, quivering in the wind like long, disheveled hair, give an eerie feeling.

A quarter of an hour later, the track comes to an end.

"Have you seen a kangaroo?" you tease.

"So, you're making fun of me. I'm off to get one for you to have a look at!"

Sylvie jumps off the tram and runs onto a path with an arrow pointing to an information kiosk. You sit down by the path. After a while, she rushes back, clutching some pamphlets, and saying there's a path down to the sea, but that it is a few hours' walk. The sun has already moved to the lower part of the forest, and it is almost four o'clock. She looks at you, but doesn't suggest anything.

"Then let's go back the way we came. In any case, we've visited a museum," you say.

The two of you get on the tram with the children, and she ignores you. It's as if it is entirely your fault. You go back to the station and board the train for Sydney. The carriage is empty, and she lies down on the seat. You examine the tourist map and find that there is a station on the way back, called Cronulla, which is right by the sea. You suggest getting off the train right away, and drag her to her feet.

The sea is not far from the station. Beneath the setting sun is the deep-blue sea with lines of cloud-white waves rolling in and charging at the beach. She has changed into her bathing suit, but she has broken one of the ties on the back and is really cross.

"Find a nude swimming pool," you can't help teasing.

"You don't know what living's all about!" she retorts.

"Then what can you do?" You say you can pull the tie from your trunks to replace it.

"Then what about you?"

"I'll just sit on the beach and wait for you."

"That's no good; if you don't go in the water, then neither of us will!"

She really wants to go in, but also wants to appear magnanimous.

"I can pull out my shoelaces," you say, rising to the occasion.

"That's a great idea, you're not so stupid after all."

With the help of your shoelaces, you manage to help her get her breasts cupped securely. She gives you a big kiss and runs into the water. It is icy cold, and you are shivering by the time the water gets to your knees.

"It's really cold!"

In the distance, on the left end of the bay, a few boys are surfing beyond the reef. Further out is the deep, ink-blue sea, lines of white waves surging up and vanishing, then surging up again. Clouds hide the setting sun, there is a sea wind, and it gets even colder. The people swimming nearby have all come out of the water, and those lying and sitting on the sand also get up and collect their things. Almost everyone has left.

You get back to the beach and put on your clothes. You stare out to sea, but you have lost sight of her; the surfers have climbed onto the reef. You are worried, and stand there looking. In the distance, surging up with the white spray, there seems to be a black spot, but it seems to be moving out to the open sea. You feel uneasy. The reflected light on the waves is no longer bright, as the sky of the vast South Pacific Ocean is drawn toward darkness.

You have not known her long, and certainly don't understand her. Before this, you had simply slept with her a few times. You mentioned that friends had invited you to put on one of your plays, so she arranged some leave and came with you. She is perverse, and you don't know if you love her, but she fascinates you. She has had several boyfriends who, according to her, were companions. "Sexual companions?" you asked. She didn't disagree, and, maybe because of this, she excited you. She said she opposed marriage, she had lived with a man for some years, but then they separated. She couldn't belong to just one man. You said that you approved. She said that it was not that she didn't want a stable relationship, but, for a relationship to be stable, it had to be stable on both sides, and that was difficult. You said you felt the same, and that the two of you had some things in common. She had to live transparently, she told you this the first time she went to bed with you and stayed overnight. She also told you of her past and ongoing sexual relationships. She said that male-female relationships were important, and you agreed. She was quite frank, and this was why she excited you.

In the distance, the surface of the sea is no longer visible, and you frantically look around on the shore to see if there are any lifeguards on duty. She comes around from the side and, seeing that you have seen her, she stops. She is pale with cold.

"What are you looking at?" she asks.

"I'm looking for a lifeguard."

"Aren't you looking for a beautiful woman?" she asks, giggling. She is shivering and covered in goose pimples.

"There was a blond here just now, sunbathing on the sand."

"Do you like blonds?"

"I also like brunettes."

"You rascal!" she softly berates you, but this pleases you.

You have dinner in a little Italian restaurant, where a white Santa Claus is chalked onto the glass window of the kitchen. Above the tables hang paper streamers in the form of dark-green pine needles. It will soon be Christmas, yet it is almost summer here in the southern hemisphere.

"Your heart's not in it. Coming with you for a vacation is really no fun," she says.

"But isn't a vacation just having a rest? There doesn't have to be a specific goal," you say.

"Then there wasn't any need to bring a specific woman, any

woman would have done." She stares at you from behind her glass of wine.

"On the beach, I was frantic and about to call the police!" you say.

"It would have been too late." She puts down her glass and, stroking your hand, says, "I deliberately gave you a fright. You're really very silly. Let me show you what living is all about!"

"All right," you say.

That whole night, you and she make wild, passionate love.

50

In this small town, the electricity was often cut, so he had lit a kerosene lamp. Writing in the light of the lamp made him relaxed, less inhibited, and so it was easier to pour out his feelings. There was a quiet knocking on the door. No one in the village knocked like that. They called out first, or called out while pounding on the door. He thought it must be a dog. The headmaster's sandy-colored dog sometimes sniffed the meat he had stewing, and would lie by his door to beg for bones, but, for days, he had not lit his stove and had been eating in the school dining room. He gave a start, quickly stuffed what he was writing into the basket of wood and charcoal by the wall, then stood behind the door to listen, but the knocking had stopped. As he turned to go back to his chair, he again heard the knocking.

"Who is it?" he asked loudly, as he opened the door a crack to look.

"Teacher." It was a woman's hushed voice, and the person was standing in the dark by the door.

"Is that you, Sun Huirong?" he had recognized her voice and opened the door.

This girl had graduated after two years of schooling and was now working in the fields in one of the villages. Official documents said that all town children, even if they were not from peasant families, had to settle in the villages, and it was up to the school to implement this. He was Sun's class teacher, so he chose a production brigade only a couple of kilometers or so from town, and where he knew Hunchback Zhao, the Party secretary. He also found her lodgings with a family where there was an old woman to keep an eye on her.

"How is it? Is everything all right?" he asked.

"Everything is fine, Teacher."

"You have become quite dark from being in the sun!"

In the dim light, the girl's face seemed black. Just sixteen, her chest protruded, and she looked healthy and strong. Unlike most city girls, she had been doing manual labor from the time she was a child, and was used to hard work. Sun Huirong came into the room, but he left the door wide open to avoid arousing suspicions.

"Is there a problem?"

"I've just come to see my teacher."

"Fine, sit down."

He had never let her come into his room on her own but she had now left school. She stood there looking behind her, looking at the door.

"Sit down, sit down, I'll leave it open."

"No one saw me come." Her voice was still very hushed.

He was in an awkward situation. He recalled being moved by a touch of sadness in her voice when she had told him that her home was a women's domain. She was the best-known girl in town. After the student propaganda team visited the nearby coal mine to stage a performance, a group of young miners came and hung around outside the classroom window, craning their necks and looking in. They started clamoring and shouting that they had come to see Sun Huirong! The principal came out of the office and chastised them, "Why do you want to see her? What's there to see?" The young hooligans mumbled, "So what if we take a look at her? She's not going to disappear if we look at her, is she?" They all jeered as they slunk off. "This is where Sun Huirong had her tits felt" had been scrawled in chalk on the stone embankment by the river, and the boys in the class were summoned one by one into the principal's office and interrogated. All of them said they didn't know anything about it, but, out of the office and in the corridor, they were sneakily guffawing. The village girls mature early, and a lot of silly talk went on among the girl students. Often there was fighting and crying, but whenever he questioned them, they would blush and say nothing. The propaganda team had to put on makeup for the performance, and Sun Huirong turned this way and that, looking in a little round mirror. She knew how to use her feminine charm. "Teacher, does my hair look good like this?" "Teacher, could you help me with this lipstick?" "Teacher, come and have a look!" He corrected a corner of her lips and said, "You look great, it's fine!" and sent her on her way.

The girl was sitting in front of him right now in the dim light of the lamp. He went to turn up the lamp, and the girl said, "It's fine like this."

She was trying to seduce him, he thought, so he started to talk about something else. "Tell me about the family." He was asking about the peasant family with the old woman, which he had chosen for her.

"I left that place a long time ago."

"Why did you leave?"

At the time, he had arranged for her to share the room with the old woman in the family.

"I'm looking after the storehouse."

"What storehouse?"

"The production team's."

"Where is it?"

"Near the road, by the bridge."

He knew the lone building by the little bridge at the edge of the village, and asked, "Are you living there on your own?"

"Yes."

"What are you looking after?"

"Some heaps of paddy-rice hay and a few plows."

"Why do they need looking after?"

"The Party secretary said that later on he wanted me to do the accounts and that I would need a room."

"Aren't you afraid?"

She was silent for a while, then said, "I'm used to it now, it's all right."

"Isn't your mother worried about you?"

"She can't keep looking after me, I've got two younger sisters at home. When people grow up, they have to fend for themselves."

She was silent again. There was moisture in the kerosene, and the lamp suddenly spluttered.

"Do you have time to read?" As a teacher, he felt he had to ask this.

"How can I do any reading? It's not like working in the little vegetable garden at home. I have to earn work points. It's not like when I was at school; it used to be so good here!"

Indeed, school for her had been a paradise.

"Then come by and visit the school from time to time. You're not far away, and when you come home, you can stop by." He could only console her like this.

The girl bent her head over his desk and ran a finger along a join in the wood. He suddenly stopped talking, he could smell the aroma from her hair, and he blurted out, "If nothing is the problem, then you had best be going back."

The girl looked up and said, "Go back where?"

"Home!" he said.

"I didn't come from home," the girl said.

"Then go back to the brigade," he said.

"I don't want to. . . ." Sun Huirong's head bent low again, and her finger went on running over the join in the wood.

"Are you frightened of staying on your own in the storehouse?" he asked. The girl's head bent lower.

"Didn't you say you were used to it? Do you want to go back to that old woman's family? Do you want me to talk to them so that you can go back?" What else could he do but ask her again.

"No. . . . This. . . ."

The girl's voice was even more hushed, and her head was almost on the table. He moved closer, but, smelling the warm, sour sweat of her body, sprung to his feet and, almost angrily, shouted, "Do you or don't you want me to go and talk to that family?"

The girl gave a start and stood up. He saw the bewilderment in her eyes, and tears glistening. She was on the verge of crying, so he quickly said, "Sun Huirong, come now, you must go home!"

The girl slowly bowed her head and stood there, motionless. He recalled that he had virtually pushed the girl out of his room. He took her by her sturdy arms and turned her around. She still wouldn't move, so he said softly into her ear, "If you've got something to tell me, come during the day! All right?"

Sun Huirong did not come again, and he never saw her again. No, he did see her once, at the beginning of winter. The night she came to the school was at the start of the autumn chill, so it was probably three months later that he passed by the Sun family house and the girl was in the main hall. She had clearly seen him, but, unlike in the past, when, without fail, she would shout out for him to come into the house for a rest and a cup of tea, she turned around straight away and went to the back of the hall.

Just after the New Year, a girl in his class was crying and had her head on the desk even after the bell for the start of class. He asked why she was crying. None of the boys would say, but when he asked one of the girls, she told him that at the end of the previous class the boys said to her, "Why be so stuck up? When the time comes, you'll be just like Sun Huirong. Just wait until Hunchback gets you pregnant, then you'll do as you're told!"

After the class, he asked the principal, "What has happened to Sun Huirong?"

The principal mumbled, "It's not easy talking about it, I don't really know the details, but she's had an abortion! Whether or not it was a case of rape, I would not hazard to guess."

It was only then that he thought back to when the girl had come to see him, maybe she was trying to get him to save her. Had it already happened prior to that? Or did the girl sense that it was about to happen? Or had it happened, but she hadn't yet become pregnant? She had not said anything of what she wanted to say, because she didn't know how to say it. It was all in the girl's eyes, she wanted to say it, but she had stopped herself. It was all in her hesitation, in the sour sweat of her body, in her movements. She kept looking at the door of his room, what was she looking at? What was she looking for when she avoided his eyes to size up his room? She could have had a very clear plan. She had come on the night when there was no electricity, so that she wouldn't be seen. She said nobody had seen her coming, so clearly she had been on the alert. Was there some secret she wanted to tell him about? If, at the time, he had shut the door and had not been so careful—she clearly wanted him to shut the door—would she have told him everything, and this tragic event have been averted? She didn't want him to turn up the lamp, could she only talk about it in the dark? Or did she have something more complicated on her mind, something that would get him to sympathize with her and save her, stop or interfere with what was about to happen or had already happened?

The people of the small town all knew that the Sun girl had been raped by Hunchback, and that her mother had taken her to get an abortion, but that was all he could find out. There was a big brass padlock on the Sun house. He visited the police station. In the past, he'd had drinks with the public security officer, Old Zhang. Zhang was chastising an old peasant who had been selling sesame oil, and had confiscated the man's little galvanized bucket and his basket.

"Grain and oil are goods that are bought and sold exclusively by the state. Do you understand that?"

"Yes, yes."

"Then why are you selling it? Don't you know it's against the law?"

"But I grew it in my own garden!"

"How can I tell if you grew it yourself or stole it from the production brigade?"

"If you don't believe me, then go and ask!"

"Ask who?"

"Ask in the village, the brigade leader knows."

"All right, all right, get the brigade leader to write a note and then come to collect these things!"

"Comrade, let me off this time, I won't sell it again, all right?"

"The state has laws about this!"

The old man squatted on his heels, refusing to budge. While he sat watching all this, he finished smoking a cigarette and thought it was unlikely that the matter would be resolved soon, so he got up and said he would come around some other time. However, Zhang was very polite, and stopped him to ask, "Did you want to see me about something?"

"I'd like to find out about the case of my student Sun Huirong," he said.

"The dossier is right here; if you want to, take it and have a look. Even if you are a teacher, you can't do anything in these matters. She's a local girl, and there are many more such happenings with girl students who have come from elsewhere. If the person and the parents don't make a legal complaint, and no one is killed, every effort is made not to take matters any further."

Zhang opened the document cupboard, found a dossier folder, and handed it to him, saying, "Take it with you, the case is already closed."

He examined every scrap of paper in the dossier. There were handwritten records of the separate testimonies of Sun and Hunchback. Hunchback had his thumbprint to his, and Sun had both signed and put her thumbprint on hers. There was also a record of the interrogation of Hunchback's wife. Attached to it, was a letter in a girlish handwriting, written to Hunchback. It had been written on paper torn from a student notebook, and there was a postmarked envelope addressed to the commune for a certain comrade who was Party secretary of Zhao Village Brigade: Hunchback's name was written there. The letter started off with "Dear Elder Brother." Hunchback was over fifty, but the girl was not yet an adult. There were only two lines in the letter, but the gist of it was as follows: I love my elder brother but it is impossible for me to see him. What happened has ended like this, but I will never have regrets. The word for "regret" had been written incorrectly, but the letter clearly bore Sun Huirong's signature, and it was dated after the matter had become public.

The record of the interrogation of Hunchback's wife said: "That slut seduced my man, the shameless hussy even wrote him a letter. The little whore only wanted to get herself merit points so that she would be able to get a work permit." Hunchback's wife had intercepted the letter and was so angry that she delivered it to the commune! However, the matter became a problem because of Dr. Wang at the commune health clinic. The record of the interrogation of Dr. Wang stated that the girl's mother had begged him to come to her home to induce an abortion. She said that if the girl went to the clinic to have it done, the whole neighborhood would know, then how would the girl find a husband later on? Dr. Wang said that he did not do illegal work like that. If word got out that he had not followed proper procedures and had privately carried out an abortion, how would he be able to continue in his profession? What was more, wouldn't rumors spread through the village and people think that he was involved with the girl himself? Dr. Wang put it quite bluntly that he was not going to do anything illegal.

How the matter came to be public was not mentioned in the materials on the investigation. Hunchback's testimony was very simple: Rape? Rubbish! He never did wicked things like that! It wasn't just his wife, sons, and daughters, that he'd have to face, how would he be able to face going on being Party secretary? Also, he couldn't sabotage the Red Flag Brigade, and he had to live up to the expectations of the various levels of leaders of the Party who had nurtured him over the years! This girl student is cunning, don't be fooled by the fact that she is young, her scheming is very adult. She was clearly inside, taking a bath, and there is nothing wrong with taking a bath. But the latch is on the inside, and the door is very solid, so if she didn't open the door herself, how could someone charge in? If she wasn't willing, why didn't she scream? How many times did it happen? Best ask her, every time it was in her bed! It wasn't in the fields. Now, can such a big latch drop off by itself? If she'd been raped, why didn't she report it earlier instead of waiting until her belly started to get big? She was trying to get a work permit, and you can't blame her, what young student doesn't want to get a job instead of working a lifetime in the fields? If a person wants merit points for a work permit, it's not an offense to give a gratuity now and then. It's the same for everyone, the brigade can only make a recommendation, it's the commune that issues the permit, he can't, can he?

As to Sun's own testimony, it was a thick wad of paper. They had interrogated her in great detail, from the cheap bath soap she used to how she was taken all wet to her bed behind the pile of hay. The interrogation could not have been more detailed, and amounted to her having been raped yet another time. The verdict on the case read: "It was the capitalist thinking of the young educated girl that was playing havoc, so she was not satisfied with working as a peasant. She should be transferred from the brigade to do manual labor in

another commune, and her thought-reform should be intensified."
The Party's verdict on Hunchback read: "Decadent lifestyle, bad
influence on society, but the memory of the Party is more severe
than punishment. For the time being, position to be retained, but
subsequent behavior to be observed."

After hesitating for a few days, he eventually spoke to Secretary Lu
and asked him to do something for Sun Huirong.

"Her mother has already come to me," Lu said. "The girl has had
the abortion, a contact in a county hospital was found, and her
mother took her to have it done. The matter has been dealt with,
and there is no need for you to be involved."

"But she is not yet an adult—" he tried to argue.

"Don't get involved!" Lu interrupted him, then followed with a
stern warning, "There are very complicated relationships among the
villagers. Does an outsider like you want to go on living here?"

This silenced him but it made it clear that he was merely eking out
an existence under the protection of Lu.

"I've already taken care of the girl, I've sent her to another commune. When the affair cools down, in a year or so, and things have
settled down, she will be given the merit points she needs for a work
permit. Her mother has already agreed to it."

What else could he say? It was all a transaction, generations have
rolled in this mud, what else can they do? For better or worse, this
place had accepted him, and he had to comply, but he understood
that he would always be an outsider.

51

Unlike Margarethe, Sylvie was bored when you spoke to her about these past happenings. She was not interested in your past. She was interested in herself, her love, her feelings, and she kept changing from one minute to the next. If you said more than three sentences to her about politics, she would cut you short. Race did not bother her, and her lovers were mostly foreigners, an Arab from North Africa, an Irishman, a quarter-Jewish Hungarian, a Jew from Israel, and, recently, you—if you counted as a lover. She said she preferred you as a friend rather than as a sex partner. Of course, there had also been French boyfriends or sex partners, but she said she wanted to get away from France, to go somewhere far away, to some place in the tropics like Indonesia or the Philippines, even Australia. She liked sunbathing, so she went to a sunny beach by the sea to start a new life, but fell into the same old trap again. She got pregnant by a boyfriend, not you, of course, and had her third abortion. At first, she wanted to have the baby, a woman had to give birth at least once, should she have it or not? The guy couldn't come out with a definite answer, and, in a fit of anger, she had it aborted. It was only later that the man said if you don't want an abortion then have the child. He wanted it! But wouldn't that have meant she would have had to take care of it? It wasn't a matter of her not wanting a child, she first needed a stable home, and she hadn't yet found the right sort of man, so she was anxious. Her anxiety was deep-seated, but it was an anxiety caused by a conflict between freedom and restriction that everyone had. In other words, what were the limits of freedom? She didn't have a money problem, because her parents had bought her a small apartment on the sixth floor at the top of a building. Outside the window were the red tiles of rooftops with chimneys, and beyond the rooftops, in the distance, was the pointed spire of a church. Paris was intoxicating, but on a rainy day it was sad, and there, in her apartment, you could only think of making love.

Saying that her anxiety was deep-seated didn't mean she couldn't find a man she could love and who loved her, she certainly didn't lack men. The men all loved her, at least for a certain period, and even after they had found someone else, they would still come from time to time. She said she wasn't a slut, and she reminded you with those very words. She wanted to do something meaningful, or, to put it more precisely, something interesting. She referred to artistic creation as being akin to giving birth. She wanted a child she could put body and soul into, even a spiritual child, and that was at the crux of her problem. But what was worth putting one's body and soul into? To be frank, only love. Yet being able to manage love was difficult, and not something determined by her alone.

When you fucked her, or she got you to fuck her, she put everything into it. But with you, once you were satisfied, that was it, and she was left feeling compromised. Of course, there were plenty of men who were good at making love, but the problem was she didn't love them all that much. What she was searching for was the ultimate in both love and sexual excitement. But that was an ideal, what people dreamed about, utopia. She was aware of this, but it made her sad, profoundly sad, it was the profound sadness of being human, an eternal sadness that could never be dispelled.

She appreciated art the way she loved men, but she could not apply herself to the creation of art. That would mean sacrificing oneself to one's work, and she thought that was stupid. She was not so stupid as to sacrifice herself for art. She wanted to live artistically, but not to be an art object for the enjoyment of others. However, she was just that, she had an abundance of youthful feminine attraction, few men could resist her, but she was not a toy for men. It was the opposite, she enjoyed men, she believed that love had to be enjoyed to be worthwhile, but love often brought her disappointment.

You could not resolve matters for her, but thought you understood her, and, striving to overcome your jealousy, told her to go and enjoy the man she loved! Like the Devil teaching Eve to seduce, you were the snake. But she didn't need *you* to teach her, she already knew, she knew long ago how to seduce and be seduced. She was much younger than you were when you were just struggling for your basic right to exist as an individual. At the age when you had not yet tasted the forbidden fruit, she was already satiated by its bitter aftertaste. At the age when you were an idiot, or striving not to be an idiot, she was already overly clever. She could not tolerate the slightest suffering unless it was for her own masochistic pleasure; she would accept suffering only if it gave her pleasure.

But don't think she was a feminist. She, like you, had no "isms," and when there was talk about feminism, she would purse her lips. You did not dare recklessly voice an opinion about feminism. You have never personally experienced male oppression, and only a woman could understand the suffering this brought, and the significance of resisting it.

In any case, Sylvie wasn't a feminist. She most definitely was not a feminist, and she said she could, in fact, be a very good wife. She could spend a wonderful sleepless night with you, be up early, and have coffee and toast made for you. Barefoot, she would bring these on a tray to you in bed. She would sit cross-legged in front of you, and be happy just watching you enjoy it. Her smiling face would beam like the sun shining into the room with the curtains open, and she would show no sign of weariness after being up all night. At such times, she would be a lovely girl, or, more accurately, a little woman with a beaming face. That is, if she was in a good mood.

But if her anxiety flared up, you wouldn't be able to do anything right, and all your glib talk wouldn't be able to placate her. So, you knew you could not marry her, the two of you could only be lovers, possibly lifelong friends. According to her, the two of you could not be partners, and this depressed you. Therefore, her severe anxiety also severely affected you, but you could do nothing about it.

You were afraid that she might commit suicide, like her friend Martina. The week before Martina died they recorded a conversation. There was an old, pocket-sized tape recorder on the table, and it was on while they were drinking and talking. Martina had put it on, but Sylvie didn't know until she saw that the little red light was on and the tape was turning, and she asked, "Are you recording?"

On the tape, Martina's speech was slurred. She had been drinking all afternoon, and, when Sylvie arrived, there were already quite a few empty beer bottles on the table. Martina often just drank beer instead of eating and drinking water. She started laughing loudly, and her voice on the tape was hoarse. Sylvie said this woman friend of hers used to have a good voice, a natural mezzo-soprano, and, before she was admitted to the psychiatric hospital, she had been a reserve member of a choir. Once, when she sang Fauré's *Requiem* at Saint-Germain Church, it was recorded by the France-Musique radio program and played on the air.

You never met Martina. She died some months before you met Sylvie. The only thing she left Sylvie was this small cassette tape, and, in the second half, the battery had almost run out as the tape was being recorded. Their voices were muffled and barely audible, and Martina's hoarse voice really sounded like a man's.

At the beginning, there wasn't anything serious. "Have a drink?"—"All right."—"I've also got half a bottle of red wine."—

"Won't it have gone off?"—"No, it was only opened yesterday. . . ."
After that, there was the sound of glasses, then some scratching
noises, probably the table was being wiped. Sylvie said Martina's
home was a filthy mess, and there was nowhere to set your foot
down. But it was only like that after she came out of the psychiatric
hospital, it hadn't been like that before. Martina said she hated the
psychiatric hospital and hated her mother; it was her mother who
had put her there. The tape also said that she came across this man
on the street and took him home. Afterward, there were the two of
them laughing, the high-pitched laugh was Sylvie's and the throaty
one was Martina's. They laughed for a long time, and then there was
the sound of glasses again. "What happened?" It was Sylvie asking.
"Did I throw him out? He hung around until the afternoon of the
next day, but was scared off after I said I'd call the police." There
was the sound of laughing again.

"How old was she when she died?" you ask Sylvie.

"She was older than me . . . by nine years, she was over thirty-
eight when she died."

"That's young. Was she ever married?" you ask.

"No, the two of them lived together, then separated."

"How did she die?"

"I don't know, her mother phoned me four days after she died
and said she had this tape. When I asked for it, her mother wouldn't
agree at first. I told her it had my voice on it and that I wanted it as
a keepsake."

"Didn't you ask her mother about it? How she had died?"

"Her mother wouldn't say much, except that she had committed
suicide. She refused to see me, even though she knew me. Anyway,
she sent the tape; Martina, of course, had my address in her phone
book."

She showed you a photograph of Martina, a young woman with
gentle eyes and clearly defined lips. Her mouth was wide-open, and
she was laughing. Probably because of her makeup, her eyes looked

more deep-set than Sylvie's pale-brown eyes. It was taken the summer when they were traveling in Spain together, almost ten years ago. At Martina's side was a lean man with deep-set eyes and a black stubble, Vincent. At the time, he was living with Martina. They had a small van and had taken along her and Jean, the good-looking young man behind Sylvie's head. Sylvie had just started university, and Jean was two years older. Jean said Sylvie was his first real lover, and she preferred to believe him. But she knew that he'd had such experiences before, of course, sexual experiences. She showed you another album, there was a photograph of Martina taken a year before she died. The corners of her lips drooped, and she looked like an old woman. Sylvie said Martina looked much better in person, that she had the sensuousness of a mature woman, a sad weariness.

It was hard for her to describe her feelings for Martina. They used to talk about everything, although, for a few years, they had avoided one another. It was after returning from Spain that she hated her, Sylvie said, she hated Martina. She and Jean had taken a tent with them, and one night it started pouring rain. They were totally wretched, and it was impossible for them to sleep, so Martina got them to come into the van. At first, Sylvie and Jean sat in the front and slept leaning against one another. Martina got her to come into the back, to sleep next to her, but then proceeded to make love to Vincent. Sylvie felt uncomfortable and pretended to be asleep. Afterward, Martina climbed into the front and left her sleeping with Vincent, she was half-asleep, and it was raining heavily outside. As it was just starting to become light, she heard Martina doing it with Jean; next, Vincent had put his hand into her clothes, and she and Vincent started doing it. The rain pelting down on the roof of the van had turned everything into a vast rustling chaos, and it all seemed so very natural. The next day, they took a room in a hotel, and Vincent requested an additional bed for the room. Martina gleefully gave the big bed to Vincent and her, she didn't object, and Jean didn't say anything. The first time she heard Jean call out while making love, she, too, called out. It was then that she started to engage in oral sex.

Life is like that. Martina and Vincent split up, she didn't love the man anyway. She never asked how long Martina had continued with Jean, but she herself no longer loved Jean, she wasn't interested in what he was doing, she already had another boyfriend.

"Do you want to go on listening?" she asks with a sarcastic look on her face.

She also said she wondered if Martina had already made up her mind to commit suicide when she was making that recording with her. And why hadn't she spoken to her about it? She no longer resented Martina for having killed herself, that had passed a long time ago, she was no longer sickened by feelings of disillusionment and anger. Was it Martina's own rotten idea, or was it a trap Vincent had set? If it was a trap, Maritna had jumped into it herself, she hated no one. Martina had savored both the intoxication and the bitterness of life, for her guilt and ecstasy were above ethics. It was impossible for Sylvie to describe her feelings for Martina, yet it was only Martina in whom she could fully confide.

"Men don't understand, men aren't capable of understanding. Don't go misconstruing the feelings between two women." She said she wasn't a lesbian, that with Martina there was never what all you men imagine, she knew what you were thinking. But she could tell you that she had a sort of longing for Martina. She knew why she had killed herself; she didn't have a mental problem, but her family insisted on her being treated for a mental disorder. It was because of the family's reputation, her mother couldn't allow her daughter to be a slut. But she wasn't a whore, she never was. It was just that no one could understand her, people just were not willing to try and understand her.

52

"The people are victorious!"

This had been announced on all the walls in Tiananmen Square. However, the victory was not the people's, it was still the Party's, the Party had smashed yet another anti-Party organization. Less than one month after Mao's death, his widow, Jiang Qing, had been arrested, and the people had been summoned to Tiananmen Square to celebrate the victory. The Party is forever right! Forever glorious! And everlasting, because it was still Mao Zedong who was sleeping peacefully in a crystal coffin for people to view.

After a deluge of old cadres were exonerated, reinstated, and promoted, some cadres he had once protected, especially Comrade Wang Qi, had given some thought to old friends, and he, this insignificant person, was brought back to Beijing. It was on that old narrow street in Dashanlan, beyond Qianmen, that he ran into Big Li, who, back then, had been in the rebel Red Guards with him. During the military-control period, Big Li was interrogated in isolation for over two years, then put into a mental institution for two or three years before being released. Big Li recognized him and grabbed him with his big hands, very strong hands, and looked at him gleefully. The people in his former workplace said he had gone crazy, and that whenever he saw anyone, he would just laugh, and this was exactly how he was. They were blocking the footpath of the narrow street, and people were bumping and knocking into them, but Big Li hung onto him and wouldn't let go, all the time with this silly smile on his face. Unable to keep looking at him, he made some idle conversation, then pulled his arms free and hurried off.

After the disbanding of the Army Control Commission, Danian was handcuffed and arrested for committing "wrong-line errors." He was interrogated by the new army officer, and, afterward, declared his crimes at a public meeting: two people had died by his own hands. In the case of Old Liu, he got together a few thugs at night, and, in the underground room of the workplace building, had tortured him to extract a confession. They had used rubber-coated electrical cables on him, and had pulverized his internal organs. Afterward, they carried him upstairs and threw him out of a window to make it look like a case of suicide. The other person killed by similar tactics was a Chinese woman who had returned from abroad. She was given electric-shock treatment, to extract a confession. A transformer with the voltage turned down had been used to get her to confess into a tape recorder that she had been sent by a Taiwanese spy organization. She was forced to give the names of the people she had recruited as well as the people in the upper and lower ranks of the spy organization. The names supplied enabled them to proceed with purging cadres in the opposition faction. The former army officer who had taken part in all this was arrested at the same time.

Wang Qi's husband, who had formerly been denounced as an anti-Party black element, was useful again, and, reinstated in the central apparatus of the Party, now took part in the investigation and punishment of new cases of anti-Party organizations. Wang Qi was promoted, but was the same as before, and seemed to be even kinder. During the army-control period, she, too, had been interrogated in isolation and kept in solitary confinement in a small room of a warehouse for half a year. The hundred-watt globe in the ceiling was kept on day and night. The light switch was outside, and the window had been nailed with cardboard from the outside, with no gaps, so she didn't know if it was day or night. She had to write testimonies over and over on the underground student movement in Beijing, known in those days as Beiping. She said she was disoriented and, if she shut her eyes, she would feel that she was hanging by the feet and spinning upside down. Nevertheless, she said she had been treated leniently and had not been subjected to physical abuse or humiliation. This was probably because she was old, and also because some of her old comrades still held important positions in the army and, to some extent, they had looked after her.

The old cadres had mostly been reinstated to their former positions. However, a small number, like the former Party secretary Wu Tao, were too old; arrangements were made for their retirement when they were exonerated, and remuneration, such as salary and housing and the allocation of work for their children, taken care of. However, a person like Old Tan, who was not a Party member but an insignificant deputy section-chief with a blemished background, remained at the cadre school doing hard manual labor until cadre schools were abolished and reverted to local governments as reform-through-labor farms for criminals. It was then that Old Tan returned to the capital. He was not old enough to retire, and had to wait around to be allocated some kind of work or other.

Lin had divorced and remarried. Her second husband was a newly appointed deputy department-head, whose former wife had died during the Cultural Revolution.

He began to publish his works, became a writer and left that old workplace. Lin had invited him to her home for a meal. Her second husband who was also there commented on literature, "The disaster that our Party has gone through really should be properly written up to educate later generations!"

Lin was in the living room with them, and there was a maid in the kitchen preparing the food. Lin was among the first to use imported perfumes; it was probably a French perfume, one of the latest by Chanel, or some such famous brand anyway.

He was in the process of getting a divorce. His wife, Qian, had written a letter to the Writers' Association, accusing him of reactionary thinking, but had not been able to produce any evidence. He explained that she had become deranged during the Cultural Revolution and was mentally unstable, and she hated him because he had initiated divorce proceedings. Following the decade of the Cultural Revolution, people wanting a divorce were considerably fewer than those wanting to get married, but divorce was common practice. The law courts, which had just started to function again, couldn't handle all the cases of miscarriage of justice, and didn't want to create new problems, so he was finally able to extricate himself from the marriage. He apologized to Qian for having committed her youth to the grave. Chairman Mao's Cultural Revolution alone could not be blamed. He himself was also to blame, although this could not compensate her for her lost youth. Fortunately, the anti-Party spy case against Qian's father was suddenly dropped, and she was able to leave the village and return to be with her father.

He received a letter from Lu, which said, "All the good trees of the mountain have been cut down, and there is no place left for a decaying tree." Lu had turned down an appointment to chair the new Discipline Investigation Committee of the local Party. He said he had retired, just like that. He wanted to build a house on the mountain to live out his old age.

A year later, he had the opportunity to travel south for work, and he made a special trip to see this benefactor who had once protected him. He first went to the county town where his old schoolmate Rong was still living in his thatched hut. In the interim, the roof had been rethatched, but it was again due for replacement. Rong now had another son. In the county town, family planning was not as rigorously enforced as in big cities, and the inspector for the family register was an acquaintance. In any case, Rong had already been living there for twenty years, and his wife was a local, so, after a slight delay, the child was given a residential permit. Rong was still working as a farm technician, and his wife was still selling merchandise in the cooperative shop at the entrance to the county town. She had tried to get a transfer to the department store in the little street behind their house; it was closer and would have been ideal for looking after the two small children at home. She had not given the cadre in charge enough gifts, and wasn't successful. Rong was even more taciturn than before, and there were long periods of silence, when they just looked at one another.

The bus from the county town arrived at the little village, and, as always, people started to surge on board before everyone had got off. The bus left, but he didn't go to the little street or the school. He was afraid of running into people he knew, then being dragged off for a meal or something. It would not do to visit one family and not another, and he thought that if he went from one place to another, it would take a couple of days. He stood at the bus stop and looked around for someone he knew, so that he could ask where Lu had built his house.

"Hey—" a young man from the timber cooperative with a cigarette hanging from his lips recognized him and came over to shake hands. During the concerted militia training, they had done shooting practice together, then got to know one another while drinking and bullshitting together. The man, no doubt now a minor cadre, did not intend to invite him home for a meal, but said he was due at the timber cooperative. He had only stayed here temporarily, and, having left the place, was of little interest to anyone; he was just an outsider.

However, he found out that Lu's new house was on the other side of the river, on the mountain behind the flatland where the coal mine was located. After crossing the river, there were another three or four kilometers, and he would have to walk for some time. Rong had told him that the cadres in the county town were spreading the rumor that Lu had gone crazy. They said he had built a thatched hut on the mountain and had become a Daoist, living on a vegetarian diet, and, in a quest for longevity, was refining cinnabar to arrest the aging process. Lu's old comrades, his superiors in higher echelons who had been reinstated to their former positions or promoted, were certain that his revolutionary will had deteriorated. Lu told him this after he went up the mountain and saw his old benefactor.

"I don't want to get my hands dirty again. This is fine, a thatched hut with a purple bamboo garden where I grow vegetables and read books. I'm not like you, you're still young. I'm getting old, and I am not going to do much more in life," Lu said to him.

Lu, of course was not living in a thatched hut, but in an unimposing brick house with a tiled roof, which couldn't be seen unless one climbed up the hill behind the coal mine.

Lu had taken a retirement payment for old cadres, designed the house himself, and supervised the local peasants who built it for him. The inside of the house was paved with blue-stone slabs. One of the slabs in the bedroom could be lifted: it was the entrance to a secret tunnel, which led into a small wooden hut by a stream adjoining a pine forest. It could be said that Lu had finally succeeded in preserving himself, yet, from time to time, probably because of what he had experienced in life, he still thought about possible plots against him.

In the main hall by a wall, inlaid into the floor, was an old stone tablet. Lu had some peasants carry it down from the ruins of the old temple on the top of the mountain. Much of the inscription was missing, but a rough outline of the life and thinking of the monk who had built the temple could be made out from what remained. A disgruntled graduate of the county level of the Imperial Civil Service Examinations had joined the rebellion of the Long Hairs, the Taipings. The Heavenly Kingdom of the Taipings had also aimed at establishing a utopia on earth, but internal fighting and cruel killings led to defeat. The scholar subsequently renounced the world, to live here as a monk. Books were piled in Lu's bedroom. There were internal reference publications of the time for high-ranking cadres of the Party, such as the Japanese prime minister's *Autobiography of Tanaka Kakuei* and the three-volume *Memoirs of General de Gaulle*, as well as an undated, hand-sewn edition of *The Essentials of Pharmacology* and a new edition of classical poetry.

"I want to write something, I've already got the title: *Daily Chronicle of a Man in the Mountains.* What do you think of it? It's just that I don't know whether I'll actually be able to write it," Lu said.

He and Lu laughed. This tacit understanding was the basis of his friendship with Lu, and, probably, the reason he had received Lu's protection during those years.

"Let's get something to eat with the liquor!"

Lu wasn't a vegetarian at all, and took him to the coal miners' dining room. Below the hill, at the mouth of the coal mine where there were rows of workers' huts, was the structure for the electric trolley carts. It was late afternoon, work had stopped for the day, and the mine workers were queuing with their big bowls at the food window of the big bamboo-shed dining room. Lu had gone straight to the kitchen. Suddenly, a woman's voice called out, "Teacher!"

A young woman had left the queue of grimy coal miners, and was cheerfully coming over to greet him. He immediately made out that it was his student Sun Huirong, wearing a peasant woman's gown. Her beautiful eyes had not changed, but her face and body had become rounder.

"How is it that you're here?"

He could not suppress his surprise and delight, and was about to go up to her when Lu emerged from the kitchen, gave him a shove, and commanded, "Get going!"

He instinctively obeyed. He had been under Lu's protection a long time, and it had become habit. But he couldn't help turning to look back. Anxiety, panic, despair, shame, all showed in her eyes that had sunk deeper and become darker. Her lips parted, wanting to speak but uttered no sounds. She was still standing apart from the men in the queue with their bowls, and everyone was looking at her.

"Ignore her, the slut sleeps with anyone, and she's got men fighting with knives in this mine!"

Lu was speaking to him in a low voice. He was upset, but, forcing himself to follow, he heard Lu say, "At the beginning of the month, when wages are paid and those devils have a bit of money, they go off to her house. The women in the village are all cursing and yelling about it. At present, she's working at the broadcasting station of the mine, but you can't go anywhere near her. If you say more than a few words to her, she will want you to go to bed with her, and everyone will assume that you couldn't get away and did go to bed with her!"

Half an hour later, Lu had taken out bowls and chopsticks, and poured liquor. The cook from the dining room arrived and brought out plates of quick-fried dishes, still hot, from a covered basket. He was not in the mood for drinking, and deeply regretted not having stopped to talk to Sun Huirong. But then, what would he have said to her?

You and she seemed to be from two different worlds. Although your world could never be clean, she was stuck in this coal pit, and would never be able to pull herself out. She had forgotten the distance separating you from her, forgotten her experiences, and forgotten her status as a whore in the eyes of the locals. To her, you were her teacher, she was not asking for your help, and probably she had never again thought of changing her circumstances. It was a sudden and total innocence that had resurfaced, a hazy childhood infatuation, and she was so happy that she forgot herself. As you came to this realization, you flinched from the pain of having hurt her like this, and for a long time you couldn't forgive yourself for being so weak.

At night, lying in Lu's bedroom with the secret tunnel, he listened to the sound of water flowing outside the window and the waves of wind blowing through the pine forest. Early the next day, he crossed the river and hurried to the village to get the early bus back to the county town.

You had a photograph of Sun Huirong. You had taken it at a performance of the revolutionary opera, *A Qing Sao*, by the Mao Zedong Thought Propaganda Team on National Day. It was before she had been assigned to the production brigade, when you had helped her with her makeup and lipstick. She sang the role of the heroine, A Qing Sao, who fought the bandit army of the Japanese puppet government. This opera had been prescribed in the syllabus issued by the County Education Bureau, and all the students had to learn to sing the songs from it in the music class. She had the best voice. It was impossible to know if she now had a man or was still a whore in the coal mine, which was run as a peasant collective enterprise. After you left China, the authorities sealed off your apartment in Beijing, and those photographs, together with your books and handwritten manuscripts, were all confiscated.

While you were still in China, a former student, who had gone on to graduate from university, was sent on a job to Beijing and paid you a visit. When you asked him about Secretary Lu, he said that he had died. You asked how he had died.

"Sickness, I suppose," he said. But he had only heard this.

You had never met Lu's wife. It was said that she taught at the regional teachers' college, but that she was often on sick leave because of psychological problems. She stayed with her daughter, but that could have been a means of self-preservation, to avoid being implicated. Also, a woman might not necessarily have been able to endure the life of a recluse in the mountains.

Afterward, you had a dream. The village did not have houses that were close to one another or huddled around a small street and a few lanes. It was desolate, and the houses were scattered and far apart. The school was on a hill, and it was empty. The windows and doors were all wide open. You went to look for Lu; his home looked like a village dwelling, but stood all alone, with no other houses around.

There was an iron padlock on the door. It was in the afternoon, and the setting sun was shining on the orange earthen walls. You were not sure what to do, but seemed to have come to him to work out a way of getting you out of this place. You didn't want to spend your whole life, grow old, and die in this empty school. They had told you to guard the school, grade endless homework books. You had no time to look up to think about your own affairs, although you were not sure what, in fact, you wanted to think about. As you stood before the mud wall looking at the padlock hanging on the door, you heard behind you the sound of the wind rising from the paddy fields. It was late autumn, after the harvest, and only grain stubble remained. . . .

53

The first time he ever saw the great man at such close range was in Tiananmen Square, midway between the Imperial Palace and Qianmen, behind the Memorial of the Heroes of the People. The recently completed mausoleum, constructed with heavy-duty steel-reinforced concrete, was said to be capable of withstanding nuclear bombs and point-nine earthquakes. In the crystal casket, Mao's head was really big, it was clearly swollen, and this could be seen in spite of the heavy makeup. He was five meters away, and filing past in the queue only allowed two or three seconds. There was no time to articulate what was on his mind.

He felt that he had things to say to the old man. Of course, not to the corpse of the Leader of the people in the crystal casket, but to Mao wearing only a bathrobe. Whether he had just got out of bed with some woman friend, or had just got out of the swimming pool, was not important; moreover, that such a great leader had numerous women friends shouldn't be held against him. He simply wanted to speak to the old man after he had taken off his Commander-in-Chief army uniform and his Great Leader's mask. You really lived fully as a human being, and it must be admitted that you possessed individuality, that you really were a Superman. You succeeded in dominating China, and your ghost still hovered over more than one billion Chinese. Your influence was so powerful that it spread to all parts of the world, and it was pointless to deny this. What he wanted to say was, you could kill people at will. What he wanted to tell Mao was, you made every single person speak your words.

He also wanted to say that history would fade into oblivion, but, back in those days, he had been forced to say what Mao had dictated, therefore, it was impossible for him to eradicate his hatred for Mao. Afterward, he had said to himself that as long as Mao was revered as leader, emperor, god, he would not return to that country. However, what gradually became clear to him was that it was impossible for a person's inner mind to be subjugated by another, unless that person allowed it.

What he finally wanted to say was that although it was possible to kill a person, no matter how frail the person was, that person's human dignity could not be killed. A person is human because this bit of self-respect is indestructible. When a person's life is like an insect's, is the person aware that an insect also possesses its own insect dignity? Before an insect is trampled or squashed to death, it will pretend to be dead, struggle, or try to run away in order to save itself, but its insect dignity can't be trampled to death. People have been killed off like the grass under the blade, but does the grass under the blade seek to be forgiven? People are clearly inferior to grass. What he wanted to prove was that, as well as life, people have human dignity. If preserving one's human dignity is impossible, and one isn't killed and doesn't commit suicide, then, if one does not want to die the only option is to flee. Dignity is an awareness of existence, and it is in this that the power of the frail individual lies. Once one's awareness of existence is extinguished, the apparition of existence, too, is extinguished.

Enough of all this, all this nonsense. But he had sustained himself precisely through this nonsense. Now, when he could finally speak these words openly to Mao, the old man had already been dead for some years, so he could only address them to Mao's spirit or shadow.

Mao was wearing a bathrobe, he had probably just come out of the swimming pool. He was tall and had a fat belly. His high-pitched voice was somewhat like a woman's, and he had a thick Hunan accent. His kindly benign face was just as it was in the unchanging oil portrait on the wall in Tiananmen Square. To look at, he was an amiable person. He liked smoking, was a chain smoker, and his teeth were stained black from tobacco. He smoked specially manufactured Panda-brand cigarettes with a pungent aroma. Mao also liked richly flavored foods, for example, fatty pork with chili, a point that had not been fabricated in the memoirs of his doctor.

"Friend," Mao said. Mao sometimes addressed people as "friend" and not always as "comrade" because he had many young women friends, and, of course, he couldn't be ranked with them. The only man in China who succeeded in having Mao address him as "friend" was Lin Biao. Later, when it was said that Lin Biao's plane went down at Öndörhaan in Mongolia while he was fleeing the country, the Party took the unprecedented action of making photographs of the plane wreckage public. Among foreigners, there was Nixon. Mao had a lot to chat about with him, and, once they started talking, it went on for three hours. At the time, Mao, close to eighty, was being kept alive with injections, and talked and laughed with great gusto, so that even that intelligent Jew, Kissinger, while not adoring him, greatly admired him.

When Mao said "friend," he certainly couldn't have been addressing him, but he went forward regardless. What he wanted to ask was, "Did you really believe in the utopian state of Marx's communism, or did you just use it as a front?" Back then, he had naively asked this question, but he wouldn't have asked it later on.

"There are more than a hundred political parties in the world, and most of them no longer believe in Marxism-Leninism," Mao said in a letter to his wife, Jiang Qing, during the early part of the Cultural

Revolution. The letter, clearly also addressing the entire Party, was not bedroom talk between husband and wife, but, afterward, it was used as important evidence to purge Mao's widow, and was presented before the entire Chinese people.

At the time, he preferred to think that since Mao had said this, probably he believed it. So, the old man did want to create this sort of a paradise on earth, if it didn't count as hell. That was what he also wanted to ask at the time.

"It was only the initial stage," Mao said.

Then when will the next stage come about? he reverently asked.

"In seven or eight years, it will come again," Mao wrote in a letter to his wife, "the Cultural Revolution is a serious trial practice." The old man took another cigarette, paused for a while, then went on to write, "Moreover, after seven or eight years, there will be another movement to purge all Ox Demons and Snake Spirits. And, after that, there will be many more purges." After finishing the letter, he laughed, showing the black teeth in his mouth. According to the memoirs of Mao's doctor, he smoked three packs a day and never used a toothbrush, and this was apparent from the news documentaries of Mao in old age meeting with foreign guests.

The old man was really a great military strategist! He had hoodwinked the people of China and many people in the world. This was also what he wanted to say.

Mao frowned.

He hastened to add: You defeated all of your enemies and won every single battle in your life.

"Don't let your brains be addled by victory. I am ready to fall down and be smashed to pieces, but this is of no consequence. Matter is not destroyed, it only disintegrates." Mao had written this in that no-longer-secret family letter subsequently made public by the Party.

Only your wife was smashed. You, old man, still enjoy good health. People still go to visit you in your mausoleum, and this is irrefutable testimony to your greatness, he said to Mao's spirit or shadow.

"Believing I will live two hundred years, I set out to swim three thousand *li*."

You wrote poetry from your early years, and it must be said that you were a great writer of classical poetry, but your tyranny is without precedent, you destroyed all the writers of the country, and it is in this that you were great. He said that he, too, did a bit of writing, but that he had to wait until after the old man was dead.

"In my person, I have, first, the spirit of the tiger, and, second, the spirit of the monkey."

He said that, in his case, he had, at most, a minute amount of the spirit of the monkey.

The old man gave the hint of a smile, as if he had squashed some insect. He stubbed out more than half of a cigarette, indicating that he wanted to rest.

Mao lay in the crystal casket, and it seemed that the Party flag covered his body, he couldn't remember too clearly. In any case, the Party led the country, and Mao led the Party, it really wasn't necessary for him to be covered with the national flag. In the long queue filing past Mao's remains, he probably had these unformed words in his mind, but didn't dare to pause. After he had walked past, he didn't dare look back, afraid that the people behind would notice the strange look in his eyes.

Writing freely about it now, this is what you want to say to this emperor who ruled as dictator over one billion people. Because you are insignificant, the emperor in your heart can only be the dictator of one person, and that person is yourself. Now that you have said this publicly, you have walked out of Mao's shadow, but this was not an easy thing to do. You were born at the wrong time, and encountered the era of Mao's rule, but your being born in that era had nothing to do with you, and was decided by what is known as fate.

54

You no longer live in other people's shadows, nor treat other people's shadows as imaginary enemies. You simply walked out of their shadows and stopped making up nonsense and fantasies. You are now in a vast expanse of emptiness and tranquility. You came into the world naked and without cares, there is no need to take anything away with you, and even if you wanted to, you wouldn't be able to. Your only fear is unknowable death.

You recall that your fear of death began in childhood, and that your fear of death then was much worse than it is now. The slightest ailment made you worry that it was an incurable disease, and, when you fell ill, you would think up all sorts of nonsense and be stricken with terror. Your having survived so many illnesses and even disasters is purely a matter of luck. Life in itself is an inexplicable miracle; to be alive is a manifestation of that miracle. Is it not enough that a conscious physical body is able to perceive the pains and joys of life? What else is there to be sought?

Your fear of death came about when you were mentally and physically weak. There was the feeling of not being able to breathe, and you were afraid that you would not be able to last long enough to take your next breath. It was as if you were falling into an abyss, this sensation of falling was often present in dreams during your childhood, and you would awaken in fright, drenched in perspiration. In those days, when there was nothing wrong with you, your mother used to take you for numerous hospital tests. Nowadays, even under your doctor's instructions to have tests, you often procrastinate.

It is clear that life naturally ends, and when the end comes, fear vanishes, because fear is itself a manifestation of life. On losing awareness and consciousness, life abruptly ends, and there can be no further thinking and no further meaning. Your affliction had been your search for meaning. When you began discussing the ultimate meaning of human life with the friends of your youth, you had hardly lived. However, it seems that having savored virtually all of the sensations to be experienced in life, you simply laugh at the futility of searching for meaning. It is best just to experience this existence, and, moreover, to look after it.

You seem to see him in a vast emptiness, with a faint light coming from some unidentified source. He is not standing on any specific or defined patch of ground. He is like the trunk of a tree, but has no shadow, and the horizon between the sky and the earth has vanished. Or, he is like a bird in some snow-covered place, looking here and there, occasionally staring ahead, as if deep in thought, although it is not clear what he is pondering. It is simply a gesture, a gesture of aesthetic beauty. Existence is, in fact, a gesture, it is striving to be comfortable, stretching the arms, bending the knees, turning to look back upon his consciousness. Or, it may be said that the gesture is actually his conscious mind, that it is you in his conscious mind, and it is from this that he is able to gain some fleeting happiness.

Tragedy, comedy, farce, do not exist but are aesthetic judgments of human life, which differ according to the person, the time, and the place. Emotional responses are probably also like this, and what is felt now and what is felt at some other time can fluctuate between being perceived as sad and being seen as absurd. And there is no longer any need for mockery, for it seems that there has been enough self-ridicule and self-purification. It is only in the gesture of tranquilly prolonging this life and striving to comprehend the mystery of this moment in time, that freedom of existence is achieved. It is through this act of solitarily scrutinizing the self, that others' perceptions of one's self lose relevance.

You do not know what other things you will do, or what else there is to do, but this is of no consequence. If you want to do something, you do it. It's fine if you do it, but it doesn't matter if you don't. And you don't have to persist in doing something. If, at a particular moment, you feel hungry and thirsty, you just go and have something to eat and drink. Of course, you still have your own opinions, interpretations, inclinations, and you even get angry, because you are not so old that you don't have the energy for anger. Naturally, you still become indignant, but it is with little passion. And while you still have the capacity for feelings and sensory pleasures, then so be it. However, there is no longer remorse. Remorse is futile and, needless to say, harmful to one's self.

For you, only life is of value, you have a lingering attachment to it, it continues to be interesting because there are still things to discover and amaze you. It is only life that can excite you. That is just how it is with you, isn't it?

55

One day, passing Drum Tower around dusk, he got off his bicycle and was about to go into a small eatery when someone called out his name. He turned. A woman stood there, looking at him. Uncertain about smiling, she was biting her lip.

"Xiao Xiao?" He wasn't sure.

Xiao Xiao gave an awkward smile.

"I'm sorry." He didn't know what to say. "I didn't think. . . ."

"You can't recognize me, can you?"

"You're more robust. . . ." In his memory, she was a young girl with a slight build and small breasts.

"I'm a peasant woman?" the woman asked sarcastically.

"No, you're just more sturdy!" he hastened to add.

"I am, after all, a member of a commune. But I am not that flower turning with the sun; it withered and died!"

Xiao Xiao was caustic. She was referring to a song in praise of the Party, which compared the members of a commune to a sunflower that turned with the sun. He changed the topic, "Are you back in Beijing?"

"I'm trying to get a residential permit. I've put down that my mother is ill and needs me to look after her, I'm the only child in the family. I'm dealing with the formalities for getting back to Beijing, but I haven't got my residential permit yet."

"Is your family still at the same place?"

"The place is a shambles. My father is dead, but my mother has come back from the cadre school."

He knew nothing of Xiao Xiao's family circumstances and could only say, "I went to the *hutong* where your house is, I went to see . . ."

He was talking about ten years ago.

"How about coming to my house for a visit?"

"All right." He agreed without thinking, although he hadn't originally intended to. That year, he had cycled many times through that *hutong* in the hope of running into her, but he didn't say this, and simply mumbled, "But I didn't know your house number. . . ."

"I didn't ever tell you." Xiao Xiao remembered very clearly. She had not forgotten that winter night when she left before daybreak.

"It has been a long time since I've lived in that house. I was in a village for almost six years, and I am now living in a workplace dormitory."

This explained things, but Xiao Xiao didn't say if she had also tried to see him. He pushed his bicycle, walking for a while in silence beside Xiao Xiao, until turning into a lane. He had gone through this *hutong* on his bicycle many times, from one end to the other, then had gone into another lane, circled around, and come back from that end of the *hutong*. He had noted each of the courtyard gates, thinking that he might bump into her. He didn't know Xiao Xiao's surname, so he couldn't make inquiries, he thought Xiao Xiao had to be a name her classmates and her family called her. The *hutong* was quite long when it came to walking through it.

Xiao Xiao went ahead, through a gate leading into a big courtyard shared by a number of families. On the left, was a small door with a padlock hanging on it, and, next to it, a coal stove. She opened the door with a key. Inside was a big bed piled with folded bedding, the rest of the room was a mess. Xiao Xiao quickly grabbed the clothes from a chair and threw them onto the bed.

"Where's your mother?" He sat on the chair, and the springs in the seat cushion squeaked noisily.

"She's in a hospital."

"Why is she in a hospital?"

"Breast cancer, it's already spread to the bones. I hope she will last the year and a half it will take to get my residential permit issued."

After such a response, he couldn't ask anything else.

"Like some tea?"

"No, thanks." He had to try to think of something to say. "Tell me about yourself—"

"What about? What's worth talking about?" Xiao Xiao asked, standing right in front of him.

"About your years in the countryside."

"Didn't you also stay in the countryside, don't you know?"

He started to regret having come. The cramped room was a total mess, and destroyed the image of the young girl he had cherished in his mind. Xiao Xiao sat on the bed and looked at him, frowning. He didn't know what else he could say to her.

"You were my first man."

All right. He thought of her left breast, no, it was his left hand, so the tender red scar was on her right breast.

"But you were so stupid."

This hurt him. He immediately wanted to ask her about the scar on her breast to get back at her, but he asked instead, "Why?"

"It was you who didn't want it. . . ." Xiao Xiao said calmly, her head hanging.

"But at the time you were only a middle-school student!" he explained.

"I became a peasant woman a long time ago. It was soon after I had been sent to the countryside, not even a year. . . . People in the village couldn't be bothered with things like that!"

"You could have reported it—"

"To whom? You're really stupid."

"I thought . . ."

"Thought what?"

"I thought at that time you were a virgin. . . ." Thinking back to that time, he had thought this, and so he didn't dare to defile her.

"What were you afraid of? It was I who was afraid. . . . You were just a coward! I knew that, with my family background, nothing good would come of me, it was I who presented myself at your door, but you didn't have the courage to take me!"

"I was afraid of taking responsibility," he was forced to admit.

"I hadn't told you about my parents' situation."

"I could have guessed. It's too late now, how can I put it. . . ." He said, "I'm married!"

"Of course, it's too late. I can also tell you that I'm a slut. I've had two abortions, two bastards that I didn't want!"

"You should have taken precautions!" He also needed to say things that would hurt her.

She snorted in derision. "The peasants don't carry condoms. It was my own bad luck that I didn't have good parents and didn't have anyone to turn to for help. Anyway, I can't keep going on like this in the village."

"You're still young, don't be so negative and cruel to yourself. . . ."

"Of course, I have to go on living. I don't need you to preach to me about that, I've had enough of being preached at!" She laughed, laughed really hard, her hands gripping the edge of the bed, her shoulders shaking.

He laughed with her, as tears welled in his eyes. Xiao Xiao stopped him. Suddenly, he seemed to see in her face the gentleness of that young girl of the past, but, in an instant, it had vanished.

"Would you like something to eat? I've only got dried noodles. Wasn't it dried noodles that you made for me?"

"You made it," he reminded her.

Xiao Xiao went outside to cook the noodles on the coal stove, shutting the door behind her. He cast his eyes over the mess in the room. Even her dirty underwear was among the clothes she had thrown onto the bed. He had to completely destroy the dreamlike image that evoked tender feelings in him, he had to be debauched, he had to treat the woman like a slut he had picked up, a whore who had been used by the villagers.

Shoving aside things like grain-coupon booklets, keys, and other odds and ends, Xiao Xiao put the noodles on the table. He embraced her from behind, pressing his hands onto her breasts, and got the back of his hands slapped, but it was not a genuine slap.

"Sit down and eat!"

Xiao Xiao was not angry, there was no emotional reaction. Her relationships with men were probably like this, and she had become used to it. Xiao Xiao ate her noodles with her head down and said nothing. He knew she had sensed what he had on his mind. There was no need to talk about it, there were no obstacles.

Xiao Xiao quickly finished eating, pushed away her bowl and chopsticks, and, head held high, stared blankly at him.

"Should I leave now?" he asked. That was how hypocritical he was.

"Do whatever you like," Xiao Xiao said flatly, without moving.

He got up and went over to her. He took her head in his hands and tried to kiss her, but Xiao Xiao turned away and put her head down. She would not let him kiss her. He put his hand down her shirt and felt the woman's breasts, which had become big and plump.

"Get into bed, then," Xiao Xiao said, heaving a sigh.

He sat on the edge of the bed and watched the woman bolt the door. The switch was by the door, but the light hanging from the ceiling pasted with yellowing old newspaper did not go out. Xiao

Xiao ignored him, and, straight away, stripped. He gave a start; for a moment, he did not see the scar in the shadow at the base of her breast. While he was untying his shoelaces, Xiao Xiao got on the bed, spread the bedding, then lay on her back and covered herself.

"Aren't you married?" the woman said, staring with her eyes wide open.

He made no response. He felt humiliated and wanted revenge, but he couldn't understand why. He roughly pulled away the bedding and threw himself on the woman's body. What came into his mind was the body of that other girl in the production-brigade storehouse by the road, all his repressed violence poured into this woman's body. . . .

Her eyes closed, Xiao Xiao said, "You can relax, even if I were to become pregnant you wouldn't need to worry about it. I'm used to abortions."

He examined the skin and flesh of this woman who was a stranger to him. The pink nipples and the protrusions dotting the dark-brown aureoles were hard, but the breasts were white and soft. It was then that he saw the inch-long, pale-brown scar below the breast. He didn't touch it, and stopped himself from asking how she had got it.

Xiao Xiao said nothing frightened her anymore, and it didn't matter to her if the neighbors wanted to talk. However, he said he was married, and if the neighborhood committee reported him to his work unit, his application for divorce would fall through. When he put on his clothes, Xiao Xiao was still lying in bed, she seemed to be smiling, but the corners of her mouth were turned down.

"Will you come again?" Xiao Xiao asked. "I never see any of my former school friends and I'm very lonely."

He didn't ever go back to Xiao Xiao's home and even avoided going past Drum Tower. He was afraid of bumping into her and not knowing what to say to her.

56

It was with difficulty that he pulled off the mask he had put on his face. This false skin was a sheath of molded plastic, mass-produced to standard specifications, elastic, and able to stretch and contract as required. Wearing it gave the appearance of an upright, correct, positive character, which could be deployed in various roles—whether for the masses, such as workers, peasants, shop personnel, university and office personnel, or intellectuals, such as teachers, editors, and reporters. By putting on a stethoscope, one became a doctor, by replacing the stethoscope with a pair of glasses, one became a professor or a writer. The glasses were optional, but the mask was obligatory. Only bad elements in society, such as thieves, hooligans, and public enemies of the people, were entitled to rip off this mask. This was the most commonly used mask, probably made of high-density polyethylene and indestructible even if hammered.

He toyed with the mask, scrunched up his eyes, uncertain if he was still capable of normal human expressions. However, he refused to put on some new mask, such as political dissident, cultural broker, prophet, or member of the new rich.

Having removed the mask, he could not help feeling somewhat

awkward. He was tense and didn't know what to do, but, for better or worse, he had discarded hypocrisy, anxiety, and unnecessary restraint. He had no leader, because he was not controlled by the Party or some organization. He had no hometown, because his parents were dead. And he had no family. He had no responsibilities, he was alone, but he was free and easy, he could go wherever he wanted, he could drift on the wind. As long as others did not create problems for him, he would resolve his own problems, and if he could resolve his own problems, then everything else would be insignificant, everything else would be inconsequential.

He no longer shouldered any burdens, and had cancelled emotional debts by purging his past. If he again loved or embraced a woman, it would only be if this was what she wanted, and she accepted him. Otherwise, at most, it would be going for coffee or beer in a café, having a chat, a bit of a flirt, then each going their separate ways.

He wrote because he needed to. It was the only way he could enjoy total freedom; he didn't write for a livelihood. He also did not use his pen as a weapon to fight for some cause, and he didn't have a sense of mission. He wrote for his own pleasure, talking to himself so that he could listen to and observe himself. It was a means of experiencing those feelings of the little life that remained for him.

The only thing in his past he didn't break with was the language. He could, of course, write in another language, but he didn't abandon his language, because it was convenient and he didn't need to look up words in a dictionary. However, conventional language did not suit him, and he had to look for his own voice. He wanted to listen intently to what he was saying, as if he were listening to music, but he found language always lacking in refinement. He was certain that one day he would abandon language and rely on other media to convey his feelings.

He admired the agile bodies of some performers, especially dancers. He would love to be able to use his body to freely express himself: to casually stumble, fall over, get up, and go on dancing. However, age was unrelenting, and he could very well end up injuring himself. He was no longer capable of dancing, and could only somersault about in language. Language was light and portable, and it had him under its spell. He was a carnival performer in language, an incurable addict, he had to talk, and even alone he was always talking to himself. This inner voice had become the affirmation of his existence. He had already formed the habit of transforming his feelings into language, and not to do so left him feeling unfulfilled, but the joy it brought him was like groaning or calling out when making love.

He is sitting in front of you, looking right at you, and laughing loudly in the mirror.

57

The place is New York. On the first day, it is ten degrees below zero, and snowing, and the very next, it suddenly turns warm. Dirty lumps of ice are everywhere, your shoes become soggy, and you have to buy a pair of heavy boots because of the lousy weather. . . . You prefer the mild Paris winter. There are large numbers of Chinese here, and, from time to time, on the streets, you hear the speech of Beijing, Shanghai, Shandong, and even the He'nan village dialect spoken near the reform-through-labor farm where you were once sent. Also, there is every kind of Chinese food you can think of, even crab-roe dumplings and hand-shaved noodles. Chinatowns are everywhere, whether downtown in Manhattan, or in Flushing, Queens. This is China, more Chinese than China, as Chinese New Yorkers construct their own virtual hometowns.

You don't have a hometown, and, in America, you do not have to put on a play with Chinese actors. You wanted local Western actors, and had hoped they would find a uniquely American woman to play the lead role. But it was after the premiere that you again saw the beautiful Linda. She was one-quarter Turkish, and you first met her at a drama festival in Italy, at the dinner following the performance of your play. She came over to your table, embraced you, kissed you passionately on both cheeks, and said, "I loved your play. If you ever come to New York to put on a play, don't forget to look me up!" You were delighted to see her so visibly moved, and had not forgotten to give the theater group her telephone number and address. However, nobody called her, and she also missed the advertisement for auditions. There are just so many beautiful women in New York, and plenty of good actors. She came to the performance, and wept after it had ended, but you were not sure whether it was because she had seen you, or the play, or because she was sorry she had missed the chance to perform in the play. In any case, you, too, were deeply moved.

You are, in fact, not so alone in the world, and have many close friends, as well as some you have just made. You find it is often easier to communicate with them than with some of your fellow Chinese. You can be more direct, and when you make love with Western women, there are fewer obstacles. In the middle of the night, you answer a telephone call from Paris, and you say that you had just been thinking of her. "What about?" she says on the phone. You say you had been thinking of the smell of her body. "Then what if I send it wet and sloppy over the phone?" she laughs. "It wouldn't be enough." You say you had been thinking of her, the whole of her, from top to bottom. "Don't you have another woman in your bed?" she asks. "Not right now, but who knows, maybe there will be one along any moment," you say. "You rascal!" she says. "But I'll still kiss you, kiss you all over!"

You're not an "upright gentleman," and don't have to put on an act of being virtuous. What you want to do is to spray your lust all over the world, turn it awash! Of course, that is sheer fantasy, and you can't help feeling a sort of sadness. But you know your sadness has been diluted, in fact, you rejoice in having salvaged your life. You belong now to that rascal, you. But you have allowed yourself to be enjoyed by the French filly that called you a rascal, you willingly gave yourself to her so that she, too, gets all wet, and you can enjoy her.

Everything in the past already seems so remote and far away, you have wandered all over the world and you are not really sad. You like jazz and the freedom of the blues. That was how you had come to write that play. One day among the props in the theater storeroom, you found an old picture frame, and you hung on it the plastic leg of a display model. You wrote on the leg "WHAT" in fancy lettering, and it counted as your signature. You poke fun at the world, and you poke fun at yourself, and it is by offsetting the one against the other that life is fun. You would like to become a piece of jazz, like that classic recorded by the black singer Johnny Hartman:

> *They say that falling in love is wonderful*
> *It's wonderful. . . .*

At rehearsal, the actors say that a black singer was shot when he got out of his car on the highway to fix something. The newspapers that day have photographs of the person killed, and, although you have never heard the man's songs, you can't help feeling sad.

It would be hard for you to love a Chinese woman again. When you left China, you dumped the little nurse, but now you no longer reproach yourself for it, you no longer spend your days reproaching yourself.

Gentle moonlight, hazy mountain, shadowy thatched huts, paddy fields after harvest in the valley, a dirt track crawling over the slope past the door of a storehouse. A rustic poem so old that it has lost its impact. You seem to see this dream scene, see the shut door of that tamped-earth building. It was there that your student was raped, no one could have saved her. She had no choice, she was hoping to earn merit points for a work permit so that she would not have to go on growing her own grain in order to be able to eat. That was the price she had to pay. She is far away, on the other side of the world, and has long since forgotten that a person like you ever existed. You lament in vain, but it is lust, rather than fond memories, that is evoked.

She says that right now she has no lust. She says she wants to cry, and, immediately, tears are streaming from her eyes. You say you are full of uncontrollable lust. But she says she doesn't want to be a substitute, says it's not she that you want to penetrate, and she can't penetrate your heart, because you're somewhere far away. You say you're by her side, that it's because tonight you're in bed with her, want to excite her, that you're telling her this story. But she says not to use her to pour out the secret pains in your heart. You say you didn't think that a French filly like her would be like that. She says so what if she is? You ask how can she possibly not know about male wickedness? But she says lying together like this is so good, she treasures her relationship with you, don't make this beautiful feeling into something dirty, just let her lie there peacefully. She goes on to say she, too, can be wild. If it was a man she didn't know, she would have let him go ahead, it's because she loves you and doesn't want suddenly to ruin her relationship with you. You remind her that she had said she was a whore. She says she did say this, and she still is your little whore, but not right now. You ask when she would be. She says she doesn't know when, but she would be your little whore, and, at that time, she would give you anything you wanted. But you haven't brought a condom, and she's afraid of getting some disease. Don't get cross with her. She says who told you to come unprepared? Where can one of those things be found in the middle of the night? If you really must, you can spray it over her, but definitely not into her. You embrace her, sniff her, and fondle her all over. You rub your semen, her tears, and your mixed sweat onto her belly, breasts, and nipples. You ask her if she's happy. She says you can do anything you like, only don't ask. She embraces you, lets you press against her swelling breasts, and says no matter what, she loves you. Her murmuring and her breathing are right by your ear.

You open the curtains to another day. Afterward, at a café, you are sitting outside under a big umbrella. It is a Sunday, and the afternoon sun is a golden yellow. She came especially to see your play but has to rush back to Paris for the opening of her boyfriend's exhibition at six o'clock. She says she has to be loyal to him, but she also loves you. You're happy, put your hand into the sun, say you can catch a handful of sunlight. You tell her to have a go, but she throws back her head and laughs. The waiter comes out, apologizes, lunch finished some time ago, and the cook's gone. Then what is there to eat? Only ham and eggs. Then ham and eggs it is!

You say you want to write about all this, and she says it will be very beautiful. You say it was she who had given you these feelings and had helped you to turn suffering into something beautiful, all of this had weighed heavily on you. She says after suffering has passed, it, too, can become beautiful. You say she's a genuine French filly. A woman! She says this both as a correction and an affirmation. You say she's also a witch. She says she probably is. She wants you to discharge all your suffering, so that you will be a wiser person. Yes, you feel purified inside and outside, as if you've been washed and scrubbed right through. She says she wants you to have exactly this feeling, don't you think it's something very precious? You say this feeling is what she's given you, she says what she wants is you as a person and not your lust. You say you really want to rip her apart and swallow her. Then I'd no longer exist, she says, and don't you think that would be a pity?

You go with her to the railway station, and she holds your arm. You say you love her, and she says she loves you too. You say you love her very much and she says it's the same with her. Life is worthwhile, you say. Now pay attention, you're going to sing! She laughs so hard that she doubles over. She says come on the train with her! You say there is still another performance in the evening, and you can't just abandon the actors, you do have that amount of responsibility. She says she knows, not to listen to her, she just had to say it. The carriage door closes, and, as the train moves off, she mouths three words: I love you. You know she's just saying this, and, as she says, she has to stay loyal to her boyfriend. You truly love her, but you can still love other women.

You're light, and float up as if you're weightless. You wander from country to country, city to city, woman to woman, but don't think of finding a place that is home. You drift along, engrossed in savoring the taste of the written language, and, like ejaculating, leave behind some traces of your life. You achieve nothing and no longer concern yourself with things in life and in afterlife. As your life was plucked back from death, why should you be concerned? You simply live in this instant, like a leaf on the brink of falling from a tree. Is it a tallow tree, a white birch, or a linden? Anyway, it's a leaf, and, sooner or later, it has to fall, but while it's fluttering in the breeze, it must strive for freedom. You are, after all, the irredeemable prodigal son of a family that was destined for destruction. You want to be free of the ties, complications, perplexities, anxieties of ancestors, wife, and memories, and to be like music, like the jazz of that black man: "They say that falling in love is wonderful, it's wonderful. . . ."

The plastic leg bearing your signature WHAT in the old picture frame slowly rises on the stage. In the midst of singing, an old man with a sunken mouth is hoisting it up on a rope, solemnly, just like raising a flag. Your actress, a young Japanese performer, is standing elegantly at the front of the stage. She is very solemn, and presents a rose on a broken stem in both hands to the audience. Then, parting her lips, she erupts into laughter, revealing a mouth full of black teeth. This is wonderful, so wonderful!

You have already played around with revolutionary art and revolutionary people, and even if you were to play around more with them, you would not be able to come up with anything new. The world is like an unfurled, worn-out flag. In the early hours of the morning, while you are traveling by car from Provence to the Alps, a gentle stretch of mist comes toward you. You become formless and weightless, and, while mocking others and yourself, you vanish with the wind. . . .

You're just a melancholic piece of jazz, greedy and insatiable in that moist, dark cavern between a woman's thighs. So, why is this pitiful little bird of yours complaining?

You're a saxophone, moaning when you want and shouting when you want. Ah, you have said farewell to revolution! If you think crying will make you feel better, you have a good cry. You're not afraid of losing anything. If there's nothing to lose, then you're free, like a wisp of smoke, like the pure fragrance of marijuana mixed with the fishy smell of stinkweed. So, why are you still worried? Why are you still afraid? When you disappear, you will disappear. But disappearing between the voluptuous, moist thighs of a woman is wonderful and is to understand fully what is known as life. You don't need to be sad or begrudging, you can squander everything, and this is wonderful!

Tough reeds blowing in the wind. The wind on the North Sea coast of Denmark is strong, but among the clumps of reeds on the undulating sand dunes is a circle of reeds moving against the wind. You think it is a pair of wild geese, but, coming closer, see that it is a naked couple, a man and a woman. You turn to leave, and hear them laughing behind you. Beyond the desolate beach, on the dark-green sea, white-crested waves tumble as they charge toward the seaweed-covered concrete bunker left from the Nazi occupation.

You want to cry, to throw yourself onto her firm breasts wet with perspiration and smeared with semen, and to cry uncontrollably, like a child needing the warmth of his mother. You don't just enjoy yourself with women, but also seek their warmth, forgiveness, and acceptance.

Your mother was the first woman you saw naked, through the half-closed door of her lighted room. You were sleeping in the dark on the cool bamboo bed, heard the splashing water, and wanted to take a proper look. When you propped yourself up on your elbows, your bed creaked. Your mother, with soap all over her body, came out, and you quickly lay down and hid your face, pretending to be asleep. She went back to the tub, but the door was left open, and you stealthily looked at the breasts that had fed you, and the black bushy place from which you had emerged. At first, you held your breath, then your breathing quickened, and after that you fell asleep in a state of stirring lust and confusion.

She said you were just a child, and, instantly, your lust settled. Contented and sleepy, you were her obedient child. She gently stroked you, and you placidly allowed her to examine you all over with the palm of her hand. That shriveled thing between your legs, she called it her little bird. Her eyes were gentle as she stroked your head, and, deeply moved, you wanted to nestle against her, nestle against this woman who had given you life, happiness, and comfort. You equated this with love, equated this with sex, equated this with sadness, equated this with unsettling lust, and equated this with language. The need to express and narrate is a form of joy in pouring out, has no connotations of morality, and contains nothing hypocritical. It is a soaking deluge that totally cleanses you, so that you are transparent, like a thread of meaning in life, like light from behind a door behind which there is nothing, like a hazy surge of moonlight behind the clouds. You hear seagulls flapping their wings in the night sky, and see, from the depths of the darkness, the sea surging up into a line of white foam on the tide. In Italy, at Viareggio, the sea is flooded with searchlights, but the beach is deserted. You stand there, motionless, for a long time in front of the red-and-white-striped beach umbrellas.

* * *

However, at present, on this night in New York, the icy snow on the pavement is dirty and slushy. This is citizen-conscious New York, garbage-strewn New York, New York soaring into the clouds on its accumulated wealth, breathtaking New York, New York where people have to stand on the street in the cold to smoke a cigarette. The performance has ended, and you come out with her to look for a bar where you can smoke and have some drinks. She is the Japanese performer who, without speaking a word on stage, has just performed several roles in your play: a young girl just becoming sexually awakened, a dissolute woman, the mother's corpse, a nun, and a female ghost.

Walking from Eighth or Ninth Street in Manhattan to some streets past Thirtieth Street, finally, at Third, or Fifth, or maybe even Sixth Avenue—you can never remember numbers—you find a Brazilian or Mexican bar. It has a good atmosphere, and there are candles on the table, but the rock'n'roll music is too loud and not conducive to flirting. You have to shout across the table to hear what the other is saying, as you talk about art, serious art. She says she is really happy to have been able to play so many roles in one play, it was a satisfying experience, and the play seemed to have been written just for her. You curse the *New York Times*. The theater publicity person told you repeatedly that a reporter would definitely be coming, but no one had turned up even by the end of the performance. She says that with off-Broadway theaters it's always like that, it's very hard to get into their pages. Anyway, she has no regrets about having been able to work with you.

"I'll miss you," she says as she looks at her dark-blue fingernails.

The conversation turns to life. You say her nails were painted a tea color a couple of days ago. She says she often paints them different colors, and that each of the nails could be painted a different color. She also asks you how you would have liked them painted. You say blue-gray would have been best. On the stage, it would look colder, even though the play is dance and the focus is on the arms and legs. The conversation returns to art.

"Then what about lipstick?" she asks.

"Do you have black lipstick?" you ask.

"I've got all colors. Why didn't you tell me earlier?"

"That's the job of the makeup artist, I can't do everything," you say.

"But we've already had the last performance!" she sighs.

"What new performances are coming up for you?" you ask, changing the topic.

"I'll just have to wait and watch out for opportunities. There is a musical that requires actors who can dance. Next week, I've got two auditions. My father told me to come back to Japan a long time ago, but, unless I joined the workforce there, I would have to get married. My father says I won't be able to make a living by dancing, and I should be satisfied, now that I've amused myself with it for so long."

She also says her father would soon retire and couldn't support her all her life. However, her mother says it is up to her to choose; her mother is Taiwan-born Chinese, and is quite open-minded. She says she doesn't like Japan, because women in that society have no freedom. You say you like Japanese literature, especially the women in Japanese writings.

"Why?"

"They're very sexy and very cruel."

"That's in books, it's not true. Haven't you ever had a Japanese woman?" she asks.

"I'd really like to have one," you say.

"Then you will have one." Having said this, she glances over to the bar.

You pay the bill and she thanks you.

You separate at the Grand Central Station subway entrance at

Forty-second Street. You clearly remember Forty-second Street, because you changed trains here for rehearsals and performances every day. She says if she comes to Paris, she will look you up, and that she would write. However, you never get a letter from her. In your case, it's not until several months later, when sorting a batch of papers from the New York trip, that you see the address she has left on a torn-off piece of paper napkin. You send her a postcard, but nothing happens, so you don't know if she ever went back to Japan.

58

He came upon a crowd. There was great excitement and a din of gongs and drums.

"Run, run, run!" the crowd shouted.

He said he was busy, he had personal matters to deal with.

"Personal matters? No matters are as important as this! Run, run with us, run with all of us!"

"Why are you running?" he asked.

"We're going to see the good times, the good times will be here soon, we're going to greet the good times! How can your piffling personal matters be as important?"

Everyone was jostling one another, jubilant, forming ranks, shouting slogans.

"Where are the good times?" he couldn't help asking.

"The good times are ahead! If we say they're ahead, then they're ahead! If we say they're ahead, then ahead they will be!"

Everyone was saying it with growing enthusiasm and conviction.

"Who said that the good times were ahead?" He was jostled, and had to run as he asked.

"If everyone says they're ahead, then they're ahead. If everybody says it, it can't be wrong. Run with us, the good times are definitely ahead!"

The crowd loudly sang good-times songs. As they sang, their spirits were uplifted, and, as they sang, their morale rose. He, who was stuck in the crowd, also had to sing; if he didn't sing, he would be eyed with suspicious stares all around.

"Hey, what's the matter? Is something wrong with you? Are you a deaf-mute?"

If he wanted to show he didn't have a physical disability, the only thing he could do was to sing loudly with the crowd, he had to sing as well as keep in step. He had to keep in step, because, if he were half a step slower, the heel of his shoe would be trodden on, and he would lose his shoe. If he were to get under people's feet to pick up his shoe, wouldn't people's feet run over his head? He would just have to leave behind the shoe he had lost. The foot that had lost the shoe would be trodden on, so his other foot could only hop and stumble along. Anyway, he would have to keep up, keep singing with everyone, and keep singing loudly in praise of the good times.

"The good times are ahead, the good times will soon be here! And the good times are simply good, and the good times will always be ahead!"

As the singing became more rousing, the good times became even better. With the hot waves of the good times seething, and the singing more fervent, the good times would come faster.

"The good times will be here soon! Let's go and welcome the good times! Charge into battle for the good times! Die without regret for the good times!"

Everyone had become feverish, gone crazy, and he, too, had to go crazy, even if he wasn't, he had to pretend to go crazy.

"Trouble, there's shooting!"

"Who's shooting?"

"Is there shooting up ahead?"

"Rubbish! The good times are up ahead, how can there be shooting up ahead?"

"Rubber bullets?"

"Flame throwers?"

"Tracer bullets!"

"Arrgh—"

"Blood? People are getting killed!"

"Charge into battle for the good times, break the enemy ranks for the good times! What greater glory than to sacrifice oneself for the good times! Become martyrs for the good times! Uggh—"

The crowd did not think that assault rifles, machine guns, would strafe and fire in bursts, fire in bursts and strafe. It was like frying soybeans, like letting off crackers. Everyone was like a homeless dog, and ran off in all directions, some were killed, others injured. Those who were not killed or injured fled like birds and animals. . . .

Agitated and grief-stricken, he managed to escape to a dead-end alley, where the bullets couldn't reach. Gradually, he again heard voices in the distance. Sure enough, it was another crowd of people beating on gongs and drums and, faintly in the distance, they also seemed to be shouting slogans. When he listened carefully, they, too, seemed to be talking about the good times, but, when he listened again, they seemed to be arguing. The good times will soon be here, no, for the time being they have been delayed, but they will come. The good times are sure to come. Sooner or later, they will come. . . . He hurried away. The good times terrified him, and he would rather sneak off before the good times had come.

59

You are in the military port of Toulon on the Mediterranean coast, a place you had learned about in geography lessons in middle school. You're sitting in a big tent erected on the harbor for the book fair. Like the hundred or so invited writers seated behind rows of book-stalls, you're next to your own book, holding a pen and waiting for book buyers who want a signature. But all the people passing by are looking at the books and don't notice the writers whose names are hanging there on the placards. For writers, it's not the same as with singing stars. Hysterical fans queuing for autographs mob Johnny Hallyday when he gets off the helicopter, and his bodyguards and the police have to yell and shove to keep order. You are beyond the pairs of roving eyes, and people look but don't see you. They pass right in front of you, sometimes stopping to leaf through the books with your name printed on the cover. But what does your name sig-nify? People inevitably seek self-identification in books, the light from their eyes is refracted from the book to a person's heart.

Luckily, you don't have anything to do, and have time to amuse yourself by taking in all these pairs of worried, or blank, searching eyes. A good-looking young woman is moving in the crowd, her chestnut hair casually swept into a bun, but there is a deep frown on her forehead and a startling sadness in her face. Her big eyelids droop wearily, probably from a sleepless night. Maybe she couldn't get the man she was in bed with to stay, but, in the case of such a fine-looking woman, it was more likely that the man wasn't able to get *her* to stay. Otherwise, she would not be on her own, wandering at the book fair early on Sunday morning. She eventually comes over to your stall, but picks up a book by someone else alongside, then, without looking at the introduction on the back cover, puts it down, then leafs through another book. She is not thinking of buying a book, maybe she doesn't know what she wants to do. She puts down the book and picks up your book, but she is looking somewhere else. Her eyes eventually return to your book, the book in her hand, and turn to the back cover, but, without reading more than a couple of sentences of the brief back-cover blurb, she puts it down, not noticing that the author is right next to her. She is right in front of you, the deep frown still on her forehead. The sad expression delicately roaming her face is wonderful to look at, and is more alive than any book.

What sort of people would read your book? When you wrote it, you couldn't have imagined that you would one day be sitting at this seaside book fair, facing potential readers. These people don't need to be concerned about, or go to the extent of buying, your perplexities. Luckily, the person selling the books is the owner of the stall, and you are merely a live decoration. Having lost your vanity too early, you are too much of a bystander, you are just an idler. Anyway, there are so many books in the world, and they are still being mass-produced, so whether there is one more or one less is not important. You don't rely on selling your books for a living, and it is because you don't make a living from it that you wrote it. Still, this is a book you had to write.

You clip the pen in the top pocket of your jacket, get from the proprietor a few sheets of writing paper, which you stuff into your coat pocket, then set off for a stroll around the harbor. The bright sunshine in Toulon seems to resonate, yet the cafés, bars, restaurants, and outside seafood stalls along the little street by the old port are virtually empty. However, this Sunday, on a main street into town, there are crowds at the morning market where they are selling all sorts of everyday items ranging from fruit and vegetables to clothing. There are large numbers of Arab vendors, and also a Chinese take-out kitchen. These people do good business, and this probably annoys the extreme-right National Front municipal government. In the center of town, they, too, have a book fair, and it is having a slugging match with the book fair organized by the leftist regional government that has invited you. You can't escape politics, can't escape it anywhere. Suddenly, you sense Margarethe's anxiety, it is as palpable as the bright resonating sunshine, and you can feel it by snapping your fingers.

You have no intention of going to see what new things they have at their book fair. The stereotypical tunes of nationalism are the same everywhere, so you go back to the harbor and sit in a café to write something.

Humans are frail, but what is so bad about being frail? And yours is precisely a frail life. The Superman aspires to replace God, and is fiercely arrogant in his ignorance, so you may as well be a frail, ordinary person. The almighty God created a world such as this without properly planning for the future. You do not plan anything, do not rack your brains thinking about futile things, but simply live in the present, not knowing how it will be from this instant to the next. But aren't these instant-by-instant transformations beautiful? Nobody can escape death, and death provides an end, otherwise you would become an old fogy who, devoid of compassion or shame, would perpetrate heinous deeds. Death is an end that can't be resisted, but the wonder of being human lies before that end, so squirm as you transform.

You are not Buddha or a reincarnated bodhisattva possessing

three bodies and six faces, and capable of going through seventy-two transformations. Music, mathematics, and Buddha are all existences born of nonexistence. The concept of numbers, the organization of music, and the variations in scale, pitch, and beat, Buddha or God, and beauty are all abstractions drawn from nature's myriad phenomena that defy description. All of these are intangible in their natural form. This self of yours, too, is an existence born of nonexistence. Saying that it exists brings it into existence, and saying that it doesn't exist turns it back into a mass of inchoate nebula. Is this self that you are striving to create so very unique? Or, in other words, do you have a self? You squirm in limitless karma, but where is all this karma? Karma, just like frustration, is your creation. So, there's no need for you to busy yourself with creating this self, and even less to give birth to existence from nonexistence just in order to identify with that self. You may as well return to the source of life: this instant that is full of life. What is eternal is this instant. You perceive, and, therefore, you exist, otherwise you are nebulous unconsciousness. So, live in this instant and feel this gentle midautumn sunlight!

The leaves in the park are turning yellow, and, looking down from your window, you see the ground covered in fallen leaves that have become dry but have not yet rotted. You are getting old, but wouldn't want to return to childhood times; the noisy children you see down below in the parking lot have no idea of what they want to do. Youth is precious, but by the time those children know what they want, they will also be old. You do not want to go through all the torment a second time, of struggling against vanity, anxiety, uncertainty, and chaos. You do not envy them, but you envy the freshness of their lives. However, the freshness of life of childhood ignorance is lacking in that limidity of consciousness and self-awareness, and you deeply appreciate this instant in time and this solitude that is free of all sham. This limidity, like the bright shapes reflected in a murmuring autumn stream, evokes a calm in your inner mind. You will not again charge forth to judge or to establish anything. Waves ripple, and leaves tremble on trees, then fall, so, for you, death should be a natural occurrence. You are heading toward it, but before you come right up to it, there is time enough to stage a play for a duel with Death. You have plenty of time to enjoy to the full this bit of life that remains to you, your body is still capable of feeling, and you still have lust. You want a woman, a woman whose thinking is as lucid as yours, a woman who is free of the bondage of the world. You want a woman who rejects the ties of a home, and does not bear children, a woman who does not follow vanity and fashion, a natural and totally wanton woman. You want a woman who does not want to appropriate anything from your person, a woman who will, at this instant of time, enjoy with you the joys of being a fish in water. But where is such a woman to be found? A woman as solitary as you, yet contented with being solitary like you, will fuse your solitude with hers in sexual gratification; it will fuse in caresses and one another's looks, while you are examining and exploring one another. Where is such a woman to be found?

60

Enough! he says.

What do you mean? you ask.

He says enough, put an end to him!

Who are you talking about? Who is to put an end to whom?

Him, that character you're writing about, put an end to him.

You say you are not the author.

Then who is?

Surely, it's clear, himself, of course! You are only his conscious mind.

Then what will happen to you? If he is finished off, will you also be finished off?

You say you can be a reader, you will be just like the audience watching a play. The he and you in the book are not of any great significance.

He says, you are really good at detaching yourself!

Of course, you do not shoulder or acknowledge any responsibility—moral, ethical, or the like—toward him. You are just an idler with some free time, who happened to have the opportunity of focusing on such a character. But it is enough and you, too, are weary. So, if he is to be finished off, then so be it. In any case, he is a character, and, sooner or later, there would have to be a conclusion. He can't be disposed of like garbage just by your saying that he's finished.

But people are garbage, and, sooner or later, have to be eliminated. Otherwise, the world, with its excess of people, would have created a foul stench long ago.

Is that why there is fighting, rivalry, war, and, therefore, all kinds of theories?

Stop rationalizing! It gives you a headache.

You're a pessimist.

Pessimist or not, the world will remain the same, it's not decided by you. You're not God, and nobody can control it. But even the ending for such a character in a novel has to be decided. Is his death to result from a serious illness or a heart attack, or will he be strangled, stabbed, gunned down, or killed in a car accident? This will be decided by the author, and is not up to you. In any case, he seems reluctant to kill himself, but you have really had enough, you are just a game he is playing with language, and, once he finishes, you will automatically be released.

However, he says he is playing a game with the world because he can't stand the loneliness. You and he became fellow travelers, but you are neither his comrade nor his judge, nor are you his ultimate conscious mind, whatever that may be. You simply care about him. For you and for him, the interstices of time and circumstances provided distance, although you have had the advantage of time and location. With that distance—in other words, freedom—you were able to observe him at leisure. He was a spontaneous being, and his sufferings, in fact, were self-inflicted.

So, all right, you bid him farewell and go off. Or, rather, he must say good-bye to you. Is anything more to be said?

Buddhists talk about nirvana, Daoists talk about sprouting wings, but he says just let him leave.

At that instant, he stops, turns back to look at you, and, just like that, you and he go your separate ways. He had said that his problem was that he had been born too early and so brought much suffering to you. If he had been born a century later, for example, in the new century about to arrive, no doubt these problems would not have existed. But nobody can predict what will happen in the next century, and, furthermore, can one know if this next century is, in fact, new?

61

Perpignan is a city in the French border area adjoining Spain. A friend you have just met at the Mediterranean Literary Center asks if you get homesick, and you reply categorically that you do not. You say that you had cut off those feelings long ago, completely! In the square opposite the restaurant, a little cake-and-ice-cream shop celebrating its first day of business is decked out with lanterns and colored streamers to attract customers. A small brass band is playing with great gusto, it is jolly music, and an old woman is doing a local Catalan folk dance. The Southerners' passion and the heavy roll in their French make you feel close to them.

This early summer night brings a festive atmosphere, and, with the cheerful brass pipes as well, is it also celebrating your new life? You have finally won joy in living. The proprietor of the restaurant comes to you with a book for your signature. He says his wife loved your novel and now wants to go on a trip to China. You smile.

You will not go back. Not even in future? someone asks. No, it is not your country. It exists in your memory only, as a hidden spring gushing forth feelings that are hard to articulate. This China is possessed by you alone, and has nothing to do with the country.

Your heart is at peace, and you are no longer a rebel. You are now an observer, and not anyone's enemy. If anyone wants to make an enemy of you, it no longer concerns you. For you, looking back has been a time of quiet reflection, so that you can get on with your life.

When you left China, you had brought with you a photograph that had been lost between the pages of a book. He was thin and had his head shaved. You look closely at the old yellowing photograph that you had somehow managed to keep. It had been taken thirty years ago in that reform-through-labor farm known as a May Seventh Cadre School. You want to see if his eyes will tell you anything. His shaved head, looking like a gourd ladle, was held high. He was proud, somewhat arrogant, even as a convict, and this had probably saved him from being crushed. But there is now no need for any arrogance. You are now a bird that is free and can fly wherever you want. There seems to be virgin land up ahead, well, at least, for you it is new. Luckily, you still have this sort of curiosity and don't want to be immersed in memories. He has already become footprints, which you have left behind.

Using this instant of time as the starting point, for you, writing is a spiritual journey, either in deep reflection, or talking to yourself, and you obtain joy and fulfillment in the process. Nothing frightens you anymore, for freedom eradicates fear. Let the sterile writings you leave behind erode with the passage of time. For you, eternity is not of pressing significance. This bout of writing is not your goal in life, but you continue to write so that you will be able to experience more fully this instant of time.

This instant of time is in Perpignan, after breakfast. As cars drive by under your window, illuminated shadows glide past the milk-white globular streetlights, but before there is time to see what sort of car it is, the illuminated shadow has vanished. Many shadows are illuminated in the world, but they will all vanish. You savor the shadows illuminated in this instant, so you also savored this he as a shadow that had been illuminated, and it amazed you. Oh, his shadow that was illuminated has flashed by and vanished!

It is beautiful music, Schnittke. Right now you are listening to *Concerto Grosso No. 6.* In this elegant piece, the frustrations of life are gracefully sublimated into high notes, which are released by the long chords of the violin streaking by like lightning. There is no need to try to understand the life of your contemporary Schnittke, but, from a conversation you had with him, each note he wrote echoed in harmony with the high notes of the violin.

Outside your window is the bright sunshine of early summer. Eight hundred years ago, Perpignan, this city in the East Pyrenees, was a city-nation with a constitution that enshrined magnanimity, peace, and freedom. It was a city that received refugees, and the local Catalans took pride in this. However, the editorials of special editions commemorating the eight-hundredth anniversary of the city write about "eight hundred years of democracy and freedom, today under threat."

You didn't imagine you would ever come here, and, even less so, that readers would ask for your autograph. A youth asked you to write something in your book for his girlfriend, who, he said, couldn't come. You go to write, "Language is a miracle that allows people to communicate, but people often fail to communicate with one another." However, you only write the first half of it. You can't just write anything you feel like at the expense of another's good intentions. You are free to make fun of yourself, but you must not make fun of language.

Music must also be like this, and it is best to remove unnecessary ornamentation. Schnittke had a compulsive need to do this, he did not flaunt music, he was minimalist and left many spaces, every phrase conveyed genuine feeling, there was nothing contrived or gratuitous. You must only speak when you have something to say, if you do not, then best be silent.

The illuminated shadows of one car after another flash by the globular streetlights, and on the other side of the street, plane trees and palms grow in a quiet little park. This region is the home of the French plane tree, a species that roots from cuttings, and has virtually spread throughout the world. It also entered your memories and grew everywhere along the streets and in the parks in the city where you lived as a child. The first girl you kissed, Little Five, was leaning against the shiny trunk of a plane tree that had shed its bark. It was also summer, but hotter than here.

It is good to be alive, and you sing a hymn to life, sing it because life has not treated you badly in everything. But sometimes life still makes your heart tremble, like this music with its crisp, fine drumbeats and the sound of the horns.

Not long before Sylvie's friend Martina killed herself, she picked up a drifter from the streets and took him home for the night. Finally, she killed herself. She said on the tape she had left behind that she could not bear the psychiatric hospital, and that her death had nothing to do with anyone. She was sick of life, killed herself, and that was the end. You do not know what your end will be like, and there is no need to plan an end. Should neofascists one day come to power, if it is still a magnanimous city that accepts refugees, will you escape here, to Perpignan? You are not going to fantasize about disaster.

To say that people are born to suffer, or that the world is a wasteland, is an exaggeration. Disasters have not been entirely your lot, so you are grateful to life, and this gratitude is akin to thanking God, but who is your God? Fate? Coincidence? You think that it is this consciousness of your self, this awareness of your own existence, that is to be thanked, for it was through this that you were able to save yourself from your predicament and suffering.

The big leaves of the palms and the plane trees are trembling. A person cannot be crushed if he refuses to be crushed. Others may oppress him, and defile him but, as long as he has not stopped breathing, he will still have the chance to raise his head. It is a matter of being able to preserve this last breath, to hold onto this last breath, so that one does not suffocate in the pile of shit. A person can be raped, woman or man, physically or by political force, but a person cannot be totally possessed: one's spirit remains one's own, and it is this that is preserved in the mind. Schnittke was uncertain with his music, and he was groping in the dark; seeking a way out was like searching for light, but he relied solely on that small point of dim light in his heart, and it was this feeling that was indestructible. Pressing his palms together to protect that point of dim light in his heart, he slowly moved through thick darkness, quagmire, not knowing where the path lay, yet carefully protecting that point of dim light. He was patient rather than obstinate. His tough resilience wove a cocoon; like a larva, he played dead and closed his eyes to endure the weight of the loneliness. But those delicate tinkling bells, that point of awareness of existence, that point of beauty of life, that gentle light, that spot of pulsating in the heart gradually began to radiate outward. . . .

On the bare branches of the tallow tree in front of the door, a few frost-lashed, withered, dark-red leaves trembled. He felt compassion for the youthful glow of that helpless young woman, the gurgling of the stream, the black mother hen on the single log bridge, head down, pecking, then looking up to stare. They were all projections of his self. Even the lust aroused in him by that sexy girl flirting with him and mocking him had made him keep his grip on life, made him hold his breath to wait. While he could not find a way out, by seizing these beautiful specks of feeling, he was able to avoid spiritual collapse. Also, he comforted himself by masturbating, and obtained slow release by secretly writing.

There was the clean fragrance of the paddy-rice straw cushioning his plank bed in those years, and the smell of his sheets drying in the sun after they had been washed in the pond. And there was also the sweaty smell of her body, his tender excitement as he corrected her lipstick, and the tremor in his heart as, brushing her firm breasts, he seized her by her strong shoulders and pushed her out the door. She had provided him with warmth and, in his imagination, he had been intimate with her. Moreover, he had articulated all these in language, put them into his writings, in order to obtain spiritual equilibrium.

You are filled with gratitude to women, and it is not just lust. You seek them, but they do not necessarily want to give themselves to you. You are insatiable, but it's impossible for you to have them all. God did not give them to you, and you don't have to thank God, but, finally, you do feel a sort of universal gratitude. You are grateful to the wind and the trees swaying in the wind, grateful to nature, grateful to the parents who gave birth to you. You now have no hatred and are at peace. Maybe it is because you are getting old that you lose your breath when climbing a hill, and you are now frugal with what used to be inexhaustible energy. These are signs of getting old. You are going downhill, and a chilly wind suddenly starts blowing. No, you are not in a hurry to go down. The distant mountains in the mist seem to be at the same altitude, and you go down even if there is an abyss at the bottom, so, when you fall, you might as well think of the splash of the setting sun on the faraway mountain tops.

In the small harbor, on a jutting cliff, is a small church. Facing the Mediterranean Sea, stands a white cross with a black metal statue of Jesus Christ nailed to it. The wind is still and the waves are calm, there are people on the sandy beach, and children are running about. There is also a woman in a bathing suit, her eyes closed, lying in a nook in the cliff.

They say that Matisse once lived and painted here, where the sunlight is transparent and blinding. Light and color are in the paintings of Matisse, but you are walking toward darkness.

They drive you to Barcelona, the city with the bright-red Dalí Museum decked with giant eggs on the roof. Spain had produced this old naughty child and the Spanish are a happy race. Crowds throng the streets. The black-haired Spanish women all have dark eyes and high nose bridges. Afterward, you go to a village restaurant that used to be a mill. Diagonally opposite is a family seated around a table: husband, wife, and their very pretty daughter whose rosy cheeks glow through her fair skin. The girl's long, black eyelashes are not fully-grown, but one day she will become one of the sturdy, voluptuous, big girls of Picasso's paintings. She is sitting across from her parents, sulking, engrossed in her own thoughts. Maybe she doesn't really know what she is thinking. That is life, she doesn't know what is in her future, and surely that is important? She doesn't know that she too will suffer, maybe she will get wiser, as she starts to worry. Her thick long black hair enhances her fair complexion and rosy cheeks. She is probably just thirteen or fourteen. For a young girl, thirteen or fourteen years of age, already to be sulking, surely, is one of the wonders of life, just like the suffering of Margarethe. Will she become a Margarethe?

Right now you are listening to a mass by Kodály, a woman singing to an organ. People need prayer just like they need to eat and make love, and you, too, have religious feelings. Last night, the woman in the room above was crying out all the time. It was excruciating, and stopped you from sleeping the whole night. From midnight till three o'clock, she was screaming, panting, then laughing loudly. You couldn't tell if it was rape or ecstasy taking place. At first, you thought it was in the room next to your bed headboard, then you heard the noise on the floorboards above, and it seemed that they were playing sex games on the floor, maybe it was the sort of rape Margarethe had spoken about. But so what if this were the case, it was happening in the hotel room, and no one would ask questions. Afterward, you heard laughter, loud wanton laughter that even aroused your lust. However, your heart is now at peace, and there is the organ and the wonderful choir of alto and tenor singers.

Earlier, at breakfast in the dining room downstairs, you only heard polite good mornings in German. It was a German tourist group of hefty, middle-aged and elderly couples at buffet breakfast, so everyone had a plate full of diced sausage and fried bacon. They eat a lot but aren't worried about putting on weight. The thought crossed your mind that it was unlikely that these women would have been crying out in bed. They were all engrossed in eating and seldom spoke, and their knives and forks made very little noise. At a table by the window was a young woman, sitting opposite an elderly man. They had finished eating and were drinking their coffee. They were not talking, but looking out at the street. The fine weather of yesterday had changed, the ground was wet, but the rain had stopped. They did not appear to be lovers, but were more like a father on vacation with a daughter who was still not financially independent. Probably the woman who was wailing and laughing loudly last night was still fast asleep in her room.

The organ and a choir. The hotel room has stylish old furniture, a heavy oak table, dark-brown carved wardrobes, and a wooden bed with round carved posts. Outside the window, no cars are flashing past the round streetlights. It is Sunday, late morning, and you are waiting for friends to take you to the airport to catch the plane back to Paris some time after noon.

1996 to 1998, in Paris

Gao Xingjian

Soul Mountain

Winner of the Nobel Prize in Literature

'A complex, rich novel on an epic scale . . . *Soul Mountain* bristles with stories from Chinese history, folk tales, childhood reminiscences and memories of the Cultural Revolution, as well as bitter arguments and passionate sex.'

Independent on Sunday

'When he writes of his experiences in the real world, Gao transcends cultural barriers. A good story will out in any language, and when Gao is good he is staggeringly so. His writing about the Cultural Revolution is remarkable.'

Daily Telegraph

'A quirky, thick, playful monster of a book, both engaging and elegant.'   *New York Times*

'An original voice unlike any contemporary writing available in English. *Soul Mountain* is an extraordinary product of an imagination infused with European and Chinese cultures; an exploration of individual identity in a society that exalts the collective; and a daring play with voice that plunders ancient myths, philosophy, history, folk songs and memory.'

The Australian

'A true work of great literature'   *Los Angeles Times*

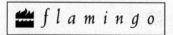

Amy Tan

The Hundred Secret Senses

Olivia Yee is only five years old when Kwan, her older sister from China, comes to live with the family and turns her life upside down, bombarding her day and night with ghostly stories of strange ancestors from the world of Yin. Olivia just wants to lead a normal American life.

For the next thirty years, Olivia endures visits from Kwan and her ghosts, who appear in the living world to offer advice on everything from restaurants to Olivia's failed marriage. But just when she cannot bear it any more, the revelations of a tragic family secret finally open her mind to the startling truths hidden in Kwan's unorthodox vision of the world.

'Kwan emerges as a splendidly vital comic character . . . and her sensibility – call it superstitious and crazy, or call it colourfully imaginative and indicative of a proper respect for the past – pervades every part of this highly enjoyable novel.'
LUCY HUGHES HALLETT, *Sunday Times*

'The story works like a dream . . . and the novel is most compelling and alive when the two sisters are sparring and squabbling. Tan has a great ear for feminine chitchat, its spikiness and hilarity, its mockery and teasing.'
MICHELE ROBERTS, *Independent*

'Resist the temptation to feast on this latest offering from Amy Tan in one voracious sitting – instead, savour it, slow time. Tan's writing rolls along effortlessly, like the best-told folklore – it's simply mesmerising.'
Elle

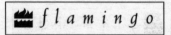

Amy Tan

The Kitchen God's Wife

Pearl Louie Brandt has a terrible secret which she tries desperately to keep from her mother, Winnie Louise. And Winnie has long kept her own secrets – about her past and the confusing circumstances of Pearl's birth. Fate intervenes in the form of Helen Kwong, Winnie's so-called sister-in-law, who believes she is dying and must unburden herself of all falsehoods before she flies off to heaven. But, unfortunately, the truth comes in many guises, depending on who is telling the tale . . .

Thus begins a story that takes us back to Shanghai in the 1920s, through World War II, and the harrowing events that lead to Winnie's arrival in America in 1949. The story is one of innocence and its loss, tragedy and survival and, most of all, the enduring qualities of hope, love and friendship. Tan's voice – her vivid characterization, her sly and poignant humour, and her sympathetic insights into human relationships – gives us a compelling novel, both painful and sweet, suffused with hopes universal to us all.

'Tan is a consummate storyteller whose prose manages to be emotionally charged without a trace of sentimentality.'
Sunday Times

'In this remarkable book Tan manages to illuminate the nobility of friendship and the necessity of humour. Give yourself over to the world she creates.'
New York Times

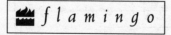

flamingo

Mira Stout

One Thousand
Chestnut Trees

'A startlingly impressive début. This marvellous – and very moving – book tells its Korean story stylishly and with great skill.'
WILLIAM TREVOR

'In 1936, Anna's mother is living a blissful, pre-lapsarian existence on her grandfather's estates. The adults around her, however, have already seen the slow stripping away of their lands and titles by the Japanese . . . and the story of the parents' survival during the war and the mother's eventual escape to the US in 1951 makes horrifying, moving and tremendously exciting reading. Stout's descriptions bring Korea's stately, cultured civilisation and heavenly landscape into sharp focus like a jewel-coloured miniature.'
LAURA TENNANT, *Independent on Sunday*

'Mira Stout not only grapples with the deep conundrum that is mixed-race identity, but also grabs with both hands the extraordinary history of turbulent twentieth-century Korea. The writing is encrusted with details like coloured sequins. An extremely ambitious first book.'
JOANNA PITMAN, *The Times*

'A warm and warming evocation of landscape and memory. Stout's lively sense of language and culture shows her to be a writer of great promise.' ANDREW BISWELL, *Daily Telegraph*

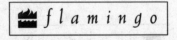

Andrew X Pham

Catfish and Mandala

A Vietnamese Odyssey

Shortlisted for the *Guardian* First Book Award; winner of the Kiriyama Pacific Rim Book Prize

'Jack Kerouac meets *Wild Swans*.' *The Times*

'Andrew Pham left his native land as a 'boat person', grew up in California and was recently impelled to return to his roots. But not the easy way: alone, by bicycle, eating and sleeping among the poor: Pham's occasionally brandished knife – and inborn streak of violence – powered him through hair-raising encounters. As he is an acute and evocative writer; the result is a rough guide to make the *Rough Guide to Vietnam* sound like the obscene lap of luxury. His tale is interwoven with a finely calibrated network of flashbacks in which war, imprisonment, escape and exile are shown to leave their indelible mark on everyone . . . Terrible and graphic, the book is as much about the future as the past: every event is scrutinised for what it may portend. But *Catfish and Mandala*'s real power is visceral. Pham records his encounters with beggars, sadists, prostitutes and simple country folk with a bursting heart and a Dickensian eye for detail. The deaf-mute boy who befriends him in Hanoi, the despairing jade-cutter who jumps from the roof of the internment camp in Indonesia, the one-legged veteran who scoops him off the road when he can't go a step further – they are all unforgettable.' *Independent*

'A powerful memoir of grief, full of both comic and painful adventures.' *Elle*

0 00 655223 4

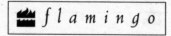 *flamingo*

Pascal Khoo Thwe

From the Land of Green Ghosts

'A luminously vivid and truly remarkable autobiography'
CAROLINE MOORE, *Spectator*

'An extraordinary tale . . . Pascal Khoo Thwe subtitles this beautiful autobiography "A Burmese Odyssey", and indeed it has all the mysterious power of something out of Homer . . . a magical story, full of richness and subtlety, told with the instinctive touch of a true writer.'
CRAIG BROWN, *Mail on Sunday*

In 1988 John Casey, a Cambridge don visiting Burma, was told of a waiter in Mandalay with a passion for James Joyce. Intrigued, he visited the restaurant, where he met Pascal Khoo Thwe, a member of the tiny, remote Kayan Padaung tribe, famous for their 'giraffe-necked' women. The encounter was to change both their lives.

Within a few months of this chance meeting, economic crises brought about by Burma's military dictatorship meant that Pascal had to give up his studies. His student lover was arrested, raped and murdered by the armed forces. He fled to the jungle, becoming a guerrilla fighter in the struggle against the government. At a moment of desperation he wrote a letter to the Englishman he had met in Mandalay. Miraculously, it reached its destination, and led to Pascal being rescued from the jungle and enrolling to study English at Cambridge University, the first Burmese tribesman ever to do so.

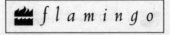